Patricia M.

The Colours of Death

HODDER

First published in Great Britain in 2021 by Hodder & Stoughton
An Hachette UK company

This paperback edition published in 2021

1

Map by Rosie Collins

A CIP catalogue record for this title is available from the British Library

Paperback ISBN 978 1 529 33670 2

Typeset in Sabon MT by Hewer Text UK Ltd, Edinburgh
Printed and bound in Great Britain by Clays Ltd, Elcograf S.p.A.

Hodder & Stoughton policy is to use papers that are natural, renewable
and recyclable products and made from wood grown in sustainable
forests. The logging and manufacturing processes are expected to
conform to the environmental regulations of the country of origin.

Hodder & Stoughton Ltd
Carmelite House
50 Victoria Embankment
London EC4Y 0DZ

www.hodder.co.uk

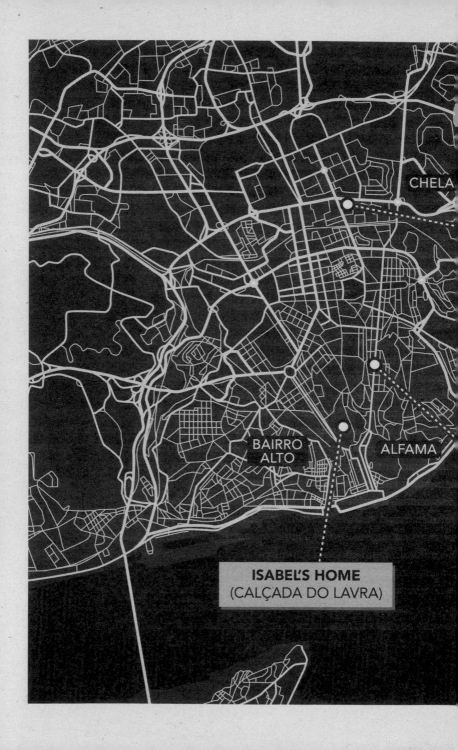

CHELA

BAIRRO
ALTO

ALFAMA

ISABEL'S HOME
(CALÇADA DO LAVRA)

1ST MURDER
(GARE DO ORIENTE)

2ND MURDER,
THE UNIVERSITY
(ALVALADE)

NATIONAL TESTING
INSTITUTE
(MONTIJO)

PRECINCT
(ANJOS)

LISBON

I

The first time Isabel heard a voice in her head, she'd tried to talk back.

It'd been different back then; the voices hadn't been as clear.

Now, Isabel stares down at the still body on the slab. The chill of the room seeps through her skin to settle in her bones and she can't help but wonder what this person's last thought had been. If Isabel would have heard it.

The emotions would have packed a hell of a punch.

The body is that of a woman, leached of colour in death, lips together and arms limp at her side. There's a jagged scar, cleaned and sewn in a crude line from the bottom of her left eye to the corner of her mouth. There's another like it on the right side. The half of her that Isabel can see above the sheet is covered in more of those neatly stitched lines. The knife had punched through her chest several times and the woman had felt every single one of them.

Yes, Isabel thinks, I would've heard this woman.

With one last sweep of the wounds, she turns her back on the body and nods to the medical examiner, who's tucked away in the corner of the room, clipboard in hand, only his eyes visible above the mask.

'Thanks,' Isabel says and walks out.

It's warmer out in the hallway. The morgue has seen better days and could do with money, but the floor is pristine, the piercing smell of antiseptic permeating the air. Coupled with the lighting that sucks the colour from the walls, it makes for a grim practice.

Isabel's steps are loud in the silent hallway, accompanied by the ticking of the clock on the wall at the end of the long room. It reads 8.15 a.m.

She signs out of the morgue with a nod to the man at the front desk, slides her sunglasses onto her face and steps outside. The fleece is soft against her neck as she tugs the collar up around her throat. The sun is bright, cold and cutting. It's the coldest winter they've had in a while, though up until a few weeks ago the temperature had been mild enough that all she'd needed was a scarf and a blazer.

Lisbon's weather had turned vicious as winter began to settle.

Her hair hasn't quite dried from the quick shower she'd taken earlier that morning. It sticks to the nape of her neck beneath the coat's collar and the rest has started curling around her face. It's like a magnet, making the iciness more acute, and she grimaces. Her car's parked half off, half on the kerb and she rushes to it, sliding in gratefully and starting the engine as soon as she's slammed the door behind her.

The heat is beginning to blast into the car when her phone starts vibrating against her hip. 'Merda,' she mutters, leaning her head back on the headrest and closing her eyes. As usual Isabel hadn't got much sleep the night before. Opening her eyes at the sound of her alarm had felt like a particular type of torture. Remembering how bad the pain had been has her rubbing her temples.

Isabel shifts on to her other hip and tugs her phone out. CHIEF flashes up at her on the screen.

'Reis,' she answers, voice still raspy from the remnants of a bad cold. In front of her car, a man stops on the street corner with his stand, huge bags of chestnuts leaning up against the cart. His hat is pulled down over his ears and air puffs out of his mouth in little white clouds as he gets ready to start serving.

'I want you at Gare do Oriente terminal, ASAP.'

In her mind's eye, Isabel is already adjusting her route. 'Okay, what do I need to know?' she asks. She puts the phone on speaker and tosses it onto the passenger seat.

'Possible Gifted murder.'

Shit.

'All right, should be there in twenty. What about my Jane Doe?'

'I'll put someone else on the case for now. If it turns out that this really has Gifted involvement, then I want my most competent inspector on it.'

'And it won't hurt that I'm Gifted myself,' Isabel says, wry.

'Exactly. Your new partner will be meeting you there.'

Isabel glances down at the phone as if she'll be able to see the Chief's expression on the other end. 'New partner,' she repeats.

'You knew this was coming,' the Chief says. 'Oh. And Reis. HR are on my case about your retesting. Get it done.'

'I will.'

2

Lisbon is buzzing at this time of the morning. Tourists who have woken up early to enjoy the clear weather mingle with the Lisboetas going about their daily business. The tables outside the café are packed with people, smiles more of a stretch of the mouth rather than genuine expressions as they snap pictures of themselves over breakfast. They seem to take to the weather much better than the locals, who huddle in their jackets, wrapped up with scarves halfway up their faces.

It's rush hour and Isabel almost doesn't make it in the twenty minutes she'd promised.

The first thing she sees is the wave of people running along the length of the station. Normally they'd be streaming into it, not fanning out from the entrance in an angry mob.

Gare do Oriente terminal is always busy, the amount of traffic it sees every day equal to that of New York's Central Station. Its white arches, made to resemble trees, gleam in the sunlight. The shopping centre further down draws huge crowds year-round. Isabel can see a flash of police tape as people shift, some turning back to the bus stops and others shuffling forward to yell. Police dot the area surrounding the bus terminal directly outside the entrance to the trains.

It takes Isabel another ten minutes to find a parking spot. It's further away from the terminal, but even from there she can hear them all. She feels the first shivers of the wall in her mind as the strong emotions batter past her car window. It's a shock in comparison to the quiet of the morgue and the still mind of a dead woman.

People never know how loudly they think.

Isabel reaches for the glove compartment instead, digs through the stupid amount of energy bars inside until she finds and tugs out the see-through pillbox. She pops the tiny powder-blue pill, eyes still on the crowd. She pulls out a bottle of water from the footwell and takes a drink to wash the pill down with. The water is icy cold and leaves her throat tingling. She shoves one of the energy bars into her coat pocket, throws the pillbox back inside and closes the compartment.

She should have taken it on the way.

It takes between twenty and thirty minutes for the pill to take effect, which means Isabel's going to be wading through the crowd unprotected except for her regular wards. The mental protective shields are instinctive now. There was a time when they really hadn't been.

It had taken Isabel longer than her peers to learn how to block out the thoughts around her on command. She'd had to do extra sessions with her assigned Guide, Rosario, every Saturday morning. Because of the extra sessions, Isabel always missed her favourite morning show.

She sits quietly for a moment, eyes closed, attention turned inward as she focuses on building her wards, one strong enough to get her through the wall of people surrounding the station. It'll be quiet beyond them.

A suspected Gifted murder is not something they need right now. In the current climate, it's a very dangerous thing.

'Well, not going to get any warmer out there,' she says to herself and gets out.

The whip of the wind is harsh enough to make her gasp and try to duck her whole head into the loops of her scarf. It doesn't help.

Crime scene tape covers both entrances to the train station and officers are positioned at the entry points. Isabel catches flashes of the yellow tape through the multitude of angry commuters. She can see each police officer at their post, some in pairs, some standing by themselves. A few of them are trying to address members of the crowd but don't seem to be getting anywhere, others have given up and are either standing there with a stoic look on their faces or talking quietly to each other.

5

As Isabel gets closer, little tendrils of thoughts begin to brush against her wards. Even though she's still quite a distance from the entrance, she feels them. They are whisper-soft at first, like the touch of a chilled breeze on the back of her neck, making the hairs on her arms stand up. They aren't strong enough, at this distance, to disorientate and bring her to her knees.

Isabel stops, eyes roaming the scene. The wind drags her hair into her face, and she tries to knuckle it away from her mouth. Rain is coming.

As soon as she hits the crowd, it's like someone turns up the dial and the volume of the angry voices echoing in her head shoots up. Isabel flinches before taking a calming breath and forcing her wall up higher. She can see it in her mind's eye, focuses on building it taller until the thoughts swirling all around her fade into the background. It takes concentration to keep them out and she's reminded that she only had a quick coffee before leaving home that morning. She's going to need some proper fuel; even with the pill's effects kicking in soon her energy will be eaten up in no time.

The crowd doesn't budge. Their yells meld together, shouted words indistinct. Isabel manages to catch a few things, questions about when the station will reopen, demands to know what's happening. There are a few 'merda's and 'caralho's thrown in for good measure but that's typical.

'Excuse me,' she says.

There's always something about her that makes people move. Isabel's never been sure what that is. Maybe they glimpse the ID dangling from her neck or maybe it's the look she gives them out of the corner of her eye when they don't move fast enough. She's not sure. She thinks, sometimes, that maybe they know she's *other*.

One of the police officers notices her. He shifts, drawing up to his full height, mouth already twitching with the need to spout something condescending. Isabel can tell. She knows the look.

'Miss—'

Isabel doesn't stop. Around her, the crowd closes up once more. She can feel them at her back, jostling and trying to shift forward. Coffee breath and the clinging smell of one too many morning smokes surrounds her.

'Inspector,' she corrects and tugs her ID badge into view. The officer leans in closer than necessary to inspect it.

She knows the exact moment he focuses on her classification. His eyes flick from her back down to her ID. He licks his lips, a nervous tic as he takes a step back and nods, trying to put his tough mask back in place.

'Problem?' she asks. 'Because I have people waiting for me and you've got enough on your hands out here.'

The man – Mateus, his ID reads – steps back. 'Good morning, Inspector.'

'Good morning.'

'I'll take you through, Inspector,' Mateus says. Isabel nods and as they go into the station makes a note to call the Chief and suggest that she see whether she can spare any other officers to hold the fort.

Everything is still functioning inside the station but the large space that should be filled with the people cramming up against the police tapes, is empty. Their steps echo as they head for the trains. She spots more officers and gets a few more grumbled morning greetings as they head up towards the scene.

The platform they emerge onto is a flurry of activity and there's a train stationed there. A small group of people is gathered at the end of the platform. All the doors on the train are closed save for the one they are standing in front of.

Leaving Mateus behind, Isabel makes her way towards them. She catches a glimpse of her reflection in the train window and winces. She looks like shit.

At her approach, the three people standing by the open doors turn to look at her.

'Reis.'

One of the three splits off and walks to her.

Jacinta tugs her mask down and hooks it underneath her chin. Her tight curls are starting to escape the hood they're trapped under. The pale blue hazard suit looks oddly complementary against Jacinta's black skin, which is ridiculous because the suit is fucking ugly.

The face itself is a familiar and welcome one, which Isabel is thankful for. There aren't many people who she's able to work comfortably with. Jacinta is one of them.

'Então,' Isabel says, 'glad it's you. I'm going on three hours' sleep and I think I'd honestly make anyone else cry. What time did you get here?'

Jacinta shrugs. A camera dangles from her hand. 'Not long. About an hour or so. They had trouble clearing the station.'

Isabel nods. 'I heard it was a bit of a shit-show. Anything compromised?'

Jacinta lets out an aggravated sigh and gestures at the train. 'They were in there when it happened. Everyone trampled all over the place trying to get out.'

Isabel hums. 'It is rush hour. They've got an angry mob outside.'

'Wouldn't want to be one of your officers holding the fort.'

'Well . . .' Isabel thinks about the dickhead outside who'd got in her face and can't bring herself to feel too badly about it. A needle of sharp pain knifes through her temple and she winces.

Jacinta's eyes narrow on her face. 'You okay?'

Isabel rubs at the spot, teeth gritting. It abates as quickly as it arrived. 'Fine.' She drops her hand back to her side and tries to smooth the pain from her expression. The first hour of the pill taking effect is always a little worse. 'So. What do we have?'

'We've done a walk-through already. Your partner,' Jacinta pauses here, arcing a brow at that piece of news, 'got here about twenty minutes ago and we've been waiting for you to arrive. When did you get a partner, by the way?' Jacinta looks over her shoulder. Someone else is making their way over.

The man is tall, Isabel thinks.

'It's new.'

8

Jacinta looks from Isabel to the man who is apparently Isabel's new partner. 'How new?'

'Looks like we're about to meet,' Isabel says, watching him approach.

'Inspector Reis?' he asks.

'Yes?'

He holds out his hand and Isabel looks down at it, then back up at his face, waiting.

His hand stays in the same place. 'Inspector Aleksandr Voronov,' he says.

Voronov. She's not a stranger to the name. Isabel takes his hand and shakes. 'Inspector,' she greets him, already trying to place it.

He looks her over, his grip firm. He's got sharp eyes.

Pretty striking looks, she thinks. Maybe not the best person to partner with if you wanted to keep a low profile. This one will turn heads: thick black hair, pale blue eyes and killer cheekbones.

'All right,' Isabel says to Jacinta, 'let's get in there.'

It's one of the older-model trains. The outside is scuffed from its long years of use and bad weather and decorated with spiked letters in green spray-paint. The interior isn't much better; its seats are worn and paint flaking. Voronov walks beside her and Isabel doesn't bother to hide her assessing gaze.

The doors to the carriage have been left open. The air carries with it a tinge of the threatening rain and the lingering smell of spilled coffee and blood. It makes her think of stepping inside a butcher's shop, the metallic tang always in the air. It seems stronger in this compact carriage, maybe because it's so out of place.

The shape of the man on the floor looks odd in the empty carriage. Still and large, slumped in the space between the seats either side of it, surrounded by shards of glass. Behind it, the closed carriage-door window is broken, glass jagged and red-stained, the door dirty, large spots of red on its surface.

As they walk through, there's a scarf discarded on the floor, a forgotten bag is tucked into the corner of a seat and an umbrella in another. They approach the body and Isabel tugs her coat tighter around her. The carriage is freezing.

'How long has he been here?' Isabel asks.

Jacinta hangs back, peering around Voronov at the body on the floor. 'We got here within half an hour of the call coming through. He was dead before we got here.'

Isabel lowers herself onto her haunches, keeping a bit of distance as she looks over her second body of the day. The two couldn't be more different.

The body lies on its side, one arm trapped beneath it and the other stretched out. Isabel can just see the side of the face. A white male. His skin looks as if it's been peeled off by a child who's mistaken it for plasticine, falling away from his face in some spots, torn and drooping, brutalised and bloody in others. The eye she can see is swollen and battered, but there's a gleam where the dead gaze still peers out at her from behind a half-shut eyelid. Like he's staring at her. The dark hair at his temples is matted with blood.

Isabel makes a concentrated effort to look away. 'What happened?'

Jacinta steps out of the aisle and wedges herself between a set of seats facing each other.

'Got a report of an emergency at the station. When we got here, the scene was barely secured, hysterics everywhere. People panicked and tried to rush out of the carriage.' She slants a look at Isabel. 'You can imagine how well that worked out.'

Isabel looks over her shoulder at Voronov, who is standing quiet, towering over Jacinta and staring down his long nose at her.

'I'm hoping that means witnesses,' Isabel says, reaching up to rub at her temple. The first pulses of a headache are beginning to settle.

Jacinta shakes her head. 'Mostly confused commuters who have no idea what in the hell happened. One passenger thought the deceased was having a fit or just losing his shit' – Jacinta gestures at the broken window on the door – 'says he up and started smashing his head against the window, alarming the other passengers. Train was packed.'

Isabel nods.

'The guy closest to him actually tried to do something about it,' Jacinta says, 'he tried to keep him from bashing his face against the door but wasn't all that successful.'

'Where is he now?' Isabel asks.

'They've taken him to the break room, him and whoever else they could catch that didn't run out of the station as soon as they got clear of the train. Think some paramedics are with him to check for damage but he seems to be mostly okay.'

'Hmm.' Isabel tears her eyes away from the one staring eye and looks around the carriage. Beneath the smell of the blood is a different smell, really subtle. Isabel frowns and tilts her head, trying to identify it. There's something familiar about it but she can't place it.

Isabel stands. 'The Chief told me it was being reported as a possible Gifted crime.' She glances at Voronov to see if there's any outward reaction to that but there's nothing.

Jacinta shrugs. 'Like I said, people don't know what they saw. The woman sitting next to the deceased says it looked like he was yanked out of his seat. She said it was like he was just plucked up into the air.'

3

The station is eerily silent as Isabel and Voronov cross it. They can hear the noise of angry protests from commuters outside. None of their thoughts reach Isabel now though.

Isabel hopes they haven't caught the attention of the press yet, though that's probably a fruitless hope. No doubt if she were to turn a TV on right now, RTP Notícias would be right in front of the station with a pretty news reporter giving them a run-down of the situation. After all, the death of one man had brought the terminal to a standstill.

Isabel tries to put that to one side now and glances at her new partner as they make their way to the break room. His strides are longer than hers, but he's shortening them to keep pace with her.

'What are you thinking about this case?' she asks, keeping her voice low. She checks that their Guide, Mateus, can't hear them. She doesn't need any more information getting out than it has to.

'That it's going to be a mess,' Voronov says.

Brutal. But Isabel doesn't think he's wrong. Not when what she's seen so far is supporting the fact that there's more to it than just a man who lost his shit.

'Odds are,' Voronov says, pulling her out of her thoughts, 'it's someone who's lost it and caused a panic.'

She arches a brow at that. 'It's possible. But seems a bit extreme for someone who "just lost it", don't you think?'

He looks at her then. 'A suicidal episode would be extreme.'

Isabel is surprised when she spots Carla and Daniel outside the break room. She hadn't expected the Chief to send anyone else – at least not until they have more information. It's a sign of how even the Polícia Judiciária is feeling the tension when, at the mere possibility of a Gifted crime, an entire team is dispatched to deal with the situation.

Carla is new in the Investigations department, having started with them in January. Gifted, like Isabel. It had been a surprise to everyone when the Polícia Judiciária had continued to recruit without any obvious discrimination. It's a dangerous game for the PJ to play. Public opinion is lying heavily with the PNP, Portugal's right-wing political party. Their anti-Gifted agenda, spearheaded by the party leader, has taken a strong hold with the Portuguese people.

Isabel doesn't know what Carla's classification is, has only spoken to her in passing. Carla works with Daniel. All thanks to the new policy, every Gifted officer in the PJ is required to have a Regular partner.

A year or so ago, on a busy Saturday afternoon, a Gifted teenage girl had levelled an entire section of a shopping centre. She'd somehow slipped through the net, her Gift level having been misclassified, which had brought Portugal's National Testing Institute under fire. Their responsibility was to properly test and determine a Gifted's affinity and level to make sure incidents like these didn't occur. Gifted people come under two affinities, telepathy and telekinesis, and their levels of power are measured on a scale of 1–10, though Gifted at the higher end of the scale are few and far between. And dangerous. Well, according to NTI and the government, that is.

No one had noticed when the girl's control had started to slip or when she started to break under the weight of her telekinesis. There'd been no Monitor on her case because they hadn't known she was a high-level Gifted.

The result had been twenty-eight people dead, eight critically injured and many more who had had to be seen to by paramedics. Public uproar had been intense. Isabel still remembers the moment when the news had broken out; she'd been scraping the burnt layer off a piece of toast in her kitchen when the news presenter's

13

voice had filtered through. They'd never shown the girl's face.

That was the point when hostilities against Gifted had become more open. The government had been quick to come forward with fail-safe policies in case another Gifted 'went rogue'.

For the PJ that meant that every Gifted officer would have to have a non-Gifted partner.

Isabel glances over at Voronov. Hence the addition to her team of one. Something else the public could thank the PNP for. Clearly, their tax money was hard at work here keeping them safe from the big, bad and corrupt Gifted population.

Daniel looks like he's just rolled out of bed; his hair is all over the place and his eyes are bloodshot. He's sucking down that cup of coffee like it's got the answer to life.

Carla looks apprehensive. She's a petite woman with a prominent nose and pretty eyes. Her dark hair is scraped back from her face and tucked into a sleek ponytail atop her head and she's huddled into her coat, wrapped tight around herself.

Isabel stops in front of them, eyebrows high as she takes in Daniel's face. 'You look like shit,' she says.

He scowls at her. 'So do you. We were on nights. Just had time for a shower before the Chief pulled us back in.'

Isabel rolls her eyes. 'All right, sorry.' She gestures at Voronov. 'You guys met?'

They all make their introductions and with that out of the way, they turn back to the business at hand.

Daniel finishes his coffee and crushes the cup. 'So, where do you need us?' he asks.

'We have a group of witnesses inside. I'm interested in talking to the passengers who sat closest to the deceased, particularly the one who tried to help him. Take statements,' Isabel says, 'and if you think we would benefit from me speaking to them personally just come and grab me. Unless . . .' She looks at Carla questioningly.

Carla shakes her head. 'No, no. I can't do any of that.'

Voronov gives them both a questioning look, which means that the Chief has been as forthcoming with him in regard to Isabel as she has been with Isabel in regard to him. 'She means that she can't look into people's memories. Which I can,' she says.

'I'm a class-two telepath,' Carla explains. 'I can only do very low-grade stuff. Nothing that would be of use here.'

Isabel doesn't bother to look Voronov's way to see how he's taken that.

The break room, they find out, isn't much of a break room. It's a tiny square with a kitchen attached and a door that Isabel assumes leads to a supply cupboard.

There's a small electric heater on and a handful of people gathered around it. The rest are sitting, hunched in on themselves, on hard plastic chairs lining one side of the room. When Isabel asks the officer present to identify the witness who had tried to hold the deceased back, he points at a young man sitting with a blanket around him. His elbows rest on his knees and his hands are clasped together. He's staring at the floor and doesn't so much as twitch when they enter. The others turn quiet and watch them, eyes wary. There's an empty cup at the guy's feet and the lingering scent of coffee fills the room.

Isabel calms her breathing, reaching out with her Gift.

Once the pill takes effect, it's like her Gift is draped over by a very thick, very dark blanket and she has to pull a little harder. She doesn't mind it. It keeps things in check and keeps her from going crazy. Literally. What she does mind is the way she's had to learn to work with a constant headache whenever she's taken the pill. Even if recently it doesn't help her quite as much as it used to, as if her body has learned to fight it off.

Voronov stops by the officer guarding the door, has a few words and a second later comes back to her.

'He says there's an office to the side of the staff kitchen we can use.'

'Perfect, thanks.' She approaches the young man in the chair and lowers herself so that she's at eye level with him. 'Hi,' she says.

It takes him a moment but then he looks up.

'Would you mind speaking to me for a bit?' She gives him a small smile as she says it, projecting as much calm as she can. 'They have a small office here so we can talk in private.'

He doesn't say anything, gathers the blanket in his hands, bringing it higher around his shoulders, and follows her.

4

'Take a seat for me, okay?' Isabel offers the witness the seat closest to the door of the office, trying to put him as at ease as possible. An electric heater is already heating the room, which should help.

'May I sit?' she asks, as she drags over one of the fold-up chairs so that it's facing him, making sure not to crowd him. From the sounds of it, that train carriage had been crowded enough.

As if coming out of a dream, he lifts his head up and looks her in the face. He's young, in his early twenties, mixed race. His hazel eyes are glassy. He blinks a couple of times and then looks from her to Voronov, who has taken root next to the door, leaning against the wall, hands in his pockets.

The witness is looking back at her now.

He's got blood on his hands. They're unnaturally steady.

'I'm Inspector Reis, that's my partner,' she keeps her voice gentle but to the point, gesturing at Voronov, 'Inspector Voronov. We're here to try and find out what happened today. I understand you were there when the incident on the train took place. What's your name?'

Out of the corner of her eye, she sees Voronov get a notepad ready.

Something flickers in the witness's expression for a moment, a quick thing, and the vagueness of his stare abates, enough awareness coming back to add some life to him. The blanket around him shifts as he straightens his shoulders, and the hands that he's got clasped together start twisting.

'Rodrigo,' he says.

Isabel nods. 'Rodrigo, I'm going to ask you some questions, just about what you remember from this morning. Can you tell me when you noticed something was wrong?'

Rodrigo's eyes drop back to his hands. 'I'm missing my class.'

Okay, she can work with this. 'You were on your way to university?'

That brings his attention back up and he focuses on her again. 'Yes. I was running late. Normally, I'm on the first train. My car's broken down, so I can't drive right now.'

'You travel from here often?'

'Yes.'

'Do you know anything about the man you tried to help?'

Rodrigo shakes his head.

'Ever seen him before?'

Rodrigo shakes his head again. Stops. His mouth turns down and he shrugs like he's confused. 'I mean, I don't think so. I didn't know him, but you know when you look at a person and get that sense of déjà vu like you've seen them somewhere? At the station, maybe. I don't know. I can't really place it.'

'That's okay. So, you were sitting near him? You guys were in the same carriage?'

'Yes. He sat down across from me. I was trying to get some last-minute reading done. Everyone was getting on and it was getting cramped. We were right at the end of the carriage near the connecting door.'

Isabel stays quiet, lets him figure his way through it. His eyebrows pucker and he looks like he can't make sense of whatever he's trying to convey to them, as if there are too many words and his mouth can't quite fit around them. He's too young for what he's seen in that carriage.

No one is ever old enough to deal with shit like this.

'I'm staring down at my book and next thing I know he's knocking me into the woman beside me. When I look up, he's already scrambling and there's someone else on the floor. Then . . . then he's h-hitting his face against the door. It made no sense but – he was screaming—' Rodrigo's breathing picks up and his eyes have gone wide like he still can't believe what he's seen. 'Just, I didn't understand. People were getting up and I thought, I don't know what I thought. Maybe he was having some kind of fit? I thought maybe if I calmed him down—' He swallows and looks down at his feet.

'What did you do then, Rodrigo?' Isabel asks, trying to draw him back into the room with them.

'I-I got my hands on his shoulders. Tried to talk to him. The lady next to me tried to get out of her seat and I tripped. But. I don't know . . .' He looks up at Isabel, shoulders hunched, looking lost, like he's still in that moment and not knowing what to do. 'I couldn't understand what was going on. Everyone started yelling and the train was packed. Then the window breaks and when I look, this guy is smashing his face in it over and over and over. I-I tried to pull him away. I even managed to get my arm around his waist but-but it was like he was possessed. The weird thing is that—' He stops, shakes his head again and rubs his hands over his face, leaving rusted specks on his chin, 'when I lost my grip on him? It's not like when someone pulls away from you, you know? Like they're straining away.'

'What do you mean, Rodrigo?'

'It felt like when I was tugging him away, something else was tugging back.'

For a moment, Rodrigo doesn't say anything else, and Isabel doesn't push. He sags in his seat, back to the same place of shock he had been in when they'd walked in. Isabel looks at Voronov and finds him staring at the kid, eyes narrowed. 'If you'd seen . . . I saw the expression on his face,' Rodrigo whispers.

Isabel snaps back to him, focusing. 'What did you see?'

'He looked scared. He looked so scared. After, I thought he wasn't in control. I mean, I know with fits or just . . . I don't know. I don't know what I'm saying.' He falls quiet then and rests his head on his hands.

Isabel eases back in her chair and watches as a fine tremble takes over the kid.

She gets up and crouches in front of Rodrigo. 'Rodrigo,' she says and hears the deep breath he takes before he looks up at her again. She doesn't feel comfortable doing this here, with a new partner she knows nothing about. But it's one of those situations where if she doesn't take advantage of it, the information will slip through her fingers.

She tugs at the badge around her neck and holds it up for him to see. 'I'm Gifted,' she says.

For a moment, all Rodrigo does is stare at the badge she's showing him. Then he looks at her, confused.

'How would you feel if I tried to take a look at your memory of what happened? You can say no,' she says, 'you're under no obligations here. Nothing will happen to you if you refuse.'

Rodrigo stares at her and Isabel can feel Voronov's eyes burning a hole in the back of her head.

'Would you be okay with that?'

Rodrigo's eyes flick over her head to Voronov but the other man remains quiet. Isabel tries to block his presence from her mind. She doesn't think any of his thoughts will make it past the blocks she has in place, both natural and reinforced by the pill, but just in case, she doesn't want anything distracting her from the young man in front of her.

'What would you do?'

Isabel gives him a small smile, surprised that the first thing she's met with isn't outright hostility. That's becoming more and more of a rarity. It's got to the point where she doesn't show her badge or her classification apart from where her job dictates she has to.

'I'd have to be touching you, just your hand would do, it helps the connection. Then I'd take a look at your thoughts. Sort of like peering in through someone else's window, if that makes sense?'

His hands curl into fists and she waits for him to make his decision. 'Does it hurt?'

'No, it doesn't. And it would only be for a moment.'

Rodrigo licks his lips. Then he nods. An aborted thing, like he wants to take it back after making the decision to agree.

Maybe Isabel should check that he's sure, but she doesn't. Voronov has seen the confirmation and that's enough for her, enough for it to hold in court should accusations be made of non-consent.

She reaches for Rodrigo's hand. Nothing too sudden, he's spooked enough. His hand is cold and at her touch he lets out a shaky exhale. She leaves her fingers there, only the tips of her index and middle finger on the back of Rodrigo's hand.

They'd explained in class once how touch could help a weak connection, strengthen it and anchor it, made easier by the transference of electric pulses.

'All right?' she asks, peering up into Rodrigo's face.

Rodrigo swallows, Adam's apple bobbing with it, and nods again.

It's quick. Most people, when she tries something like this, think there'll be pain but there's nothing like that. They'd practised under the eye of their Guide, to show how seamless it should feel to the person on the receiving end of a connection. They're supposed to feel nothing. Not even a tickle. Doesn't matter if it's done with or without touch, the receiver should never even register your presence. It's something the PNP likes to throw around in their manifestos, how Gifted telepaths can sneak into your minds without you even knowing and invade your privacy.

Isabel closes her eyes, breathes in through her nose and out through her mouth as she reaches for the connection.

It's harder opening a pathway to a person under the influence of the pill, but suddenly it snaps open through the block. Thoughts that aren't her own spill into her head. She can't hear Rodrigo's voice in them, but they carry his essence. Isabel doesn't even need to dig too deep; she latches on to his next horrified thought and follows it back to its source memory.

The train is packed.

That's the first thing Isabel notices. The feeling of claustrophobia bleeds through the memory and she can feel everyone pressing around her from all sides.

It takes a moment for her to adjust. She's sitting higher than she normally does and can't look beyond the field of vision Rodrigo has from his point of view. It's one of the most frustrating things about going into someone else's memory. It's their memory. You can only see what they saw, smell what they smelled, move how they moved, no matter how much you want to turn around and look for all the things you know will give you a clue about something.

The book blurs in front of her eyes and the next thing she knows someone is crashing into her.

It's the deceased. He's standing. Rodrigo's own sense of déjà vu overlaps with hers. She thinks she recognises the man's face too and for a moment, that distracts her.

His eyes are wide open, and she sees exactly what Rodrigo meant. The awareness is there, completely, his expression horrified. The sound of his face hitting the glass is sickening. Isabel hears a crunch and for a brief moment, the victim's eyes roll back in his head. The smell of blood is quick to hit the air and Rodrigo is standing now too, Isabel with him. She feels the victim's shoulders under her hands as she tries to pull him back but isn't strong enough. The window breaks as he puts his head through it.

Screams, sharp and acute, threaten to deafen her and the carriage shakes with the number of people pushing past each other to get out. At least that's what Isabel assumes is happening, because her eyes are still on the man who is smashing his head over and over again into the broken glass.

It isn't a fit. This isn't someone losing it. No way.

Then the smell is right there, familiar but stronger than the ghost traces of it that had been in the train when she'd done her walk-through earlier. Like burnt human hair.

Isabel withdraws from the connection. It's disorientating and she doesn't realise until she's standing that Voronov has a hand at her elbow and has helped her up.

'Thanks,' she murmurs, brow puckering as she focuses on the new memory now inside her head, sealing it, compartmentalising it.

'No problem,' Voronov says. His hand lingers on her elbow and his eyes roam her face. Then he steps back, keeping any questions he might have to himself. Isabel appreciates that. Second-guessing her in front of a witness wouldn't help. And it would piss her off.

Isabel ignores the shakiness in her fingers and knees and forces another smile onto her face.

'Thank you, Rodrigo, you were a great help. Stay here a bit longer; get your feet under you. I'll ask someone to bring you some tea to warm you up, and then they'll have to take your details in case we have any further questions. Will that be okay?'

'Yes' – it comes out faint and shaky, so he clears his throat and then speaks again – 'yes, Inspector Reis. Thank you.'

'Thank you again for your help,' she says with a touch to his shoulder. 'Rodrigo, make sure you speak to someone if you have to.'

Rodrigo puts his head back in his hands.

The knock on the door comes as she turns back to Voronov. He's staring right at her.

Well. I suppose this is where I find out if he's a prejudiced prick, she thinks.

Voronov turns away and reaches to open the door. Jacinta is standing there, a small clear plastic bag in her hand with what looks like an ID badge inside.

'Can you step outside for a quick second?' Jacinta asks.

Isabel spares one last glance for their young witness before stepping outside with Voronov and pulling the door closed behind her. She eyes the bag in Jacinta's hand.

'Is this what I think it is?' Isabel asks.

Jacinta nods but she doesn't look happy. 'Take a look for yourself,' she says, handing the bag over.

Isabel turns it around in her hand, smoothing the plastic over the front of the victim's ID card inside. The lanyard is green, the bloodstained spots darker. She sees the name next to the ID's picture and understands why Jacinta is looking so grim.

'Merda,' Isabel bites off.

Jacinta sighs beside her. 'My thoughts exactly.'

It's the head of Portugal's National Testing Institute.

Gil dos Santos.

5

Isabel slides her thumb over the plastic bag, smoothing it and scrunching it over the ID card, as she chews on another energy bar.

The title and name are printed on a white background. On the right-hand corner, along the top of the card, is the university's name and logo, on the left is the deceased doctor's photo. A man in his early sixties, full head of dark hair and square-rimmed glasses on an angular face. No smile.

The NTI was set up by the government as the main body dedicated to the study and the acclimation of Gifted people in Portugal. It's responsible for all the testing centres and the setting up of the Gifted Registry, as well as the monitoring, which keeps tabs on higher-level Gifted. They coordinate the testing seasons and although they're mostly funded by the government there is private investor money going in too. They have their fingers in a lot of pies when it comes to Gifted study and research.

And now one of its figureheads is dead – and he hasn't passed away quietly in the night.

The media is going to have a field day.

Isabel tosses it back in the evidence box, trying not to fixate on how empty it is right now and leans back in her chair. She finishes the bar and drops the wrapper into the bin. She needs a proper meal. The headache is settled square between her eyes and after reading three witnesses that morning she really needs to replenish her energy.

The light in the case room is bright and feels like it's stabbing her in the eyes despite the aspirin she'd taken on the way back to the station from Gare do Oriente.

Isabel and Voronov had made the trip back to the station separately, which Isabel had been grateful for. The familiarity of her own space had been soothing in the wake of the pain building steadily behind her eyes through the two hours or so of witness interviews.

Her head throbs with it now and she fights to keep from wincing, muttering under her breath. The problem with the aspirin is that once the headache is in place then nothing dislodges it.

The pill's job is to tamp down her Gift, forcing it under. It's what causes the headaches. Gifts aren't meant to be suppressed; though when she first started medicating Isabel had been assured that the pills don't cause permanent damage. Isabel has always wondered if anyone in power would care if they did. Sometimes she thinks she doesn't want to know the answer to that.

Isabel is still staring at the ID when the Chief sticks her head out of her office.

'Reis, come in here please.'

Isabel stands, trying to work the crick out of her neck as she does so. She nods hello to a few colleagues arriving for their shift.

They're on the second floor of the building. The station is a ratty thing that has seen better days. It needs a new coat of paint and some central heating. Isabel walks into her boss's office with her scarf still wrapped around her neck, wishing for another coffee and a sandwich.

Voronov is already seated in one of the chairs across from the Chief. Isabel takes the other one and folds her arms across her chest, trying to keep what warmth she can cling to in this icicle of a room.

'Okay. What's the situation?' Chief Bautista's got a voice that sounds like paper rasping over bumpy concrete. It's the voice of someone who has spent their entire life drinking and smoking too much but it carries across a room like crazy. The Chief is in her late fifties. Her salt and pepper hair is down; loose staticky curls that come down to her chin, cut with borderline OCD precision. Isabel always wonders if they used a ruler when they gave her that haircut.

'What did the witnesses have to say?'

'There was a young man who tried to stop the vic from bashing his head in. Obviously it didn't work, but he was pretty up close and personal during the whole thing,' Isabel says.

The Chief narrows her eyes at Isabel. 'And what did you get from him?'

'From the conversation he had with Inspector Reis,' Voronov says, 'it seems that he's not sure exactly what happened. It could have been a fit but he doesn't think it was.'

'And?'

'And,' Isabel says, sighing because she knows what look she's about to get, 'I asked for his permission to see the memory. And two other witnesses as well.'

'Reis. You know the situation we're in. You can't just peep into people's memories; we have protocols—'

Isabel puts her hands up to hold her off. 'Chief, the kid was in shock and I needed to get the most accurate possible view of the whole thing. I asked for his consent and Inspector Voronov served as a witness. No foul play. Same with the other two. I followed protocol, I promise.'

That takes the wind out of the Chief's sails but she still harrumphs as she eases back in her chair. 'In the current climate, we have to be careful with these things. Voronov,' she says, sounding like a barking drill sergeant, 'you'll need to fill out a statement detailing Inspector Reis's use of her Gift during the interviews. I want it on my desk by tomorrow morning. I want yours too, Isabel.'

'Yes, Chief,' he says.

Isabel nods.

'Carry on,' the Chief says.

Isabel thinks back on what she saw. 'A lot of the other passengers claimed he was just a crazy guy who lost it, some say he was trying to go for his bag and that's what set everyone off. Others are saying that he was having a fit and everyone panicked.' Isabel sits up in her seat and drags a hand through her hair, pulling it back from her face. 'We can't rule out the breakdown or medical condition theory yet. But from what I saw, I think we should be worried. There's a strong possibility that there was more at play here.'

'You think that maybe this was a result of someone using their Gift on him. As in someone used their Gift to physically move him? Can that even be done?'

Isabel nods. 'I don't know what kind of level a Gifted person would have to be to be able to actually influence a person's whole body like this. I'm guessing it would have to be a monitored level. To be honest, after what happened in Colombo, would it really be such a shock? I think we need to make sure we've ruled out health issues and anything else of that nature before going down that avenue. The autopsy results will be useful.'

'Okay,' the Chief says, 'you do what you need to do. Anything else I should know?'

Isabel catches the look Voronov throws her way. 'We found ID on the deceased,' she says, 'it's Gil dos Santos.'

The Chief curses under her breath. 'One of the heads of NTI?'

'Unfortunately,' Isabel says. 'He has a wife. We're going to go and see her.'

'So you're telling me we're going to have a media circus with the press circling our investigation like vultures.'

Neither Isabel nor Voronov say anything. They don't have to.

'Fine, try and keep as tight a lid on this as possible. Isabel, make sure you do everything by the book. I know you're good and you follow the rules, so don't give me that look. I'm saying this because this is going to be high-profile, and you know as well as I do that the public is in the mood for more Gifted blood. I don't want to give them anything to hang you by, understand?'

'Maybe it won't come to that,' Isabel says. 'For all we know, it really was an unfortunate incident and we'll have an open-and-shut on this one.'

The Chief sighs and rubs her eyes. 'I hope so, Reis. What about the rest of the team?'

'We've been assigned a room in case this blows up. Carla's in there setting up with Daniel. I think Jacinta's on her way. We're heading over now for a quick briefing, see where we're at.'

'Keep me posted. You can go.'

As they walk to the case room, Voronov keeps step with her.

'Today has been the first time I've seen telepathy used like that,' he says.

Isabel gives him the side-eye. 'Oh? And? Is it going to be a problem?'

Voronov stops in the middle of the corridor and Isabel does too. No one notices; they keep going about their day, immersed in their heavy caseloads.

'Should it be?' he asks.

'No. It shouldn't. Not to be an arsehole but I think as your new partner, it'd put my mind at ease if I knew that it really wasn't going to be a problem.'

'It won't be a problem.'

'Good to know,' Isabel says and carries on to the room. 'I just wanted us to be clear.'

'We're clear.'

6

The case room is halfway to set up when they all gather to go over preliminaries.

'Right, so most of our witnesses either haven't seen anything or they don't understand what happened,' Daniel says.

Isabel and Voronov are at the end of the table; Jacinta and Daniel are sitting across from them. Carla is at the desks that line the wall, setting up the binders, carefully labelling them as she goes. Voronov's rolled up his sleeves past his elbows and is leaning back in his chair, rocking back and forth in it. Everyone's got rid of their coats and the coffee pot has made the rounds.

Isabel needs that proper meal soon. She's relieved she didn't have to access too many memories. People don't usually want someone in their head and despite what most Regular people think, Isabel would rather stay in her own mind. Less energy expended; fewer horrors seen.

'Yes,' Isabel says, tapping the ID absently, 'but we have this. Gil dos Santos.' She sits up and resettles in her seat so she's facing the rest of the team. 'As we know, he was one of the heads of Portugal's National Testing Institute, so that's a big deal. They run a pretty tight ship, they're heavily involved in the organisation of the Gifted testing and they work closely with the government and the Registry. I'm sure they do more than that.'

The NTI work *too* closely with the government for Isabel's liking, and there are many things about them that aren't shared with the public. There are even rumours of experimentation and militarisation, but nothing like that has ever been confirmed.

'In any case,' she says, 'he's a big name. Not the best of starts for us. The press will be on us the moment they catch wind of it.'

The case room they've been assigned is too airy for Isabel's taste but they're lucky to have one, so she hasn't complained about it. Also, if she complained, Chief would tell her to fuck off. It's not the best idea to irritate the Chief before lunch has even taken place.

'Until we get news back from the autopsy, we won't be able to rule out the health issues angle. Ideally, that's what I would've liked it to be but after seeing those memories we need to make sure.'

'We've found something that we can start looking at,' Jacinta says. 'Gil's bag. We have his mobile phone and by the looks of it his work computer, so we can look through that, see if it throws up anything interesting.'

'We'll need to be cautious,' Isabel says, 'we don't want the media getting any closer to this than they have to, especially if we have to confirm that this was done by someone Gifted.'

Voronov hums, eyes fixed on the table, thinking it through. 'I think at this point we're all leaning towards this being a crime. We need to go over what the crime scene officers have found,' he goes on, 'check the CCTV too, see if we can spot anything there.'

'That's a good place to start,' Carla says and sets down the last binder. She has a notebook out and is scribbling in it. 'We'll look into that.'

'Are we getting any prints?' Isabel asks Jacinta. They might as well dot all the i's and cross all the t's.

'Yeah,' Jacinta says, 'I left them working on it.'

'Good,' Isabel says and pushes her chair back. 'Voronov and I are going to speak to the wife. Lucky for us Gil and his wife spend most of their time at their house in Sesimbra. We'll go and deliver the bad news. If we could get a meeting with the other head of NTI that would be great.'

'On it,' Carla says.

Jacinta sits back, pouring some more coffee into her cup. 'Okay, while Carla gets on that, Daniel and I will start going through his things. See what comes up.'

'All right,' Isabel says, getting up, 'sounds good. You good to go?' she asks Voronov.

The precinct is near the Anjos metro, not all that far from the main terminals of Cais do Sodré and Terreiro do Paço. Despite having seen better days, their building still looks new in comparison to the one across from it, with its fading tiles and potted plants on balconies. Beneath the balconies is a café, a bright red canopy proclaiming its name, with tables set out underneath. It's peak time and Isabel can see in through the door to the customers standing at the counter, drinking down their quick coffee to the buzz of catch-ups.

'Sesimbra is a bit of a drive,' Isabel says. 'I need something to eat now.' She veers away from where their cars are parked and waits for an old grandpa to drive past. She crosses the road and heads straight for the café ahead. 'Have you had anything?' she asks.

'Not since leaving the house this morning.'

'Good. I'm starving.'

It's an older café that's been there since before Isabel started working at the PJ. Isabel likes it. They always just leave her to it and they've never given her shit over being Gifted. Sure, they don't know what her Gift is, but they've known her long enough to know she has one and not care.

Old man Días is sitting at one of the small round tables, deep in conversation with a customer, gesturing at the TV suspended from the wall. The café is filled with conversations, people on breaks from work grabbing a coffee with colleagues before heading back in. The old man's wife and son are behind the counter, serving and chatting with the customers drinking there.

'Hey, old man,' Isabel calls out, heading straight for the food. The selection of cakes is spread all along the left corner of the counter, flaky custard tarts, bolas de Berlím filled to the brim with sweet yellow cream, chocolate and confectioner's-cream tarts and so many more. On the other side are the day's sandwich offerings, breaded chicken, chouriço omelette, tuna mayo and other snacks. She glances over the chalkboard with its daily menu.

Old man Días twists in his chair to look at her, bushy black eyebrows standing out against his full head of white hair.

'Ah. Was wondering about you. Haven't seen you in a while. Took a holiday?'

Isabel scoffs. 'Been busy.' She stops in front of the menu. 'What've you got?' Her phone vibrates in her pocket and she tugs it out.

'Well menina, that depends, have you eaten today?'

'Didn't have time,' she says, looking down at her phone screen. Her sister's name stares up at her. 'And we're on our way somewhere so we can't stop either, it'll have to be to go.' She presses the ignore button and puts the phone back into her pocket.

'Adriana,' he calls out to his wife, who is in the middle of taking a payment. 'Get Isabel some of the picadinho to take with her.'

Adriana looks at Isabel with a smile. 'Anything else?'

Before Isabel can answer, old man Días calls out again. 'And who's that with you? New friend? No introductions? No manners these days.'

Isabel looks at Voronov, who's been watching the whole back and forth with an amused curve to his mouth. 'Yeah,' Isabel says, 'my manners. Sorry. This is Inspector Voronov.' She slaps a hand on Voronov's shoulder and—

—*seems pretty familiar with*—

Isabel drops her hand and steps back, tries not to let it show on her face as she disconnects from the unexpected flow of thoughts. 'He's a new face,' she says, 'he'll be working with me from now on.' Not that she has much choice in that.

Old man Días starts nodding his head vigorously. 'Good, good. Not healthy always working by yourself,' then to Voronov, 'you'll take some picadinho too. Adriana, you heard that?'

'The whole street heard you,' she says, rolling her eyes before smiling at them. 'I'll make sure they're ready to go. What else did you want?'

They walk out of there with two tubs of picadinho, Isabel's mouth watering from the smell of stewed pork. On top of that, they have a huge fresh bread omelette sandwich each, a slice of tortilha for Isabel and a box of assorted cakes on top of that. Two coffees and bottles of water rustle in the plastic bag old man Días has given them. Voronov looks stunned by the amount of food Isabel is cradling to her chest as he unlocks the car door.

The car, when they get in, is freezing and does nothing to help with the pulse at her temples. But Isabel is more concerned about how Voronov's thoughts had just slipped into her mind. She'd forgotten herself. The pill holds a lot of thoughts back, but touch is like a conduit and still allows things to slip into her head if she doesn't actively have her walls up.

Isabel shuts the door in a hurry and sets the food on her lap. The heat of the containers imprints on her thighs and the smell of the food fills the car.

'Here,' she says, handing Voronov his, along with the plastic cutlery. She sets aside the rest. 'Adriana was born in Madeira. She makes the best picadinho.'

'Yes, I could tell,' Voronov says. 'The accent.'

'Hmm. As for the food,' she gestures at her bounty, 'I'm not sure how much you know about Gifted but some of us burn through a lot of energy when using our Gifts. I'm normally quite good about getting fuelled up but didn't get a chance today because of, well, you know.'

Voronov watches her peel the lid off the food; the smell of the pork and mushroom sauce becomes stronger. 'How fast do you usually burn through it?'

She shrugs. 'I'll need to eat again in a couple of hours. Longer if I don't use my Gift for the rest of the day.' She shoves a forkful of fried potato chunks drowned in sauce into her mouth and groans in bliss. 'I recognise your name,' she says. 'But I can't place it. Want to tell me where I know it from?'

'You could've asked the Chief.'

Isabel doesn't say anything right away, letting the sound of the car heater fill the space instead. She's now realising how cold her feet were before. She wriggles her toes in her trainers as warmth bathes her ankles and begins to rise steadily. 'Doesn't sound like the best way to start a new partnership with someone.'

Voronov looks at her, head tilted, considering. He's got his own tub on his lap. 'No,' he says and gives her a slow nod, 'I appreciate that. And if you want to look into my history, that's fine by me too.'

But you're not going to tell me, she thinks and gives him a wry smile. 'Fair enough. Tuck into that before it gets cold. You'll ruin all of Adriana's hard work.'

They finish the rest of their meal in silence.

7

The wind is a vicious thing, ripping the clouds from their stasis and scrolling them across the sky, solid grey and threatening. Not a drop dots the windscreen as Voronov navigates the narrow and bumpy streets of Sesimbra, the car rocking over roads that haven't seen maintenance in too long. They don't talk much during the ride. Isabel has no issues with not driving. It leaves her free to go into her own head and mull things over. Besides, it's too soon to have him in her personal spaces, so his car works out fine. The low noise from the radio, with its old-school rock ballads playing as background noise, suits her too. She stares out the window. Trees tower over them from the side of the road as they go higher up.

It takes them longer to reach their destination than it should because of a few roads that have been closed off for one reason or another. They pass several people out on the rocks fishing, comfortable as anything despite the volatile weather and the steepness of the rocks.

As Voronov rolls the car to a stop Isabel thinks she wouldn't mind doing the labyrinth of tiny streets and bad potholes every day if it gets her the view she lays her eyes on now.

She lets out a low whistle and leans forward, peering out the windscreen at the stretch of the sea before them.

The more modern builds are at the top of the hill that guards Sesimbra's California Beach. The houses aren't the most scenic; they're tall, flat, modern-looking buildings that wouldn't fit in with the old-world charm of the ones below. The way these houses have been laid out creates a stair effect, each one set higher than the one before it. Driveways divide them from each other.

'Which number?' Isabel asks, tugging her coat on.

Voronov is out of the car and looking at the houses. 'Number seven,' he says and steps back to shut the door.

Isabel follows suit and falls into step with him.

There's an odd stillness up here. No sound coming from any of the houses, no loud TV, no pans on stoves, or barking dogs, nothing. Just the wind whistling as it sweeps past and the sound of the waves crashing below. Then again, it's mid-afternoon on a weekday, so Isabel supposes it's not so odd.

This location is removed from all the life going on below, where homes are all crowded together, surrounded by cafés and shops and markets and people wandering the beach. Up here, it's all isolation and incredible views. Some are most likely holiday homes that fill up in the summer, not in these chilly months.

Isabel's hairband has given up its fight and bits of her hair have come free, whipping against the side of her face and catching on her mouth as they walk. She pushes it back, to no avail. Why had she thought it'd be a good idea to cut it so close to winter? The back of her neck is going to be frozen before they get there. She rubs at it as she considers the house. She's never been that great at this part of the job. Sorry is such a useless word when you're telling someone their loved one is dead.

Number 7 has heavy potted plants with winter-defying glossy green leaves lining the base of its walls. There's a small car in the driveway, a silver KIA, but there's enough space for two more.

The first knock doesn't get a response, but the second one does.

'Just a moment!' Loud heels clipping on the floor at a fast pace sound from the other side.

The woman who opens the door has her mobile phone in her hand and is polished to her core. Artfully dyed blond hair falls in sleek waves around her face and she has small wrinkles on her carefully made-up face. She looks from Isabel to Voronov, her expression polite but with a touch of impatience she can't quite hide.

'Can I help you?' she asks.

37

'We're looking for Mrs Irina dos Santos,' Isabel says.

'Yes?'

Voronov steps up. 'Mrs dos Santos?'

Her polite smile wavers but stays in place. 'Yes. Sorry, who are you?'

'Inspector Voronov,' he says, showing her his badge.

Mrs dos Santos glances down at it, confused. The smile falls off her face.

'This is my partner, Inspector Reis. Mrs dos Santos, would it be possible for us to speak inside?'

Mrs dos Santos pulls her hand away and some of the sleekness disappears from her posture as she takes an uncertain step back. 'What is this about?' She opens the door wider, moves aside and gestures them in.

'Thank you,' Isabel says and walks in ahead of her and Mrs dos Santos closes the door behind them, shutting out the sound of the wind. It's all dark wooden floors, the hallway they go through into the living room a long and shadowed thing, curtains open but lights left off.

'Please have a seat,' Mrs dos Santos says. 'Sorry, I just got home myself, can I get you both anything to drink?' She's smiling at them but it's strained, the corners of her mouth not quite steady.

'No, thank you.'

Voronov murmurs something along the same lines as he takes a seat next to Isabel.

Like the outside of the house, the inside is pretty modern too. Minimalist in a way that's still not seen often in Portuguese homes. Everything is in its place, as if ready for a photographer to come by and snap pictures for a home magazine.

Mrs dos Santos would've fit right in with that photoshoot on any other day, but today isn't one of those days.

She's wearing all black and the longer she stands there, the more the illusion of the make-up on her face fades away and the woman beneath shows through. The lipstick can't hide the down-ward curl of her mouth when the smile slides away and the red of her eyes becomes more prominent. Tiredness rolls off her and Isabel can feel it soaking in through her own skin.

That Isabel can feel it so effortlessly is worrying.

'Mrs dos Santos,' Voronov says, 'I'm afraid we come with bad news. There was an incident this morning in Gare do Oriente terminal and a person was killed. Your husband has been identified as that person. I'm very sorry. My condolences.'

Mrs dos Santos seems lost for a moment, eyes searching the room around them as if waiting for someone to jump out and yell out that it's a joke.

'I . . .' She sits down in a chair across from them as if in slow motion. She frowns and shakes her head. 'What? That doesn't make any sense. He—'

'I'm very sorry for your loss,' Isabel says. 'He was identified by his ID.'

Isabel isn't sure that Mrs dos Santos is listening any more. She's staring at an empty spot on the wall and Isabel feels a compulsion to look away, switch off from the first inklings of grief. Seeing it always unsettles her, pulls Isabel towards memories she'd rather stayed wrapped tightly and out of sight.

'Mrs dos Santos,' Isabel tries again, 'could you tell us where your husband was going this morning?'

'Work,' Mrs dos Santos says, her voice hollow and slow like she's coming to them from very far away. 'My husband left for work this morning. He had a meeting at ten fifteen.' She looks at them then, eyes alive and fierce. 'Have you called? Have you checked to see if he's arrived? He could've dropped his ID. Maybe this person randomly picked it up. Do you have it? Can I see it?'

It would be a stretch. Even in the state that they'd found Gil, it had been easy to connect him to the picture of the man on the ID card.

Before either she or Voronov can say anything else, Mrs dos Santos is on her feet again, pacing around the sofa and tapping one-handed at her phone before putting it to her ear and turning her back on them.

The phone call that follows is brief and furious and it's followed by a silence that has Isabel watching their late victim's wife cautiously.

'I don't understand,' Mrs dos Santos says. Her arm hangs loose at her side; her fingers are white around her phone. 'I don't understand. He was fine when he walked out of the house this morning.'

'Irina,' Isabel says.

That gets a reaction. Mrs dos Santos looks at Isabel and her eyes have the clarity of a mad person.

Isabel settles back in her seat and waits it out, lets Voronov lead so she can steady herself and her wards.

Soft as dew gathering on grass, Isabel allows her Gift to unfurl and reach for the woman sitting stiffly across from her, hating this part of her role here. Everyone is different, but willingly seeking the emotions of a person who has recently been given this kind of news is never a pleasant thing.

It's like there's a fog around Isabel's senses though, too dense for her to break through. She needs a trigger, something to make Mrs dos Santos' thoughts spike enough for Isabel to capture a snapshot of them, even if only a sliver.

'Irina,' Isabel says again. She leans forward, clasping her own hands together and meeting Mrs dos Santos' gaze. A grieving woman. That's what she has to remember here. It doesn't matter what her husband did for a living. The woman sitting in front of her is a woman who can't even comprehend the change her life is about to go through. Shock hasn't had a chance to settle in yet. Isabel gives Voronov a pointed glance. 'Maybe you should come with us. I think you need to see this for yourself.'

8

The coroner at the sign-in desk frowns at Isabel when she looks up at the window and sees her standing there. She peers over Isabel's shoulder at Voronov and Mrs dos Santos.

'Busy day?' she asks Isabel. 'Sorry, we're a bit short-staffed so we're having to man the desks as well.'

'Sure,' Isabel pencils her name in for the second time that day, 'we're here for the deceased that came in earlier from Gare do Oriente.' It feels surreal that she was here just this morning. The day has taken a toll and Isabel is trying not to think about face-planting into her sofa when she gets in. Shut her eyes, feel her headache fade away along with the clinging emotions of terrified witnesses and a newly made widow in shock.

'Your colleague called ahead. I'll walk you through.'

Mrs dos Santos is a heavy silent presence at their back as they walk. Her face is pallid, and her fingers rigid where they hold her clutch bag. Her eyes are downcast. Isabel doesn't think the woman's looked up since they got out of the car.

Voronov follows behind Mrs dos Santos and his eyes meet Isabel's.

Isabel can sense the woman's pain.

It had started to affect her halfway through the ride back. People experienced emotions differently. Mrs dos Santos' sorrow is a rusted brown red that seems to fleck the air around them, Isabel breathing it in with each inhale. Isabel checks her watch, mindful of how long it's been since she snuck in another pill before they'd left the precinct. Its effects will start waning soon. The barrier the pills provide tends to last for four hours or so. The funny thing is, the headache is still lodged right there, tucked against her left temple and clinging with a stubbornness that lets Isabel knows it's not going anywhere soon.

Right now, there's a deep-seated weight of pain that's weighing Isabel's stomach down and clenching at her chest. Something that doesn't belong in her body and mind and that has Mrs dos Santos' signature all over it. It had got gradually worse on the drive over and now it's as though the other woman's pain is a physical thing that Isabel can feel as if it were her own.

Isabel follows the coroner into the room and holds the door open for Voronov and Mrs dos Santos.

Mrs dos Santos stops when she gets inside the door. Her spine snaps straight and her sharp intake of breath is audible in the cold room.

The coroner heads to the slot furthest away from the door. The room is chilled and maybe it's Isabel's imagination, but it feels as if the room drops further in temperature when the coroner tugs the door open and pulls out the slab, revealing the body covered in a white sheet.

Isabel braces herself, mind flashing back to Gil's wrecked body and ruined face in the train carriage.

Mrs dos Santos's eyes are fixed on the covered body on the slab and she doesn't even seem like she's breathing.

Cautious, Isabel draws closer.

'Mrs dos Santos?' Isabel says, voice as soothing as she can make it. She's afraid the woman is about to bolt on them. 'Do you need a moment?'

Mrs dos Santos clears her throat and strides further into the room. Her shoulders are up tight around her neck, both hands clasping her bag in front of her. Isabel looks at Voronov and follows Mrs dos Santos until they're both standing beside the body.

The coroner glances from Isabel's face to Mrs dos Santos and Isabel watches the coroner's expression soften in sympathy. 'I'm going to pull the sheet down now.'

Mrs dos Santos takes a deep breath and squares her shoulders, before giving a sharp nod of assent.

'I need to warn you, the nature of his injuries means that the face looks significantly damaged. If you need to take a moment just let me know.'

'Okay,' Mrs dos Santos says, her voice barely above a whisper.

The coroner looks to Isabel and Voronov for confirmation. Voronov motions for her to go ahead. The coroner folds the sheet back.

Isabel has to take a deep breath at the sight of the body.

Gil has been cleaned up and there's no longer one open eye staring out at her. The cuts, scrapes and scratches to the face distort his features, the bad bruising making his face discoloured.

Mrs dos Santos flinches. She turns on her heel, a muffled sound escaping her that makes Isabel think of a wounded animal as she rushes out of the room, tripping over her feet and almost going down before she makes it to the door.

'Merda,' Isabel says and moves to go after her. 'Voronov—'

'Go.'

Mrs dos Santos hasn't gone far; she's sitting on the steps outside the morgue, head in her hands, and drawing in large gulps of air.

Isabel kneels in front of her. She touches her shoulder and if the pain emanating from the woman had been a heavy weight to bear before, now it robs Isabel of her breath, weakening her knees. Isabel grits her teeth and pushes through it. She needs to stay on track here. 'Mrs dos Santos?' Isabel watches the other woman's face, concerned, hoping she isn't going to start hyperventilating right there on the steps. 'Mrs dos Santos?'

'It's Gil,' she says.

Isabel sits on the cold steps beside her, leaving her hand on the woman's shoulder. But beneath Isabel's headache, which is making her want to nail her own head through a wall, she feels the static chaos of the widow's emotions bombarding her, bursting like morbid fireworks in her chest. Snatches of Mrs dos Santos' thoughts slice into Isabel's mind and stick to it like shards. Isabel digs her thumb into her own temple.

'Reis.'

Isabel looks up. Voronov towers over them, a questioning frown on his face.

Isabel forces herself past Mrs dos Santos' tumultuous thoughts and the dull throb of the headache. 'Can you get Mrs dos Santos somewhere warm?' she asks, standing. 'I'll be right back.'

Isabel heads back inside, and every step between her and the grieving woman is like a breath of fresh air, their connection stretching thin, and then snapping altogether when Isabel locks herself in the morgue's cramped bathroom. She takes a moment, breathing through it, before pushing away from the door to go and splash some water on her face, grounding herself by slowing her breathing and not letting herself focus on anything but the sting of cold water on her skin and the rise and fall of her own chest.

The small mirror above the sink reflects her face leached of all colour, the squint of pain to her eyes. She stays there a few moments longer, just existing in the absence of outside emotions, the rush of the running tap another layer to soothe her senses. Then she forces her back straight, pieces back together her wards as best as she can and heads back to her waiting partner.

Someone has wrapped a blanket around Mrs dos Santos and put her in the warmest room at the precinct.

It's only been a few hours since they walked into the dos Santos' home, but she couldn't be more different from the woman who greeted them at the door. Now, she sits curled in on herself, a hand clutching the lapels of the coat closed at her throat, eyes fixed on the wall in front of her, unmoving.

'Irina,' Isabel says, 'Gil. Was he an unhappy man?'

That seems to do it. 'No. No. He has his work, we're—' She chokes, coughs and presses the back of her hand to her mouth. 'We're happily married. We have friends and a good family. I don't understand. What happened?'

Isabel looks to Voronov, handing it over.

'We were called to the station this morning over a disturbance,' he says. 'As we understand it so far, your husband was injured during the commotion. From witness statements and also the nature of his injuries' – Mrs dos Santos' face loses another shade of colour at that – 'we need to determine whether your husband had a reason to harm himself.'

'What?' Mrs dos Santos chokes out something that sounds like a garbled laugh but there's no real mirth anywhere on the woman's face. Her hands curl tighter around the mug. The diamond rings littering the fingers of her left hand gleam. 'Are you trying to tell me Gil committed suicide? Is that what you're trying to tell me?'

'You don't think that's possible? That it's something he may have considered?' Isabel asks, voice still soft, still coaxing.

And Isabel gets what she's looking for. It's sharper than it should be considering that Isabel isn't even touching the subject. The pill's effect is fading. The emotions swell and the projected image is clear, a swell of affection and contentment all condensed into two hands holding each other, one bigger and long-fingered, wedding ring glinting in the light.

So, happy, Isabel thinks. At least from the wife's point of view. For all Isabel knows, Gil felt differently.

'No, Inspector.' Irina dos Santos sighs, her shoulders slump and she pushes her fingers through her hair, dragging it back from her face. It leaves the once-perfect hairstyle in disarray. 'I don't think that sounds like Gil. He was a driven man; his work took more time from him than it should have.' She can't quite meet Isabel's eyes. Probably a point of contention between them, Isabel thinks. 'No. I don't think he killed himself.'

'Is there anything of note you can tell us? Anything that you know may have upset him recently or caused him any significant problems?' Voronov leans forward, all sympathetic face and unthreatening posture.

'So that you can prove he committed suicide? I'm telling you that's not Gil. He has—' She catches herself. Her mouth trembles, but then it's back under control and she stares at them both hard.

'He was in a good place in his life, Inspectors.' She's building a wall around herself; doesn't even realise she's doing it, but Isabel can feel it, like cement pouring into a mould.

'He'd been stressed. For some time now. Don't misunderstand, he was coping. But he was upset with some things going on at work, from what I could understand. It never sounded like . . . like this would be the outcome.'

'Do you know what kind of issues he was having at work? Did he speak about them with you?' Voronov asks.

'No. Not much. I know it was in relation to Julio.'

'Julio?' Isabel asks.

'Julio Soares. Julio's father, Bento Soares, is a good—was a good friend of his – of ours. But I can't say for sure. Gil didn't discuss these things with me.'

Bento Soares. Just the name makes Isabel's stomach do a sickly turn. He's the very well-known leader of the successful PNP political party, who are quite open about their anti-Gifted rhetoric and policies.

It makes sense, considering Gil's profession and role within NTI, that he would be involved with a high-profile politician. Having a friend like Gil would have been something that someone like Soares would never pass up.

'Had Gil and Julio Soares been in recent contact?' Isabel asks.

'I'm not sure, they cross paths often, work on projects together and there are various functions that we attend where the Soares' are regular attendees also.'

'I see,' Isabel says. Any events attended by the Soares family were not where any Gifted person would want to be. 'Is there anything else you can tell us?'

Mrs dos Santos shakes her head, hands spreading palm-up as if in supplication. She looks lost and like she doesn't understand any of what's happening. 'If that's all, Inspectors, I'd like to go home. Thank you.' Her tone brooks no refusal.

Isabel stands. 'Thank you for your time. We'll be in touch about the progress of the investigation.'

'In the meantime, if you do think of anything else,' Voronov says and pulls a card out of his pocket and hands it to her, 'please don't hesitate to contact us.'

Mrs dos Santos stands up, the scrape of her chair on the floor a grating sound.

Isabel and Voronov stand too. 'Once again, we're sorry for your loss. We'll have someone take you home,' Isabel says.

Mrs dos Santos nods and without waiting for them leaves the room.

Isabel sits back on the edge of the table, tucking her hands into her pockets, and stares out the door that Mrs dos Santos left through.

9

Walking back to the case room after Mrs dos Santos has left, Isabel finds three missed calls on her phone, two more from her sister Rita and one from their brother Sebastião.

She frowns down at it, not in the mood to deal with her sister, in particular, right now. The effects of the pill are fading fast and the headache has eased from being a pulsing, living thing to an annoying ache. Isabel tries to remember if she's still got a batch of pills in her desk drawer. Taking another one will get her through the rest of the day but it'll also drag back the intensity of the headache. It's such a part of her daily routine you'd think she was used to it by now.

Every day, without fail, one at each meal if she can. She tries to never go over three pills, but with long workdays, sometimes she has to go for the fourth. They only ever last for about four hours each time; five if she's stretching it, but by then, if she's not concentrating, thoughts start slipping in.

'Go ahead and meet the others,' she says to Voronov, 'I'll be right there.'

Voronov gives her a long look. 'Sure. We'll wait for you.'

Isabel makes it quick and gives the room a sweep, but no one is watching her when she sits down at her desk and yanks open her drawer, rifling through everything until she finds the spare box that has been flattened under the weight of paperwork she'd dumped on top of it. She takes out a pill and pops it in her mouth, goes to the water station and washes it down.

When she gets back to the case room, Carla is already there and so is Daniel.

'Jacinta?' Isabel asks as she pulls out a chair and sits down beside Voronov.

'She's checking on forensics, seeing what updates they have for us,' Daniel says.

'Okay,' Isabel says. 'The wife says he was happy, no suicidal inclinations, and as far as we know, no health issues, but we're still waiting for confirmation on that. Though I don't think we need it, at this point. The only thing of note she brought up is that Gil was stressed with work and there'd been an issue with Julio Soares.'

Carla sighs. 'Bento Soares' son?'

'Unfortunately for us, yes. The Soares' aren't the most Gifted-friendly family. I'll look into what exactly Julio Soares does that would have him working with the National Testing Institute,' Isabel says. 'We're going to need to speak to him as well, see if there's something there.'

'We can help there,' Carla says, and Daniel slides a paper onto the table. Isabel and Voronov lean over to see.

'What is this?' Isabel asks.

'List of numbers on Gil's phone, recent log, takes us as far back as last month.' Daniel leans over and taps at the last number with his pen. 'That's the last call Gil received yesterday. And I've already checked it – the number is registered on his phone under Julio Soares.'

'Oh?' Isabel looks back up at Carla. 'Great. Let's give him a call.'

'I'll contact him,' Carla says, 'he works at the university. If we have any difficulties reaching him, I can always try him there. In the meantime, we have been given the go-ahead for Célia Armindas, the other head at NTI, so she would have worked closely with Gil. If this is related to NTI she might know some-thing. She's expecting us at nine thirty a.m. tomorrow.'

Isabel breathes out, rubbing at her temple absently. 'Okay, not too bad. Any other updates?'

'We're combing through Gil's diary commitments for today. There's a note in his paper diary but it's a few letters pencilled in, doesn't say what it is. We're also checking the papers he had on him at the time. Looks like he was making some comments on a preliminary study. It doesn't look relevant, but we'll keep going. Here, this is it. Take a look.'

Voronov reaches across the table and drags the diary over. Scrawled in pencil in that day's slot is: HSL – 14.15

'All right, well that doesn't mean much,' Isabel mutters. 'Maybe Armindas can shed some light tomorrow.'

'We're working on getting his laptop, check what he might have on there as well.'

'Nothing on his cloud calendar?'

'Not that we could see,' Carla says.

'Anything from the station?' Voronov asks.

Carla shakes her head. 'Not yet. They've been on damage control since this morning so it's chaos over there. I've requested copies of all CCTV footage, see if we can spot anything there.'

'Look,' Isabel says, and her tone has everyone's attention on her, 'we'll need to be prepared for what might be coming our way, especially with the Soares' name thrown into the mix. When,' she crosses her arms, 'and I do think it'll be a when, not if, the autopsy report comes back and we know for sure this wasn't an underlying health condition, we'll officially have a murder on our hands committed by a Gifted individual. From what the witnesses said, we're looking at a telekinetic who has possibly used their powers to physically move Gil dos Santos' body enough to kill him, something not documented anywhere as having happened before. We'll have to be ready for the press and PNP if this gets out.' She pauses and looks at each of them in turn, stopping on Voronov, locking eyes with him before she goes on. 'When that happens, we are a team. Not one piece of information leaves our mouths unless it's to each other or the Chief.'

For a moment the room is quiet as the enormity of this case settles over them all.

For his part, Voronov hasn't looked away from her, and there's a small unamused smile on his face that tells Isabel her message has been received.

'All right.' Isabel eases back in her chair, linking her hands behind her head. 'Looks like we're going to have to sit on this one overnight.'

The sky is darkening as Isabel eases her way out of traffic and into the smaller roads leading to the older district. Investment in the area in recent years means that these cracked wall buildings and steep pavements are interspersed with scaffolding where renovations are taking place.

As usual, it takes at least a ten-minute search to find parking, but Isabel manages to tuck her car into a spot off the square and then begins the trek up the long narrow street to her home. The tram, with its bright yellow and brown roof, waits at the bottom of the slope as passengers get on. People tired from work, nestling into what seats they can find. Papers crinkle open and plastic bags filled with groceries rustle as they're set at people's feet. It'll be a while before the tram makes its way up and past her house, and by then it'll be packed to the brim.

Isabel walks up the steep cobblestone pavement, glad she'd thrown trainers on when she'd left in a hurry that morning. She hates walking up the steep road in smart shoes. It always feels too slippery even after living here for four years.

Lisbon is built on hills, more than the seven hills of myth, and the sloping streets have always been a part of it. Isabel loves them, but in the back of her mind there's always a voice telling her that one day she's going to fall.

When she gets inside the house she's enveloped by cool air, and shivers. Toeing off her trainers, she goes straight to the heater and flips the switch on, tries not to think too hard about the gas bill that's headed her way.

Her place is small, what they call a T1 apartment. A one-bedroom, though the bedroom itself is a pretty decent size and, since she doesn't get other visitors that often either, the small living room and kitchen work well enough for her. There's enough space for a newish TV and the shelves in the living room are packed mostly with plants. She put a nail on the wall and hung a wire hanger off it for the ivy to climb and curl all over it. The bottom shelves are packed with old paperbacks that she needs to trade for new reads and her comics are squished in between. She doesn't have an armchair, just an old terracotta-coloured sofa that she falls asleep on way too much and a chair to one side of the low coffee table.

She stares at the plants as she holds her hands over the heater, waiting for the warmth to start rising in gentle waves and lap at her palms. She can't bring herself to take her coat off yet.

Isabel thinks about what tomorrow will bring, the way the case is unfolding and what this will mean for Gifted in general. She sighs. They don't need this on their plate right now. Following the Colombo incident, a wave of discrimination against the Gifted community had swept over Portugal. There had always been an edge of mistrust between regular people and Gifted, but it hadn't been blatant, and Isabel would go as far as saying that it was mostly fine. But what happened then ripped open a whole new rift, one that had been greatly aided by the PNP and their followers.

But right now Isabel has other, more immediate problems at hand. She needs to call her brother Sebastião back – that's not so bad. But she needs to call Rita, her sister, back too and she's not as keen to follow that one up.

She pulls her phone out and scrolls through the missed calls, and remembers she hasn't given Voronov her contact information. Fuck. She sighs and rubs at her head hard, wanting the headache to disappear. It doesn't matter that it's a part of her daily life; she wants a break from the pain.

As much as it annoys her to do it, she'll have to squeeze in a visit to the clinic tomorrow. She can't put it off with HR on the Chief's case and these headaches escalating this way.

Great.

A loud rustling outside her windows draws her attention and she tosses the phone onto the armchair.

The room might be small, but Isabel loves that her living room window overlooks the winding sprawl of the city. Directly in front of it is a thick crop of trees and dry bushes surrounding a disused basketball court. It's hard to get to. Sometimes teenagers manage to find their way up it to drink a few beers, or smoke weed. She'd kill for some of that right now.

Isabel already knows what she's going to see as she peers down over her windowsill. A four-legged creature freezes and looks up, eyes reflecting the light from the window. It's one of the mongrels that wander around in the threadbare woodland. The two of them are always here, even in the unbearable heat of summer. Except this time, as she looks around for the second, she doesn't see it.

Something twists in her chest and she looks back down at the dog.

It's not too far down; close enough that someone would only need a good boost up to grab onto the window ledge and haul themselves in. This dog has a permanently floppy ear and a rough circle of black fur around one amber eye. The rest of him is brindle.

'Where's your friend, hmm?' she asks, as the dog continues to look up at her. She can see his ribs. She wonders what happened to the other one and then tells herself not to think about it. No point. 'Wait here. I'll bring you something to eat.'

She goes back and digs into her pathetically empty cupboard, drags out a can of sausages and pries it open. When she gets back to the window, the dog is gone. She blocks the sense of helplessness out and tosses the sausages down anyway. He can't have gone too far. Hopefully, he'll smell the food and return.

Dialling her brother's number, Isabel tucks her phone between her shoulder and cheek. She wanders into the kitchen and dares to unzip her coat as she sets a pan filled with water on the stove and starts peeling a lemon, dropping the pieces of its skin into the water.

Sebastião picks up on the third ring. 'She lives.'

Isabel snorts. 'Shut up. Don't you have sermons to go and see to instead of harassing a poor working woman?'

She can practically hear the eye-roll from his side. 'I've been trying to reach you.'

'I know,' she says. She finishes with the lemon, tosses the knife in the sink, and sticks the skinned lemon in the fridge, the smell of it clinging to her fingers. 'We've picked up a sticky case.'

'All right. Well, be careful.'

She sighs. 'I'm always careful.'

There's a pause there. 'Not always.' Before Isabel can say anything, Sebastião continues, 'Rita's been trying to contact you.'

'I know. I've seen her missed calls.'

'They want us to go to dinner with them. Apparently, they have big news.'

'You mean they want *you* to go to dinner. I doubt my mother actually wants me there.' Isabel's sister Rita might, Isabel can believe that. Though to be honest, she doubts even that. Her sister is too much under their mother's thumb to step out of her safety zone and try to maintain a proper relationship with Isabel. It happens sometimes, but Rita's moments of bravery are few and far between.

Both her mother and sister make more of an effort with Sebastião. Which is funny considering he's not her mother's child. But Isabel can forgive that one; Sebastião is easy to adore.

'I'll be coming too.'

Isabel leans back against the counter, eyes on the pot as bubbles start to appear at the bottom of the pan. 'You usually have about as much time for their invitations as I do,' Isabel says.

'Rita sounded like she really wanted us to come.' His sigh is loud and clear through the line. 'Call her.'

'Sebastião . . .'

'Someone has to be the bigger person, Isabel.'

Yeah and it's always me, she thinks. 'All right, I'll call her. And you're going?'

'Yes, I've already told her I'll be there.'

54

Isabel groans. 'Sebastião.'

'Isabel.'

'Do you even know what it's about?'

'As clueless as you are.'

'I hate you sometimes.'

'Liar.'

10

Instead of calling, Isabel texts her sister. Rita messages her back asking her to please come to dinner because she has 'important news'. Isabel replies, agreeing to go, and doesn't check her phone again until she's out of the shower and settling down to a bowl of hot bean soup and buttered toast. She really needs to go and buy some food for the house. She pulls the booted-up laptop onto her lap and types Gil's name into the search page.

Most links that come up are related to scientific journals and studies and papers. As one of the heads of NTI, he has weighed in on a lot of things related to Gifted history and evolution. There are reams of pages of that, and some YouTube videos of him speaking that Isabel watches a couple of minutes of before clicking back out when it doesn't turn up anything too important.

Ah. There.

An article on a joint project between NTI and the university, involving Professor Julio Soares. Isabel clicks on it.

It's about a study to determine whether the ability to reduce or increase a Gifted's level would be beneficial to the control and mental and emotional well-being of Gifted individuals.

Isabel arches a brow at that and scans the rest of the page.

They're working with a new trial drug and documenting the results, with the aim of modifying Gifted classifications. According to the article, they think that the difficulties experienced by Gifted individuals are because anything below or above a number five classification creates an imbalance in brain activity, which can lead to mental and emotional complications. They use the components of the S3 pill as their starting point.

S3 – Isabel's own regular not-so-miracle pill, designed to suppress someone's Gift.

The idea makes Isabel's skin crawl. Interesting that not one of the people heading the project is a Gifted individual themselves.

She comes off that page and searches for Gil and events.

She gets a couple of talks and lectures, a science convention that he'd been due to attend as a speaker. There are a few other things, some charities and funding parties. Nothing that brings up where he might've been going this morning. Not that Isabel had expected to find that online. They'll have to check if he has any other computers or laptops he used, speak to his colleagues and to Mrs dos Santos, see if the computer is a company asset. He might have another one that's personal.

Isabel makes a mental note to check on all of that tomorrow.

She watches a bit more of another video of Gil talking. He hadn't been the best speaker but clearly knew his stuff. She'd heard him on the news a couple of times and it had always left her cold listening to him talking about Gifted as subjects rather than people. Although Gil dos Santos claimed to have their best interests at heart, he had treated Gifted more as a problem that needed to be fixed.

Isabel finishes her soup and toast, sets it aside and sits for a while before going at the search again.

Aleksandr Voronov.

She stares at the headlines that fill the screen. They're all from three years ago.

Ah. So, that's where she'd recognised it from.

Aleksandr Voronov testifies against Gifted partner!

Criminals infiltrate the PJ: Gifted Police Officer turns back on PJ as his role in organised crime ring is exposed by partner.

In one article, there's a picture of the courthouse, crowded with journalists and police officers trying to hold them off. That might be the back of Voronov's head going into the courthouse. She can't tell for sure. Too many other people in the photo.

Aleksandr Voronov had been a celebrated name by the Regulars in society when the news had broken. A Gifted officer, Mario Seles, had been turned in and, after an investigation by the Internal Investigations Unit, was found guilty. All the evidence had been provided by Voronov.

It had been big news at the time. Isabel had been in her first year as Inspector. She remembers she'd felt grateful for having already passed her exam. The board of examiners have since used Seles' case as a point of reference for all Gifted.

There's a picture of Voronov coming out of the courthouse on the day he'd been in to give evidence.

What isn't mentioned is the rumour that had spread like wildfire through all the Lisbon departments, a rumour that the evidence had been bullshit and Voronov had turned on Seles for being Gifted, that it had all been yet another thing done to discredit the Gifted community.

Isabel sits back and stares at the article until it blurs.

What she knows for certain is that the Chief isn't a bigot and fights tooth and nail for the people who work under her, no matter who or what they are. But no one is right all the time. And now Isabel's going to be stuck with a partner she can't trust.

It'd be easy for Isabel to get her back up and put Voronov in his place. But fair is fair, and since there's a chance that Voronov isn't a rat, then Isabel is going to do her best to make sure they work well together. She's going to have to be smart about it and watch her own back until she knows one way or the other.

She glances back at the screen. There are no mentions of him in anything else. Not for the past three years, nothing after the case that ended with his partner being put away.

Isabel closes her eyes and lets her head fall back. It feels like the blood is pumping through her head in time with the headache, throbbing badly at her temples. It hasn't improved. She hasn't even had the smallest reprieve. Normally it abates by the time the pill's effects begin to run out but this time it remains, steady and rhythmic, until Isabel feels like hitting her head against a wall a couple of times might be a great alternative.

She kneads at her right temple, where the worst of the pain is collecting, and forces herself to open her reports folder. She still needs to finish off the report for the case she was working on before Gil dos Santos died and set in motion a series of events that Isabel isn't feeling particularly eager about seeing through.

Nothing good can come of a case where the son of a right-wing politician who has made his contempt for Gifted well known gets thrown into the ring of the investigation.

II

THEN

Isabel watches the other children waiting just like her.

The sterile smell of the reception area isn't nice; it makes her stomach swoop down and she has to swallow over and over as her mouth fills up with saliva. She feels like she's going to be sick. But she doesn't want to do that. Her dad is still inside the room with the doctor lady who had taken Isabel through her tests and Isabel doesn't want to make a mess.

The others are sitting with their parents and waiting to be called in by one of the doctors. They are all here for the test results.

Her mum hadn't been able to come because Rita's sick, and Sebastião, their brother, had exams this week, so Tia Simone hadn't let him come either. But that's okay; Isabel told him it was fine because she's strong. And she is. That's what Dad always tells her.

Isabel looks at the table in the middle of the room. It's covered with kids' books and magazines and, on one side of it, colouring-in pencils with broken leads and felt tips with missing lids. There are a lot of yellow pencils and some of the markers have had their tips squashed. Isabel hates it when that happens. It's why she doesn't like Rita playing with her pens at home; she always presses too hard and breaks everything.

The door opens and Isabel looks up.

Her dad shakes hands with the doctor lady. Dr Carvalho, she'd told Isabel her name was. She looks over at Isabel, giving her a gentle smile and a wave.

Isabel doesn't smile but she waves back. She hopes they can go home now. The tests had been long and scary. And she's hungry. It's been so long since they were last given a snack. She hadn't been allowed anything else because they said it could ruin the tests.

Something odd happens to her dad's face when he turns to look at Isabel. It's like his face breaks for a second, and Isabel stands, hands fisting at her sides, because it looks like Dad is going to cry.

Isabel swallows again and rubs her hands over her jeans. Her mum had said she was allowed to wear her favourite clothes for this, so the jeans she's wearing are her best ones. They have flowers on the pockets and her top has a picture of her favourite sailor moon.

But then Dad smiles and walks over to her. Dr Carvalho calls out the next patient's name.

'You okay? We didn't take too long did we?' Dad asks, patting her head and picking up her bag. They'd asked them to bring comfortable clothes for the test and Mum had packed up Isabel's favourites for that too. Her dad takes her hand.

Isabel shakes her head. 'Did she say something bad?' she asks. She holds Dad's hand tighter. Her heart is beating so fast and it scares her.

Dad kneels in front of her, smiling and shaking his head. Isabel loves it when her dad smiles like that.

He brushes her curls away from her face.

'You did fine. The doctor was just explaining to me what the results mean.'

'Is it bad?'

'No,' he says, 'but remember what we talked about?'

Isabel nods. 'Yes. You said we needed to know where the voices were coming from. If I was special.'

He nods. Dad has dimples. Sebastião and Rita have them too. Isabel doesn't, but she doesn't mind. Mum says Isabel has Dad's eyes. Isabel thinks she's right. When Isabel looks in the mirror they're big and soft brown just like his.

'Okay.' He takes out a paper from his pocket and unfolds it. It's pale green and when he opens it up Isabel sees the same symbol on the top of the page that she'd seen on top of the building when they'd walked in yesterday morning. 'This says that you're Gifted.'

Isabel feels her whole body flush cold and then hot. She stares hard at her dad, can't even open her mouth. She squeezes his hand tight.

Because she hadn't wanted that. She hadn't wanted that. No one wanted to be Gifted. She doesn't want to think about what her friends will say.

'Dad,' she says and her voice is weird. Her throat hurts. It feels too tight.

Dad takes her other hand and rises so that he can take the seat next to hers.

'Então, Isa,' he says, voice gentle, 'you don't have to be scared. Okay?'

She can't look at her dad then, she's so scared. She's so scared and her heart won't stop beating so hard.

'People don't like Gifted,' she says. 'They don't like them.'

Her dad ducks his head a little to look at her. 'Do you not like people who have different Gifts?'

'Everyone at school said it. And Mãe sometimes . . . when they talk about it on TV.' Isabel's mouth feels so dry and her chest hurts. 'Mãe – is Mãe going to be upset?'

Her dad sighs and then hugs her. He's warm and smells nice. Sebastião had taken Isabel with him on Father's Day and they'd picked a cologne for their dad together. Dad wears it all the time.

'It'll be okay. You've just been given a gift, that's all,' her dad says, 'it's going to be fine. We're going to learn more about it together, okay? I bet you're going to think it's really cool once you know how to use it properly. I promise I'll help, okay?'

She nods against his shoulder, doesn't want to look up yet.

'You're a gift to me Isabel, understand? You're a wonderful gift to me.'

But then seven months later her dad is dead, and Isabel's best gift is taken away from her.

12

Portugal's NTI headquarters is situated on the outskirts of Lisbon. Every Gifted who's been registered and has received their classification has passed through here. That is its main function.

The walls surrounding the building need a new coat of paint. The graffiti stands out, words in bright pink and blue bubble writing, caricatures of politicians, contorted in angry expressions and waving their fingers in the air. Whoever threw up the graffiti is amazingly talented. Isabel's not so impressed by what's in the speech bubbles though: **WE DON'T ENDORSE ABOMINATIONS!**

Isabel looks away, rolls the stiffness out of her shoulders and fixes her gaze straight ahead as Voronov drives through.

They're met at reception by Célia Armindas herself.

Célia Armindas, now the only head of the NTI, is a tall woman with elegant wrists poking from the sleeves of her pristine lab coat, wavy white hair parted in the middle and sensible shoes. A gold watch dangles from her wrist when she shakes Isabel's hand.

'Inspectors,' she says, shaking Voronov's hand as well, 'you won't mind if I ask to see your badges.'

'Of course,' Voronov says. Armindas' eyes flicker over his behind the wire rims of her glasses. She then takes Isabel's in hers, focusing on the classification printed there.

She gives Isabel a tight smile. 'Inspector Reis, you've spent more time inside our walls than your partner here.'

Isabel smiles back, polite, even if her teeth are gritted and she's not sure if it comes off looking like a grimace. 'That was a long time ago.'

'Of course. Would you like to follow me to my office? I've had some refreshments sent up for us.' Her smile falters. 'Though I understand this isn't exactly a social call. Please.' She turns on her heel and leads them in.

Isabel wants to turn right around and walk back out but follows, walking a little behind Voronov and forcing herself to look around.

It hasn't changed much. More security measures in place, but the smell is the exact same and it makes the sandwich Isabel ate for breakfast turn in her stomach.

She remembers it too well. Her first glimpse of it. She'd been on a school trip. They'd taken a coach and she remembers the long ride, the wrapped sandwiches her mother had made, the stickiness of the peach juice she'd spilled on the way over. The second they had walked into the reception area, led by their teachers, the place had smelled like everything had been washed in antiseptic from top to bottom. It had left her feeling off.

Of course, they hadn't got to see anything important then. They'd been taken into a cool room that had shown them an animated explanation of the differences between Gifted and Regulars, and about the test. They'd made it sound so non-threatening.

It's what comes after classification that they don't tell you about. The video didn't cover that part.

Isabel's second time in this building had been for the test. There weren't as many test centres back then and the bulk of them took place right here at NTI.

They call it a test as if it's just the one thing, but there are three stages. The first one determines whether a person has an ability and, if they test positive, they get put through the second test. Officially, there are two categories that Gifted fall into, telekinesis or telepathy. Officially, because the whispers that there might be other categories have never been proven. Just urban legend, according to scientists.

As soon as they know an individual's classification, they take the subject into the third round to determine their level.

Isabel had tested as a five. The first time.

She prefers not to think about those hours. They aren't her best memories.

Dr dos Santos hadn't been the head of NTI at the time of her test, but he'd risen to the position soon after. He'd also produced a lot of research on suggested treatments for Gifted who couldn't control their powers, and for those Gifted who belong to the higher classification, eight through to ten.

Higher-classification Gifted are few in number. Most think that's a good thing. They don't get to stay out in general society for long enough to alarm the public before they're taken away by Monitoring. For many years it was a flawless system.

Then Colombo happened. The Gifted girl in question had been seventeen at the time and was apprehended a few days later, neutralised with tranqs like an animal and hauled away. The trials had been kept out of the public eye. No one had seen or heard of the girl since the day of her arrest.

The building is huge and quiet. The route they take to Armindas' office is the tourist version. Not the one Isabel had seen when she was younger.

In no time, they're sitting in a plush office with a gorgeous view and a sofa area for guests. As promised, there's coffee at the ready, a tall jug of water, and cakes that some poor soul had been sent to get.

The sofa Isabel and Voronov sit on is a bit on the small side and Isabel tucks herself closer to the arm. Voronov, like most men, seems to take up more room than necessary. She feels the weight of the headache, a shadow of a thing tucked in tight behind her eyes.

'Coffee or water? I can have something else brought in if—'

'No, thank you,' Isabel says. She doesn't glance at the offerings. Doesn't consider it, doesn't trust it. Voronov also declines.

'Oh, well, please help yourselves if you change your mind,' Armindas says and pours herself a coffee, leaves it black and cradles the delicate cup in both hands. A thick gold band on her left thumb winks in the light. 'Forgive me but I feel like I need a bit of extra energy.' She drains it in one before setting it down and pouring another. 'Your colleague explained your visit over the phone. Are you sure it's Gil?'

Well, that's to the point.

'We believe so, yes,' Voronov says. 'You two were close?'

Isabel forces herself to concentrate as the headache builds. She finds herself squinting at the other woman. It's a bright, spacious room and, despite the dark sky outside, the overhead lights are strong enough that it's starting to feel like sharp little pinpricks are jabbing at her eyes.

'We've worked together for a long time,' Armindas says and tucks her wavy white strands behind her ear, 'a very long time. We both started working here in the same year, for the same team. I made head first, if you can believe it. Gil followed shortly after. Gil was an extremely intelligent man; he did great things in his time here.' There's a pause. She takes another sip of her coffee. 'He was certainly a good friend.'

There.

Isabel tilts her head, like a dog catching a scent of something. Something not quite right. But she can't pinpoint what it is with the constant pulse of the headache muddying everything for her.

'Can you tell me what happened to him?' Armindas asks.

'I'm afraid we can't disclose that at this time. We're trying to find out a bit more about Gil, about his life, if there's anything that may have happened recently that may have caused him to feel under pressure maybe?'

Armindas is quiet for a moment. Isabel can see the wheels turning.

'No. I can't say that there's been anything that has stood out. It's that time of year when we start prepping for the January tests, there's a lot to get done and it can get stressful. A lot of administrative work and of course, implementing changes to the tests as we evolve. There have always been some adjustments to make and countless reviews of the changes to make sure they're safe to go through with.' Armindas sighs. 'After Colombo last year, the whole system has had new regulations implemented.'

'You're referring to the young Gifted woman who lost control at the Colombo Shopping Centre?' Voronov asks.

'Yes. It was a great tragedy. The government were keen for us to look into preventative measures.'

Isabel keeps her face blank even as she feels those words crawl under her skin and leave a bad taste in her mouth. 'Preventative measures and new regulations, you say. What kind?'

'Just in regard to classification levels,' Armindas quickly moves on, waving the question away, and Isabel has to physically keep herself from grinding her teeth at the dismissal.

'But aside from that,' Armindas continues, 'there weren't any issues that I know of, or that he's discussed with me.'

'Personal projects? Things that he might have been working on outside of the scope of NTI?'

'No. Not that I know of.'

'When did you speak to him last?' Isabel asks.

'Day before yesterday. He had a meeting the next morning, and we had a call scheduled to go over some of the data.'

'Who was the meeting with?'

'The European Gifted Union. We meet and present to them any major findings or incidents that have occurred. It's a standard thing, happens twice a year.'

'And he sounded normal, nothing out of the ordinary that you could tell?'

Armindas shakes her head. 'No. We went over everything and made the necessary changes to his delivery but it was all fine. I'm sure he told me he'd be having an early night because he was getting the first morning train to make sure he arrived on time. It was a normal conversation, there was nothing wrong that stood out to me.'

'And around what time was this?' Voronov asks.

'I was still in my office and left around eleven thirty that night. We were on the phone for a while. I think we finished our call around eleven ten?'

Voronov nods and notes it down. 'You said he was working on something with you over the phone, do each of you have company assets that you take home? Computers, tablets etc?'

'Yes, we do. We each have a laptop to work from home on NTI matters; our tech team has ensured secure servers. We deal with a lot of sensitive information, so we're not really allowed to use anything else.' After a pause, Armindas licks her lips, a small nervous tic. 'Inspectors, I'm sorry, but these questions . . .' She spreads her hands, 'they're making it seem like maybe there's more to this. That you don't think this is an accident.'

'We're investigating all possibilities, that's all, Ms Armindas,' Voronov says, 'at the moment this is as much as we're able to give you.' He glances at Isabel, eyebrows lifting. 'We saw that in Gil's diary there was an entry marked under yesterday's date that said "HSL". Do you know what that could be? Do you know if Gil had any other work or personal engagements after his presentation?'

'No.' She frowns. It calls attention to how wide and thin her mouth is. 'No, I'm afraid I don't.'

'One more thing,' Isabel says, 'what can you tell us about Julio Soares? Do you work closely with him?'

Isabel feels the uptick of something from Armindas, a feeling that's instantly caught and tamped down before she can identify what it is.

Armindas works her shoulders in a small circle, head tilting with the movement as if trying to work a crick in her neck. 'Yes. He's a long-time contributor to our studies here at NTI. He has one of the sharpest minds I've seen in a long time.'

'According to Mrs dos Santos, he and Gil were having some issues. Would you know anything about that?'

'No, Inspector, I'm afraid I don't know anything about that,' she says, and there's a touch of defiance in the uptilt of her chin.

'Hmm. Thank you. In that case, could you take us to Gil's office? We'd like have a quick look.'

Armindas sits back in her chair, twisting the ring on her thumb round and round. 'You won't be able to take anything.'

Isabel arches an eyebrow at that. 'We weren't planning on it, Ms Armindas. But rest assured, should we need anything from his office we'll be sure to get a warrant first.' Isabel stands and motions ahead of her. 'Shall we?'

She wants to get into that office and get out. She needs cool air and a dark space to get control of this thing. Then she'll have to figure out what it is about this case that has sent her stress level spiralling enough to trigger a reaction of this nature.

The blinds in Gil's office are drawn. They block out all but slivers of pale white that cut through the room, wall to wall in perfectly even lines.

Isabel scans the wall for a light switch as Voronov strides into the room.

Armindas' assistant hovers outside, hands clasped in front of her. She's been put on watch duty. If the intent was to make Isabel and Voronov feel uncomfortable then Armindas is going to be disappointed.

Isabel finds the switch and flicks it on.

Voronov stops in the middle of the room and looks around. He looks over at Isabel, as if to say 'well?' Isabel shrugs and turns her attention to their surroundings.

The room itself is smaller than Armindas', not as grandiose, but it's super-sleek. It smells of air freshener and the worn scent of coffee. The entire left wall is floor-to-ceiling shelving, packed tight with books.

No seating areas. Just two chairs on the other side of Gil's desk. A lamp hovers over the computer monitor, and when Isabel rounds the desk, there are Post-its stuck along the bottom of the screen. She ducks her head to read over the scrawled notes. Gil had a doctor's handwriting. Which is to say, very beautiful but near illegible.

Post-its aside, Gil's desk is neat. Everything in its place, pencils clustered together and sharpened to tidy points, black pens together, blue together. Everything has its place and even the mug that's on the desk is washed and set upside down, gleaming under the light.

'Tidy,' Isabel says as she takes a closer look at the Post-its.

Voronov hums in agreement.

A few reminders that are nothing special. A phone number with what looks like an English area code, someone's name scrawled beneath it. A neon green Post-it has a note relating to his wife; what looks like the name of a restaurant, along with a date and time a few weeks ahead. Celebratory dinner of some kind maybe. Isabel notes it down and looks at the last one.

HSL – 14.15 It's followed by yesterday's date and nothing else. Isabel plucks it away from the monitor and it unsticks loudly. Voronov comes to peer over her shoulder at it.

'Yesterday?'

'Hmm,' Isabel says. 'This was what we saw in his diary too, wasn't it? What do you think?'

'Wife didn't mention anything. Neither did Armindas,' Voronov says and shifts to block the assistant's line of sight before taking the note from Isabel.

HSL. Someone's initials? A place?

The day before, Mrs dos Santos' depiction had been one of a happy marriage. Maybe it was happy because Gil was having additional needs met elsewhere. It happens. Or it could be something completely different. Maybe Julio Soares might know what it stands for. That would definitely be an interesting interrogation.

Voronov tucks the Post-it into his notebook. 'Don't think we'll be able to look through much with the assistant watching us like a hawk,' he mutters, glancing around. 'And we'll need a warrant for his computer.'

Isabel digs her thumb into her brow, pressing against the throb there. 'Yeah. Let's get out of here.'

The less time she has to spend in here, the better.

13

'Are you okay?' Voronov asks.

Isabel glances over at him.

He's got a thicker coat on today, the inside fleece turned out at the collar where it cradles his neck. His hands are easy on the wheel as he navigates the early morning traffic back into central Lisbon.

The rain has arrived, drops peppering the window and the roof of the car. Isabel wants to close her eyes and go to sleep. If she managed a full hour of sleep the previous night, she'd be surprised. Right now though, as the clouds open up and load down on the city, she finds herself wondering about the two strays and how they'll fare. Neither dog had returned, or at least she hadn't heard anything for the rest of the night. In her hurry to get ready and leave this morning, she'd forgotten to pop her head out of the window to see if at least the food was gone.

'I'm fine,' Isabel says.

'Okay. These headaches you have, are they normal?'

She cuts a look at him.

Voronov calmly shifts gears as he coasts into another lane. 'I understand it being none of my business, but at the very least I need to know if they're bad enough that they'll affect you while we're out on the job.'

Isabel huffs. 'It's fine. It won't hinder anything.'

Voronov's silence is the equivalent of telling her she's full of shit. And if he wasn't maybe a little bit right, then she'd rake him over the coals for it; but the truth is that although she's used to coping with the headaches, they've been off-kilter lately, and the way her Gift had leaked yesterday even while under the effect of the pill worries her too.

73

'What did you think of Célia Armindas?' he asks, breaking through her thoughts.

'I think that she's a smart lady with a cool head. She's going to play her cards close to her chest, which doesn't bode well for us – but hopefully we'll be able to find enough pieces on our own.'

'Maybe she'll feel differently about talking to us once we have more to go on.'

'Yes. There were a few moments in there where I felt something . . .' she says, 'no thoughts or anything, but a spike when we brought up Julio Soares. These are powerful people. She was nice enough today, but she'll turn if we start getting in her face too much. I don't want them to start talking about lawyers. They'll block us and then we'll have no room to move.'

'When you say they, are you thinking about Julio Soares too?'

'Oh, absolutely. And getting an appointment with him isn't going to be easy. The Chief is going to love this.'

'Julio Soares?' the Chief asks.

'Yes,' Isabel says and winces when the Chief yanks a drawer open and pulls out a packet of cigarettes and a lighter. She pops one of them between her lips, fiddling with the light to get a flame going long enough for it to catch. 'Chief . . . you're not supposed to smoke in here any more.'

The Chief keeps trying to light it. 'Who's going to report me, Reis?'

'Not me.' Isabel pushes up from her seat. 'Anyway, I'm going to see if I can get something booked in with him sooner rather than later. If Julio is anything like his father, I don't want to agitate him any more than necessary. Oh, hope it's okay but I'm ducking out for a couple of hours, got a medical today. I'll come straight back to the station after.'

'Isabel.'

She stops, hand already on the door handle, cursing her shitty luck. 'Yes?'

'Voronov. Any thoughts so far?'

74

Isabel pauses, wondering how frank she should be. 'It's only the second day. I'd be lying if I said I feel comfortable with having him at my back given his history. I guess time will tell.' Despite wanting to get the call to Soares out of the way, she turns to look at her boss. 'I'm curious as to why him of all people, what with his record and all the rumours.' She kind of expects to be told to fuck off.

The Chief gives her a sober look. 'Because I don't think the rumours about him are true.'

Isabel's not sure what to say to that.

They'll have to wait and see.

14

The day has turned sunny and sharp and the tourists are out in full force.

The emotions that drift towards Isabel aren't too intrusive; pure bubbles of excitement tinged with anxiety here and there, but nothing more than that. Isabel breathes a sigh of relief. She was feeling oversensitive from the headache that plagued her all night. Emotions she can handle; as long as their thoughts stay out of her head right now, then she's good.

The pill always brings with it a sense of claustrophobia, as if she's choking off a part of herself. In a way, she is – it's a form of walling a part of herself in, a reminder that what she does to keep her power manageable isn't the natural way of things. But right now, having the barrier it provides in place is the only thing allowing her to get through her morning. Even if she's going to pay for it anyway. A vicious circle.

Isabel stops for a coffee and her eye catches on the newspapers displayed on the nearby kiosk. She grabs her drink and heads over.

'Bom dia,' she says, and reaches for the newspaper, fishing out a euro from her pocket. ''Brigada.'

The man tips his head to her. 'Have a good day, menina.'

Isabel doesn't look at it until she's on the metro and by then she thinks she shouldn't have bothered paying for it – she can see the same headline staring at her from all around the carriage. Despite the protection of the pill being in place, she pushes her natural walls higher, just in case, brow puckering with the effort. She glances down at her own paper as it shakes and shivers with the movement of the metro.

'Well, that didn't take long,' Isabel mutters and scans the rest of the article briefly to see if anything else has made it on there, but luckily no one's managed to get a hold of hers or Voronov's names yet.

That should improve the Chief's mood.

Isabel tucks the paper under her arm and closes her eyes, breathing out.

The clinic is quiet when Isabel walks in. It's mid-afternoon and there are a few people sitting in the waiting room, some flicking through magazines. A couple of older ladies have their romance novellas out for the wait.

The receptionist, a young woman called Susana, looks up from the computer and smiles at her in recognition.

'Inspector Reis, how are you? It's been a while since we've seen you.'

Isabel smiles back. She's always liked Susana. 'Thanks Susana, I'm doing well. What about you? They made you the boss of this whole thing yet?'

Susana laughs. 'Not yet,' she says, wry. 'Though you'd never guess if you saw what I do around here.'

'I have,' Isabel says, 'and I believe you. Is Michael busy today?'

Susana glances down at the computer. 'He's booked up, but he should be on break right now.'

'Should I call ahead and come back some other time?' Isabel doesn't relish the idea of going back to work like this, but she might not have a choice.

'No,' Susana says, 'go ahead. I'll buzz him to let him know you're on your way.'

'But if he's on break—'

Susana waves that away. 'You know he always makes time for you.'

Yeah. Isabel forces a smile to her face.

When she gets up to Michael's floor, he's already at the door, waiting for her.

Michael Campos, Isabel's personal doctor. Also, her ex-boyfriend of two years.

His effect is instant, her body becoming stiff in her awareness. She can't be at ease in his presence. Not any more. If she had a choice, she wouldn't be here at all. He's in his white doctor's coat. He's not much taller than her, short and messy light brown hair, large hazel eyes and dimples that flicker gently as his eyes light on her.

'Hey,' he says, and waits at the door until Isabel reaches him, hand warm on her upper arm as he leans in to kiss her on either cheek.

Isabel stands there, awkward and wanting to step away but not wanting to be rude. Although the break-up hadn't been pretty, they hadn't walked away hating each other either. It had been two years. They'd now been apart as long as they'd been together.

'Hi,' she says, stepping in when he moves back, 'sorry to come in without calling.' Her gaze flicks over the desk that sits by the windows and at the half-eaten sandwich on it.

Michael closes the door behind her. 'I don't mind.'

Isabel doesn't comment, going to one of the chairs on the other side of the desk that Michael keeps for his visitors and patients.

'It's not like you though,' he says, going around to his side and sitting down, 'are you okay?'

Isabel eases back in her chair. 'Yeah. I have a bit of a situation happening. I don't think S3 is working as it should.'

She takes him through it all, explains that her dosage is up to three or four pills a day and about the crushing headaches, how they'd been manageable before but that now they're even bad enough that her partner has started to pick up on them. 'I can't

78

have people at work thinking I'm not okay. You know that's a dangerous situation for me.'

'No, of course not.' He leans forward on the desk, eyes tracking her face, concern clear there. 'Are there any other symptoms? How bad are the headaches?'

She takes a deep breath and shrugs. 'Six on a good day. Mostly a seven.' She's learned to function through it. 'It's not tamping down my Gift like it was before. And HR is on to the Chief about my retesting.'

He nods and stands up, tugging at the stethoscope around his neck. 'All right, we'll do some quick checks and make sure it's not something else throwing the S3 out of whack.'

'Okay.'

'You'll need to lose the coat.'

Isabel turns her face away as she shrugs out of it, irritated that she has to be here at all.

'Are you taking anything for the pain?'

'Aspirin, but it doesn't work.'

'I'll ask Susana to schedule in a retesting to make sure it's on file in case anyone comes sniffing around.'

'Thank you.'

'Can you face me for a bit?'

Isabel hates this part, but stays still while he shines a light in her eyes and checks her ears, manages not to fidget when he takes her wrist in his hand for her pulse.

'I'll need to listen, now,' he says, touching the stethoscope.

Isabel twists in the chair and stares at a point over his head as he lowers himself in front of her, fitting the earpieces of the stethoscope into his ears. She braces herself and lifts up her top.

The stethoscope is cold when it presses against the bare skin of her chest. She ignores it, focusing on his quiet instructions on her breathing. Then she stands so he can put it to her back. The cold air makes the hairs on her back rise, she can feel the sensation. He's too close. She can feel the heat emanating from him and for a moment, she thinks she feels him breathing against her hair and instinctively pushes her walls higher.

'All right . . .'

Isabel steps away and tugs her top back down. She sits down and starts rolling up her sleeve without making eye contact. When she sticks her arm out and he doesn't automatically move to take her blood pressure, she forces herself to look at him again.

He's already turning away from her though, jaw locked tight.

'So. You have a partner now?' he asks, getting the cuff out and wrapping it around her arm. 'When did this happen?'

Isabel shrugs. 'I've just been paired up with him for a new case. Don't know if the Chief wants us to keep working together after that.'

'Do you get along with him?'

Surprised by the question, she looks at him. 'It's early days.'

Michael nods and starts the pumping. She feels the cuff tightening on her arm. 'And he's okay about you being Gifted?'

She thinks about the Chief and can't help smiling. 'I suppose he's getting as much choice in the matter as I am. Whether he has an issue with me being Gifted, well he hasn't shown it yet.'

When she looks back at him, Michael is watching her with a peculiar expression.

'Okay, I think we're good with this.' He unwraps the cuff and tugs it off.

Isabel rubs at the spot where the cuff had been, trying to get rid of the sensation of tightness still on her skin before rolling down her sleeve.

'Have you spoken to your sister lately?'

Isabel pauses in shrugging her coat back on and frowns. 'Rita? Why?'

Michael puts everything away and shrugs his shoulders.

'You've been talking to Rita?' she asks, unsure of what she's feeling.

'We've bumped into each other a couple of times,' he says and sits back down, scribbling something down on a notepad that already looks filled with other little notes.

'No. I haven't seen her in a while. I've been busy.'

'Right. Work.'

It's the way he says it.

It brings with it echoes of bitter silence and passive-aggressive doors shutting in the quiet of her apartment.

And this is part of why they were here, like this. Too many scenarios like this one, as well as his inability to understand that sometimes she needed to be alone. To breathe and not have someone else's thoughts pouring into her head in the middle of the night. He'd always taken it so personally. Her work, her need to have a day off from everything and everyone. Attempting to explain had always ended up in these silences.

Imagine if he knew just how clearly she could hear him in those moments when her wards slipped and there was no pill to keep his thoughts out.

'Look, I'm clearly taking up your time. What should I do about this?' she says, getting to her feet and tapping her head.

Michael doesn't look up. 'Your vitals seem normal. If anything, you just seem tired. I want you to keep a diary for me of the headaches. Jot down your log times for the S3 and the times the headaches start, when they intensify, when they calm down, when they go away.'

'Okay.'

'We might have to mess around with your dosage. I don't want you taking more than you have to.'

'Okay. Are we changing it right away or . . .?'

'Let's give this two weeks. Come back then, we'll look at your log and see what we can do. But if it gets worse, don't wait, just come back. It might be a bit risky, but if we have to, I can arrange for off-the-record tests.'

'All right. Thanks. I know—well. Anyway, thanks. I'll let you get back to your lunch.'

Michael nods and leans back in his chair, watching her walk to the door. 'It was really good seeing you, Isa.'

Her mouth tightens at the nickname. 'You too, Michael.' She doesn't look back again as she leaves.

15

When Isabel gets back to the station and the case room, she finds Voronov sitting in her chair and rifling through papers.

'What's up?' Isabel tosses her bag under her desk, motioning for Voronov to lean forward so she can drape her coat on the back of the chair. She casts her eyes over what he's looking through and relaxes when she recognises them as the little documentation they have so far.

'We've had a witness come forward. The owner of the bag. Carla got her settled in interview room three, sweet-talked her into waiting to speak to us.'

Isabel's mouth forms a small O of surprise. She hadn't expected anyone to come forward. Despite the constant pressure of her headache, curiosity gives her some much-needed energy as they head to the interview room.

Luisa Delgado is a curvy young woman in a flattering yellow dress that clashes with the weather outside. She tucks her brown hair behind her ear as her gaze darts from Isabel to Voronov. She's got her bag back already and is clutching it to her chest like they might yank it out of her hands again. The coffee she either requested or was offered sits on the table in front of her, still full.

'I'm Inspector Isabel, this is my partner Inspector Voronov, thank you for your patience. We really appreciate you taking the time to speak to us.' Isabel holds out a hand and continues speaking as Luisa starts to reach out to shake it. 'I want to make you aware that I'm Gifted, but please, understand that I'll respect your boundaries. I gain nothing from something that is not freely given in this scenario.'

Despite her words, there's a hesitation on Luisa's part before she forces a tight smile to her face and shakes Isabel's hand.

Isabel wasn't lying when she told Luisa she wouldn't poke into her head, but she isn't above using the short contact to get a deeper read on the woman's emotions. Nervous. Uncomfortable. Luisa doesn't want to be here.

Not unusual for people who aren't used to being in a police station. It never helps when a short trip where you just expected to grab your bag and leave turns into being asked to wait and interviewed as a witness. Probably the last thing this woman had wanted.

'Miss Delgado,' Voronov says reaching across the desk too.

'Are you also Gifted?' Luisa asks.

'No, I'm classified as Regular.'

Luisa nods but doesn't say anything else.

'Miss Delgado – or would you prefer Luisa?'

'Luisa is fine, thank you.'

'No problem. Luisa, we'll be quick. We understand that you were sitting near the victim during the incident that occurred early yesterday morning at Gare do Oriente.'

'I was by the window,' Luisa says.

'Okay. Did you notice anything out of sorts before the incident took place? Anything that seemed strange to you?'

'No. I had my earphones in. I didn't realise anything was happening until the young man got up to try to subdue him.'

'You didn't by any chance see the victim take anything? Drink anything or use any kind of substance?'

Luisa shakes her head.

'May I ask where you were headed?'

'It was my day off. I work at a bank in Lisbon. I'm a manager there. Days off are a little scarce right now. I was going to spend the time with some friends who live in Coimbra.'

'Luisa,' Voronov says, scooting forward in his chair. His voice is kind and the frosty blue of his eyes seems to warm. 'What

84

happened after the incident? You weren't with the other witnesses.'

Luisa swallows and starts fiddling with her bag handle. 'I panicked. When the other young man started to try and hold him back, the train was still on the platform and I ran. I didn't even realise I didn't have my bag until I tried to get a cab home. I had my phone in my coat pocket and I contacted my boyfriend to pick me up. Luckily, he was in the city and came to get me right away. I'm sorry I didn't come forward,' she looks from one of them to the other, 'but I really didn't see anything suspicious before . . . before.'

'Of course. Luisa, can I ask you one more thing?'

Luisa's grip on the bag tightens but she motions for Isabel to go ahead.

'Normally in that kind of scenario it's hard to remember everything in detail. Things can get quite confusing and what we're able to recall isn't always accurate. It's the same for everyone. Our mind does what it has to do to cope with the situation. Would you be open to letting me look at your memory of that morning? It'd be helpful to us, I could maybe spot something that's buried just a little deeper than what your mind picks up when it's remembering.'

Luisa's face pales and she sits back from them. 'I'm really sorry' – she licks her lips and shakes her head – 'but I don't think I can do that.'

Damn it. 'That's fine too, I understand. But if you change your mind, please contact me. Memories get fainter with time, so it'd be useful to take a look as soon as possible. But as I've said, we won't force you, of course. It's completely up to you.' Isabel pulls a card out of her pocket and hands it over. 'This is my contact number, both at the station and also my working phone. It's always on me, so if you remember anything, have any questions or change your mind, feel free to contact me on those numbers okay?'

Luisa takes the card from Isabel's fingers and shoves it into her pocket. 'Thank you, I will.'

Voronov stands when Luisa does. 'I'll show you to reception so we can get you signed out.'

'Thank you,' Luisa says, then, giving Isabel another one of her nervous smiles, 'thank you again, Inspector.'

Isabel nods at her and meets Voronov's eyes before he opens the door and leads her out.

As soon as Isabel senses they're out of earshot, she groans and rests her head on the table. She'd been hoping for a little more from that. Their meeting with Armindas earlier that morning hadn't produced as much as she'd hoped either. They know Gil was headed to a morning presentation with the European Gifted Union. They know that Célia Armindas had spoken to him the night before but experienced nothing out of the ordinary. But that spike of emotion during their interview with her hadn't felt normal and had left Isabel wanting to pick at it a little more. And then they have HSL at 14.15 and that Julio Soares was possibly the last person to speak to Gil alive.

One of those has to bear fruit.

A rap on the door makes her look up. Daniel's leaning against the doorframe. 'Some good news for you.'

'Really?' She sits up.

'The witness didn't pan out?'

'Couldn't wait to get out of here.'

'Isn't that most people who come in?'

'True. Anyway, what is it?' Isabel stands and tucks the chair back in. No point staying here.

Daniel walks out with her. 'Julio Soares' PA got back to us. You guys have a date with him tonight.'

Isabel stops. 'Tonight?'

'Yes. Apparently, there's some kind of a fundraiser function he's attending. His diary is booked up for the rest of this week and next week so this is the only point where he can fit you guys in. Try to get there early. He made sure to stress that he wants to get this over and done with before his speech.'

Isabel rolls her eyes. 'Of course he does.'

16

The event turns out to be not too far from the police station.

The university's Social Sciences and Humanities building is still fairly new, and boasts one of the best rankings in Europe. Its glass front that would normally allow a visitor to see into the building shows nothing but the reflection of the setting sun.

It takes Isabel and Voronov fifteen minutes to find a parking spot among all the BMWs and Mercedes. The place is littered with luxury cars there for the charity event.

'Looks like it'll be a bit high-profile,' Isabel says.

'Looks like,' Voronov says.

The reception area is empty apart from the security guard. He's dressed sharp; suit black and bow tie neat and stiff at his neck. He must have been employed just for the event, Isabel thinks. She doubts that the university generally employs people to stand at the door and bow people into the building. He opens his mouth, and then shuts it again when they show him their badges.

'Have a good day, Inspectors,' the guard says and steps aside, holding open the door.

Right at the entrance, there's a huge A3 programme on fancy paper with fancy writing, detailing the times and the names of speakers and other entertainment. The first speaker is scheduled for 6.30 p.m.; in about fifteen minutes.

We're going to stand out like a sore thumb, Isabel thinks. Going by all the cars outside, this is probably nothing less than a black-tie event.

'And to think, I have a new dress sitting in my wardrobe that would've been perfect for this occasion,' she says, tone dry as flaking paint.

Voronov snickers but doesn't say anything as they ascend the steps, following the helpful arrows telling them where the ball is taking place. 'Maybe next time,' he says.

They're not even halfway up the stairs when the thoughts start to batter against her wall. She can feel the protection provided by the pill creaking under the weight of them. Too many people, too many thoughts in one place. Maybe a few months ago she wouldn't have felt a thing after taking the pill, would have been sealed off from all the thoughts around her, but now she can feel it strain. It's as if she's standing at a door between her and all these thoughts, hands pressed to its surface, and against her palms, where she once would have felt nothing, the door vibrates under her fingertips with the thrum of all the voices clamouring to flood in.

She knew they were going to be in a place packed to the gills, but it's not like she can pop a pill every hour, not if she wants to remain a functional human being. Isabel stops at the top of the stairs and takes a moment, closing her eyes and centring herself. In her mind's eye, she's standing, bare feet digging into warm sand, on an island only large enough for one. That island is surrounded by nothing more than green-blue waves and a velvet black sky.

A touch to her elbow makes her blink back into the room.

Voronov is looking down at her, a crease on his forehead. 'Are you all right?' He drops his hand from her arm.

Isabel nods and taps her temple. 'Sometimes it's better to take a moment to prepare before going into a room like that,' she says, jerking her chin in the direction of the noise and music that's now humming along the corridor.

Voronov doesn't say anything for a moment. 'Is there anything you need me to do?'

Isabel glances at him. She hadn't been expecting any gesture of support. Yes, he's her partner but as far as Isabel is concerned, she is still watching out for her own back. And there's a long way to go before she even feels comfortable considering trusting this man, with his history.

She shakes her head. 'No, thanks. I'll be fine. But I think, once we locate Julio Soares,' she says, considering, 'it might be a good idea for you to take the lead.'

He tilts his head in question.

'He might be more forthcoming if he's not being questioned by a Gifted inspector.' She's fully expecting to meet with hostility the second she shows him her ID.

'All right, I have no problem with that.'

The main event is in a large hall that looks as modern as the building's exterior. They've built in a temporary stage where the band is situated. The music is slow jazz. There's a microphone stand too, but at the moment the space in front of it is empty. A woman in a sweeping black dress and a man in a tux stand off to one side, speaking to each other. They've both got large cards in their hands. They're probably the masters of ceremonies for the night.

Men and women in crisp white blazers cut through the swarm of people here and there, drinks and canapés balanced perfectly as they circle the room.

'Hmm. This won't be a quick find,' Isabel mutters. Now that she's in the room, she can feel the walls of her defence shake under the onslaught. She can't hear their thoughts. Not yet. But she can *feel* them. It's not unlike a stampede. The vibrations of it are there underfoot.

'Should we split up?' Voronov asks.

'Yes, I'll call you if I find him.'

He moves off in the opposite direction, tall form disappearing quickly into the crowd.

Isabel braces herself and does the same.

The close proximity of so many people makes her grit her teeth, but Isabel forges on, keeping her face blank as her eyes do a sweep of every face she sees, trying to pinpoint where the man they're looking for might be. She's seen a photo of him. A quick search of the university website had turned up a picture, which she and Voronov had agreed would do the job.

Professor Julio Soares, well known not just for his politician father but also for the strides he's made working in partnership with NTI and his research work in the Gifted field. There is an entire section on the university website dedicated to his achievements. It's an impressive work history for someone only in their early forties. Useful.

Isabel picks up conversations here and there as she squeezes past people, paying attention to anything that might be of use.

The music continues, mixing in with the buzz of a hundred conversations happening at the same time. Isabel can feel the pressure of all the thoughts swirling in the room, the way they crowd around her, butting up against her walls looking for a crack to slip through.

Isabel's been circling for a few minutes when the song ends. There's a brief vacuum of silence before the rush of applause swallows it whole. The woman who had been at the side of the stage is now standing in front of the mic. She's wearing a big red smile, clapping too despite the cards she's holding. Her salt and pepper hair is swept to the side in an elegant up-do, her long neck draped in a glittering necklace.

'Thank you, thank you, don't we have some wonderful entertainment tonight? I want to thank the university once again for hosting us this evening.'

Isabel tunes her out, trying not to get frustrated when the faces in front of her seem to blur one into the other.

Then someone familiar catches her eye. Célia Armindas, in a sleek red dress showcasing her delicate collarbones. Her waves of white hair have been pulled back into a slick style that pulls into a compact knot at her nape, but her expression, which had been a mask of politeness when Isabel and Voronov had questioned her at NTI, doesn't look so polite now. Her mouth is twisted and angry, spitting words at the man who has her by the elbow. His back is to Isabel so she can't get a good look at him.

They're tucked into a darker corner of the room. They must be speaking in a low tone because even though the music has stopped playing, Isabel can't hear so much as a whisper from where they are. Isabel cuts through the crowd, eyes fixed on Armindas.

Armindas is trying to tug away, mouth trembling in her attempts to keep her face blank. When her gaze lands on Isabel, her expression morphs. Isabel isn't sure if it's a trick of the light, but Armindas' face seems to pale; her mouth snaps shut on whatever she'd been about to say.

Isabel continues to barrel through the crowd.

Armindas yanks her arm out from the man's hold and turns her back on both him and Isabel before storming off. The man turns. Isabel's eyes narrow. Professor Soares.

Isabel has almost reached the professor when she feels it.

It raises the hairs on the back of her arms. Isabel freezes.

Fingers on the back of her neck.

Isabel spins to smack the hand away.

There's nothing there.

People mill about but they're talking to each other; no one's looking at her other than to send curious looks as they take in her clothes and the fierce look on her face.

There's no one near enough to have touched her.

She tries to rub away the sensation. She feels on high alert but doesn't know why. The barrier she put up is still in place, nothing there but the thoughts of the people around her still beating at it.

Dropping her hand, she turns back to the professor, who is now watching her, eyes wary. Isabel closes the distance between them.

'Professor Julio Soares?' she asks.

Julio Soares stands straighter and smooths a hand down the lapels of his suit. 'Yes.'

Isabel leans in so that she can keep her voice low. 'Inspector Reis. Our department contacted you about us dropping by to have a word.'

Something passes over Soares' face then but it's too quick for Isabel to catch. Distaste, irritation? 'Right, yes.'

'Do you know if there's a quieter place here where we can go? A little more privacy. I'm positive you'd also be grateful for the discretion.'

For a moment Soares does nothing but stare at her, eyes like granite. Then he gives a curt nod. 'If you'll follow me.'

'Thank you,' she says. She takes her phone out and sends Voronov a quick message: **Found him. Heading left off stage.**

Voronov catches them as they exit out through a door that had been covered up by heavy drapes, which presumably had been put up as part of the decoration for that night. Soares sweeps it aside and ducks under. Isabel and Voronov follow.

The door opens and the cold envelops them. Isabel hadn't realised how hot it was in the hallway and now she shivers as she feels the change of temperature, it bathes her throat and face and slips up her sleeves.

The corridor is dim, only emergency lights glowing green in the dark. Julio seems to know his way and he leads them on, the noise of the charity event growing quieter behind them. They stop at a door that opens to what looks like a lecture room.

The blinds haven't been pulled down and the lights from outside throw slabs of pale yellow over the worn seats of the hall.

Julio goes only as far as the first row of seats before turning to face them.

Voronov closes the door and the relief, for Isabel, is immediate. The force of the thoughts climbing on top of one another, trying to beat their way through her defences, falls off, becoming nothing more than a feather-light weight leaning against them instead. She lets out a quiet breath and flexes her shoulders, trying to get the tension tightening up her shoulders and neck to loosen and disappear.

'What can I do for you, Inspectors?'

Julio Soares is one of those perfectly turned out men, all clean-cut lines in his tailored black suit. His face isn't as striking as his father's, which is often plastered all over TV and campaign billboards. Julio's is a little easier to forget. Thin mouth, a head of strong dark hair brushed back from his face. The artful touch of stubble adds a little character but doesn't hide the cleft in his chin.

Isabel settles in, tucking her hands into the pockets of her trousers and leaning a shoulder against the closed door. 'We're here in relation to the death of Gil dos Santos,' she says, 'we understand you'd been in contact with him fairly recently.'

'I'm not sure how you think I can help. This couldn't have waited?' His arms are folded across his chest and if looks could kill, well.

'Sadly, no,' Isabel says. 'I'm sure you'll understand, especially as you knew Dr dos Santos. His wife said your families are quite close.'

'They are,' Julio says. He doesn't give them any more than that.

In the pictures on the website, his looks hadn't quite marked him as Bento Soares' son. But meeting him in the flesh is different. He gives off the same aura. It's the way he stands and looks at someone. Like they're not fit to lick the heels of his shoes.

'How often did you work with Gil?' Isabel says.

'The university does a lot of work with National Testing. I've collaborated with Gil on quite a few projects.'

'Any problems?' Isabel asks.

'No. We work – worked – well together.'

'I see,' Isabel says.

'We've been to see Mrs dos Santos,' Voronov says. Like Isabel, he's remained standing. He's a few feet away from her, hands tucked into his back pockets, face a calm mask of politeness. 'She says Dr dos Santos had been feeling a little stressed lately. That you and he were having some issues. Can you tell us about that?'

Julio's eyes flick between Voronov and Isabel but she stays quiet and waits. It will be to their advantage if Voronov does most of the questioning with this one. If Julio is anything like his father, then having a Gifted questioning him will get his back up. Isabel doesn't want to give them an excuse to discredit anything she does.

Some people would say she's being paranoid but she'd rather err on the side of caution.

'There's nothing to tell.'

'No?' Voronov asks. 'Mrs dos Santos seemed quite certain that there was some kind of tension between you and her husband.'

'Look, I don't know what you're trying to imply—'

Voronov puts a hand up, a small, pacifying smile on his face. 'Professor, please. We just want to build a bigger picture of what was taking place in his life in the lead-up to Dr dos Santos' death. We're trying to understand what happened exactly, and so we need to know more about his state of mind at the time of death. If he had any problems, we need to be aware of them. That's all, I assure you.'

Julio is quiet.

Although it's faint, Isabel can just about make out the voice of the master of ceremonies who had been talking as they'd left the hall.

Finally, Julio says, 'They weren't issues. It was a professional disagreement, that's all.'

'What about?'

Julio blows out a harsh breath. He shifts, turning his face away from them. He runs a hand through his hair, a little roughly. 'We work together on some of the Gifted who are monitored, for case studies et cetera. As I said, nothing major, we were disagreeing on a particular diagnosis. We're both stubborn men and experts in our field. We don't like to be wrong. Our egos got in the way. That's it.'

'I see.'

Although Julio sounds calm and is looking them both full in the face, Isabel thinks there's more here. There's a rigidity to his mouth and the line of his shoulders is a little hunched, like he's bracing himself and can't wait to get out of the room. Maybe because someone he knows well, a friend even, has died and he's not sure how to cope with it. Maybe it's something else altogether.

'Were you close?' Isabel asks. 'Outside of work,' she clarifies.

Julio's mouth tightens, thinning out his lips. 'We ran in the same social circles. And yes, our families are close. We've had the occasional drink after work when there was a shared project. But beyond that, no.'

Isabel nods. Then she says: 'That was Dr Armindas I just saw you speaking to. She seemed upset.'

A rise of hostility washes over her so fast it leaves a bitter taste in her mouth.

Oh, she thinks, and feels anticipation lick at her.

Although Voronov doesn't say anything, Isabel can tell his attention has been grabbed as well. Voronov shifts. It's subtle, but his body is now facing Soares and he's leaning forward.

'Do you also work closely with Dr Armindas?' Isabel asks.

Julio frowns. 'Yes. I've worked closely with both Célia and Gil. Our fields have a lot of overlapping goals and theories.'

'That makes sense,' Isabel says. 'The conversation you two were having out there seemed a little heated.' And considering that Célia Armindas came across as quite a composed woman, it must've taken some doing to get her that agitated.

Julio straightens from where he'd been leaning against the armrest of the seat. He adjusts his suit jacket with quick sharp jerks at the hem and lapels. 'We were discussing a private matter.'

Isabel acquiesces with a nod of her head.

'We would appreciate it if you could give us a run-down of the last time you spoke to Dr dos Santos, when you last saw him.' Voronov tugs out his notebook and it seems to dawn on Julio that they mean now rather than later.

'Look. I'm happy to help, really. But I don't have time for this right now, I'm needed outside. I thought this would be a quick conversation. Obviously, I was mistaken.'

'No problem. We'll come and see you at your office tomorrow then,' Voronov says, tucking his notebook back away. He smiles. 'Or you're welcome to come and see us at the station tomorrow instead?' He takes out a small card and holds it out to Soares. 'In the meantime, if you think of anything else, please contact us. Any information is appreciated.'

Isabel pushes away from the door. 'Thank you for your time, Professor.' Then she opens the door and stands back to let Voronov go through. When she glances back at the professor, he's staring down at the card. 'Have a good night.'

She follows Voronov out of the room and as they emerge back out into the corridor, the door they'd used earlier to gain entry into the corridor opens again, letting in two people and the swell of noise and thoughts that had been sealed behind it.

The blast of thoughts makes Isabel wince and she touches her fingers to her temple reflexively. She doesn't hear anything specific, but what had only been a distant thrumming when she'd walked in earlier is now a growing rumble. The pill is beginning to wear off. *Merda*.

'Oh.'

The new, unfamiliar voice makes Isabel refocus. She stops next to Voronov and takes in the man who has just joined them in the corridor. He is in his early thirties perhaps. His voice is pretty deep. Next to him, holding on to his arm, is Luisa Delgado, the witness who had left her bag on the train.

Luisa's hair is a little straighter and she's swapped out the yellow dress for a formal bronze gown that hints at her ample curves. Her make-up exaggerates her doe eyes and makes her look even more spooked.

Isabel blinks at her. Not someone she'd expected to see here.

Luisa is staring at Isabel and Voronov, eyes flicking from one of them to the other.

The man with Luisa speaks. 'Professor, they're looking for you.'

Isabel looks over her shoulder to see that Julio has followed them out. He still has Voronov's card in his hand.

'Yes, yes. I'm coming back now, thank you, Gabriel.' Soares looks back over at Isabel and Voronov. If anything, he looks even more apprehensive now. 'Rest assured, I'll be in touch.'

Voronov smiles again. 'We'll be waiting.'

Isabel heads back into the hall, braced this time, Voronov right behind her. As they pass Luisa Delgado and her date for the night, Isabel nods at her. 'Good to see you again, Miss Delgado, we hope you enjoy your evening.'

Everyone is clapping and there are a couple of wolf-whistles here and there. There are four people standing on the stage, all impeccably dressed and laughing and clapping too. It takes Isabel a moment to realise that people are bidding on them. She rolls her eyes.

'Would be nice if we can make it out of here with all our toes intact,' she calls over the noise.

'Walk faster, then,' Voronov says.

'What does it look like I'm doing?'

They reach the exit and Isabel hears someone announce Professor Soares, who is apparently joining the auction. When she looks over at the stage again, Professor Soares has a smile plastered over his face.

Voronov motions her ahead of him. 'Let's grab something to eat,' he says, 'I'm starving.'

That's something Isabel will gladly get behind. 'I'm up for that. Did you see the way Luisa Delgado looked when she saw us there? I think she thought we were stalking her. Poor woman.'

She's stepped out of the room when she feels it. The imprint of a warm hand on the back of her neck once more, fingers pressing into her skin with gentle force.

Isabel stops and spins around, eyes scanning.

'Reis?'

Everyone is facing the front, riveted by the lively auction, laughter and cheers swelling in the room. Julio is joking, his voice booming thanks into the mic in his hand.

'Reis?' Voronov grasps her shoulder.

Shit.

Shit.

17

'I've never been so glad to get out of a place,' Isabel mutters.

'I can't say I disagree,' Voronov says, unlocking the car.

People are still arriving for the function, more cars pulling in and circling around looking for an empty spot. Isabel's phone is buzzing in her pocket. The screen lights up the interior of the car when she pulls it out. Her brother's name shows on the screen. It continues to vibrate in the palm of her hand.

Voronov pauses before starting the engine. 'You're not answering?'

Isabel gives him a look.

She sighs and shrugs off her jacket, tosses it into the back seat and rolls up her sleeves.

Her phone buzzes again, but it's with a message this time.

Isabel, don't forget to call me about the dinner, okay? Rita xxx

'Did you think he was lying to us?' Voronov asks.

'I don't think he was telling us the whole story, no.'

Voronov relaxes into his seat, dropping his hand from the keys. He turns to her. Half of his face is cloaked in the dark of the car and the other is thrown into sharp relief by the streetlights. The blue of his eyes is swallowed by the shadows.

'I saw the exchange between Julio and Armindas. She went past me when she was storming off.' He thinks about it. 'She noticed me when I greeted her, she wasn't pleased. I'd say she looked scared.'

'Of Julio?'

'Of me.'

Voronov leans back against the car door, shifts around as he tries – and fails – to stretch his legs in the cramped space. She can hear the sound of his fingers scratching over the growth of stubble on his face. 'Or,' he says after thinking about it a bit more, 'of my presence there.'

'Did you manage to hear what they were arguing about?'

Voronov shakes his head. 'Though I do think it was probably about our case. From her reaction and the way Julio was when we spoke to him,' he shrugs, 'there's no way to know unless we get it out of one of them.'

The rumble of the engine fills the silence while Isabel thinks. She decides to go ahead. 'There's something else,' she says.

Voronov doesn't say anything, but she knows she has his attention, can feel his eyes on her.

'Soares didn't notice.'

'What do you mean?'

Isabel shifts in her seat, bringing one leg up and under her, her knee digging into the stick shift. 'I showed him my ID. He didn't even blink at it.'

'Should he have?'

'Given that his father hates Gifted and apples don't generally fall far from the tree? The whole family has been out on campaigns with him. Him spotting the classification on my ID should've generated some kind of a response.'

Voronov remains quiet, taking in what she's saying. 'So was he distracted or was he already informed about it?'

Isabel watches as a woman in a brilliant gold dress sweeps out of the car in front of them and takes her time making sure there isn't one thing out of place before placing her hand on her partner's arm and allowing him to lead her inside.

'They were arguing about something,' Isabel says. 'I didn't get near enough in time to hear what it was about, but she looked pretty pissed off with Julio. Didn't appreciate it when he grabbed her.'

'And then . . .' Isabel reaches up and touches the back of her neck. Unease settles over her. The remembered sensation makes her feel like gravity has disappeared and her stomach doesn't know how to adjust. 'I felt something. Like a touch on the back of my neck. Twice. When I turned around, there was no one there. Which is . . .'

His eyes narrow on her. 'You think there was a Gifted there. A telekinetic? But using their power to touch someone without consent – that's grounds for arrest.'

Isabel leans her head back against the seat. 'It is. Or my mind was playing tricks on me.'

'Or maybe the person we were looking for was in that room. But to draw attention to themselves that way? To taunt? And why you?'

That would have other implications. Voronov's suggestion implies that if Gil dos Santos' killer was in that hall, then they had known who Isabel was and what they were there for.

'Maybe we should go and pay Armindas another visit tomorrow, see if we can get out of her what happened in there this evening. We might get something useful.' Voronov sighs.

'We can hope. Something's not right.' Isabel lifts her hand and rubs it over the back of her neck again. She can still feel that phantom touch, making her skin crawl. 'I want a copy of tonight's guest list,' she says. 'I'll ask Carla to find out the—'

Her phone starts ringing. 'Speak of the devil,' she says and takes the call. 'Was just talking about you.'

'Yeah?'

'This function that Julio Soares is at right now; I need you to contact whoever organised it. We need a copy of the guest list.'

'Okay. I'll get on that. I've got something for you guys.'

'Hang on.' Isabel puts her on speaker. 'All right, go ahead.'

'So, it turns out that Gil's personal laptop wasn't on him that morning. It's not in his office and not at home. Mrs dos Santos says he takes it everywhere. It's smaller than his work one.'

Voronov looks thoughtful. 'Could've been stolen. But then

why not take everything else too? Would've been easy to do in the middle of all that commotion. Is there any way to track it?'

'Not the laptop no, but since Gil's cloud can be accessed from any of his devices, Daniel has managed to log into that.'

Isabel leans forward. 'And?'

'It was accessed for the last time the same morning he was killed. Log-off time was eleven thirty-four a.m.'

'Long after Gil is dead,' Isabel says.

'Exactly. Good news is we have an IP address for that last log-in and we've been able to track down the location.'

'Okay, so Gil's laptop is gone, and someone logged in to one of his devices after he died.' Isabel looks at Voronov. 'You good to check this out tonight?'

'Yes.'

'All right, Carla, send it to us. We're done here, so we'll go check it out. See what we can find.'

'Okay, sending it now. And one more thing, I contacted Monitoring to ask if they could send someone over to answer a couple of questions about the technicalities of the crime. They're sending someone to us tomorrow. They made sure to tell us we're lucky. Apparently, this woman is one of the best.'

'Maybe I'll actually feel lucky if she helps us get somewhere. Thanks, Carla, we'll keep you guys posted.'

The location Carla sent turns out to be a café in Estoril, close to the church by the Memorial Park, fifteen miles away in Greater Lisbon.

Voronov parks the car and as soon as they step a foot outside of it, the wind tries to flatten them.

'Jesus,' Isabel mutters, turning her collar up to shield her throat. She left her scarf at the station and she's hating herself for it right now.

Isabel looks around; despite the reason for them being there, she lets herself enjoy the charm of the lit-up city around her.

Estoril and Cascais have always been beautiful places. Of course, she's considered riff-raff around these parts, but she can ignore that long enough to enjoy the polished surroundings.

'You good?' Voronov asks.

'Yes. Let's go.'

She falls into step beside him as they follow the directions that Voronov's phone is giving them in its robotic female voice.

'It's been a while since I've come this way,' Voronov says, doing what Isabel had been doing a few seconds ago and taking in the view.

'Same,' Isabel says, hunching her shoulders against the wind. 'Don't have much reason to come down here.'

Voronov glances at her. 'My sister lives around these parts.'

'Oh?' She glances at her watch. 7.26 p.m. 'There probably won't be much for us to do after this. I can go back on my own if you want to stick around for a bit.'

The smile he'd had on his face disappears. 'It's all right. Another time maybe.'

Isabel glances at him, surprised by the abrupt change. Had she hit a nerve? 'Sure.'

They make the rest of their way in silence. Isabel wonders if she's overstepped; but she hadn't been the one to volunteer the information. She watches him, curious, but doesn't say anything else.

The place Carla has sent them to is, surprisingly, still open. It looks like an internet café.

Isabel peers through the window. There is a food display and counter at the front, with mostly empty trays of sweet pastries at the top and savoury finger food on the lower shelves; pataniscas, little triangles of xamuças, pasteis de bacalhau and more, all laid out on beds of lettuce and tomato, plus metal tubs of sandwich fillings. Just looking makes Isabel's mouth water and reminds her that she hasn't had anything to eat yet this evening.

The rest of the space is taken up by small round tables. Most of the occupants have their laptops open, earphones in. Further back, she can make out a row of computer desks along the back wall, some of which are occupied too.

'Smart,' Isabel says. 'This is why Carla didn't mention an IP address.'

Voronov pushes the door to the café open and motions for her to go ahead.

Isabel resists rolling her eyes, telling herself that he's being polite, not that he thinks she can't open doors on her own.

The guy at the counter, who'd been on his phone as they walked in, glances up, startled. Isabel examines the ceiling. With this much valuable equipment around, there should be a certain level of surveillance. If they're lucky, this place does well enough for the owner to have put in proper security, though it's not unusual for businesses to go for the bare minimum. Times are tough for everyone.

'Boa noite,' the guy says.

Voronov walks over to the counter. 'Hey.' He turns so his back is to the rest of the café and shows the guy his badge. The guy puts his phone away like they're about to bust him for playing Candy Crush while on shift. 'We just needed to have a look around, maybe ask some questions. Is your manager here?'

'No. I'm the only one on shift now, the manager's in again in the morning,' he says, looking from Voronov to Isabel, fidgety all of a sudden. 'What's this about?'

Isabel points to the ceiling and whirls her finger around. 'You have any cameras here?'

He nods, looking like he's forgotten how his tongue works. 'Y-yeah, we do.'

'How long does the footage run?'

'A-about a week.'

'Okay,' Voronov says. 'We're going to need a copy of it.'

'Uh, I can't authorise that?'

'Then I suggest you call someone who can,' Isabel says, 'and we'll need to know who was on shift Thursday morning too.'

The guy glances back down at the badge Voronov still has resting on the counter and gives them a jerky nod, before abandoning his phone and turning away to get them what they're asking for.

18

The Gifted Registry is notoriously difficult to get information out of, even when it comes to investigations. And with good reason. They hold the records of all the Gifted in the country – date of birth, location, power levels, next of kin, names of their Guides and Monitors if applicable – anyone with a Gift above a level 7 requires monitoring.

They know there was at least one Gifted person present at the function last night. Running the list of guests through the Gifted Registry's database would be the way to ferret them out.

The database holds the kind of information that would be dangerous in the wrong hands. So, it makes sense that the amount of paperwork Isabel and Voronov had to go through in order to file a vetting request makes Isabel want to put her head through a wall. Having to do this at all leaves a bad taste in her mouth and it doesn't help that she has a foreboding feeling in regard to this whole case. With society's current distrust of Gifted, an investigation like theirs could very well tip the state of affairs into something that the Gifted community won't be able to recover from easily. Hunting one of her own—well. Isabel's been trying not to examine it too closely.

They'd queued up for close to an hour in the frosty early morning to get their hands on the forms – queues being another highlight of Portuguese bureaucracy – and spent hours filling them out. With the request granted, they'd be able to identify anyone Gifted they might want to talk to. But there would be a long wait before they got the results.

In the meantime, Isabel and Voronov start poring over the guest list. 'You really think the person involved attended?' Voronov says.

Isabel sets the paper down on the desk and then eases back, folding her arms. The heating in the room has gasped its last breath and their section is freezing. She has her scarf wrapped around her neck and her fingers are chilled. They've been waiting since the previous day for the facilities staff to turn up and take a look.

'I told you about the feeling I had yesterday, like someone had touched my neck when we were leaving?'

'Yes.' Voronov rests his arms on the desk, blue eyes intent on her.

'It happened at the beginning too, just after we arrived. I thought it was my imagination the first time,' she says, rubbing her hand over the spot. If she focuses hard enough, she feels as if the hand is still there, the sensation lingering. 'But then it happened again, when we were leaving. Both of those times, there was no one there when I looked.'

'Are you thinking someone of a significant level?'

'For the touch to feel that real? I'd say yes. Unless I'm imagining things.'

'Which you're not.'

She pauses, then nods slowly. Voronov hadn't questioned what she'd relayed to him yesterday but despite that, she'd still expected scepticism. But there was none of that. Not that she could sense; and her Gift aside, Isabel considers herself to be a good people-reader.

'Which I'm not,' she concedes, 'so then I'd say they'd have to be fairly strong. I mean, quite the coincidence to have someone who is a powerful telekinetic in the same room as two of the people involved in our investigation, no? An investigation where the only person who could've committed the crime has to be on the higher Gifted levels. Once the Registry come through for us then we can know for sure who in that room could've pulled a move like that. But for now, it's good to look at the possibilities.'

That's when she hears a commotion.

Frowning, she looks round, aware of Voronov doing the same at her side.

Bento Soares has stormed through the station, into the room full of busy police officers, all of them a little too cautious and surprised to tell a senior politician to calm the fuck down. He's walking at a click ahead of Laura, the station's front-facing officer, who has chased him into the room. She looks equal parts worried and pissed off. Bento glances down at Laura and hisses something at her that Isabel can't hear. Even from the other side of the room, Isabel can see the hard look Laura gives him before turning to sweep her eyes over the occupied desks.

Isabel catches her attention and gives her a small nod. 'I think this one's for us,' she says, easing away from her laptop and stretching her arms above her head to try to work out the tension slowly pouring in between her shoulder blades.

Voronov gets to his feet, face placid and polite as Bento Soares makes a beeline for them, his sharp steps cracking on the glossy polished floor over the commotion of the station.

Isabel ignores the trepidation she feels trickling down to her stomach and keeps a calm mask on her face. This is not a man you want to show weakness in front of, not when he hates the very thing you are and is actively campaigning to have you locked up for being born.

'Mr Soares,' Voronov greets him smoothly, intercepting Bento and bringing the threatening stride to a halt.

Voronov is taller than Soares, and the politician has to tilt his head back to look at him. He narrows cold grey eyes on Voronov but otherwise shows no outward reaction.

'How can I help you?' Voronov asks.

Isabel rises from her seat and leans back against her desk, crossing her arms over her chest.

'Inspector Reis?' Soares snaps.

Isabel smiles. She hopes it looks like a smile anyway. 'That would be me, Mr Soares.' She sticks out her hand for him to shake.

Soares looks from her to her hand and reluctantly takes it. His hand is clammy, his grip tight and meant to cause discomfort.

Isabel works to suppress a grimace, not at the strength of his grip, but at the unpleasant emotions that come off the man like one giant wave of negative energy. It seeps in through their connecting palms and Isabel wants to yank her hand back and go stick it in a basin full of sanitiser.

'And you are?' Soares asks, when he releases her hand, eyes flicking to Voronov.

'Inspector Voronov. I'm Inspector Reis' partner. What can we do for you?'

Soares sends a cool look around the room. 'Is there a private place where we could have this conversation?' He manages to keep the sneer from taking over his mouth completely.

Isabel just stops herself from suggesting that if he's so worried about the press then maybe barging into the police station might not have been the best way of keeping a low profile.

'Of course,' she says instead, nodding. 'Please follow me.'

The room Isabel chooses is down a long corridor at the back of the building and far away from prying ears. They pass the Chief's closed door on their way.

Someone's left the windows open, which would normally piss her off but, as she doesn't really want to offer Bento Soares any type of comfort, she's happy to let it slide. There are a couple of desks pushed up against the side of the room, chairs tucked underneath, and an old landline phone sitting on a table, its wires running behind it and into the wall.

Once they're all inside Voronov pulls the door closed.

'Mr Soares, would you like a seat?' Isabel asks, gesturing towards one of the uncomfortable-looking plastic chairs.

'No, thank you,' he says, biting out the words. 'I want to know why you're targeting my son in a murder investigation.'

Voronov comes over to Isabel's side and sits on the table, fingers curling around the edge as he stares calmly at the irate man in the middle of the room. Isabel remains standing, her hands in her pockets, trying her best to keep a look of concerned interest on her face. She badly wants to tell him to fuck off.

'A murder investigation?' Voronov asks. 'And I'm afraid we can't disclose the details of the case with you, Mr Soares, unless you are personally involved with it yourself. I can assure you no one is being targeted.'

'My son is involved.'

'Your son, yes,' Voronov says. 'And he invited us to meet with him. He was fully aware that we were going to be present at that function.'

She'd been wrong when she'd thought that his son had the same energy as the father. No. Bento Soares fills the room with how he holds himself alone.

The thing with Bento Soares is, he's not your typical politician. He's not a man who sweats it out in suits, folds of neck fat spilling over his collar and buttons straining at the middle, as is the case with most of Portugal's politicians – they're more attached to their big expense accounts than they are to the people they're meant to serve. Soares isn't like that. Strong bone structure, body filling his expensive suit perfectly and salt and pepper hair neatly trimmed. A quick glance down and Isabel sees that even his nails are manicured.

It's amazing how much poison people will swallow when the face of the one holding it out to them is pleasing to look at.

So there's no red flush or heaving breaths as his anger builds. In fact, most people wouldn't even be able to tell that he was anything other than mildly displeased right now.

But Isabel senses it.

It reminds her of inhaling fumes at a petrol station. That lingering smell of fuel. That's what his anger tastes like as it transfers over to her. It's not quite a rage. He's not at that stage. But he is *angry*. And indignant.

'If I may,' she says, oozing as much calm as she can, 'I can assure you that your son is not being targeted in any way, shape or form within our investigation. At the moment we are just trying to gather as much information as possible, as is the case with any investigation.'

Bento Soares slides his cold gaze to her. The anger changes into something else, thick and full of smoke.

'Inspector Reis. I am on very good terms with the PJ. I know exactly what this case is about. It would do you well to think whether you are the best person to be put on this case. We wouldn't want an inspector who cannot remain impartial.'

Fucker. 'I don't understand what you mean, Mr Soares.'

'People talk, Inspector Reis. I'm very well aware that this is an investigation on a Gifted crime and that you yourself are Gifted.'

'Ah, I see. I'm sure the department appreciates your concern, but you can rest assured that Inspector Voronov is here to make sure that impartiality is maintained. Just as it's my job to do the same. However, should you still have concerns, I'd be happy to direct you to my superior. Is there anything else we can help you with? I'm afraid we do have a case to get back to.'

Soares looks from her to Voronov and back again.

'Try not to step on any toes, Inspector Reis.'

'I'll do my best.'

With that, Soares gives them each a nod, sends one last icy glance Isabel's way and then turns to the door.

'I'll see you out,' Voronov says.

Isabel sends him a sharp look, but he isn't looking her way. Instead he's opening the door for Soares.

Isabel leans back against the table and sighs. She rubs at the bridge of her nose, eyes scrunched shut and tension vibrating in every muscle of her body.

She'd known this was a possibility. That someone high up the food chain would throw her Gift in her face during this investigation. She hadn't expected it to be the man doing his level best to drag Portugal back into the dark ages. She'd never expected to actually come face to face with the arsehole, and it has left her off-kilter.

She looks up when she senses Voronov come back into the room. She wonders what he said to Soares as he escorted him out. She wonders if she can trust him.

She wishes she hadn't taken that pill this morning, so she could find out.

But those are not things she can do anything about. So, she stands instead.

'Let's get back to work,' she says, then walks past him and leaves the room.

19

The woman who Monitoring sends to meet them is Dr Nazaré Alves. Her glasses are round and swallow up half of her face and her hair looks like it's been pinned up in a hurry. She's dressed in an oversized pale-pink soft sweater, grey trousers, and white Converse. She's a bit flushed in the face as she shrugs out of her big Puffa jacket and sets a steaming paper cup that reeks of strong black coffee on the table.

Isabel watches her through narrowed eyes. This woman looks like she's just stepped out of a university. Not what Isabel had expected; but still, she keeps her guard up, the mistrust of anything related to Monitoring a knee-jerk response.

'Inspectors,' Dr Alves says and reaches over to shake their hands.

'Doctor,' Isabel says. 'Please take a seat, can we get you anything?'

Voronov has gone back to standing by the window, back resting on the wall, arms folded once more as he waits for the doctor to get settled. Isabel takes a seat at the table with her. The door to the room is closed but she can still hear the sound of everyone on the other side getting on with their work.

'Thank you for coming at such short notice, we appreciate your time.'

Dr Alves waves it away as she reaches for her cup and nudges her glasses up her nose. 'It was on my way, so I don't mind. I've only got one more case to check on today. How can I help you, Inspectors?'

'We just need to pick your brain for a bit.'

Dr Alves quirks a smile. Dimples pop up and Isabel finds herself feeling oddly charmed by them. 'Literally or figuratively?'

Out of the corner of her eye, Isabel catches the sharp look Voronov tosses the doctor's way.

Isabel smiles, amused and safely behind the comforting wall of her pill. 'I won't be diving into your head, with or without permission.'

The dimples stay. 'Of course.' Dr Alves keeps her cup in her hands and leans her elbows on the table. 'Based on the non-disclosure forms, I'm guessing this is in relation to a case involving a Gifted?'

'At the moment we're just exploring all of our avenues. We're not sure what it is yet,' Isabel says. 'The case we're dealing with right now is a little odd. There's a possibility that the victim was being controlled by an outside force.'

Interest flares, bright and focused, in the doctor's gaze. The smile disappears and Isabel can see the scientist in the woman rush to the forefront. 'From which ability branch? Telekinesis or telepathy?'

The kind of control over someone else that would be needed for this theory to be true is a terrifying prospect, and not one Isabel likes thinking too closely about. It makes her skin crawl. She forces herself to re-examine the memory Rodrigo shared with her. She remembers the helplessness in Gil's eyes. He'd been fully aware.

That doesn't mean that there *wasn't* someone in his head – a telepathic Gifted, controlling his body through his mind. Was that even possible? Even if someone had taken a hold of him from within, then Rodrigo would have been able to hold him back. Isabel remembers it, the way Gil's body was yanked around. Definitely an outside force then, not someone else guiding his body.

'Telekinesis. Though, we're not ruling out anything at this point.'

'Hmm, okay.' Dr Alves set her cup aside. 'Talk me through the incident.'

Isabel doesn't mention names or places; she knows the woman in front of her would make the connection to the dos Santos case in no time.

When she's finished, Dr Alves stays silent. 'That is . . . I mean. This is unheard of.'

Voronov moves away from the wall and takes a seat next to Isabel, hands tucked into his pockets, one leg crossed over the other and a pleasant expression on his face. 'What classification would someone have to be? To have that kind of control over another person?'

Dr Alves considers it, pursing her lips and twirling the cup in her hand. Then she lets out a loud breath and shakes her head. 'What you're asking me is . . . frankly, very alarming. I'm trying to get my head around it.' She plucks the lid off the coffee and downs the rest of it in one go. When she's done, she takes her glasses off and rubs at her eyes.

When Isabel glances at Voronov, he shrugs.

'Okay.' Dr Alves says it like she's made a decision. 'Let's say that this person was harmed by someone with an ability. I agree that it's leaning towards a telekinetic Gifted. But the level for something like this is . . .' She blows out another breath, looking as if she's at a loss and puts her glasses back on, squinting at both of them. 'The level necessary to control another living being is immense. A class ten.'

Isabel blinks, her heart slamming against her chest. 'A class ten,' she repeats.

Dr Alves nods. 'Yes. Maybe a nine. Maybe.'

'Portugal has never registered a class ten. It's a rarity. Even if you go by continent it's rare,' Isabel says.

'Yes, yes, all of this is true. The highest we've registered in the last ten years is an eight. But no system is perfect. There have been cases in the past where a Gifted's ability continued to grow and wasn't monitored correctly. It was a disaster.'

Beside Isabel, Voronov stirs. 'You're talking about the case from two years ago,' he says, 'the massacre in Colombo.'

'That's one example, yes.'

'What class was she? In the end? Did they even test her for it?' Isabel asks.

The smile Dr Alves gives her isn't so nice this time. 'I'm sure they did. Not that they'll ever say. They kept those records confidential.'

'What's the highest registered class we have right now?' Voronov asks.

'In Portugal? A couple of eights. Some sevens. For specifics, you'd have to put in a special request with the Registry. I won't be able to tell you anything more than that.'

'Of course,' he says, giving her a respectful inclination of his head.

'Is it completely impossible for a seven or an eight to do something like this?' Isabel asks.

Dr Alves mulls it over. 'I can't say with certainty that they couldn't. They'd have to have superior control of their Gift, of course. For lack of a better explanation, their ability would lack the brute strength required to do something like this. It would have to be down to mastery of their Gift, and it would likely take a lot of years to achieve that and the help of a very seasoned Guide. I don't imagine someone would be able to achieve that on their own. So, the likelihood of that happening is extremely slim.'

Still. Not impossible is still something.

'Right,' Isabel says. 'Doctor, hopefully it won't be necessary but we might need a bit more of your expertise. Would you be willing for us to put you down as a consultant for any future queries? It makes it easier on us,' she adds with a smile, 'to keep those non-disclosures to a minimum.'

This time the dimples are back. 'I'd be happy to.'

A rap at the door breaks up the conversation. Isabel glances up to see Carla popping her head through the open door.

'Sorry to interrupt,' she says, flicks an apologetic smile at Dr Alves.

'That's okay,' Isabel stands, and Dr Alves does the same. Voronov stays seated and waiting. 'We were wrapping up.' Isabel turns to Dr Alves. 'Thank you again for your time. We'll be in touch.'

'Not at all.' Dr Alves nods a goodbye at Voronov. 'I'll see myself out.'

Isabel opens the door wider for her and Dr Alves slips through with one last smile.

Carla waits until she's out of earshot, then steps into the room, easing the door closed behind her.

'Julio Soares is here.'

'Oh, good. I was beginning to think we were going to have to hunt him down,' Isabel says.

Voronov joins them at the door. 'Has he been here long?'

'Five minutes, at the most. But apparently he's a very busy man.' Carla rolls her eyes.

'All right.' Isabel checks the time left on her bracelet. Not that she needs to. The intensity of the headache has dropped, meaning it won't be long before the pill wears off. She's got maybe forty minutes. Fifty, if she's optimistic. 'Tell him we'll be right there.'

20

When they enter the interview room, Julio Soares has his back to the door and is staring out the windows.

Isabel's not sure what it is he's looking at because the views from their building aren't all that inspiring.

He has the same sharp eyes as his father and when he turns them on her and Voronov, Isabel can't help the way her chin tilts up a little more, the way her chest opens and her shoulders square. Through the buffer of the pill she can feel worry, discomfort and irritation peel off of Julio. None of which are unusual for someone summoned by the police to come in for a statement.

'Mr Soares,' she says, 'thank you for coming in. Please,' she gestures at the padded chairs tucked into the small table in the room. 'Can we get you any coffee or some water?'

Voronov closes the door quietly behind him and moves to rest back against the windows. He's got his sleeves rolled up above the elbows, impervious to the chill in the room.

'No thank you. I'd appreciate it if we could get through this as quickly as possible, Inspectors, my schedule is very tightly packed.'

'Of course. I appreciate that you were a little distracted last night so in the interest of full disclosure, I'm Inspector Reis and this is my colleague Inspector Voronov. Mr Soares, for your information, you're also in the presence of a Gifted officer, which would be myself.' Isabel takes out her ID and slides it across the table. She isn't sure if he just didn't notice yesterday. Either way, she doesn't want to take any chances considering today's visit from Soares senior.

This time, Julio pays attention. He picks up Isabel's ID and takes a good long look at it before glancing back up at her. He flips it back closed and holds it out to her, not a flicker of anything on his face. 'Thank you, Inspector.'

'We understand you worked closely with Gil,' she says and tucks away her ID.

'Yes. Our work overlaps quite often and the NTI does a lot of work with my university. We partner up more often than not.' Soares resettles in his seat, slipping his hands into his pockets and crossing one leg over the other. Despite what Isabel can sense, he looks the picture of composure. The polo and khakis make him look like he's about to walk into a lecture or onto a golf course.

'What is it that you do, exactly, Mr Soares?'

'I'm a neuroscientist specialising in Gifted development. I lecture at the university twice a week and work as a consultant for the NTI and other institutions.'

'That's a lot of years of study,' Isabel says, 'how long have you been working with NTI?'

'A very long time. I've been involved with the NTI since graduating and then more extensively throughout my PhD. A good seven or so years.'

'And you've been working with Gil recently on a project, correct?'

Julio shifts in his seat and rests his elbows on the table, steepling his hands together and looking from Isabel to Voronov. 'No. Wrong. There is no project. I've been consulting for them on a round of tests for a pharmaceutical company.'

Isabel shares a look with Voronov and he comes forward, pulling out the empty chair next to Isabel and taking a seat too.

'Mrs dos Santos said there have been some tensions between you and her husband recently. That this was causing Gil some stress,' Voronov says. 'Can you tell us why Mrs dos Santos might have got that impression?'

'No idea.'

Voronov narrows his eyes and leans forward, mirroring Julio.

Isabel waits, ready to pick up whatever emotion might come out of this, something that might give her more clues as to what is going on here. Because something is, even if Julio doesn't want to admit it.

'Does Mrs dos Santos have a reason to make this up?' Voronov asks.

Julio's expression remains blank. 'I'm not saying that she made it up. I'm saying that I think she's made a mistake. Which is understandable considering the circumstances.'

'You know them quite well don't you. Old family friends?' Voronov asks.

'Our families are close, yes. But the relationship between our families was long-standing before I came along.'

'It sounds like you slid right in, if you know them well enough to comment on their relationship.'

'I suppose. How is this relevant?'

Isabel cuts in, voice soothing. 'As we explained yesterday, Mr Soares, we're trying to paint a bigger picture of Gil and his life. It's helpful to know as much as possible, even something that might seem inconsequential.'

The look Julio turns on Isabel is sharper, his whole body tight now as his placid mask slips. 'Don't patronise me, Inspector. This isn't building a bigger picture. What do you think I've done here?'

'Nothing,' Isabel asks, 'why? Do you feel that you've done something that we would be concerned about?' She leans forward. 'You were his last phone call, the day before he died. What did you talk about?'

It's as if the emotions that have been rolling off of him, irritation, resentment, just go still, like ripples on a lake disappearing and leaving nothing but a glassy surface.

'I don't really recall,' he says.

'You don't?' she asks. 'It wasn't really that long ago. A couple of days.'

'My days have been busy.'

Voronov tugs his notebook out and flips back a couple of pages. 'The call was about ten minutes long. Mr Soares, you're sure you don't remember what you discussed?'

And like that, the stillness of that lake is broken and a ripple breaks out on the surface again. It's fast, there and gone before Isabel can pin down what kind of emotion it was.

'We were gearing up for the function, which I was heavily involved in planning. As I've said, I'm sorry, but I don't remember. Gil was making a trip for this presentation, I think we touched on that at some point and on whether he'd be able to attend the function. Beyond that,' he looks hard at Isabel and then at Voronov, as if daring them to question him again, 'a little chit-chat, which, as I've said, I don't really recall.'

'Hmm.' Isabel lets her gaze rest on him. He knows she's a telepathic Gifted and she lets that sit in the quiet of the room for a moment, and as the seconds tick by, despite him not wanting to show it, she spots the way he just about keeps his hands from clenching, flexing his fingers out instead before letting them rest on the table once more. She's not reading his thoughts, can't without his permission, and he knows that. But he knows that she could.

But she's also aware that pushing him too far might result in her being targeted. After all, his dad has already come looking for blood.

'Julio,' she says, and takes a little pleasure in the displeased downward flicker of his mouth at the familiarity, 'do the initials HSL mean anything to you?'

'No,' he bites out. But there is that little ripple again.

'Nothing, at all? In relation to a time, or place perhaps?'

'I've told you no, Inspector.'

Yes, you have. And you're lying, and you're not sure if I can tell or not. 'Isn't this a friend of your family's, Julio? I would've thought that in a situation like this, you'd show a little more . . . willingness to help, no?'

The chair drags against the floor as Soares pushes away from the table. He doesn't stand up but stays there, palms flat on the table, glaring at them.

'I lost a colleague, a man I respected very much and worked closely with. I expect you to have a little respect, Inspector.'

Isabel rests back against her chair, folding her arms as she considers him. 'With all due respect, if that is really the case, why not take the time to talk to us yesterday?'

Soares' chin draws up like he's bitten into a lemon and Isabel is sure that if it didn't mean getting his ass arrested, he might've thrown a punch her way. 'Inspector, I'm sure you do very good work here. But in what I do, funding needs to be secured. Maybe it seems harsh to you but I can't afford to let projects fail; a lot of people rely on these functions to fund their departments for the next few years.'

'Hmm. We had a visit from your father today,' she says, 'very well-known man. Very upset, disproportionally upset, about our wanting to speak to you.'

'Any parent would be upset if the police were hunting down their child for something unrelated to them.'

Apparently scheduling something in with someone's PA equals hunting someone down.

'You said you'd been consulting with the NTI on a round of tests for a pharma company.' Voronov hasn't moved throughout the whole exchange, still has his attention on Soares like he didn't just throw a very restrained hissy fit. 'What kind of tests? For which company? And who were you working with specifically?'

A muscle ticks in Soares' jaw. 'The project was under Gil's supervision, but myself and Armindas were also consulting. I'm afraid anything beyond that is confidential and I won't be able to disclose without a court order.'

'Okay,' Isabel says, 'thank you. I have one last question for you. Do you know of anyone, patient or colleague or other, who may have had any issues with Gil?'

'No. I don't.' He looks from Isabel to Voronov. 'Is that all?'

Voronov nods and stands up. 'For now.' He puts his hand out and doesn't even blink when Soares seems to shake it far more aggressively than necessary. 'We'll be in touch. We thank you for making the time to come in, Mr Soares.'

Soares doesn't reply. He shoots an unimpressed look in Isabel's direction and stalks out of the room, back ramrod straight and head held so high Isabel wonders how his neck doesn't snap from the weight of all that self-importance. The apple definitely doesn't fall far from the tree.

'What do you think?' She chews on the inside of her cheek, going over the brief interview they've just had.

'I think there's probably quite a bit he's not telling us,' Voronov says, 'but whether it's relevant to our case or not, I'm not sure.'

21

Tia Simone's house always smells of bolinhos secos, all cinnamon and warmth.

Isabel raps her knuckles on the door's glass panels. That same smell wafts out of the kitchen window that's left open all year round come rain or shine. Isabel's headache is lighter and maybe she's imagining it, but it feels like the familiar scent of the biscuits soothes the lingering discomfort.

She hears her aunt's voice but can't make out what she's saying. 'It's me, Tia.'

When the door swings open though, Isabel finds her brother standing there, eyes crinkling at the corners from the smile stretched across his face. 'What time do you call this?'

Isabel scoffs and steps up to kiss him on the cheek. 'I call it, I-have-a-job-time. Where's Tia?' She shuts the door behind her. 'Have you been here long?'

Sebastião steps back to let her pass.

Her aunty's apartment is in one of the older buildings in the area, but it's large and not cramped like some of the older apartments here. The entrance leads down to a long, narrow corridor that takes them past the door to the kitchen and into the open-plan dining room and living room. The same dark wooden furniture that her grandparents bought when they moved in decades ago adorns the place still.

From where she stands, Isabel can see over the stretch of dining area to the heavy blankets discarded on the sofa. The TV is on, a commercial playing loudly and showing a woman with teeth too white to be natural. On the coffee table, a tea towel has already been laid out along with a small jar of sugar and some spoons.

Isabel turns in to the kitchen, where Sebastião has stolen a stool at the table tucked into the corner by the window. Her aunt is at the oven and the blast of heat as she opens it warms Isabel's fingertips. Tia Simone tugs out a tray packed with bolinhos secos, the thick wool cardigan hanging over her shoulders. Her hair is a mass of black and white that's been tightly tucked into a French braid.

'Hey, Tia,' Isabel says, laying a hand on the other woman's shoulder and dropping a kiss on her cheek.

Tia Simone sets the tray down carefully on the stove before turning to pull Isabel into a hug and kissing her temple. 'Então linda, you okay?'

'I'm good, Tia, you?' She peers over her aunty's shoulder at the bolinhos on the tray. 'You want me to start the tea?'

'Sebastião is having coffee.'

Isabel rolls her eyes and spears her brother with a look. 'Since when does that even go with bolinhos? Heathen.'

'Watch your mouth,' he says, grinning.

'Why? Because you're a man of the cloth?'

'Isabel,' her aunty says, drawing her name out in warning.

Sebastião's grin is unrepentant. Isabel rolls her eyes again, shrugs out of her coat and tosses it at him. 'Make yourself useful.'

The three of them work quietly on setting up. Atop the fridge, playing old kizomba through static, sits the ancient radio, one of the few things their grandad brought back from Angola that had stayed with the family and never quite been replaced.

'How's Rita? She hasn't stopped by in a while,' Tia Simone says.

'Not sure, I've been working a case pretty hard,' Isabel shrugs. 'Thought work was going to calm down but it looks like I'm going to be elbow-deep in another one that might blow up in our faces.'

'Isabel,' Tia looks up from where she's stacking the bolinhos on a tray, 'I know your work is important, but you need to make time for your family.'

'I try, Tia,' she says, the lie slipping from her lips without any guilt whatsoever. 'I'm here aren't I?'

'Oh, yes. You're here all the time. But when was the last time you spoke to your mother?'

Sebastião winces. 'Tia.'

Tia Simone waves it away. 'I know Maria isn't the easiest person to get along with, but family is family and we have to try.'

Isabel has nothing to say to this that her aunt would want to hear, so she leaves the water and the chamomile to steep and roots through the cupboard instead. She takes out three mismatched mugs.

They used to spend a lot of time here at her tia's house when her dad was alive. And then her dad, a police officer like Isabel, had died in the line of duty. That had been nearly seventeen years ago.

This was the place that her grandparents had scraped money together to buy, so dinners and family get-togethers had always been hosted here. Along the way, people would bring gifts or things from wherever they'd gone off to – Tia Simone had spent some time in Switzerland, working in the fields there – and added to their grandparents' collection. You'd find them displayed all over the house.

Then slowly, slowly, things had changed. After Isabel's dad died, her other two aunts moved back to Angola, which had changed a lot in the last decade and where there was the promise of an easier life. Her Tia Simone had stayed here. Sebastião's mum had passed away when he was two and then later, with their dad gone as well, he'd become fiercely attached to Isabel and Rita. So, Tia had stepped up to be his carer and remain in Portugal.

Isabel's grateful for that. She wonders if she would've been able to survive the years after her father's death without her aunty and her brother.

Chances were slim she wouldn't have ended up in a Gifted ward somewhere.

'Isa.'

'Hmm?' Isabel blinks to bring herself back into the room. 'What did you say?'

Tia clucks her tongue and shakes her head. 'All right, you two go sit down. It's too early to start dinner and I have another batch to put in the oven.'

Sebastião follows her out, nudges her with his shoulder. 'Have you spoken to Rita yet?'

'I messaged her.'

'You know she won't leave you alone until you talk to her properly?'

'Yes. Funny how that works. I love that when I reach out they can take their time about replying but if it's the other way round . . .'

'Isa.'

'Yes, I know, Sebastião.' She toes off her shoes and slips under one of the blankets.

Sebastião drags one of the chairs out from the dining table and turns it so that he can sit and face Isabel.

The space is large but the dining table takes up a chunk of it. It has six chairs tucked around it and Isabel knows from experience that at a squeeze it can seat more.

'Maninha,' Sebastião sighs and leans over to squeeze Isabel's shoulder, 'someone has to be the bigger person.'

'Ugh, shut up. Just for that you can go finish making the tea.'

Sebastião smiles. 'Of course.'

Isabel watches him get up and walk back into the kitchen, listens for a moment to the sound of her brother and aunty chatting.

With a grunt of frustration, she hitches up her hips to fish her phone out of her pocket. She scrolls through her contacts until her sister's name comes up.

Resigned, she hits the call button.

She hates being the bigger person.

Each one of Isabel's exhales manifests in little white puffs of air as she makes her way home.

It's a quieter night; the cafés are open but their buzz is a little softer.

She sticks her hands into her pockets, curling her fingers into the warmth.

The sky is clear, free of clouds, and the stars stud the deep dark of night. She's still warm inside from the chamomile tea they'd had at the end of the evening, full of the stew they'd had for dinner and the bolinhos they'd followed it up with. Isabel had dozed off on the sofa, tucked under the blankets.

The streetlights spotlight the way up to the turn of the road, cobbles gleaming under the yellow.

The tram sits, eerie at the bottom of the long road up with its lights off, all shadows within shadows as Isabel walks by it.

Sebastião dropped her off around the corner from her place. She left her car at the station, which feels like a blessing in disguise right now. She doesn't relish hunting for parking spaces at this time of night and then making her climb up the hill. She really wants to duck into the shower and then slide into bed.

The road up to her place is deserted, though she can hear laughter from further up, knows that the courtyard beyond her place is probably filled with teenagers hanging out.

Isabel pats at the pockets of her jeans and coat as she climbs, fingers a little numb as she searches for her keys.

She's maybe halfway up when she feels something, like a stirring in the back of her mind.

She hadn't taken another pill after dinner. With Sebastião dropping her off there had been no need for the extra support. Taking pills late at night when she isn't working guarantees a sleepless night.

But still. She hadn't expected to sense anything.

Not now on a quiet street.

The houses along the way buzz with the low sound of the TV, the clanging of someone cleaning up a kitchen and a door closing further up the street. But there is no one outside of the barrier of their house walls, or close enough to even slip through her defences.

Isabel looks over her shoulder at the slope of the road but there's no one there.

She digs deeper into the pocket of her coat and her keys jangle in the silence and fall into her hand, cold where they press against the centre of her palm. Isabel stays where she is, eyes seeking out the shadowed corners in the doorways because there isn't anywhere else someone could tuck themselves into.

She's tempted to think that her mind is playing tricks on her. But she can still feel it, huddled in the back of her mind, something that doesn't belong to her but feels familiar.

From the tram?

Isabel gathers herself. The keys cut into her hand as she focuses on the intruding weight at the back of her head. Tries to feel it out. As she fixes her attention on the empty tram, it seems to swell.

'What . . .'

The hairs stand up on the back of her neck and she starts forward.

Inside the tram, something changes.

Isabel stops.

Had something moved?

She moves into the middle of the road so she can speed up, eyes zeroed in on that one spot towards the back of the tram where passengers would be able to hop on and off. The streetlights don't quite reach it.

That's when it happens again. She sees it, like a re-forming of the dark within. Isabel's step falters and she stops in the middle of the road. Discomfort lodges in the centre of her chest and for a moment she hyper-focuses so hard, white noise fills her ears.

A door to her left opens, light and noise spilling out, and she jerks, snapping round to face the woman who stops outside of her house to give Isabel a look.

'Boa noite,' the woman says, words slow, a disapproving dip to her brows.

Isabel dips her head in apology. 'Desculpe, boa noite.'

The woman nods and steps down from the stoop, makes her way down the road, leaving the door ajar behind her as she carries the black bin bag towards the big collection area.

Isabel turns back to the tram. She makes herself put one foot in front of the other, shifts her grip on the keys as she goes.

When she reaches the tram she leaves enough space that she can walk a circle around it without getting too close, constantly checking back to that open hop-on-hop-off point, acutely aware of how vulnerable the space between her shoulder blades feels as she peers in through the windows, only to see nothing but empty benches.

She circles back to the open point and stands there, staring into the dark and empty space.

She sees dos Santos' open eyes, looking right at her.

She shakes the image out of her mind and steps back, unable to keep her gaze from tracking back to the tram, knowing that it's empty but feeling as if the moment she turns her attention away, something will be there.

'Sleep, Isabel. You need sleep,' she murmurs, backing up.

Whatever had brushed against her thoughts is gone. She can't feel it there any more.

Still, as she makes her way home she keeps checking over her shoulder, but sees nothing.

Eventually, she wills herself to turn her back on it and makes the rest of the climb to her door.

She double-checks the lock on the gate and closes the distance to the door in record time.

And if she stares out of the window into the street for a little too long before going into her apartment, well. No one will know.

22

THEN

'Isabel?'

Isabel pulls her gaze away from the sway of the trees outside and faces the woman across from her again. She tucks her hands between her legs and begins to trace the rug's blue pattern with her eyes.

It's her third time sitting across from the woman in front of her and she's still not sure she likes it. But her dad has asked Isabel to try. So, she tries.

The woman's name is Rosario and she's Isabel's stage Guide. She'll be with Isabel until she turns eighteen.

Isabel still isn't sure she understands what that means, but mostly they sit together and talk, every Saturday from nine to ten thirty in the morning.

'So, have you been practising?' Rosario asks. Her chair is big and looks super-soft, and her big green hoop earrings catch the light pouring in from the window. They swing a little every time Rosario moves her head and her hair is tangled around them.

'A little,' Isabel says. 'But sometimes I try, and I can still hear thoughts.' She frowns and scratches at the centre of her palm with her thumbnail.

'At home?'

Isabel nods. 'And outside too. Sometimes when I go shopping with Tia Simone and Sebastião I'll hear other people. Little voices. But they go away quickly.' She shrugs. 'Sometimes, they hurt my head. Dad or Tia Simone give me paracetamol and it goes away.'

'I see.' Rosario scoots to the edge of her seat and peers into Isabel's face. 'And what about your mum and your sister? Do you hear their thoughts too?'

'Yes.' The word is little louder than a whisper and after she says it Isabel clamps her lips together. She doesn't want to talk about it.

'Okay. We can talk about that another day, okay?'

'Okay.'

'What about the exercises we've been doing? Have they been helping you?'

Isabel shakes her head. 'I think I'm doing them wrong.'

'Okay, well we can work on that.' Rosario shifts from her chair and sits on the fluffy carpet. Her skirt settles around her in a circle and it reminds Isabel of girls in movies and how their skirts twirl around them when they spin.

Isabel, reluctant, slides off her chair and sits down too, folding her legs and sitting upright with the chair against her back.

'We've talked about why it's important to learn wards, haven't we?'

'Because they help protect our thoughts and keep us healthy.'

'Exactly. Because although our minds have a natural barrier that helps us to keep other people's thoughts out, we have to build on it and make it stronger. Some people think louder than others, don't they?' Rosario smiles. 'And do you remember how we create a ward?'

'We have to use our imagination.'

Rosario smiles at Isabel like she's caught her out on something. 'See? You know the basics. So why don't we start by trying a little one, hmm? So, let's close our eyes.'

Isabel closes her eyes and takes a deep breath. They've practised a few times already. In through the nose so it puffs out your belly and out through the mouth until your tummy tucks in.

'Okay. Now we have to build a wall. Brick by brick. Your wall can be any colour you want. And you have a mountain of bricks.'

Isabel's bricks are bright green, the kind of green that glows, and they're all stacked into one big mountain.

'Isabel, we build one by one.'

It's hard at first, Isabel tries to hold on to the image of the bricks but it keeps slipping away from her. But then Rosario doesn't speak again, and Isabel settles on the dark of her eyelids. She is distracted briefly by the noises outside of the room – shoes clipping on the varnished floor, doors opening and shutting further down, a phone ringing over and over – and then she settles, and the image isn't slipping away from her any more.

When Rosario speaks again her voice is soft and quiet, like she's coming from far away. 'There's someone standing on the other side, Isabel. And they're trying to speak to you. But you just want a little quiet. Do you want a little quiet?'

'Yes,' Isabel says and there it is, the first line of glowing bricks.

Beyond the line, her imagined person-on-the-other-side stands. But Isabel is focused on building her wall and doesn't think about the tops of their familiar, work-worn brown shoes.

'You keep building. Add another line. And then keep going until you can't see the other person.'

Isabel does. She keeps adding, line by line by line until the height of the wall reaches up to the other person's hips and higher. It becomes harder as she gets to shoulder level and she has to concentrate really hard. Her eyebrows pucker and she grinds her teeth together.

'Can you still see them, Isabel?'

Isabel clenches her jaw and looks into her mother's eyes over the wall.

She pushes in the final bricks, the glow consuming her mum's expression and blurring it until the final brick slots into place and all Isabel can see is green.

'No.'

23

The day dawns with a message from her sister reminding Isabel yet again about the dinner later on that night.

Isabel hides a yawn behind her hand and rubs absently at the pulsing at her temple as the door to the case room opens to let in Jacinta.

'Sorry, sorry, I'm here,' Jacinta says eyes scanning over everyone else present and grabbing a seat.

Following the relaxed evening at her tia's house, feeling energised and centred, Isabel had messaged everyone late the night before asking them to make it in a little earlier so they could squeeze this meeting in. Carla, bless her soul, had brought a box of sweet treats that sat in the middle of the desks Isabel and Voronov had pushed together.

Isabel had managed to wring two portable heaters out of facility management's hands when she'd arrived and the room was warm enough that she'd rolled up the sleeves of her top past her elbows. The back of it is still a little damp from having her freshly washed hair plastered to it, which she had now tugged into a half-hazard knot at the top of her head. The artificial heat lends a certain smell to the room, like Isabel can smell the toastiness of the warmth radiating from it.

Isabel waves Jacinta's apology away, the words that accompanied it garbled because of the croissant clenched between her teeth, flakes of it dusting the corners of her mouth and falling on her as she pours herself a cup of coffee.

Instead of taking a seat, Isabel sits on the edge of the table, knee half drawn up. She takes another bite of her croissant and nearly burns her tongue on the coffee before starting.

'Sorry for calling you all in early, and I know I sent that message pretty late last night. But,' she rubs her thumb over the arch of her brow, thinking, and sighs, 'I think we need to pause and see where we're at, agree on our next steps.'

As the weak sunlight filters in through the blinds, Isabel goes over the interviews they've had with Mrs dos Santos, Armindas and Julio. They still don't know what HSL means – it could be nothing – Armindas apparently didn't know anything but then has an argument in the middle of a function with Julio, who, according to Mrs dos Santos, hasn't always had a smooth-sailing relationship with their victim. And on top of all of that . . .

'He lied,' Isabel says and chews on the last chunk of her croissant.

'Julio did?' Jacinta asks.

Isabel washes it down with the coffee – a little too bitter for her taste. She makes a note to not let Voronov make it again. 'Definitely withholding information, especially in regard to the last phone call he had with Gil.'

'Did he slip up or something?' Daniel asks, stretching across the table and trying to hook the coffee pot with his fingertips. Isabel is happy to watch the struggle and keeps drinking her own. When she looks up she finds Voronov watching her with an arched eyebrow, and she can't help giving a twitch of a smile in response.

'No. I read it in him,' she says, and it changes the atmosphere in the room.

It's not that her colleagues have an issue with it. They wouldn't be working with her if they did and Isabel wouldn't want to work with them either. But there's always a sense of unease that slips into a room when someone talks about using their Gift. It's the elephant in the room. You know you're Gifted. They know you're Gifted. They know you sometimes use it. But that's usually as far as it goes.

Considering what this case revolves around, it's something that they'll need to get as comfortable with as possible. She's not about to let any of them shy away from it.

'Carla,' Isabel says, 'I'd like you to be here for any interrogations or interviews where I can't be present. We don't need permission to read emotions and I want as many authentic reactions as we can get without crossing the line. Especially with Julio.'

Carla nods. Her hair, which always seems to be up in the same high, tight ponytail, swishes with the movement.

'Won't that be risky?' Jacinta asks. 'Considering their stance on Gifted and how Bento Soares came storming in here. They won't react very well to that.'

Isabel shrugs. 'Thankfully for us, the investigation isn't about making them comfortable. But you're right. We'll have to watch our step where they're concerned. And maybe we're barking up the wrong tree, but right now Julio Soares is standing out.'

Of course, Isabel thinks, the fact remains that he's not Gifted himself. But if there is a motive serious enough there is no reason why Julio couldn't have gone out of his way to get a Gifted to do his dirty work for him. They just need to figure out exactly what the disagreements between Julio and Gil, and between Julio and Armindas, had been about.

Julio comes from money and his profession means he's come into contact with countless Gifted individuals, ones whose levels he'd most probably be well acquainted with too.

'Actually, Carla, do me a favour. Contact his secretary again, find out what he was scheduled to do the morning of Gil's death – a map of his day would be great. And check with her to see if there's anything in his diary similar or in relation to HSL. Ask her if she knows anything about it too.'

That set, Isabel asks Jacinta to update them on the crime scene processing.

Jacinta runs them through the details quickly. Nothing found at the scene that pointed to someone having committed a crime. The crime scene shows that someone repeatedly bashed Julio's face into a door. He died of severe blunt-force trauma.

Isabel crosses her arms, shoves up the sleeve that had fallen back past her elbow. 'That supports the theory that this was a crime committed by a Gifted telekinetic.'

'Definitely. Good news is,' Jacinta says, 'we've still got Gil's car, which we've started processing. It might be a long shot, I know. But maybe it could turn up something useful.'

'Right.' Isabel chews on the inside of her cheek, trying to hide her disappointment. She hadn't thought they would get much on the train carriage, but she'd been hopeful.

Voronov, who's been sitting quietly and taking in all the information, sits forward. 'And what about the CCTV footage from the station?'

'Chasing that today,' Daniel says.

'Keep us posted.'

It's going to be a long day.

24

Isabel didn't start out being able to hear people's thoughts. It was all feelings. All these feelings that didn't belong to her. But she is a telepathic Gifted. Her talent manifested later than usual. Not surprising considering they should never have manifested to begin with.

Both her parents were Regulars, and so is her sister. Initially it'd looked like Isabel was heading the same way. At thirteen though, in the middle of playing a school basketball game, the most horrendous pain had hit her and the pressure on the backs of her eyes had spread through to the centre of her head. The pain had been crippling.

Isabel remembers her dad rushing onto the court, a dark shape against the court lights, his arms tight around her and his voice shaking as he'd tried to stay calm.

Through a fog of strong painkillers, she remembers the nurse telling her mum and dad that she was fine, telling them this sometimes happened with Gifted when their talent began to manifest.

Isabel's father accepted her wholeheartedly. Her mother had never looked at her the same way again. Her sister – well. They talked.

For all the drama, though, her official classification on her passport reads as:

Grupo	Telepatia
Nivel Internacional	5
País de Origem	Portugal

The PJ had been happy to take on a telepath. Back then the more Gifted they'd had in their ranks the better. It had kept the balance.

Now, wherever there is a Gifted officer, there'll be at least twice as many Regular ones to ensure that they're not breaking any rules.

The fear being a Gifted sometimes generates, although unwanted, can be useful. She's not above letting it intimidate people into telling her what she needs to know.

Isabel is stepping out of the taxi when her phone starts ringing.

'Reis here.'

'Isabel, it's Carla.'

Isabel starts walking towards the roads filled with small restaurants. 'Hey, what is it?'

'Got a few things for you.'

'Tell me.'

'Medical history for Soares came in. We now know for certain that he had no other pre-existing conditions.'

Isabel stops. 'So, it's all the confirmation we needed. This is officially a Gifted crime.' She breathes out a careful breath.

'Yes, it looks like it.'

'All right, call Voronov and let him know.'

The restaurant is a little thing tucked into the back streets in the surrounding area of Restauradores.

There are tables outside and Isabel can hear the strumming of a guitar drifting out of it. The streets are busy; there aren't as many tourists here, but still enough to fill the streets with a buoyant mood. The locals are strolling, having a quick drink and unwinding after a day's work before heading home for a late dinner. Isabel should be doing the same and wonders why her sister booked the restaurant for so early. The Portuguese are late eaters, having dinner around nine or sometimes even ten in the evening.

After the meeting she'd called first thing that morning, they'd spent the day going over witness statements, trying to spot anything they might have missed and speaking to station staff who had been in the middle of their shift before it had all gone to shit that morning. It'd been a day filled with too many voices and little progress and to be honest, Isabel was looking forward to having a drink.

At least the place isn't too upscale, because all she could find was a black shirt to offset the jeans and plain, comfy flats. Her hair is still damp against her cheeks and she knows it's going to curl out of control as soon as it dries.

Isabel gives the waiter who greets her at the door a tight smile. Despite her not wanting to be here, the inside of the restaurant smells amazing and her mouth waters.

'There should be a table for seven o'clock under Reis?' she says.

The waiter smiles at her. 'Of course, the rest of the party has arrived. This way.'

All feelings of warmth die a quick death, though, at the sight that greets her when she's shown to her table. The only face that she's glad to see is Sebastião's and if looks could kill, she thinks that the rest of the table would be six feet under. Because her brother doesn't look pleased, and it's not hard for Isabel to see why that might be.

Through sheer will, Isabel keeps her mouth from dropping open. She tightens her hand on the bag hanging from her shoulder and smiles.

Her mother is watching her with a bland expression, which is better than some of the looks Isabel has got from her in the past. She is sitting with her back straight, eyes flinty behind her glasses. Rita is also sitting unnaturally straight, and when she spots Isabel, she plucks up her crisp folded napkin and starts to twirl it in her fingers. They look alike, except Rita has always worn her hair longer. Right now, it's swept into a complicated up-do on top of her head and she's wearing a pale rose dress that sets off her dark skin to perfection. The smile she gives Isabel is tense.

But, more than her mother's death glare, and Rita's obvious nervousness, Isabel is pulled up short by the fourth person at the table.

Michael.

He doesn't quite meet Isabel's eyes and he doesn't move the arm resting along the back of Rita's chair, fingers brushing the bare curve of her shoulder. Isabel tugs at the scarf around her neck. It feels too tight.

Rita's smile is still in place and Isabel wants her to drop it.

Isabel approaches the four, wishing strongly she'd never bothered to show up.

'Mãe,' Isabel greets her mother, and kisses her on her soft cheek. She gets nothing in return, just a stiffening of her mother's shoulders in response.

'Isabel, I'm so glad you came.' Rita stands up and hugs her tight. Tighter than usual, tucking her face into Isabel's shoulder like she used to do when she was little and had got into trouble. Despite everything, Isabel can't help responding to that and wraps her arms around her sister.

Over her shoulder, Isabel stares at Michael's face and is stumped when he still refuses to look at her.

'Hi,' Isabel says as she pulls away and takes the empty seat between Rita and her mother. 'Michael. Hope you're well.' That's the best she can do. She doesn't smile when she says it.

There's an awkward silence at first.

'We haven't ordered yet, we were waiting for you,' Rita says, settling back into her seat. 'You want to get something to drink?'

Isabel doesn't need the prompt; her hand is already in the air trying to catch the waiter's attention. Maybe it's because it's not too busy, or maybe their service is just that fast, but there's a large glass of red wine in front of her in under two minutes.

Isabel swallows. Fuck appearances. She sets her glass down, rubs her hands on her thighs and looks around the table.

'What's going on?' she asks.

Sebastião doesn't speak. His jaw is locked tight, a muscle ticcing in his cheek. He hasn't spoken a word since Isabel walked in.

'Well.' Rita looks to their mother, who nods at her, a kind smile on her face, encouraging. 'I meant to tell you. I really wanted to tell you earlier but . . . but it's so hard to catch you when you're free and it felt like there was never the right time but—' Rita drops her gaze and Isabel notices that in the time it's taken for her drink to arrive, Rita's shredded the napkin to pieces. 'Michael and I have been seeing each other.'

Isabel blinks down at her glass. 'Oh.' She takes another drink. 'You've been seeing each other. Right.' She considers waving the waiter back over and asking for the rest of the bottle.

When Rita glances back up at her, her pretty face is pale. 'I was going to tell you—'

'You didn't. But okay. So, you've been seeing each other.' Isabel shoots Michael a mocking look. 'I guess there's something about this family tree that must be doing it for you, hmm?'

'Isabel. You weren't invited here to be crude.'

The first words that her mother has spoken to her in months. Isabel schools her expression into something blank. 'Of course.' She tightens her grip on her glass but doesn't drink again. She hasn't eaten enough to keep going and not end up shit-faced. 'Okay. Why now then?'

'Isa.' Small pieces of napkin fall from Rita's fingers as she clasps her hands together. She presses herself into Michael's hold, not seeming to realise she's doing it. Michael shifts closer and she nestles herself into his side. 'I know, and I want to explain. But this, this isn't new. We've been together for some time now and,' she glances at Michael but he's looking at Isabel now, 'we're . . . we're getting engaged.'

Sebastião grits his teeth, face turned away from the table.

'Olha-me esta merda,' Isabel mutters. She forgets about checking her drink intake and reaches for her wine while chuckling under her breath and shaking her head in disbelief. 'Married?' She drains her glass, wonders why she bothered to sit down. 'You're marrying my ex who you didn't actually tell me you were dating. Well, okay then.' She smiles at Rita and Michael, razor-sharp and none of it touching her eyes. 'Congratulations.' She stands up; slinging the bag she hadn't quite set down back onto her shoulder.

Sebastião pushes back from the table as well, striding around to come and stand behind Isabel.

Rita's hand curls around Isabel's arm as she makes to leave. 'Isabel, please—'

Isabel rounds on her, face like stone, words clipped. 'Stop. Think carefully about what you're about to say.' She points at Michael. 'If that's what you want then you go for it. But don't invite me here, throw this at me and expect me to act like this is okay. This is *not* okay.'

Rita flinches back from her, letting go, face turned away from Isabel and hands curled into tight fists. There's a pretty band on her ring finger.

Isabel considers paying for her drink for a moment but then thinks, *screw it*. That's the least they owe her. 'Excuse me.'

Neither Sebastião nor Isabel speak as they walk out of the restaurant towards Isabel's house. Sebastião is quiet and stiff beside her. They're not allowed to get very far before they hear her mother calling out to them.

Isabel stops, praying for patience.

'Isabel.' Maria is breathing hard from going after them and her cheeks are red, though Isabel doubts that has to do with chasing after her.

Isabel's mother is a beautiful woman. She's aged well, no sign now of the ravaged woman she had been for the first few years after her husband's death. Isabel wonders if she misses him still. Isabel definitely does.

'What you did in there was out of order,' her mum starts.

Sebastião lets out an incredulous laugh. 'For the love of God, Tia Maria!'

Isabel chokes out a laugh and points at herself. 'What I did? Are you serious right now? What planet are you from?'

Maria glances around and then, when she realises that Isabel is drawing attention to them, levels a glare at her. 'Your sister wanted to tell you her happy news. You could have accepted it gracefully. Be grateful that at least someone is willing to overlook your madness, the Lord knows Michael tried.'

'That piece of—' Sebastião starts.

Isabel waves a hand to cut her off. 'Enough. I'm going home. I don't have time for your hate speeches right now. Go back to Rita, wouldn't want to make you look at the devil's spawn for too long.' She sneers at her mother. 'It might be catching.'

Her mother doesn't need any more prompting. She spins around, delicate skirt fluttering around her dainty figure. All black. Her mother hasn't worn colours since her husband died.

For the first time, that fails to make Isabel feel anything other than bitterness towards the woman who didn't love her enough to see beyond their differences.

25

It takes two cups of strong coffee the next morning to get Isabel functioning.

She walks into work with a third steaming cup in her hand.

She'd stayed away from her pills after arriving home last night. She'd stayed away from another drink too. Not that it did her much good.

After she'd left the restaurant yesterday and gone home, she'd spent most of the night staring at different parts of her bedroom. Eventually she'd given up and dragged her bedding to the sofa, where she stayed curled up and wide awake until the early hours. The last time she had looked at the clock before finally dropping off, it had been 4 a.m.

There had been ten missed calls from Rita on her phone when she'd woken up, and three text messages. All of them went unread and unreturned.

Isabel's not even sure what had hit her the hardest. That her sister had gone behind her back, that Michael had even dared to go there, or that her mother remains the same woman she became after Isabel tested Gifted, taking any excuse she can to tear her down and go against her.

Voronov looks up from his desk as she walks in. He takes in her face.

Isabel sets her coffee down on her desk and shrugs off her coat. 'What?'

'Nothing. Good morning.'

'Morning.' She drapes her coat over the back of her chair and sits down, feeling like her entire body is one big weight. She takes another sip of the sweetened coffee. She doesn't normally take it with sugar, but she can't afford to skimp on energy. 'Did Carla call you last night?'

'Yes. She told me about the medical history.'

Isabel sighs. She digs the heels of her hands into her eyes, rubs hard for a moment.

Voronov arches a brow. 'Well,' he says slowly, 'CCTV for the car park at Gare do Oriente came in half an hour ago. Daniel has started viewing it. The Chief is waiting on us, she wants an update.'

Not what Isabel would've chosen to do on two hours of sleep. Her eyes already feel like they've been dipped in sand. 'Sure, no time like the present.'

They find a car.

Hundreds of cars are parked in and around the station during rush hour. It's a hub of activity and there are three colour videos of that morning, from different parts of the cark park.

It's 3 p.m. when Daniel calls them into the room. He's isolated the stretch of footage they need to look at and Isabel, Voronov and Carla settle in to see.

The CCTV isn't that clear, too pixelated.

Gil is already parked – they can see his Jeep in its bay on Carla's screen – but he doesn't get out right away. While he's in there, an older Peugeot circles the car park three times, despite there being quite a few spaces available.

At 6.20 a.m. on the CCTV, Gil gets out, hovers outside the door for a moment before heading towards the station. That's when the Peugeot reverses into a parking space three down from Gil's Jeep.

The driver leaves the car and walks in the same direction. Shorter than Gil, with a dark jacket that hits them about mid-ankle, white, dark hair. It's impossible to tell if it's a man or a woman.

The call goes through to 112 at 6.59 a.m. And five minutes later a spread of people come into the frame, some running, some speed-walking past. Jacinta had said that many people had made a break for it that morning.

'All right, rewind it and pause. See if we can catch a plate number for the Peugeot,' Isabel says, words half muffled by her hand. Her cheek aches from resting on it for so long.

They pause the CCTV on the back of the car. There are good shots of the licence plate but the pixelated video doesn't pick up the number properly.

'How long will it take to clean this up?' Isabel asks.

'Depends, it might not even be possible,' Daniel answers, frowning at the image.

Two hours later, Isabel is banging on the glass of the snack machine outside in the hall; the headache feels like it's cleaving her head in two. Voronov pokes his head out of the case room and motions for her to come back in.

'It's registered to a Luisa Delgado,' Carla says as Isabel walks back into the investigation room.

'Luisa Delgado.' Isabel narrows her eyes. She looks at Voronov, who is staring at Carla. 'We spoke to her,' Isabel says. 'She also happened to attend that function.'

'Is that the witness who came back for her handbag?' Carla asks.

'Yes.' Isabel looks at the small figure on camera where they've paused the video. 'She said she called her boyfriend to pick her up because she'd left everything on the train. Said he didn't take long to come and get her. But if she has her car there, then why would she call her boyfriend to come and get her?'

'Car keys in the bag, maybe? There were keys recorded in the logged contents.'

'Maybe,' Isabel says, frowning. 'Fast-forward it. Let's see if she gets back in the car.'

Isabel chews on her lip as she mulls it over. Any other person would have mentioned the car. People usually spill as much detail as they can, irrelevant or otherwise, when they're trying to get the police off their backs. So why hadn't Luisa done the same?

They all watch the tape intently but Luisa doesn't get back in her car.

'She should've mentioned it,' Voronov murmurs. He's standing next to Isabel, hands tucked into his pockets and eyes on the screen.

'Yes. She should've.' Isabel chews the inside of her cheek and twists her hair into a makeshift bun, thinking it over. On the screen, the image is fixed on the image of Luisa's vehicle, lonely in its parking bay, the darkness of evening made into a grainy charcoal-black around it.

Voronov's still examining the frozen image. 'We need to speak to her again.'

26

They get to the bank where Luisa Delgado works just as it is closing. Despite the hour and the clouded sky, the streets are still well lit. Even in winter months, the sun sets late here. There's a tired quietness in the air.

Isabel eyes Voronov in disgust. She's bundled up to the point where her chin barely clears the top of her layers, while he's walking upright, smart coat on with a thin scarf around his neck that might as well not be there.

One of the other bank employees is on their way out, a cigarette and lighter in hand. She startles as Isabel goes to open the front door. Throwing a cautious look over her shoulder, she pulls the door open. 'Good evening,' she says. Her name tag reads José Fátima. 'I'm afraid we're now closed for the day.'

Isabel digs out her police ID. 'Sorry to bother you when you want to get home. Is Luisa working today?'

Fátima glances down at Isabel's ID, looks up at Voronov where he's towering behind her and then back at Isabel. 'Yes, but we're in the middle of closing right now.'

Then should you really be sneaking out for a cigarette break? Isabel thinks. 'I see.'

Voronov steps forward, a smile on his face. 'Actually, you might be able to help us.'

Fátima shifts back, looking uneasy now, but there's enough curiosity on her face that Isabel knows she's going to cave. The curse of the Portuguese. They love a good gossip.

'We have to finish setting up for tomorrow too, but I have a few minutes.' She steps out and lets the heavy glass door swing closed behind her.

The whole front of the bank is made out of sturdy glass and they can easily see in. It's a wide-open space with marble flooring that reflects the bright ceiling lights. Tall potted plants dot the corners of the large room and the walls are painted maroon. A few other employees at their desks peek over, their curiosity obvious, but they keep their distance as they go about setting up for the following day.

'Thank you for your time,' Voronov says, again with that smile.

Isabel resists rolling her eyes as José Fátima stops short of melting into the floor. Isabel doesn't blame her really, but still.

'How can I help? Like I said, Luisa won't be available right away, she's overseeing the cashing up.' She lights up her cigarette. She's dressed in a prim grey pencil skirt with a white shirt and a navy blazer.

'And we're happy to wait for her. How long have you worked with Luisa?'

'Oh. A few years now. She was already a member of staff when I started here.'

'And how is she, here. Good colleague?'

'She's a good manager, always friendly.' She stops short, and then seems to think better of holding back. 'Well, she's been a little quiet recently. And, well,' she shifts as she smokes, 'she's been having a rough time of it, which is a shame. She's a nice woman.'

Isabel tilts her head, interest piqued. 'Rough time, how?'

José Fátima's cheeks go a blotchy pink then and she drops her eyes. 'Um, well, just some personal things.'

Voronov steps in again. 'Could you explain a little more for us? Don't worry. This won't go beyond us, if that's what's concerning you.'

José Fátima hesitates. 'It's just that she's always been an immaculate manager. Rarely made mistakes and totally reliable. She knows this branch like the back of her hand. But then about a year ago things changed a little. She started becoming forgetful.

A few days she didn't show up to work and then couldn't remember – I heard she was seeing a doctor for it and that it might be some kind of condition. I'm not sure. We get along and we're friendly but we're not close. She is well-liked by everyone and we worry that it might get too much for the higher-ups.'

Odd. 'Forgetful in what way?' Isabel asks.

'Little things. We noticed that sometimes you'd mention a conversation from a day ago or ask her about something that we'd already discussed or a particular client, and she would go blank. It was a little sad and we guessed maybe she isn't okay but, obviously that's a personal thing, you know? It's her business. It's a shame though.'

'That does sound like a shame,' Isabel says. 'Well, thank you Fátima and sorry for taking up your time. Please can you let Luisa know that we're waiting for her for a quick word?'

'Of course, and it's no problem.' She quickly finishes her cigarette before stubbing it out and heading back inside.

Yeah, Isabel thinks, the whole bank is going to know the police are here for Luisa. Fátima is clearly the type who likes to spread things around.

Isabel and Voronov wait for Luisa.

'Difficulty recalling things?' Isabel shakes her head.

'Might explain why she didn't want to consent to you looking through her memories.'

Valid point. 'Maybe,' Isabel says. She pulls out her phone and checks the time. 'Think we have time to grab a snack from around the corner or something before she comes out?'

He shakes his head but doesn't say anything, mouth curling up at the edges.

'What?'

'Where does it all go?'

The humour takes her by surprise and Isabel's mouth curls in amusement before she can help it. She shakes her head and gives him the finger.

*   *   *

Luisa doesn't look pleased as she walks outside to find Isabel and Voronov waiting for her.

'Inspectors, this is my workplace. Do you know what kind of impression you're giving my staff?' She's tugging the belt of her coat closed around her waist as she talks. 'Interrogating them about me?'

Inside the bank, the other tellers are shooting looks out of the glass doors. They've all clearly finished for the day but are taking their time pulling on their coats and standing around, chatting, casting them the most unsubtle looks Isabel has ever seen. Fátima is among them. Surprise, surprise.

No rain has come down yet, but the wind is a brutal thing. Luisa's dressed a little fancier today. Her gold watch dangles from her wrist like a bracelet and diamond earrings glint at her ears.

'Sorry we had to intrude like this,' Voronov says, 'I hope you understand that the nature of our investigation means we have to move as quickly as we can on any potentially new information. I know we asked you to contact us if you felt you could help us any more, but we needed to double-check.'

'No, I'm sorry Inspectors, but I can't.'

'I understand, but we do have a query. You drove to the station that morning.'

Luisa tucks her hair behind her ear again even though she did that a few seconds ago. Her face is pale and she looks seconds away from bolting from them. 'Yes, I did.' She doesn't say anything else. Isabel stays quiet, letting Voronov handle it.

The woman will only get more nervous if Isabel steps in. She'd become more withdrawn at the station when Isabel had identified herself as Gifted – they don't need to make the situation worse.

'You're not in trouble. But your car was parked outside Gare do Oriente station and when we spoke to you, you didn't mention this to us. You said you only had your phone and you wouldn't have been able to get a taxi because your money was in your bag.'

Luisa frowns. 'Yes – I mean. No. I drove there, yes. But once I left the station, I forgot my bag like I told you. I didn't have my keys.

And even if I had had them at the time, I wouldn't have wanted to drive. I was too shaken up for that.' Her eyes keep darting, back and forth, back and forth. Isabel watches it all through narrowed eyes. How shifty can you look while attempting not to look shifty?

'I see,' Isabel says. 'I'm sorry; but we found it odd that you didn't mention it. Gabriel Bernardo is the boyfriend you mentioned? The one who picked you up from the station that morning? Is this the gentleman you were accompanying the night of the function?'

Luisa steps back; pulls her coat tighter around her. 'Yes, what about him?' The look she gives Isabel has some backbone to it this time.

'Do you go to these functions often?'

'Yes. I accompany him to them all the time. The invite was actually for him. His parents run in those circles and his profession means that they're an important part of his social calendar. They're very close to the Soares family. Gabriel's dad works in politics too.'

'I see. If you attend these things often, you must have spoken to Gil at some point, no?'

'Gil dos Santos?' Luisa asks. 'I don't know, in passing, maybe.'

'Why not mention this at the station when you spoke to us there?' Isabel asks.

There's a spike of emotion that hits Isabel hard just then. Bright and sharp. Luisa broadcasts it so loudly that Isabel feels it hit her in the chest.

'I don't know,' Luisa says, 'like I said, we've only spoken in passing.'

'But you knew who he was, is what I'm saying.'

'I don't—I wasn't . . .' Luisa folds her arms over her chest and stands up straighter. 'Look, I've told you what I know.'

Except you haven't, Isabel thinks.

'It was just a coincidence that we were even in the same carriage. I didn't realise and then when I did, he was—he was—' Luisa cuts herself off. 'I don't have anything else to tell you.'

Yeah. Big coincidence. Anyone else would have stayed behind to find out what had happened, not run away at the first opportunity. Not unless you had something to hide.

Voronov steps a little closer and dips his head a little to catch Luisa's eyes again. 'That's okay, Luisa, you've been helpful. Can I ask one last thing?'

Luisa nods, probably because she knows she doesn't have much of a choice.

'I understand you were maybe confused at the time. When did you call your boyfriend to come and get you? Do you remember the time?'

Luisa's face goes blank and she stares at them.

'Luisa?' Voronov prompts when she doesn't say anything.

'I don't—I don't remember.' She seems to come back into herself. 'Everything . . . it happened too fast,' she says.

Isabel keeps her eyes on her and then, softly, asks, 'Luisa, if you felt okay with it, I could take a look at your—'

'No!' Luisa jerks back and away from them, the skin around her mouth going white and her eyes seeming too big for her face.

Isabel holds up her hands in apology and nods. 'It was a suggestion.'

Luisa doesn't budge, keeps staring at Isabel like the other woman is about to attack her.

Isabel eases back so she's standing slightly behind Voronov, trying to make herself less threatening. Luisa's reaction was intense. Too intense. Way more defensive then she had been when they'd interviewed her the first time around.

She's still staring at Isabel.

Voronov shifts into Luisa's line of sight and smiles reassuringly. 'Okay, thank you. We'll leave you to get on with your day.'

Luisa nods but doesn't say anything. She stays rooted to the spot, arms wrapped around herself, and watches them until they get into the car and drive off.

Isabel's chewing on the inside of her cheek, mulling that whole interaction over.

'When you asked her if you could look into her memories the first time, the response was less . . . volatile,' Voronov says.

Isabel pushes her hair back from her face and leans her head back on the headrest, closing her eyes for a moment. Which turns out not to be the best thing because it has her seeing bright spots against the black of her eyelids that throb in time to her headache. She has to blink a couple of times to clear her vision.

'There's something not right there,' Isabel says.

'Did you pick up anything from her?' He asks it casually, straight out. The lack of tiptoeing around the fact that she has a Gift is refreshing. Or suspicious. Is he fishing? Beyond knowing that she can look into someone's mind and access memories, or that she can sense people's emotions, he doesn't know much else about her powers. Is he trying to find out how much she can do and to what extent she can use them?

But when Isabel looks over at him, Voronov's focused on the road.

'Nothing useful,' she says, 'hopefully Carla will have something better for us.'

'Julio's secretary wasn't as helpful as we would have liked.' Carla sighs and sits on the table.

The precinct is unusually quiet at this time of day and their floor is practically empty, so they're all at Isabel's desk, except for Jacinta who is still with the team processing Gil's car. So far, no news from them.

Voronov's shed his jacket and has rolled his chair over so they don't have to talk too loudly. It's incredible how put-together he still looks at the end of a working day. Daniel on the other hand looks like he's been working through the night, bags under his eyes and sucking down coffee like it's his lifeline. He's staring off into space like he's vacated the premises, but Isabel knows he's listening. It's his MO.

'Great,' Isabel mutters. She's hungry and she can feel her body slowing down, mind going sluggish. They should've stopped for food on their way back from Luisa. She wonders if she has any more emergency snack bars at her desk.

'But.' Carla smiles.

That gets Isabel's attention. 'Oh?'

'She tells me that the morning Gil died, Julio was due to attend a departmental meeting at the university he works at, but then at the last minute he had her send his apologies to the chair.'

Voronov rolls closer. 'What time was the meeting supposed to take place?'

Carla grimaces. 'This is where it becomes a little less helpful. His meeting was for ten thirty a.m.'

Which would've given enough time to get from Gare do Oriente to his workplace, plenty of time, Isabel thinks. Him cancelling the meeting doesn't mean much.

'What about HSL?' She catches her hair in one hand and tugs on it, frustration eating at her. 'Any mention of that anywhere?' she asks. 'Did she have any clue what it might mean?'

Carla shakes her head and her ponytail swishes along with the motion. 'She did agree to send me a copy of his schedule in the month leading up to the day of Gil's death, which we've already received. I've started looking through it.'

'Okay, thanks.' Isabel rubs at her eyes. 'Unless Jacinta has something for us, we should call it a day. Start fresh tomorrow. I need food.'

'I think Jacinta doesn't have long to go,' Carla says, 'is anyone up for grabbing some food and a drink?'

Isabel's stomach is only too happy to agree to that idea.

27

'God, we haven't done this in too long,' Jacinta groans, next to her.

It hadn't taken Jacinta long to join them. The search of the car and the forensics hadn't turned up anything useful, to everyone's disappointment.

'Tell me about it,' Isabel says.

The music in the bar is upbeat and sounds familiar; something that Isabel is sure they must play over and over again. Isabel smiles at the bartender as he slides a tall glass of rum and Coke her way. She takes a drink from it and sighs in satisfaction.

'That's hitting the spot.'

'Amen,' Jacinta says and touches her glass to Isabel's.

The rest of the team has gone to find a table and everyone is in the process of getting his or her drinks.

'So,' Jacinta says.

'So?'

'How's the new partnership going?' she asks.

Isabel shrugs. 'It's going.'

'Oh?' Jacinta sighs and looks at where Voronov is standing by the table talking to Daniel, who is already sitting with a drink in hand next to Carla. 'Are those anti-Gifted rumours proving true?'

Isabel glances over her shoulder at him. 'No, not as far as I can tell.' She can work with him easily enough. But is she at ease in his presence? Sometimes. In the back of her mind she can't help wondering if he's figuring her out, gathering what he can to maybe use against her at some later time.

'I suppose we should've known it wouldn't be an issue. The Chief can be an arsehole but she looks after her people.'

Isabel can't argue with that.

They have quite a few empty pool tables in the bar, which Isabel is surprised by. She hasn't played in a long time.

'Want a game?' she asks, pointing at the tables with her drink.

Jacinta looks at the table. 'Hmm, maybe in a bit? Let me sit down and let this drink go to my head. I need to unwind; this case is throwing everyone off-kilter.'

'I know.'

'What about you? How's it going with your sister?'

It's not. Her phone hasn't stopped buzzing with texts and missed calls since the dinner, although it has slowed down in the last couple of hours. She's ignored all of Rita's messages, meaning that her phone has the annoying notification number constantly on the screen that makes her twitch.

There had only been one message from Michael. That one she hadn't left as a notification. She deleted it right away, not having read one word of it.

Jacinta has been around as a friend long enough that she's met both of Isabel's siblings, and although her opinion of Rita hadn't been a bad one, she'd mentioned to Isabel that they seemed like polar opposites. She had also been around during Isabel's relationship with Michael. In conclusion, currently, Jacinta isn't impressed by Isabel's sister at all.

'Haven't replied to her,' Isabel says, gaze roaming the menu scrawled in white chalk on the strip of blackboard above the bar. 'Don't want to speak to her, to be honest.' She feels as if her entire body is sagging under the weight of the conversation, just talking about it exhausting her. 'I'm angry but, she's still my sister. I don't want to say something I can't take back.'

'You? Say something without thinking? Never.' Jacinta pats her hard enough that her drink spills. 'Oh look; your new partner is coming over. God, he's pretty isn't he?'

Isabel looks at Voronov making his way through the room and can't help the teasing curl to her mouth. 'He is. Think the Chief was trying to do us a favour?'

Jacinta snorts. 'Don't say that near Daniel, I think we'll bruise his ego.'

'His ego is big enough.'

'Yeah well, let me go visit with his ego so you can have a drink with Voronov. Can't believe you hadn't taken the man out for a drink yet. What kind of partner are you?'

'A tired one,' Isabel calls out to her and takes another sip, because she knows from experience that although alcohol doesn't take the headaches away – depending on how much she has, it could end up worse in the morning – the floatiness that comes with a small buzz can help a bit.

'Tired of what?' Voronov asks as he takes the stool next to her and motions the bartender over.

'Her bullshit,' Isabel says and turns back to the bar.

'Vodka, neat, please,' he says.

'Because I'm not actually an arsehole I'm not going to comment on how that's a cliché,' she says and tacks on a request for a bifana sandwich to the end of Voronov's order before the bartender can walk off.

'Didn't you do that anyway?'

'Did I?' She hitches herself up onto a stool. 'Which part of Russia is your family from? You are Russian, right? I assumed, by your last name. Or am I wrong?'

Voronov thanks the bartender and pays for his drink before replying. 'My grandmother is from Novosibirsk.' His pronunciation is crisp.

'Mum's side? Dad's side?'

'My mother's.' He takes a drink, then frowns and stares down at it.

'What? Not good?'

'It'll do,' he says, still frowning. 'I have better at home.' His eyes meet hers over the glass and Isabel doesn't look away.

'Okay,' she says, 'nice to know where I can go for good vodka.'

'Just being friendly,' he says with a shrug.

Right. She glances at the others and sees that they're deep in conversation.

She grins. The rum is warming her up and she's eager to get another. A second one will put her in a good place. 'You play pool?'

'Yes. You want a game?'

'Yeah. Let's do it.' Isabel nods at the bartender. 'Can we get one of the tables, and two more of the same, please?' She slides a note across the counter, waving Voronov's protest aside, and follows the bartender over to the cues and the pool balls, sipping her drink as she goes.

The cue is a familiar weight in her hand. It always reminds her of her dad standing beside her, explaining how to make her shot. She still doesn't play as well as he used to.

Setting her drink on the edge of the pool table, she chalks the tip of the stick and watches Voronov set the game. He lifts the frame up and off and gestures for Isabel to go up first.

Isabel shrugs and throws the chalk at him. She rounds the table to break.

'So,' she says as she leans over to line up her shot, 'you seem to be settling in without any problems.'

'Is that how it looks?'

She takes the shot, the crack of the balls dispersing across the table loud. She sinks a stripe and stands back from the table to survey her next one. 'Yeah. Why? Am I wrong?' She rounds the table and lines up her next shot.

'No, I haven't had any problems but don't think you feel the same.'

Her ball rebounds off the pocket's corner. She straightens and looks at him, arching a brow. 'No problems here.'

'Hmm.' His eyes sweep over the table. 'I get the sense that you're not convinced.'

'About what exactly?' Her words are muffled by the rim of her glass.

He pockets the first ball, then a second, but misses the third, blocking what would've been an easy one for her. He walks around to stand in front of her, holding the cue firmly with both hands. 'About having me as your partner.'

'Wouldn't that be my problem?' she asks.

'Ours,' he corrects, 'since we're meant to watch each other's backs.'

'Oh,' she says slowly, nods and finishes her drink. Gripping her cue, she turns back to the game at hand. 'Are you worried I won't have your back, Voronov?'

He inclines his head and a smile curls over the corner of his mouth that has no humour to it.

Isabel sets her cue down and leans against it, ignoring the game for now. At their table the others are laughing, unaware of the nature of the conversation taking place just a few steps away from them. 'Sorry to be blunt' – she's not really – 'but from what I understand, I think I might be the one that should worry.'

'And why is that?'

Brave. Okay. It's not like he's not aware that rumours about him being dirty and framing his partner made the rounds. 'I'm talking about the situation with your Gifted ex-partner. Sorry if I'm not too comfortable with that.'

She doesn't wait to see what he has to say, turns her attention back to the game at hand. It's not until she's cleared another two balls and missed the third that she notices he's watching her with that smile still on his face.

Isabel leans against the pool table again, crossing an ankle over the cue and wrapping her arms around it. 'Something funny?'

'No. I'm just surprised you had the balls to say it to my face.'

Isabel scoffs. 'No balls here. Your turn.' The music in the bar changes abruptly to a headbanger and they both share a look.

They play on in silence until Isabel takes the game, a smirk on her face as she straightens, because winning is winning and she's not going to pretend. It's a close enough game though.

He tilts his head at her in acknowledgement and nods at her empty glass.

'Another drink?'

Probably not the smartest thing for her to do. The strength of the pill is dissipating. The headache has faded into more of a mellow thing. She should be taking herself home. But she doesn't do this often and sometimes she misses it, having a simple night with a few drinks and good conversation with her colleagues.

She follows him back to the bar. 'So why homicide? You were in narcotics before. Change of scene or couldn't stay in there any more?'

He leans on the bar and nods. 'You're very blunt.'

The conversation is briefly interrupted by the bartender. Voronov pays for their drinks with a thanks and slides them over to her. She murmurs a thank you.

'A lot of people think they know what happened,' he says.

Isabel hitches herself back up on the stool. 'Don't they?'

'People like to make up their own narrative.'

'Ah,' she watches him carefully, 'and by people do you mean the press or your ex-colleagues?'

He stares at the drink in his hand. 'Depends on the perspective of the listener. You've already made up your mind which narrative you believe.' He flicks a glance up at her. 'Haven't you?'

Maybe. She doesn't say that though.

The smile he gives her isn't as pleasant then.

He toasts her.

'Here's to you making up your own mind.'

28

The names they'd sent into the Registry had come in.

They hadn't stayed out too long the night before but as they crowd around Daniel where he's set up on the PC, she has to hide a few yawns behind her hand. She's a little resentful that Voronov turned up looking sharp-eyed, despite knocking back quite a few vodkas himself. Carla had stuck to soft drinks all night so she was fine too, but Daniel, as always, looks a little worse for wear, so that makes Isabel feel a little bit better.

They've locked the door to the room; the odds of someone walking in unannounced are slim but she doesn't want to take any chances on whatever they discover in this room leaking to the rest of the precinct.

Someone at that function had known Isabel was working Gil's case. And that same someone had been a telekinetic Gifted and had reached out that night to her specifically. A taunt? It didn't matter. The action spoke of arrogance. Isabel wants to know who in that room had been capable of doing that. After receiving the list of names of everyone who had attended that night, they'd requested a vetting by the Registry and had been waiting for them to come back.

'They could work on being a little faster.' Isabel takes a bite out of her sandwich, frowning around the mouthful when tuna mayo squishes out of the sides to coat the sides of her fingers.

Daniel looks from the sandwich to her and frowns.

'Gifted genes. Sorry,' she says.

Daniel snorts and shakes his head, then hooks his foot around the chair next to him and yanks it out for her.

'Nice of you to get some for the rest of us too,' he says.

Isabel takes another huge bite right in his face and then nods in the direction that Voronov had gone a while ago. 'Sorry, he got it.'

Daniel's eyebrows jump up and almost hit his hairline. 'Oh?'

She flips him off. 'Show me what they've given us?'

He winks and grins at her like a little boy before turning back to what he's actually supposed to be doing. 'Okay, here's what they sent us.'

Voronov comes back into the room and Isabel motions for him to come over.

Daniel goes silent, ducking his head, eyes fixed on the screen as he clicks back and forth.

Isabel runs her eyes down the guest list on the screen, finding two of the names she's most interested in: Julio Soares and Luisa Delgado.

With Julio she's not expecting any surprises, but it pays to be thorough. Now, with Luisa – well, Julio isn't the only one who has something he's not telling them. During their last conversation, it felt like her reaction to Isabel's suggestion to view her memories went beyond the average person's aversion to having someone poke around their head.

'Once everyone is tested by the NTI,' Daniel says, 'the results are logged by the Registry nationally. This list should tell us the Gift and level of everyone who attended that night, if any. It can probably tell us a lot more, depends how much the Registry decided to share. They like keeping a tight hold on their information.'

Understandable. The risks associated with giving people unrestricted access – even the police – would be huge. All it would take was someone with a little prejudice having a bad day.

Isabel feels like she's holding her breath as Daniel moves the cursor and starts scrolling down the page of names.

They're listed in alphabetical order by surname, and followed by the date of the testing, Gift category and classification. In the case of those who don't have anything, they just have N/A in place.

Isabel eases away from the screen. 'She's Gifted.'

Voronov rests his hand on the back of her chair and leans in to see too. 'That's not enough,' he murmurs, 'her level doesn't have enough power to be able to control someone to the extent of the crimes committed, at least not if we base this on what Dr Alves explained.'

'I know,' Isabel says, chewing the inside of her cheek as she stares at the results in front of her. Why hadn't Luisa volunteered the information herself? But in any case, as Voronov has pointed out, she's a lower-level Gifted. She wouldn't have the kind of power needed to move a whole person.

Isabel frowns.

They check Julio Soares' name and, predictably, he's a Regular.

At her side, Voronov straightens. 'Wait. Stop there,' he tells Daniel, 'scroll back up, slower this time.'

Daniel quickly scrolls back up to the top of the list.

When she sees it, Isabel throws out a hand for him to stop.

ARMINDAS, CÉLIA – TELECINÉTICA – 7.0 INTL

The same Célia Armindas who is an NTI head, and who hadn't mentioned a word of her Gift to Isabel and Voronov when they'd spoken to her.

Isabel stares at the screen. She sets down her half-eaten sandwich.

Daniel gives a low whistle.

Well. She hadn't expected that. 'All right,' Isabel rubs a hand over her mouth, 'let's get everyone in here, I want any new updates ready to be reported on. We need to focus this investigation.'

Isabel sits on the edge of the table, one leg drawn up. She's tied her hair back from her face and is ignoring the bits that have escaped the elastic to curl at her nape. She's rolled up the sleeves of her jumper but keeps having to adjust the collar because of the label scratching the back of her neck.

Jacinta and Carla have joined them and been briefed on the findings in regard to Célia Armindas and Luisa Delgado.

Isabel rubs the irritated patch of skin. 'Okay, so the classifications took a turn we weren't expecting, so I want us to start looking at motivation, anything that has stood out to us as not seeming right or any new evidence.'

It's edging into mid-morning, but they've turned all the lights on, the gloom from outside doing its best to spread into the room.

Célia Armindas, currently the only head of NTI following Gil dos Santos' death. They know that Célia and Gil got their positions within months of each other, and that both had been working there for some months before that, in the senior testing team. She has a doctorate in Neuroscience and, like Gil, also specialises in research into Gifted. No partner, no kids, has an aunt who lives in Germany but that's about it.

Then there's Julio Soares. Son of a well-known anti-Gifted party leader, renowned professor and researcher at one of Portugal's top universities, a confirmed Regular, frequent partner to the heads of NTI on projects and at odds with Gil prior to his death, over an undisclosed issue. And last call on Gil's phone records. Clearly withholding information.

And finally, Luisa Delgado. A strange and vague presence in this whole thing. Present at the scene of the murder, failing to mention that she knew the victim, and then there's the speedy getaway. Gifted, which she failed to tell them too. Her overreaction to Isabel's request to view her memories was also interesting.

All three of them had been there at that function.

'I want to come back to Luisa Delgado,' Isabel says. 'But let's focus on Célia and Julio for a second. Célia conveniently forgot to tell us she's Gifted. Ascends the NTI food chain to become one of the heads of the institution, which is . . . unusual in itself.'

Carla's smile is bitter-edged. 'That's one way of putting it, I guess.'

'Why?' Voronov asks.

When the others look at them askance, Carla explains. 'The NTI isn't viewed fondly by most Gifted people. Historically, it was set up as a mode of controlling numbers, keeping tabs.'

The NTI has always worked closely with the government and their earlier years are now locked up in classified documents, but there's a lot of speculation about experimentation on unwilling subjects. This apparently started during the NTI's early years, shortly after World War One, and ramped up at the start of World War Two. At the time, they wanted to find a way to identify higher-level Gifted, supposedly so they could be used on the front lines and for intelligence gathering.

'Yes. They like to pretend that didn't happen.' Isabel gets up to go and pour herself a coffee.

'Obviously,' Carla continues, 'a lot has changed since then. Now the NTI's supposed main priority is to ensure the well-being and safety of Gifted people in society.'

Isabel nods. 'Except for the part where their systems and policies seem to cater more to reassuring non-Gifted that we're not a threat and can be controlled,' she mutters, swishing the coffee in the cup. 'For someone of Célia's level to willingly want to work for this institution is practically unheard of.'

Isabel finds it odd that a Gifted like Armindas could take up a position of power without the press tearing into it. And a level 7 at that. These things don't have to be disclosed to the public – but one could argue that it's in the public interest to know that one of the heads of NTI is Gifted themselves.

There would be riots, Isabel thinks.

Isabel thinks about Célia's obvious comfort in her shiny office, and her own dread walking into the testing centre. She can't help feeling a touch of resentment. The coffee, when she finally takes a sip, is lukewarm and weak. She gives Daniel an unimpressed look. 'Did you make it like this on purpose or something?' She ignores the middle finger he puts up in her direction.

'And then there's Julio,' Voronov says. 'But we know Julio isn't Gifted.'

Isabel nods. 'Gil, Célia and Julio worked together often. There could be various causes for motivation for both of them. And Julio doesn't necessarily need to be Gifted himself. How many Gifted has he come into contact with throughout his career?' And he comes from money, she thinks. People who come from money have ways of doing things.

'Bento Soares would have a heart attack,' she says out loud, rubbing absently at the pressure pulsing in her temples. 'Carla, see if you can speak to someone inside NTI. I want to know what their employees think of the relationship between Gil and Célia, their impressions of both, and of Julio.'

Voronov stands from the table, scratching idly at his neck. 'I think we'll have to be a bit more careful looking into Julio. I'll see if I can speak to anyone who works with him at the university – if I need to speak to him in person at any point, I'll make sure to have Carla or you with me.'

Isabel nods. 'Daniel, can we contact the Registry again? If she's a level seven then she should have an assigned Monitor. See if you can get their name. Might come in useful at some point.'

'I think they'll want a warrant, but I'll find out.'

'Good, thanks.' She downs the rest of her coffee down with a grimace and ignores Daniel's eye-roll.

'All right. I want to look into Gifted levels. Think we'll need to know more about what exactly is possible. Let's get to it.'

29

God, Isabel hasn't been in one of these since she was a child.

Her dad used to bring her to Salão de Jogos all the time. Whereas regular cafés might have a pool table here or there, a Salão de Jogos catered exclusively to people wanting a little additional entertainment with their bica or bagaço, which meant a lot of games: pool tables, darts, maybe some pinball machines depending on the clientele.

Dr Alves is holding the door open. She looks even more like a university student today, in her shock-pink Converse, black jeans and oversized hoodie. Her hair is piled on top of her head again and she patiently waits for Isabel to finish climbing the stairs.

'Something wrong?' Dr Alves asks.

Isabel shakes her head. 'No. Just haven't been to one of these in a very long time.' She tilts her head, curious. 'Thanks for meeting me last minute. This isn't what I was expecting out of tonight.' Isabel had squeezed in a trip home for a fast shower and made it here by 8 o'clock. She really needs to stop rushing out of the house with wet hair; if Tia Simone finds out, Isabel's getting a slap to the back of the head.

'Trust me, you'll understand much better after this,' Dr Alves says and her dimples flash in her cheeks. She pushes the door open wider and the strong smell of coffee and – pizza? – spills out, alongside the sound of loud voices and music.

Isabel steps inside and lets the door fall closed behind her.

It's a big place. The centre of it is taken up by the counter, bigger than in regular cafés as it houses more alcohol. Posters above it proclaim the pizza they sell here too, and an entire glass section shows off the sweet confections and sandwiches.

The right side of the room is framed by large windows that let in the dying evening light and it's filled with small round tables and wooden chairs, most of them occupied although Isabel can see one or two empty ones. The other half of the room is filled with a handful of pool tables, two pinball machines, two dartboards sections, a foosball table, and a few tables nearer the door, with painted-on chessboards on their surfaces.

The room is mainly filled with men, some standing at the counter having a chat, a few playing draughts. The pinball machines and foosball machine are both surrounded by teenagers.

'Come on,' Dr Alves says and starts weaving her way towards a free table in the corner with Isabel following.

Isabel shrugs out of her coat as she goes. She'd managed to pin half her hair up and put on a loose pale blue turtleneck sweater over her sports bra – after the day she's had she wants comfort. Her ankle boots are worn and soft and the black skinny jeans she's wearing are just as worn. It works.

'Still not sure why we're here,' she says as she lays her coat on the back of her chair and sits down.

'You haven't noticed yet,' Dr Alves says, amused, and pushes her glasses up her nose, 'besides, if we'd done this at the office not only would we not have the benefit of you seeing this for yourself, it would also mean we would have been on the clock and not allowed to have a drink. I don't know about your week, but I want to end mine with a beer, thanks.'

Isabel laughs, surprised. 'Okay, I won't complain then. But what is it that I haven't noticed?'

A waitress approaches their table, pulling a notebook out of her apron.

'Why don't you tell me what you want to drink and then take a good look around while I put in an order. You want some pizza?'

Isabel's smile slows and changes and she eases back into her chair. 'Dr Alves, this is starting to feel a little like a date.' Which she wouldn't mind in the least, Isabel decides, because she really, really likes those dimples.

As if on cue, they appear again and Dr Alves laughs. 'Pizza or not?'

'Sure.'

'Anything you don't like?'

Isabel shakes her head. 'No, not fussy. And I'll have a Super Bock, thanks,' she says, and then twists in her seat to see what exactly Dr Alves is talking about.

Mostly there's just people talking, and Isabel is doubly glad she made sure to take a pill before she left the house. The room is filled with emotions, but nothing dark, at least not overwhelmingly so. There's a calmness here that is unexpected, people relaxed and enjoying themselves, unwinding at the end of a long week. A few spikes of stress from different points in the room but nothing to make Isabel want to rush to get out of here.

She starts to shake her head. 'I don't—'

It's the thud of the dart hitting the board that pulls her attention away. Normal in a place like this except – she feels like she missed something. She twists further in her seat and registers absently Dr Alves thanking the waitress.

The darts players are a man and a woman, a couple by the way the woman is teasing before dropping a kiss on his cheek as he takes a step closer to the board for his turn.

Isabel narrows her eyes, confused about what caught her attention when everything looks so—

The man lifts his hand but it's palm side up and fisted, the tip of the dart peeking out between his middle and index finger. And then he flicks his hand open and the dart cuts through the distance to pierce the board with a loud thud.

Isabel blinks.

What?

'You saw it?'

Dr Alves's voice is closer than it had been and Isabel glances over her shoulder to find that she's drawn her chair closer to Isabel's. There's a smile playing at the corner of her mouth, a little wry.

'Yeah,' Isabel says and then looks back around to watch as he repeats the same thing again with the other two darts, the exact same way. An open flick of his hand and the darts firing out of it like a giant super-powered magnet is calling them home. Not that any of them land anywhere near the bullseye and his partner is laughing at his side. 'Gifted. He's using his Gift to play,' she says, and then she registers what she's said, what she knows is definitely true, and tenses up, eyes darting all over in anticipation of someone walking up to the couple and starting trouble.

But there's no one.

Everyone is minding their own business, carrying on with their evening as if two people aren't blatantly displaying their Gift in the room.

'Relax.' Dr Alves curls a gentle hand around Isabel's shoulder and draws her to look back around. The smile is gone now as she takes in Isabel's expression. 'Don't worry, this place is a little different. They don't tolerate that kind of crap here, and that couple aren't the only ones playing this way. Take a look at the people playing draughts,' she says with a nod of her chin.

Isabel looks. It takes a little time because one of the players is considering their move, but when they do make the move they don't touch the pieces at all. The piece moves quietly across the board on its own to settle on a black square.

'See? They're not the only ones.'

Isabel settles back in her chair, bewildered. She's so used to seeing the hostility that she's shocked that there are still places like this where people can relax and just be, comfortable enough to show their Gifts in such a way.

'This is a nice place,' Dr Alves goes on.

When Isabel finally peels her attention away from the players and looks at her, not knowing what to say.

Dr Alves shrugs. 'I understand your surprise. There aren't many places with this level of openness any more. The owner's daughter is Gifted herself.'

Isabel shakes her head. 'It's been a while since I've seen a place as . . . relaxed as this.' Or maybe I don't go out enough to actually see these things, she thinks.

'I understand that. We both know that the world isn't getting any easier for Gifted.' Dr Alves looks over her shoulder at the players. 'If it were me, I don't know that I'd feel comfortable exposing myself like this, even in a place that is supposedly "safe".'

Isabel nods.

'But I am surprised that you aren't aware of these kinds of places,' Dr Alves says.

The waitress comes back then and places their beers on the table, tells them the pizza will be out in twenty minutes. Isabel murmurs a thanks as she picks up her bottle and takes a swallow.

Isabel sighs. 'I guess I should be. Maybe I need to get out more,' she jokes.

Except that's not it entirely. Even when places like this were abundant, Isabel hadn't gone. Hadn't experienced it, not really. In her mother's eyes it was bad enough that she was Gifted. Isabel had never dared flaunt it in her face. Anyone she'd hung out with had always been Regular; it had even bled into her romantic relationships – she knows that. Didn't like to admit it, but it was there. A deep-rooted thing that she can't quite make herself look at because if she does, she's scared of what she'll find.

'Still,' Isabel says, 'I understand why you picked this place.' She gets up and shifts her chair so that they can both face the players. 'Their control is something else,' she says as she sinks lower in the chair, stretching her legs out before her and crossing them at the ankle. She picks up her bottle again.

Dr Alves nods. 'Most telekinetics actually learn to have a decent control over their Gift quite early on.'

'As opposed to telepaths?' Isabel touches the mouth of her bottle to her temple, indicating herself.

'In a way, yes. Telekinetic Gifted in general are viewed as less intrusive. They can't enter anyone's mind; they can't sense emotions. They're like a Regular person.'

Isabel arches an eyebrow. 'Except for the part where they can move things without touching them.'

'True. But that's an obvious thing, people can at least defend against it. It's a thing that can be seen.'

Is it? Isabel thinks about Gil dos Santos and she's not sure that's a true statement. Or that anyone, after details of his death come to light – because the press will uncover it eventually – will believe that that's true.

'And telekinetics in general are able to practise their Gift more. A simple game of marbles in the playground, getting a pen from across the room. Little things. They may not seem so big but it's a daily practice of control.'

Isabel nods her head at the players. 'Like them? Where does their Gift factor in, level-wise? How exactly does it work?' Isabel is familiar with her own Gift, with how it works for her; she knows enough from her lessons with Rosario to understand the weight of the different levels in the telepathy ranks. She's never given much thought to the mechanics of telekinetics.

'I'm not sure what level they are. What they're showing here could be less than their actual level. But the ability they're displaying here would be maybe a three. The items they're moving are relatively small.'

Isabel frowns. 'So, what, it's down to weight? What about distance?'

Dr Alves nods. 'Weight, distance – both of those things play a big part in it. The bigger or heavier the object, the bigger the fight to disrupt the gravitational pull. It's a lot. You have to lift it and then carve out a route for it, and move the object in that direction, while fighting that pull. Quite draining for the Gifted in question, depending on their level.'

'I see.' Makes sense. 'So,' she twists in her chair and sets her bottle on the table, leaning closer and lowering her voice, 'something like the Gifted girl in Colombo. How does that happen?'

Dr Alves pauses at that question. 'She was misdiagnosed.'

Isabel tilts her head. 'Diagnosed? She wasn't ill, Doctor,' she says.

'No,' Dr Alves says, 'poor choice of words. But something must have gone wrong with her test, and they registered her at an incorrect level.'

'Yes,' Isabel says, 'that much I know. But I'm not asking about what the test got wrong. She levelled a whole floor in a shopping centre. That isn't even in the same realm as them.' She jerks a thumb at the players. 'If throwing a dart with your Gift makes you a three, how do you measure what that girl did? Did they even test her eventually? When we talked at the precinct you said it would take a ten to cause an incident like what happened in the carriage.'

Dr Alves takes a deep breath. 'That's right.'

'And this only assumed control of one person,' Isabel says.

'Yes.' Dr Alves leans forward, crossing her arms on the table. Her voice goes quieter too. 'Let's say that what happened in the carriage was caused by a Gifted, by your own analysis and that of your team a deliberate attack, correct?'

'Yes.'

'Which points at control. An incredible amount of control. In fact, a greater amount of control than it would take to do what that girl did in Colombo. That incident was caused by a lack of it. She was overwhelmed and that was the outcome of not knowing how to handle that kind of level. It's why so many Gifted level seven and above are monitored. Because control is much harder at that level of power, and that kind of incident is the consequence of not being able to handle it. I don't know what the results of her retesting were – we both know the government is never going to release that. But it's a ten. It couldn't be anything less.'

Then Dr Alves leans in a little bit further.

'But Isabel,' she says, and the dropping of Isabel's title takes her by surprise, 'imagine this. Imagine someone who is a ten, who can do that kind of damage simply by not having control. And now imagine them with total control of all that power. And now imagine that we have no idea this person exists.'

Someone with that kind of power but with the control to wield it at will?

The waitress arrives with their pizza and Dr Alves settles back in her chair.

Isabel finishes her drink and asks for another one. The smell of red onions and cheese is strong and makes her mouth water. She reaches for a slice.

She doesn't want to think about it, if she's honest.

Armindas is a 7. By what Dr Alves has said, it sounds to Isabel like that's high enough for her to be able to pick up Gil and send him flying into a window. Though then they have another problem. Armindas wasn't in that carriage. Not that they know of. Not that they can prove with their current evidence, anyway.

The waitress puts a full bottle in front of her and Isabel toasts Dr Alves.

Isabel picks at the corner of the label on the bottle, the softened paper damp with condensation and rolling under her thumb. She sighs and takes a bite of the pizza.

Imagining someone like that—

Just her luck that it seems like that's exactly the kind of Gifted they might be dealing with.

30

Isabel gets to the precinct around 10 a.m. the next day, to the sight of Voronov closing the Chief's door quietly behind him as he leaves her office. And though Isabel has never had any reason to fear anything from the Chief and she doesn't think that will change now, it still makes her uneasy.

Voronov pauses when he spots her coming down the hallway, hand still on the door handle.

Isabel nods good morning and heads straight to her desk without waiting for him.

It had been close to midnight when she'd got home the night before. After the novelty of good conversation and a few drinks in a place she'd felt comfortable enough to relax in, she'd felt too mellow to go out for a run. There had been a voicemail on her phone from Rita, but Isabel had left it, slipping into a T-shirt and then straight into bed.

She'd been feeling an unusual quiet peace and hadn't been ready to give that up so quickly.

Waking up to the shrill sound of her phone alarm this morning had been a surprise too. Rarely did she experience the luxury of an uninterrupted night's sleep. But she'd set the time for earlier so she could squeeze in a short run before work. She could've done with a little more time though, she thinks as she speed-walks into the precinct coffee-less and food-less, with nothing but one of her pills lining her stomach and the start of that familiar ache at the base of her skull. Not the best thing to do.

She didn't feel too bad about being late either, considering she'd been out until that time for work reasons. Well, mostly. She doubted the Chief would say anything about it anyway.

Outside the sun is as bright as the cold is biting, and the light shines through into the precinct, outshining the room's artificial light and drawing the eye to the old windows.

Isabel shrugs out of her coat as she goes, the soft soles of her boots tapping on the freshly varnished floor; the smell of the varnish fills the air and the floor is so shiny that it reflects a near mirror image of Isabel up at her. They must've done it overnight. The heat from rushing warms her cheeks and the back of her jumper is a little damp from sweat.

'Morning.'

Isabel glances up at Voronov and rests her hands on the back of her chair, absently smoothing her coat into place. 'Hey.' The end of her scarf snags on the wheels of her chair and she jerks the chunky wool up with a yank and drops it on the seat.

'How did it go last night?'

Isabel leans back and folds her arms, looking him dead in the face. 'It went fine. Did the Chief have something for us?'

To his credit he doesn't miss a beat. 'Unrelated to the case.'

'Hmm.' She pushes off the desk and switches on her PC. 'Any updates?'

'Some,' he says, 'Daniel has already spoken to the Registry. They're not going to talk about Célia's Monitor, not without a warrant.'

Shit. She'd known it was a long shot. 'Want to bet she'll know we're sniffing around by the end of the day?' And probably make a fuss about it too. Célia didn't strike Isabel as the type of woman who would take this lying down. She was the type of woman who had made it to the top of the top very early on in her career. That takes a certain degree of cut-throat.

Voronov nods. 'They work too closely together not to have a mutual beneficial agreement going on between their two agencies.'

Not to mention they were snooping in her place of work too. No. She definitely won't take that lying down.

Briefly, Isabel fills Voronov in on Dr Alves' mini Gifted lesson from the night before but when she finishes, she sees him giving her a peculiar look.

'What?' she asks. Her stomach growls, loudly, and she scowls before yanking open one of her drawers and scouring the contents. Shit. She's forgotten to stock up on energy bars. She'll have to duck back out.

'You're Gifted yourself,' Voronov says.

'And?'

'I guess I assumed you'd be more familiar with levels and what Gifted people would be capable of doing.'

Isabel sits down and spins the chair around to face Voronov. The tail end of her scarf falls back over her seat and she huffs before picking it back up. 'I know more than a regular person, yes. But I'm not an expert. We're individuals,' she shrugs, 'our experiences are different, and just like Regulars we learn differently. What's easy for me isn't easy for someone else, even if they're the same level as I am. So how can I know what a higher level than me would be capable of? And with a different affinity at that?'

Voronov tilts his head in agreement.

'Your previous partner was Gifted,' she says and sharpens her focus, curiosity winning out against her need to bury other people's emotions as far away from her as possible, 'what was his affinity?'

His face remains unchanged. There's no spike of anything and Isabel wonders if he's one of those people who just has natural barriers. Some people do, those who have less reactive personalities, used to processing and calculating their next step. Jacinta is like this too and it's rare that Isabel is bombarded with emotions from her. At least not when Isabel's under the protection of S3.

'He was a level two telekinetic.' His voice is even, not even a ripple of discomfort.

'Did you learn anything from him about Gifted? It seems like a lot of this is pretty new to you, too.' And yeah, she's still fishing but it's true. Most people won't learn more than what they're told

179

by the newspapers. Isabel herself is guilty of not having looked beyond her own nose.

That gets a reaction. A little smidge of emotion that slips out, murky, like water stirred over dirt. She thinks that without the pill she could have played her fingers through it, cleared the soot to see what lay beneath.

It feels like bitterness.

'He never talked about it and he didn't use his Gift in front of me,' Voronov finally says.

That surprises her. She opens her mouth to ask how long they had worked together for, but she's interrupted by Carla popping up on the other side of Isabel's desk. 'Can I borrow you both for a moment?'

Isabel's disconcerted for a second because something's different about her. She realises that for once Carla's wearing her hair down. Its thick, dark length is straight as a razor, accentuating the sharp angles of her face.

Voronov and Isabel share a glance as they round the desk to follow Carla to the case room. As soon as they get in there, Carla slips in behind them and shuts the door. The room is stupidly cold, the windows having been open overnight, presumably to air out the smell of the floor varnish, which is even stronger in this small space.

'What's up?'

'I went to NTI yesterday to see who I could get something out of. Lingered for a bit because they didn't want to let me past reception,' she smiles wryly, 'not even when I flashed my badge. Apparently, they had big names in the building yesterday and no one else was allowed in. Didn't stop me from standing outside and having a few words with the security guard and the receptionist.'

'Oh?' Isabel drags out a chair and sits down, crossing her arms. 'Good?'

Carla pushes her hair back from her face. 'Good enough. That argument you both mentioned seeing at the function? According to the security guard it's not the first time and there's been friction. Everyone there seems to have witnessed it at one time or another.'

'Célia and Gil?'

Carla shakes her head. 'Actually, it's a little more than that. The security guard was talking about Julio Soares. Says that once Gil stormed out of a meeting with Célia and Julio. No one overheard what it was about but apparently neither of them were happy with Gil. That was about two weeks before Gil's death.'

'Anything after that?'

'No. Julio steered clear of the facility and according to the filtered-down gossip, the relationship between Gil and Célia was strained. Meetings were kept short. They said Célia kept making attempts to speak to Gil but he was keeping himself to himself and refusing to engage unless he had to.'

'Anyone have any clue what they're all arguing about?'

'No, that's where the information stops. Sorry.'

'No,' Isabel reaches out to pat her on the arm but she's staring at a spot on the floor, not really seeming to see it, 'no this is still good. We know both Célia and Julio aren't telling us everything.' Finally, she glances back up at them both. 'We need to get back in there and speak to her.'

31

The look on Armindas' face tells Isabel that she hadn't expected to see them again, at least not so soon.

She braces a hand on the desk as her secretary shows them in and pushes to her feet. Her white hair is dragged back from her face and she's in an expensive-looking beige pencil skirt and silky blouse. It's a testament to the good heating in this place that she can get away with wearing that in these temperatures.

'Inspectors.' She's frowning. 'I didn't get a call to say you were coming. I'm afraid I don't have time at the moment, I have a conference call scheduled in ten minutes' time and I have to finish preparing.'

'I'm afraid we might make you a little late for that, Ms Armindas.'

Isabel didn't think Célia's spine could get any straighter, but now it does. Isabel can see her visibly reining in her instinctive response. The chin goes up and Célia comes as close as she can get to literally looking down her nose at them. Quite different from the welcome they'd had the first time around.

'All right. But please,' she glances at her watch, 'make this as quick as possible.'

This time Isabel takes the lead. 'We did a check on the people who attended that function we saw you at on Friday. We were checking for Gifted people who might have attended. You can guess who came up.'

Armindas gets it right away. 'I don't have to disclose my classi-fication. I operate under the law and have never missed a check-in with my Monitor.'

'But you were somewhat aware of the nature of Gil's death. Why not come forward? Give full disclosure? Didn't you say you were friends?'

'Because I have done nothing wrong. And please keep it down, I like to keep my personal business separate from my work.'

'Why were you and Julio Soares arguing the night of the function?'

'It was a private matter.'

'Yes. That's what he said. What about Gil? With so many projects surely there were some late nights working in the office, no?' Isabel arches a brow.

The cool slickness that Armindas wears like a shield slips and the flush of emotion billows out, burnt orange and washing over Isabel like stinging wet sand. The skin around Armindas' mouth goes white and her right hand curls tight where it rests on the table.

Just as quickly as it arrived, the swell disappears. Isabel can't help but be impressed by how quickly Armindas gets herself under control.

'You can't use your Gift without my consent. I'll report you to your superior and you can kiss your career goodbye. So, if that's what you're attempting to do right now, Inspector Reis, I suggest you stop there.'

At Isabel's side, Voronov stirs. It's a small movement but Isabel feels his sharpened attention as he stares Célia down.

'Rest assured, Dr Armindas, my level isn't that high, I'd need to make bodily contact to tap into your head. Besides, at your level, I'm sure the wards you were taught by your Guide are a lot more sophisticated than the average person's. You'd feel me trying to find a way in.'

Armindas doesn't deny it. Jaw working, she sinks down onto the edge of her desk chair. With controlled calm, she claps her hands on top of the desk. She exhales through her nose twice and then glances back up at them.

'My disagreement with Julio related to a case that Gil, Julio and I were working on together. With Gil gone, Julio wanted to take the research in a different direction that I didn't agree with. That's all. It's a privately funded project, unrelated to NTI. We were talking about how to manage the project now that Gil is no longer with us.'

And that's what he chose to focus on the day after his colleague and family friend bashed his brains in? 'I thought their families were close and that there was mutual respect between Gil and Julio,' Isabel says, 'seems pretty cold that Gil hasn't even been buried and that's his primary concern. No grief?'

'Everyone grieves differently, Inspector.'

'There wasn't much of that going on from where I was standing on Friday night,' Isabel says. She slides into one of the guest seats on the other side of Célia's desk. 'What about you? Have you been busy since Gil's death?'

'What are you implying?' Célia spears her with a look that would have left lesser people feeling shredded to the bone.

Isabel shrugs. 'You're head of NTI. So was he. Surely with him gone there's been an increase in demand for your time, a logical assumption wouldn't you say? Unless that makes things easier, being the only person with authority here now.'

Célia's eyes widen as she takes in Isabel's meaning, as if she can't believe the audacity. Then her laughter cracks into the silence, her head falling back with it, and the light catches on the delicate gold necklace around her neck. It stops as fast as it came, a short, non-humorous thing, and she's openly staring at Isabel, head shaking lightly.

'Inspector, in regard to my relationship with Gil, your insin- uations are disrespectful to both myself and his widow. We were close colleagues, we trusted each other's judgement and stood as a unit. Were we friends outside of that? Of course. That was a natural evolution of our partnership over the years. And no. I had no wish to control NTI on my own. As I said,' her words come out clipped, as if each one is chased by a full stop, and her hand is clenched where it rests on the desk, 'we stood as a unit and together we were able to reform NTI and what it stands for.'

Isabel smothers the urge to snort at that last statement. Nothing has changed. They have a cleaner image now, that's all. As far as Gifted are concerned, there are no positive associations with the NTI.

Voronov comes forward. 'Given what's come to light, we're going to need to know your whereabouts at the time of Gil's death.'

The fight seems to go out of Armindas then. She swivels the chair to face the view behind her. Isabel feels something different this time, like a restriction around her throat.

Then Armindas ducks her head, giving it a brief shake, and it's gone again, just like earlier. Armindas really does have excellent control. But the metallic taste it leaves behind on Isabel's tongue has a name.

Fear.

'I'll have my assistant email you a copy of my schedule,' Armindas says. 'Now, I need to ask you to leave. I'm already late for my appointment.'

Voronov inclines his head.

'Inspectors?'

Isabel pauses at the door. The defeat had been momentary because when they turn, Armindas is giving them a vicious look.

'If you have to speak to me again for whatever reason, make sure next time that you book an appointment. Or I *will* call my lawyer. Understood?'

Isabel hunches her shoulders against the wind as they step out of the building. It whips at her face. 'What we need is access to her Monitor. Which I don't think we're going to get.' Isabel stops, thrown, as Voronov opens the passenger door for her, and just about squeezes in a thanks before he rounds the car to the driver's side. She's really not used to these kinds of gestures.

'Why?' he asks as he slides in and starts the car. Warmth starts to blast through and return the feeling to her fingers that just the short walk from the building to the car had stolen. 'We have no evidence tying her to the incident and it'll be covered by doctor–patient confidentiality.'

Isabel can remember the inside of that carriage as if it were her own memory. The force with which Rodrigo had tried so desperately to hang on to Gil. A level 7 is enough to have done it, she thinks. With enough practice. Enough control. Célia is an extremely intelligent woman and Isabel thinks she's very capable of having honed her Gift to that level. But they'd need to be able to place her at the scene. Dr Alves had been clear that distance played a clear factor in a telekinetic's level of control and you can't move what you can't see.

'So what are you thinking?'

Isabel lets her head fall back on the headrest. 'That we don't have enough.'

32

Looking at Irina dos Santos, Isabel thinks that had she walked past her on the street she wouldn't have recognised her. Oh, she's still very put-together, in exquisite three-inch heels and a dress that looks like it's worth more than Isabel's entire wardrobe. She carries a navy wool coat in her arms and every hair on her head is in place. But the make-up can't hide it. The slump in her shoulders and back, like they're giving under a great weight. And her eyes, full of burst blood vessels and listless.

'Irina,' Isabel draws out a chair for her, 'how are you?'

Voronov closes the door behind him and rounds the table to take the seat next to Isabel's.

'Coping, Inspectors.' Irina sets her black wide-brimmed hat on the table and the coat on her lap. 'At least the funeral kept me busy. Do you have any updates on the case? I don't understand what's taking this long.'

Isabel sits down too. The room is oppressive, Irina's emotions filling it to the brim with grief so thick Isabel feels it like a weight on her chest. She doesn't even have to try to reach for them; they walked into the room right alongside Irina and spilled out.

'I understand this is distressing for you,' Isabel says, 'but it's a little complicated. Your husband had no illnesses and as per your own words, there was nothing that would have indicated that he would take his own life. Especially not in such a manner.'

'So what now? What else could it have been?'

'We're still trying to understand that. Irina, you told us that Gil was having disagreements with Julio, but could you tell us about his other relationships? I understand he enjoyed a successful run as head of the NTI, managing it alongside Célia Armindas. What was their relationship like?'

Irina touches her fingers to the brim of her hat, flattening the material against the pockmarked table. 'They worked well together, there's not much else to tell. Together they worked hard to modernise NTI's ethics. They went through some tough times together at the beginning and I believe they were also friends.'

'Believe? You're not sure?' Voronov asks.

'I wasn't really involved in Gil's work life that way. I attended work functions with him and of course we sometimes hosted parties at our home, but I had little meaningful interaction with his colleagues.'

'Gil and Célia didn't have contact outside of work matters?'

'They did occasionally, a few dinners after work I suppose. There was the odd time where, if they happened to be working on a particular project, they would use Gil's home study. Or sometimes they would go to Célia's.'

Interesting.

'Before you ask,' Irina says, a little life returning to her eyes, 'no they weren't having an affair.'

'And Julio? Was this something that Gil did often with him as well?'

'Sometimes, yes. Why are you asking me these things? What does this have to do with Gil's death? Do they know something? How— I don't understand.'

'We've heard reports that recently there were disagreements happening between the three of them, that Gil may have been taking a more aggressive stance against Célia and Julio. We wanted to know if there's anything that he may have said that could be related to it, that maybe you didn't take notice of at the time but might seem relevant now?'

'No. I've already told you what I know.' Irina grips the rim of the hat in her hand, her eyes dry and wide as she looks from Isabel to Voronov. 'I really hope that you know what you're doing, Inspectors. I've lost my husband; I don't need you poking around our lives trying to prove that he committed suicide or that he had an affair.' She sweeps the hat off the table and stands, back ramrod straight and eyes fixed on a point above their heads.

She tells them to contact her if they have more information and leaves the room.

Isabel sits back and groans.

Voronov sinks back into his chair and rolls his neck, hand rubbing at it, grimace on his face. 'Asking a widow if her husband was having an affair with his colleague was never going to go down well.'

No, it wasn't. Isabel sighs. And something tells her Irina won't be as willing to help them in the future. She's grieving and without someone having been there with a knife or a gun, or a physical fight, this simply doesn't feel tangible to her.

In a way, they're facing the same problem.

They're solving a crime where there has been no contact. There are no fingerprints to chase, no blood under fingernails or intoxication. They're trying to pin down what is, essentially, a ghost.

Church on a weekday afternoon is quiet. The space around it is empty save for a few elderly men, sitting together on a bench, canes in hand, a greying black dog at their feet. They're watching the world go by. Slowly.

Isabel had slipped out of the precinct for a bit; the headache had been peaking and after a catch-up with the Chief on what was happening on the Jane Doe case and bringing her up to speed on the investigation, she'd decided she may as well put what was supposed to be her lunch hour to good use and go see her brother.

Isabel nods hello to the group of old friends as she walks past. The sun, despite its blinding presence, seems to sharpen the cold as it beats down on her. She feels the dampness beneath her arms, her cold sweat uncomfortable, and she wonders if she has anything to change into in the car.

Sebastião sits on a bench beneath one of the trees that is still clinging to a few of its leaves. He has a sandwich in his hands and a thermos beside him. When he spots Isabel coming down the steps that lead into the little courtyard, he waves her over.

'Well, this is surprising,' he says, smiling. He takes another bite of his sandwich.

Isabel stops to peck his cheek and drops down on the bench beside him. 'Is this what priests do all day? Just lounge around outside, hmm?'

He snorts. 'Like you'd know. When's the last time you set foot inside the church?'

She thinks of the open casket and the way the silver had glinted on the cuffs of her dad's shirt.

Isabel tips her head up to the sun, stretching her arms along the back of the bench and her legs out until she feels the pull in the backs of her thighs and knees. She lets the sunlight soak the memory from her. 'Got a short break and you're disgustingly nearby, so I thought I'd come and say hello.'

Sebastião lowers his sandwich, concern softening his smile and lining his forehead. 'Is it the death at Gare do Oriente? The one with the head of NTI?'

'Hmm. Me and my partner are the ones on it,' she says. She can't comment on the case and he knows that. Though she supposes if she were telling him in confession then maybe there'd be a loophole in there somewhere.

'A partner? You? Is it going well?'

She see-saws her hand side to side.

'Is he a Regular?'

Isabel snorts. 'What, you think they'd let two Gifted work together unchecked on such a big case?'

Sebastião frowns down at his sandwich before taking another bite.

'It's too cold to be sitting out here,' she complains, and then takes out a cone filled with chestnuts, 'but look what I brought you.'

Sebastião chuckles and takes the cone from her. The smell of roasted chestnuts is sweet in the air and somehow manages to make the courtyard feel more welcoming, a little homier. Isabel scoots over until they're pressed shoulder to shoulder, trying to leach off some warmth.

'Rita called me. She said you haven't returned her calls.' He sighs. 'You're going to have to talk to her again.'

'Yeah,' Isabel says, 'I know. I don't want to, but I will.'

'What are you going to say?'

Isabel shrugs. 'What can I say? Anything I say will just make her cry and you know I can't handle that. You're better at handling her than I am.'

He chuckles. 'You could say I get to practise my listening and comforting skills every day here,' he says, indicating the pretty little church with his chin.

'Don't know how you do it,' she says.

'I just have to listen. I don't know how you do what *you* do, but I know you do it well.'

'Not sure about that right now,' Isabel says and then groans and drops her face into her hands. 'Now I'm the one complaining to you.'

Sebastião laughs and shoves at her shoulder. 'I'm your older brother, you're supposed to come to me for advice.'

She peeks at him over her fingers, letting him know what she thinks of that. 'I'm not one of your flock, you idiot. You can't fool me with that expression. Wonder what they'd think if they knew you used to routinely terrorise me.'

Every time their dad had taken her to see Sebastião at Tia's house, Sebastião would spend the better part of that time scaring the shit out of her. How her heart didn't give out she's not sure. But then her powers had started coming in and without even knowing it at the time, she'd begun to be able to sense him getting closer, his excitement bubbling out of him in sunlight yellow. It'd been impossible for Isabel not to sense the emotions, even at that age.

'Your Gift put an end to that,' Sebastião says, recalling the same thing.

She smirks. 'I love how confused you got when it started happening.'

191

'Don't gloat, it's not a good quality in a person.'

'Sure it isn't.'

He picks up a roasted chestnut and peels back its case and the skin that has become dry and flaked with the roasting. She follows suit and when she pops it into her mouth it's heaven. They're firmly in winter now but she thinks that chestnuts always taste like autumn.

'I think those were the only times you used your Gift without being ashamed of it.'

Isabel takes another chestnut and peels it free, chewing it slowly as she thinks about it. If anyone else had broached the subject, she knows it would've got her back up. But with Sebastião she doesn't need to guard herself. Sebastião has seen her at her lowest; there's nothing that she needs to hide from him.

'It's not that I'm ashamed. I know what I am. I just know how everyone else feels about it. Just like every other Gifted person out there.' She smiles at him. 'It's hard to believe that anyone would willingly choose to be like this, knowing what's in store for them.'

'It might help if you had someone else to support you,' Sebastião says and she can hear the talk coming.

'I have you to support me.'

'Sorry sis,' he snorts, 'I can't support you that way.'

'Sebastião.' She glares at him. 'You did not seriously just say that to me.'

He snickers and pops a chestnut in his mouth.

She shakes her head, muttering. 'You're disgusting. If only everyone knew.'

That makes him start laughing.

'Besides, I have a partner now.'

'Yeah, that you don't even trust,' he says pointedly, 'and anyway, that's not the kind of partner I was hinting at.' When she gives him the look of death again, he holds his hands up. 'All right, all right. I'll stop. How is it really going, though, with the new partner?'

'He's quiet . . . and efficient. He's not afraid to go toe to toe with people who carry a certain weight. He doesn't take bullshit.'

But he's also got a sketchy past, which she's still not convinced isn't deserved.

'Ah, an important quality in anyone having to deal with you on a daily basis.'

'Jesus, you're so annoying. Don't understand why I put up with you.'

'You love me.'

'You're my brother, it's more of an obligation.'

'Yeah, yeah.'

They finish the rest of the chestnuts in silence.

'Isabel?'

'Hmm?'

An old lady hobbles into the courtyard square, a blue plastic bag in her hand as she heads to the grass area. She reaches into the bag and starts to throw breadcrumbs onto the grass and the cobbles. Pigeons flock to the food, their wings fluttering, so many of them converging on the woman at once that Isabel wonders how she isn't panicking under the sudden swarm. A moment later the old lady emerges from the mass of fluttering birds.

'Your Gift. How are you coping?'

Isabel gives him a tight smile. 'The headaches got worse. I had to go and see Michael about it. I went before the whole,' she waves her hand around, 'dinner fiasco.'

His expression darkens at the mention of Michael's name. Isabel thinks that Michael should be grateful that Sebastião chose to be a man of the cloth because otherwise he probably wouldn't have made it out of that dinner without eating Sebastião's fist.

'You know he's the only one who's fully aware of my situation. He's the only one that can help me right now.'

'Don't. I hate that you have to rely on that arsehole. I never liked him.'

Isabel snorts. 'Liar. You loved him. You were praying we'd get married and have babies.' It sobers her when she remembers that her sister will be doing that with Michael now.

Funny thing is, Isabel doesn't *want* that with Michael. Not any more. Even back when they were together, she'd only ever thought about it in passing. Never seriously.

'He'll never betray me like that,' she says, 'don't worry about it.'

'I don't trust him, Isabel.'

'I know. But if he outs me, then he goes down with me. Michael loves his career too much to tank it like that. And I don't want that for him either. Have to be forgiving, right?'

Sebastião doesn't look impressed.

'But,' she sits up, tucks her hair behind her ear, 'to answer your question, I don't know what's going to happen with my Gift. I know it's changed a lot. It's stronger,' she says, voice low as she scrapes her heels over the courtyard's bumpy surface. She can still hear the sound of the pigeons' wings as they compete for their morsel of food. 'I'm scared,' she admits. 'But there's nothing I can do about that. I just have to figure it out. Do the best that I can.'

Sebastião sighs and then wraps an arm around her and tugs her into a warm hug. 'Ai, ai maninha,' he says. 'We'll figure it out.'

She leans her head on his shoulder and nods. 'Yeah, we will.'

Thank God for Sebastião.

The buzzing of her phone in her pocket breaks the moment and Isabel sighs, pulling away and giving Sebastião an apologetic smile.

'Inspector Reis,' she says.

'Isabel,' Carla says, 'HSL. We've figured it out. Full phone records came in and he was getting calls from a particular number and when we traced it, we found out that it's the main number for Hospital de Santa Luz.'

Isabel sits up. 'And?'

'It's in Coimbra. Same city he was on his way to the day he died. The presentation he was giving to the EGU was taking place there, not too far from the hospital. He didn't have an appointment and wasn't booked in for any visits, but according to their records he was a regular visitor.'

Coimbra. Isabel runs her thumb up and down the bridge of her nose, thinking. That morning, Luisa had said that's where she was headed too. Meeting some friends in Coimbra.

'Who has he been going to see?' Isabel thinks back to the conversation with Irina dos Santos. If your husband regularly visited a hospital to see someone and had been heading that way on the day of his death, would it not have been something to mention? Why keep that kind of thing from your wife?

'The patient's name is Mila Ferreira.'

A woman. Okay. Maybe the wife really didn't know about this. That name hadn't shown up in their investigation so far. Who the hell is this person? 'Do we know what she's in for?'

Mila Ferreira, Carla informs her, has been a patient at the hospital for over a year, following an accident at her home. No family visitors to speak of, no friends visiting either. And the oddest point is that despite her being in hospital for that length of time, she isn't on life support.

'How can that be?' Isabel asks.

'They don't know. Her case is confusing everyone. Everything functioning as it should but she's not waking up.'

'Thanks, Carla. Can we start looking into who she is? I want to know why Gil's been making regular trips up there and not even his wife seems to know about it.'

'Oh, Isabel?'

'Something else?'

'There was another number there that drew our attention. A couple of weeks ago Gil made a call to Luisa Delgado, a long one.'

That roots Isabel to the spot and for a moment she's hyper-aware of the sun on her face. The birds have quietened down.

'I'm on my way back.'

Isabel hangs up. Sebastião is watching her with a wry smile. 'Leaving me already?'

'I have a hot date,' she says and slaps his arm when he snorts. 'Besides, don't want some poor soul wandering in for confession and you're not there.' She bends down to peck his cheek. 'Talk soon.'

'All right. And look after yourself please.'

Isabel waves a hand over her head in acknowledgement as she goes, her mind already on Luisa Delgado and how she is going to explain her way out of this one. Except she clearly won't talk to them. And there's that loss of memory going on that seems a little too convenient.

And it hits her; their way in.

The boyfriend.

33

It's gone 8 p.m. when they reach Gabriel Bernardo's apartment building. It's a nice one in an even nicer part of Lisbon. The streets are quiet and the streetlights haven't been on for long.

Isabel finds a parking spot and leans against her car, hands in her pocket as she waits for Voronov to arrive.

She tilts her head back, eyes pinned on the sky that hasn't unleashed its threat of rain yet. The day had slowly transitioned, the sun chased out of the sky by wind and clouds while her and Voronov had gone over the new information and tracked down Gabriel Bernardo's address. Isabel feels restless.

Luisa had said that her boyfriend also moved in the same circles as Gil and from what they'd seen at the function, it was clear he was on good terms with Julio Soares too. It was he who had gone to fetch Julio, with Luisa in tow that night. But Isabel doesn't want to get her hopes up too much.

Isabel hears car doors slamming shut nearby, followed by laughing voices.

It's another five minutes before Voronov arrives, sliding into a spot a couple of cars down from her.

He gets out. He's changed out of the clothes he was wearing earlier, meaning he's stopped at home. Isabel feels a little grubby when she sees his wet hair, clean T-shirt and jeans that he's sporting with a lighter jacket. She arches a brow at him.

'Going somewhere after this?'

Voronov brushes a hand over his wet hair and shakes his head. 'No, squeezed in a quick workout before coming here. Haven't had the time. For all I know we won't even be going home after this' – he shrugs – 'but I wouldn't mind grabbing a drink afterwards. What about you?'

Isabel eyes him, considering. 'Yeah. Sure. If we wrap up here, I wouldn't mind.' Although on paper the PJ projects an image of inclusivity and equality, in practice not everyone working there is that tolerant. Isabel doesn't really have the right temperament to put up with that kind of attitude. Voronov is new and considering they're still feeling their way around each other, drinks is probably the least intrusive way to figure out if they'll be able to stand each other in the long run.

Gabriel Bernardo lives on the fourth floor, apartment 50. They take the elevator up. It's a higher-end apartment complex. The corridor is well lit, the paint on the walls fresh as the day it was done, the numbers on the doors they pass gleaming under the lights.

They stop outside number 50. Isabel raps her knuckles on the blue door and stands back with Voronov to wait, letting her gaze wander over the potted plants that line the wall either side of the door.

It doesn't take long.

Isabel has a brief recollection of him at the function. He'd looked a little more put-together then as he'd stood with Luisa under the mood lighting of the event.

Gabriel has recently turned thirty, according to the information they pulled from the police database. He's barefoot in a T-shirt and shorts, his wavy brown hair pulled back from his face into a stubby ponytail, and there is a shadow of stubble along his cheeks and jawline. The skin beneath his eyes looks worn and thin and a green sheen has settled in, giving his dark eyes, their colour a green-edged hazel, a sunken look. His mouth is pressed into a flat line as he looks from one of them to the other.

'Mr Bernardo, we're sorry for the late hour. Thank you for agreeing to see us,' she says. 'I'm Inspector Reis, this is Inspector Voronov. May we come in?'

Gabriel steps back inside and opens the door wider, motioning them in.

The apartment is a big, open-plan space. The curtains are pulled back to reveal a pretty view of Lisbon. The only lights come from the kitchen side of the room and from the muted TV. There are papers and notes on the coffee table and an open beer bottle next to them.

'It's not a problem,' he says, his voice low, eyes downcast as he moves to hover over the sofa. 'Call me Gabriel. Please, take a seat. Can I offer you anything to drink?'

'No, thank you,' Isabel says, nodding in thanks.

Voronov declines too.

They both sit but Gabriel remains standing. His hands don't stay still, and he shifts from foot to foot. His eyes look bloodshot.

'We just have a couple of questions,' Isabel says. 'Is that okay?'

Voronov takes over the conversation then. Isabel asked him to before they headed out here. She figures they might as well put this partnership to its best use. Voronov taking the lead would leave her free to focus on Gabriel, glean what she can from his responses. His emotions.

'You were present at the function on Thursday with Luisa Delgado, correct?'

'Yes. Most of my colleagues were there that evening helping out.'

Voronov nods. 'Does Luisa attend a lot of these functions with you?'

There's a spike of emotion, sharp and stinging. Something that isn't sadness and isn't sorrow. But the expression on Gabriel's face remains the same, a mask of upset with a little bit of confusion thrown in now.

'Since we got together, yes, she usually attends these functions with me.'

'Luisa's car was seen the morning of Gil dos Santos' death. It was parked in Gare do Oriente station. Luisa tells us you picked

199

her up after what happened at the station and she left her car there. You were pretty fast getting there. Can I ask what you were doing before she called you?'

There it is. That spike again, the colour of beetroot. It leaves an earthy taste on Isabel's tongue, and she keeps her eyes on Gabriel's face.

'I was nearby, Inspector,' Gabriel says, frowning. He looks from Voronov to Isabel and back again, confusion and defensiveness evident in his stance, the set of his jaw and his scrunched eyebrows. 'I had a meeting with a visiting professor from London. He'd agreed to answer my questions for my thesis.'

'I see.' Voronov leans forward, hands clasped together, and continues, tone still calm and a touch apologetic, put upon. Isabel can't feel anything even close to pity or understanding coming through him towards Gabriel. There's a solid wall of concentration. 'Gabriel, it'd be really helpful if you could provide us with the name of the professor you were meeting that morning. This is so we can make sure that everything is in order.'

'That's not a problem,' Gabriel says. 'I know why you're here, but I don't know what I can contribute.'

'You're doing fine, Gabriel,' Voronov says. 'How long have you and Luisa been together?'

'Just over a year, our anniversary is in January.'

'And you said she normally attends these functions with you. To your knowledge has Luisa ever spoken to Gil dos Santos? A conversation here or there, anything like that?'

Gabriel frowns. 'I can't say for sure. Everyone networks heavily at these things and Luisa isn't the kind of person to just stand on the sidelines. I'm sure there were occasions where they spoke to each other, but mostly Luisa tends to stay with me. Why are you asking me about her?'

Isabel cuts in. 'We're following up on some statements, Gabriel. This is us trying to get a better understanding of those present on the day of Gil's death. I'm sure you understand.'

200

'Sure.'

'We understand Luisa seems to suffer from some lapses in memory,' Isabel says.

The look he cuts her way is assessing and his shoulders square up, as if he's getting ready to do battle. 'She's seeing someone for that.' And then he doesn't say anything more on the subject.

'Hmm. Do you have any idea why Gil dos Santos would be calling your girlfriend?'

'What?'

Isabel doesn't reply, lets the question sit and is pleased when Voronov doesn't rush to fill the silence either. It doesn't take long, a few seconds maybe, but to Gabriel it must feel longer. He shifts on the spot, looking from one of them to the other.

'He called her? Did she say that?' he finally asks.

'No. But we've seen his phone records.'

'You seem to be quite familiar with Julio Soares too. Did you also know Gil dos Santos well?'

'No,' Gabriel says, 'as I said, you network a lot at these functions, but I knew Gil more through Professor Soares. They worked together a lot and sometimes we'd cross paths and make small talk but nothing beyond that. He was a nice man. I met his wife a couple of times too. As far as I could tell they were both very nice people.'

'And what do you do?'

'I work for a pharmaceutical company. I help develop new treatments. I'm also currently doing my PhD at Professor Soares' university. They have an amazing reputation for their work in the Gifted field.' He looks at Isabel. 'You're Gifted aren't you?' he asks. 'I saw your classification on your ID.'

'Yes. Does it make you uncomfortable?'

Gabriel shakes his head. 'No. Can I ask what your Gift falls into?'

Isabel watches closely for his reaction. 'I'm on the telepathy spectrum.'

Something shifts in his gaze. 'I heard they suspect that the incident on the train was as the result of a Gifted. Is it true?'

'That's something we can't comment on at this stage in the investigation,' Voronov says.

'I can understand that. What can you do, if you don't mind my asking?' Gabriel asks her. 'They say higher-level Gifted telepaths can hear people's thoughts without skin-to-skin contact.'

'As someone working in the Gifted field, I'm sure you can appreciate that it's not that simple. You said you've worked with Julio Soares. How would you say he's been since Gil's death?'

'The professor? He's diligent,' Gabriel says and chews on his lower lip as he thinks about it, 'he hasn't missed any classes, I don't think. There really hasn't been an opportunity for me to speak to him properly but when I visited the university a couple of days ago, he seemed tired, a little less put-together than usual. But given the circumstances, I'd say that's normal. He was close with Gil.'

They ask him about Célia too but it's the same as his relationship with Gil. Casual acquaintances, enough for a conversation but nothing beyond that. Isabel asks him if Julio Soares has ever discussed anything with him regarding his projects with NTI or his working relationship with either Célia or Julio.

Gabriel folds his arms and shakes his head. 'No. He doesn't discuss any projects related to the NTI. All of those are all heavily protected by confidentiality clauses. He'd be in a world of trouble even just breathing a word about it.'

Isabel stands and nods over at Voronov. 'Okay. If you think of anything that may help us in our investigation we'd be grateful if you'd get in touch.'

Voronov passes over a card as Gabriel stands too.

Isabel holds out her hand and Gabriel stares at her for a moment. Then he clasps it in his.

Can you hear me?

Isabel stills. It's a small reaction and only lasts a second. And then she's withdrawing her hand and giving him another polite smile. 'Thank you again.'

She turns her back on him.

His eyes burn a hole in the back of her head.

34

Isabel is standing in the kitchen, towel over her wet head. She stirs the papa de milho, watching it thicken as the wooden spoon cuts through the yellow consistency of the semolina flour. Its sweet scent fills the space. She hasn't had this in a while but for some reason she'd woken up craving its nostalgic taste and smell. Her dad used to make it for her and her siblings for breakfast.

She's feeling loose from her run. Her head is quiet. She hasn't taken the pill yet and she wants to enjoy the pain-free feeling for as long as she can.

The night before hadn't given her the results she'd wanted. And although she'd still ended up grabbing a quick beer with Voronov, both of them had been quiet, mulling over the conversation they'd had with Gabriel Bernardo.

She switches off the flame and takes her favourite bowl down from the cupboard, a pretty porcelain thing with a vine pattern running along the rim in silver and pours herself a portion. Grabbing a tea towel to cradle the hot food, she takes it to the living room and sits down cross-legged on the sofa, the heat of the papa de milho seeping through the tea towel and into the palm of her hand. She needs to remember to water the plants before she leaves and check to see if there's any sign of her strays. She's bought some treats to drop out of her window for them.

She turns the TV volume up and flicks through the channels before giving up and settling on the morning news.

It's ironic that this case is making her think about her own Gift so much. Hard to avoid thinking and worrying about it when this case is firmly embedded in the Gifted world.

She'd been wondering since Dr Alves' show-and-tell whether it would've made a difference if Isabel hadn't lost her dad so soon after getting her classification.

Maybe she would have learned how to mess around with her Gift for fun as a way to learn her limits.

She's never felt that there was anything playful about her Gift. It had been one layer of misery after the other.

She still remembers how things had been before her Gift began evolving. She'd been able to sense emotions and hear thoughts, but only if she was touching someone. Then it had started to change, emotions free-flowing around her, easy for her to grab and identify. She hadn't been too worried.

It was when the *thoughts* started to float to her too that she started to become uneasy.

At first it had only been snatches of them. At the supermarket, in the café, at work. In bed.

The times when it had happened when she'd been in bed with Michael had been the worst. It left her feeling uncomfortable in her own skin, like she'd taken something against someone's will. And there were things she hadn't wanted to hear, that had made her feel guilty.

Things that came and went so quickly that she'd been able to ignore it. They'd steadily grown clearer though. And then, at one of Michael's work parties, that changed.

It's funny that she remembers it so clearly. She'd been angry that night, dealing with a hard case, working hours of overtime, and they'd argued. She hadn't wanted to face a room full of people she didn't know or care about on top of all of that. It was around the time that their arguments had become more frequent. Isabel had started withdrawing, physically. Hadn't known how to address the issue.

Isabel had replied to the person as if she had heard their words out loud. She was lucky they just hadn't realised what was happening. She'd been able to play it off as her being confused. She'd thought it was a one-off.

But it kept happening. Over and over to the point where she'd started to get paranoid, watching anyone she was speaking to intently to make sure the words were actually coming out of their mouths.

It was Sebastião who noticed. She's so thankful for that. Had it been anyone else—

Soon after that Isabel had started taking the S3. Meditation and strengthening her wards hadn't been enough. Michael had seen her struggling but he'd thought her Gift had been wearing her down, that the emotions were too much. She'd been happy to let him think that. He'd never realised that now she had no need to touch people, that thoughts just slipped into her mind.

The headaches hadn't been so bad then. The suppressants had done their job, and everything stayed normal, and if sometimes she got an annoying pressure right between the eyes when she took the pill, then that was fine. She could handle that.

Until it got worse. Until a pill a day changed to two, to three, to four and the headaches became a splitting pain that she'd somehow learned to live with.

She and Michael had been done by then.

The news presenter is doing a report and she catches sight of the university on the screen. There's a short stout woman talking to the presenter on location.

Isabel spoons a bit of papa de milho into her mouth and the soft sweet taste has her melting back into the sofa even as she tries to pay attention.

'—students have been sent home and the university is refusing to comment on—'

From the kitchen, Isabel hears the telltale sound of her phone vibrating on the counter. Cursing, she gets to her feet and jogs the short distance, spoon dangling from her mouth and her bowl of breakfast still in her hands.

It's the Chief.

'Morning Chief.'

'Reis, I need you to come in ASAP. Julio Soares has been found dead.'

35

As Isabel and Voronov pull up to the university, there's a hum along the line of Isabel's mind. She glances at the watch on her wrist. It's only been a few hours since she's taken her S3.

Its protection is definitely starting to fade faster but she has spares on her and Voronov's thoughts aren't leaking into her head even in the small confines of the car, so she has a little time. Isabel knows from past experience that even when people are zoned out, there's a constant stream of consciousness going on behind their eyes, a natural flow. They're processing things, working them out, without even realising they are going through the day in a never-ending stream of words and images.

Unlike with the death at the station with the crushing crowd of rush-hour commuters, the university's car park is near empty. Professor Soares had been discovered as the first classes of the day had started, but the students had already been cleared from the building.

Isabel feels in her pocket for the familiar edges of the small pillbox there and some of the tightness in her neck abates when the pads of her fingers rub over the corners. Voronov opens the door on his side and she follows suit.

Isabel can smell the rain in the air. It's not coming down yet, but the sky is swollen with it. It's been one of those dreary weeks.

The building looks very different from how it looked the day of the party. Maybe it's because of the circumstances that they are returning here under. Death has a way of changing the look of things. Or maybe it's because the car park isn't loaded with expensive cars and suited people opening doors for them.

Julio Soares' lab is on the third floor and the elevator is out of order.

They take the stairs in silence, both keeping to themselves.

The body is already covered up. Jacinta looks up from the notes she's making when they walk in. She nods over to the whiteboard.

Somehow, it feels more brutal here than it did in the train carriage. Isabel can't quite pin down why.

The whiteboard is filled with equations. Some are in blue marker, some in black, some in the corner in green marker and a couple of things in red here and there. There seem to be bloody fingerprints on the board too. Isabel can see where they have rubbed out some of the numbers and left red stains. On the floor directly beneath it, is a small pool of blood.

'Same thing?' Voronov asks.

Jacinta nods and puts her pen down on top of her notebook. 'Yes. No one trampled through the scene this time though. But from the looks of it, similar trauma to the head. Neck is broken too. From what I can see, I'd say he was thrown against the board repeatedly.'

A flash of memory takes Isabel out of the room for a moment. Rodrigo's eyes following the helpless clash of an out-of-control commuter crashing against the door over and over again.

Isabel pushes the image away and focuses on the scene in front of her. The overhead lights are strong, washing everything in bright white light.

It's a modern classroom and still has that shiny new feel to it. A lot of gleaming white. Most of the equipment is out of sight and blue, wheeled stools are tucked into the spaces beneath the work-stations. Isabel thinks they look like an accident waiting to happen.

The ceiling is lined with water sprinklers and the door to the classroom is a heavy-duty one. Right at the back of the room is an emergency exit leading outside. Isabel walks over to peer through its small, square window.

There's a set of old-looking emergency stairs leading down, though they're high up enough that she can't see down them to where they lead. Like most fire doors this one looks like it can only be opened from the inside.

'Going to take a look at where this leads to,' Isabel calls over her shoulder to Voronov, who's being brought up to speed by Jacinta, 'keep it propped open for me.'

She pushes the bar down, bracing herself in case she sets off some kind of alarm, but everything stays silent as the door gives with a rusted noise. Isabel steps onto the landing of the emergency stairs. A glance up shows her that the stairs continue all the way to the top of the building. They're metal and it's just the steps and the rail. The whole thing shakes as she starts down, but it's sturdy enough that she doesn't worry the whole thing will collapse and it doesn't take too long to reach the bottom. The third floor isn't all that far up.

It leads to what looks like another car park. It makes sense that this would be an assembly point – a wide area, room enough to accommodate a large section of the university. A campus this size would have more than one place to park, though Isabel thinks that the majority of the student body must travel in by public transport. Cheaper, with all the tolls on the bridges and other major roads coming into the city.

This car park is emptier than the one out front.

Isabel steps off the last step, hand trailing off the railing. She follows the corner of the building to see how far the space stretches and finds herself at the front of the building again a couple of minutes later.

Huh.

She heads back to the emergency stairs and pulls out her pill-box as she goes, sliding it open and picking up one of the tiny powder-blue pills. She pops it, grimacing as she realises too late that she has no water to wash it down with. It sticks, right against the back of her throat, and she swallows convulsively to try to get it to budge. It's slow going and she has to use a finger to dislodge it. By some miracle it does go down, but she swears she feels the slow drag of it all the way.

Isabel tucks the box back into her pocket and climbs back up.

It's not until she reaches the second floor that she notices Voronov waiting for her at the top, arms resting on the railing and eyes locked on her.

Isabel doesn't do much other than nod in acknowledgement and continues on her way up. The slam of her heart against her ribcage doesn't show anywhere on her face.

Had he seen her take it?

Relax, even if he did see, what's the issue? You could've been taking anything.

Voronov stands back to allow her room to get back to the door. He holds it open for her.

'Thanks,' she says.

After they've taken a good look around, they head back out to find the dean of the university standing waiting for them. She's a tall woman, taller even than Voronov, by an inch or so. She has blond hair, grey at her temples in a lovely way. Fine lines bracket the sides of her mouth and her skin has the papery softness that comes with age and too much sun. The skin at her throat is darker and looks rough.

'Inspectors,' she says, shaking their hands, grip short and firm, 'this is a tragedy. What can we do to help? Professor Soares was one of our very best.' Her face is calm but there's an unusual wideness to her eyes and as soon as she stops shaking hands with them, she clasps them together. Her shoulders are rigid and she's emitting this nervous energy that reminds Isabel of *formigueiro*, that feeling of itching beneath the skin. 'What happens next?'

Soares has been taken away, the blood now the only thing left of him. Probably for the best, Isabel thinks, the dean wouldn't be as composed right now otherwise.

'A copy of Professor Soares' schedule would be useful. In the meantime, could you tell us about this morning?'

'Yes, we can provide that. I'll see if I can get someone to send it over to you.' She blows out a long breath and shrugs her shoulders, as if unsure where to start. 'As for this morning, I'm not sure. Any evening sessions would take place in the lower labs – these are used for lecturing only and sometimes evening guest lectures. Professor Soares' car was already in the car park when our cleaners got in today. They're always the first ones in.'

'Around what time do the cleaners start?' Isabel asks.

'They start at five a.m. First lectures of the day are from nine a.m. onwards.'

'So, there wouldn't have been any students up here?' Voronov asks.

'Not necessarily. It's possible that there could have been meetings scheduled with students for before classes, or evening one-to-ones last night – some lecturers try to accommodate students as best as they can – but I wouldn't know the specifics of that. We could check his diary but not all student–teacher appointments are logged via the student portal.'

'Did the professor have a secretary or admin working with him?'

The dean shakes her head. 'No, our lecturers don't have individual administrative staff, though there is a team admin allocated to each department. Depending on the workload, maybe two. His department is supported by two admins. I believe one of them is currently on annual leave. Again, I'll have to check that,' she says.

Voronov nods. 'We'll also need the schedules of the professor's colleagues in the department and those of any of the students who attend his courses.'

'Of course.'

'This section will remain closed off for the time being. We will keep you briefed on what happens next. Do you keep a log of who uses the faculty car park?' Isabel asks.

The dean nods. 'Yes. Security logs the comings and goings.'

'We'll need a copy of that too,' Isabel says. 'We'll be in touch.'

36

The Soares' have several properties but their main place of residence is in Estoril.

They drive past mansion after mansion on a road lined with tall trees, all overlooking a generous view of the sea. Voronov cracks a window to let in air as the windows start to fog up, and Isabel catches the briny scent of the water.

She wraps her scarf a little tighter around her neck. The station Voronov has left the radio on stops the mix of old-school rock ballads to start relaying the first segment of the midday news.

'Think they'll be there?' Voronov asks.

'Hopefully someone will.' Isabel glances over at him. 'I think it's best if you lead once we get there,' she says and rubs a hand over her hair, pushing it back from her face and wondering if she has a hairband stashed somewhere. 'He knows I'm Gifted; it might be harder for us to get the information we want if I'm the one leading.'

Voronov doesn't say anything.

Isabel knows he's seen the propaganda; it's kind of hard to miss. If anything, she is probably still sounding too optimistic about what's about to happen.

'I think we're here,' Voronov says and slows the car.

Isabel takes in the house that they're parking in front of and gives a low whistle. It's not like she's not aware that the other half live in a different way to her, but seeing it isn't the same thing as knowing. 'Nice place. Think they all fit in there?' she asks and gets out of the car.

Outside the air is crisp and Isabel wishes she'd remembered to put her jumper in the wash because she's missing it now. Her other ones all have holes in them.

The pavements are narrow here, barely-there things running along the string of extravagant houses, and they quickly cross the road.

The Soares' house stands out. Grand and built in a late Portuguese Gothic style, it's set in the middle of a vast garden that is probably tended to every day given its pristine state. It sits on the downward slope of the road they're on and the view from it must be stunning.

This is a place of serious money.

'After you.' Isabel motions Voronov ahead of her and, when he gives her a look, arches a brow. He starts towards the house and she falls into step with him.

Even the front door is an intimidating thing. Huge and built in dark wood, it's outlined by an arch of light-brown stone slabs that contrast with the cream-coloured paint of the house walls.

The knocker sounds like it doesn't belong against the backdrop lapping of the waves below.

The door opens quietly on well-oiled hinges and a small woman stands there, peering up at Voronov and looking startled. Who wouldn't, the man is huge.

'Yes? May I help you?' The woman spots Isabel standing behind Voronov and relaxes. The clothes she wears are simple and reserved and her shoes are sensible. The hands she has clasped in front of her are work-worn.

The help, then, housekeeper, maybe.

Voronov holds up his ID and Isabel does the same.

'We're from the PJ,' he says. 'I'm Inspector Voronov and this is Inspector Reis. We'd like to speak to Mr and Mrs Soares. Are they home?'

The woman takes a step back, hand fluttering to her chest. 'Of course, please.' She gestures them inside. 'If you wait here, I'll call Mr Soares for you.'

They step inside and Isabel closes the door behind her. Saying that the hall is spacious would be an understatement.

The housekeeper's steps echo on the stone flooring as she walks away and disappears through another arch further down the hall.

Isabel looks around. Everything is perfectly in place. She wonders if people in this house are allowed to sneeze.

The sound of a man's voice comes from somewhere deeper inside the house. Isabel stands up straighter, calming herself and waiting. It isn't every day that you come face to face with someone who openly hates your kind.

The housekeeper returns, and she's followed by Bento Soares.

Even at home relaxing, Soares looks ready to welcome guests. He's dressed in a dark blue polo shirt and beige chinos, thick salt and pepper hair combed carefully into a side parting and a clean-shaven face. Shoulders straight, grey eyes focused, he walks to them in sure strides to stop in front of Voronov.

'Inspectors. Let me be blunt. I don't appreciate you interrupting my day.'

'Mr Soares,' Isabel greets him. He doesn't offer her his hand and she's happy to let it slide. She wants to touch him about as much as he wants to touch her. 'We apologise for barging in.'

'Then why are you?'

Isabel reminds herself that no matter how much she detests the man, they're here to inform him that his son is dead.

'I'm afraid it's about your son,' Voronov says, 'is there a place where we could speak privately?'

Soares says, 'Follow me.' He doesn't wait to see if they follow, leading the way to a set of sprawling stairs that take them up to the second floor of the house. The corridor is dotted with balconies. It's all very pretty. Curtains blowing in the breeze, windows and balcony doors open. It turns the corridors cold, and the house itself is unnaturally quiet. Isabel wonders where everyone else is.

'Will your wife be joining us, Mr Soares?' she asks.

Bento Soares looks at Isabel over his shoulder, not stopping. 'My wife is away at the moment.'

'I see.'

Soares stops outside a set of open doors and motions them inside. He closes them behind him and makes his way to the desk, settling himself behind it, then gestures towards the two seats across from it. 'Please,' he says.

When they're settled, Soares glances from one of them to the other.

'Why is the PJ sending two inspectors to see me? And why would my wife need to join me? Your investigation isn't related to me, or,' he pauses there and spears Isabel with a look, 'my son.'

Isabel doesn't respond.

Voronov gets straight to the point. 'Your son's body was discovered in the early hours of this morning.'

Isabel watches, tense; ready to catch whatever slips out.

It's as if the muscles of Soares' face ice over. His eyes become distant.

He stands and walks over to the cabinet on the far side of the room. He opens it and just stands there.

'Mr Soares?' Voronov asks.

Soares jolts. Then he takes out a decanter and a glass, pours in the amber liquid. When he walks back over, the smell of whisky wafts in the air. He sits back down.

As he takes a gulp, he stares Voronov down. 'I'd offer you a drink, but you're on duty. But I can call for something with a little less kick, if you prefer?'

Isabel keeps her face expressionless. 'Mr Soares, do you have any other children?' she asks.

'Two daughters.' He downs the rest of the whisky and sets the glass down with a thump. It's heavy and expensive like everything else in the room.

'Sir, we're going to need you to come with us, so that we can confirm the identity.'

The flash is quick, so quick that Isabel is overwhelmed by it, like an explosion of glass that she can't guard against. She manages to stifle her gasp, fingers tightening on her pen as the emotion spears into her.

It's only a few seconds but it feels like it's an age before the room comes back into focus. She's still holding her pen tightly. The ink has bled on the paper where the point digs into the page. She looks up. Voronov is calm next to her, still watching Bento Soares. But Bento is watching her, a peculiar expression on his face.

'Feeling okay, Inspector?' he says softly, but something has shifted in the room.

'Fine. Thank you.'

'Are you sure it was my son you found?' he asks, not looking away.

Isabel thinks of the mess that was found in that classroom, of the way that they've lost yet another person and still haven't got a clue how the killer even managed to get near the victims.

'Yes,' she says and out of the corner of her eye she sees Voronov shoot her a look.

'Will you come with us and make an official identification?'

Bento blinks at Voronov. 'Julio is dead,' he says.

Neither of them reply.

'No.' Bento puts his hands on the desk and stands. 'No. Not until I see it with my own eyes. Show me.'

'We'll take you now,' Voronov says.

Isabel is already striding to the door, phone in hand, calling ahead to let the morgue know they're coming.

Bento insists on following them in his own car.

When he's in the same room as his son's body and sees his face, the streak of grief is blinding, and Isabel has to step back from it. It feels too much like being cleaved in two. And there's a discomfort there too, that she feels from seeing a man she considers hateful displaying such human emotion.

It's something she's not ashamed to admit she hadn't wanted to see.

She stands quietly by the door with Voronov as Bento Soares stands over his son's body and his shoulders shake, proud head lowered. But he doesn't make a sound. He doesn't have to.

Isabel feels it all.

37

THEN

Underneath Isabel's hat, her hair sticks to her head.

The windows on the bus are open but it's still boiling inside.

Isabel looks up from her seat at the back of the bus. All the other kids are shifting around in the heat too, but they're quiet, like her, and she wonders if they feel the same ache that she has brewing in her stomach. She wants to go home.

Isabel shoves up her hat to scratch at her head through the tight plait Tia worked her hair into that morning. Thinking about it . . . hurts.

Isabel's mum usually does her hair every morning, always when Isabel is brushing her teeth after getting dressed for school. On the weekends, she always sits down on the floor in the living room to watch TV and her mum does her hair while they watch TV together. But Dad had come last week and Isabel had heard them talking; her parents' voices had been loud hissed words that she couldn't quite make out from where she sat with Rita at the kitchen table, the chamomile on the pot in the stove perfuming the room.

Later, her dad had helped Isabel finish her homework. Mum hadn't looked at either of her children. She had got a chopping board out, wrapped an apron around her waist and gone to the fridge to start preparing dinner.

Isabel's dad had asked her if she'd like to take a walk with him. He'd bought her an ice cream at the café. He said her mum wasn't well and that it might be better for Isabel to stay with Tia Simone and Sebastião for a little while.

When Isabel had asked if Rita was coming with her too, her dad had wrapped an arm around her shoulders and hugged her into his middle. 'She'll come on the weekends,' he'd said.

Isabel likes staying with Tia and Sebastião but Rita hasn't stayed over yet.

The bus jerks and jostles around her as it rolls over a bump on the road. Isabel looks up and freezes.

They've reached the gates of NTI. The last time she'd been here was to do her first test, a month ago. But what she'd seen as her class bus had rolled up to the gates had been nothing like this.

In front of the gates is a crowd of people, spread all along the length of it. Isabel stares, half rising off her seat, clutching at the one in front of her to see. The other kids are doing the same and the bus, which had been completely quiet until now, fills with questions and unease. Isabel can hear the bus driver swearing.

'Okay, I need everyone to stay calm.' The lady escorting them is Ms Pontes, a representative of the NTI who is meant to oversee their session today, to shepherd them from the affinity test that determines what kind of ability they have to the one that measures their classification. Isabel had been allowed to stay in the room with her dad while Dr Carvalho explained what would happen next.

When they leave here today, they'll all know what they are. Isabel already knows her affinity. She's never been able to move things. She wonders which of the other kids around her will be a telepath like her. Which will be telekinetics.

She wonders if their parents, too, had sat them outside a room and had hushed conversations with emotions so strong Isabel had felt them like a pain in her chest.

Right now, Ms Pontes is giving them a wide smile that Isabel doesn't believe. Ms Pontes has her back to the wide front windowpane of the bus, head hunched to keep from hitting it on the roof, hands gripping the tops of the seat so hard that it looks like her fingers are punching through the upholstery. 'Everyone please sit down; we'll be through to the testing centre soon. Remember that we'll need to line up in alphabetical order.' She smiles through all her words, a wide stretch of her lips, but she's speaking through her teeth.

Isabel looks over Ms Pontes' shoulder.

The group of people have pickets, large white signs waving in the air in time to the shouts. There are so many voices yelling at the same time that it's hard to hear what they're saying, but Isabel doesn't need to. She's heard those words before, hissed across a street at a passer-by walking with hunched shoulders, steps speeding to get away, or aimed at the supermarket cashier as someone switches queues.

Words pop out from the signs and Isabel's eyes eat them up, each one making the ache in her stomach worse.

Unnatural.

Unholy.

Aberrações.

Vicious slashes of red make up the words, angry block capitals that scream their presence against the white of the page.

Isabel's staring so hard her eyes sting. Her own hands are clenched where they're braced over the top of the seat above her. She can't make her knees bend, can't make herself look away. She just skips from sign to sign to sign.

They need to be stopped!
They will take over our world!
What about our privacy?
They can control you!

She thinks about her parents. She thinks about their hushed conversation behind closed doors. She remembers the ice cream melting in her hand, dark brown and sticky, making her hand smell like chocolate as her dad sat beside her and explained she'd be staying with Tia for a while.

She thinks about how her stomach ached the same way that it does right now, but now it's so much worse because Isabel thinks that maybe the conversation she hadn't been able to hear coming from the kitchen had used some of the words she sees being waved at her now.

'Isabel, please sit down. We need to think of safety first and you all need to be in your seats. Okay? Sit down, please.'

Isabel's knees are stiff and she drops her gaze as she forces them to give until she's sitting down again.

Ms Pontes turns to speak to the driver. She's got her phone in her hand and she's dialling.

The boy sitting next to Isabel has his head down.

'They don't like us,' he says.

Isabel stares straight ahead and doesn't say anything.

38

Bento Soares agrees to give them access to Julio's apartment, something Isabel is thankful for because she wasn't looking forward to having to do battle just to get inside and check the place out.

So the next morning she and Voronov are there first thing.

Julio Soares' apartment is about a thirty-minute drive from the university. The building has a concierge at the front, and they're shown to Julio's apartment by an immaculately dressed lady. 'I've been instructed by Mr Soares to wait here while you look around.'

'No problem,' Isabel says.

Voronov steps inside and Isabel follows.

A quick look around reveals an open-plan kitchen and living room, a large bedroom with en suite bathroom, and a study. There's a veranda that overlooks a small park set between the apartment buildings and when Isabel looks over the edge there are kids running around and teenagers clustered on the benches, loud laughter bouncing up between the buildings.

Isabel comes back inside and takes in the space.

'I expected more books,' she says, and wanders back over to the study.

There are two shelves above his desk. The desk itself is messy, papers left in disarray, an unwashed mug of what was once maybe coffee but is now caked and looking like it's about to come to life all on its own. Isabel leafs through some of the papers, skimming over the notes. Julio's handwriting is a lot more legible than Gil's, large and clumsy looking.

There are no pictures on his desk. Some books are stacked haphazardly on top of each other and there are two leather-bound journals, one set on top of the pile of books and the other open and facing down, a pencil peeking out from beneath it. She flips it over, flicking through the pages quickly, but they seem to be just general notes.

'Seeing anything interesting?' she calls out.

'No.' The wooden floor groans under the weight of Voronov's steps. 'You?'

'It's messy,' she says, 'but significantly more understandable than Gil's work desk.'

They keep looking through the room, going through desk drawers and the bookcase, but don't find anything of note.

'I'm going to take a look at the rest of the place,' Isabel says and after getting a nod from Voronov, who continues looking through the papers on the desk, she slips out and follows the elegant corridor away from the living room and wanders into the bedroom.

The shutters in the room are down and the bed is unmade. Everything is decked out in shades of blue. Two suit bags hang from the top of the closet and a pair of battered-looking trainers are discarded beneath the armchair by the window.

The en suite is mostly tidy, smelling vaguely of cologne. There's a used towel on the floor by the sink and the laundry basket is full. She comes back out into the bedroom and surveys the whole room. There are some books on the bedside table and bottles of cologne litter the top of the chest of drawers. Nothing that stands out.

She looks inside the top drawer of the bedside table. She finds some pens, a small notebook, a half-empty box of condoms and small bottle of lube. Nothing out of the ordinary for a healthy single man.

Turning back to the closet, she leaves the suits where they are and opens the other wardrobe instead, eyes sweeping the contents there. She spies a black shoebox tucked into a corner and half under a scarf that has been dumped there unceremoniously. She kneels to take a quick look. When she takes the lid off she pauses.

Inside there are a stack of empty envelopes still in their packet with the university logo on them, and a handful of other university-branded stationery. But beneath that is a brown leather notebook. Isabel tugs it out. At the top right-hand corner is a label that's been stuck onto the leather; it says: Patient 2, Notes 2.

There are only a couple of lines of writing on the first page. Isabel flips back through pages of notes, some of which slip into shorthand here and there. Julio's writing changes, sometimes slanting, tighter together and crowded, like he rushed it, and in other parts scrawling, as if he'd been thinking each and every word through as he'd written them on the page.

Isabel brings the notebook up closer to her face.

It's an entry dated only a month ago and a section of it catches her attention.

> *Test conducted 12th October confirms increase in level from the last retesting. Level increase unclear due to subject's category duality. Have begun designing tests to isolate the separate ability categories and measure each individually—*

Isabel stares down at the notes. Category duality.

What? Category . . . as in affinity?

'Isabel?'

> *—discord within the group. GDS unconvinced of subject's stability and no longer wants to continue with study, showing concerns that subject can no longer continue to function without a Guide. I proposed assigning a new Guide at our meeting – GDS against this decision. Cited subject as too unstable. CA shows concerns but is willing to continue monitoring subject – I share her reluctance to discontinue monitoring of Patient 2. This is new ground. If we're able to find a way to isolate the two categories and measure this, it will enable us to develop targeted tests that might let us catch the presence of secondary abilities—*

*   *   *

She sets the shoebox down and rises from her crouch. 'Voronov, read this.' She holds it out to him and is surprised her hand is so steady. 'Tell me I'm misunderstanding what that's saying.'

GDS is clearly Gil dos Santos and CA is probably Célia Armindas. Was this the privately funded project Armindas had referred to?

Voronov stays quiet as he reads through the page but his expression gets stonier as he tracks the words. 'He's talking about a Gifted who is both,' he says, and looks up, his expression for once open, 'both telepath and telekinetic? That's possible?'

'We need to get back to the station,' Isabel says.

Voronov shuts the journal and frowns down at it. 'I think it'll be a good idea to have Dr Alves weigh in on this.' He looks grim. 'But if we've understood even half of that then . . .'

Isabel's thoughts exactly.

When they reach the precinct, they make a quick trip to the café for a bite to eat. They've been on their feet too long and without a decent break; her shields are waning.

'Looks like we have a no-witness situation this time around,' she says as they walk in. She keeps quiet, just nodding hello to the regulars on her way to the counter. She calls out to old man Días, asking for that day's specials, Voronov trailing behind her.

They end up with squid stew, sitting in the small, cramped area around the side set up on the uneven cobbles that trap the chair and table legs whenever they move. It has a small heater and a canopy to buffer the tables from the wind. It's a cosy little section despite the fact that it's winter. Not many people come out here at this time of year and Isabel always takes advantage of that. It's cold, but not cold enough to cancel out the effect of the heater. Especially with a bowl of stew in front of her, curls of steam peeling away from it and into the crisp air, and over that the smell of lemon from the carioca de limão she ordered too. It's always a comforting drink for her.

Isabel takes in the smell of the food appreciatively before digging in. She almost burns her tongue off. The flavour explodes in her mouth, tomato and that saltiness that only comes with a seafood dish. She starts to feel warmer before she's even swallowed.

Voronov makes a sound of approval after his first spoonful as well and for a while they eat in silence. They're halfway through when Voronov eases back from his food, pops open his water and looks her right in the eye.

'What are the pills for?'

Isabel keeps eating, only flicking him a quick glance. She takes another forkful and then sits back, chewing on her mouthful, watching him. She takes a napkin and dabs at her mouth, then picks up a small packet of sugar and rips off the corner. She pours it into the tiny cup of hot water. The lemon peels sit at the bottom of the cup and she watches as they're buried under the white granules of sugar. She stirs it in. It's only when she has the cup nestled in the palms of her hand, heat burning through it to the skin of her palms, that she starts to speak.

'Does it matter?' she asks, and her tone hides the fact that she's suddenly hyper-aware of the beat of her heart, which feels too heavy. She sips at the lemon sweetness and sets the cup back down before returning to her food.

'It's not the first time you've taken them,' he continues, digging into his food as if Isabel hadn't just attempted to shut him down.

She sets her fork back down and stares him down. 'You going somewhere with this? Because if not, how about we drop this conversation and finish our food? We've still got things to do.'

Isabel's phone vibrates on the table between them, and she thanks God for the distraction. She picks it up to see a message from Jacinta.

'We need to go,' she says. 'Turns out they've got something from the camera outside the lab.'

'What about the journal?'

226

Isabel sighs, rubs at her temple and winces when that makes the headache shoot a little deeper. She shakes her head. 'I think we should talk it over with the team and the Chief. The repercussions of what was in that journal coming out aren't good ones. It's better if we get a handle on it as fast as possible.'

It would be worse than Colombo. If the public ever suspected that there was someone walking around, unknown to them and with the capability to command both telepathy and telekinesis – well— Isabel wouldn't put it past people to go on a rampage.

'We'll need to tread carefully. It explains Armindas' and Julio's vagueness when talking to us. This— what they were doing is . . .' She finishes her carioca de limão. 'Fuck. Let's go.'

39

This time they're not so lucky.

The news of Julio Soares' death is being reported all over the evening news. That Professor Soares, son of Bento Soares, was murdered in the early hours of Thursday morning and that the case is currently being investigated by the same two inspectors who are working on Gil dos Santos' case, leading to speculations of a link between the two.

The only saving grace is that they haven't connected either Isabel or Voronov's names to the case yet and the word Gifted isn't mentioned once. But Isabel doubts it'll be long before it gets to that point.

The door to the case room is closed tight and they've drawn the blinds down for good measure. The room is stuffy and they've had to crack open a window to let some freshness in.

The Chief sits at the back, arms crossed, cup of coffee in front of her as she waits along with the rest of the team.

Isabel stands with Voronov at the front of the room.

'We found this journal at Julio's place.' She slides the journal across the table to the Chief. 'We're still going through it, but it's significant. It seems as if Gil, Célia and Julio were working on an unnamed subject. From the looks of it, it doesn't seem to be above board. It mentions that Gil had become concerned about the subject's instability. Julio notes he and Armindas were not as convinced as he was.' Isabel takes a deep breath and drops the bomb. 'It also states that the subject in question has tested as having dual categories for their abilities.'

Daniel leans forward. 'Sorry, what? What does that mean?'

Carla's mouth gapes open. 'But that's impossible. Right?'

'We can't say for sure,' Isabel says, answering Daniel, 'but we think it's referring to a Gifted's affinity. Mine and Carla's, for example, are telepathy. Célia's is telekinetic. We think this is talking about someone who has both.' Following that no one says anything else.

The Chief is flicking through the journal, stopping in some places before continuing and then stopping again, all the while tapping her free hand on the edge of the table.

Isabel leans back against the wall behind her. 'Like I said, we didn't have a chance to go through the whole thing but it might prove significant. And if nothing else, it shows that these three are involved in something that is clearly not above board. Julio makes it clear that they are keeping this from Monitoring.'

The Chief rubs at her eyes, then sighs with her whole body. 'Okay. I want this kept between this team. Not a peep outside of this room. Everyone understand that?'

There's a chorus of assent.

'Bento Soares is riding us hard. His son is dead. So now we need to move even faster. It's only going to get worse because he *will* take this over our heads to the higher-ups and there will only be so much I can do if he does. I need something to give them when that happens. So what do you have?'

'At the moment we don't have enough. Célia Armindas is the only one of a high enough level to have been able to move a person and at the moment, we don't have her at either scene.' And with the reported disagreements between her and Gil, the argument Isabel and Voronov had witnessed at the function and now, the contents of that journal, things aren't looking great for her. But they might have another problem on their hands. 'But we have to consider that two of her colleagues are dead and they've all been doing something they shouldn't have.' Isabel looks at the Chief. 'Maybe it might be good to just have someone keep an eye on her.'

The Chief gives her a jerk of her chin. 'All right. Anything else?'

'Viewing the recording from outside the labs today.'

'The internet café's finally got back to us with their CCTV as well,' Carla chimes in. 'We'll see if there's anything of note on there. Hopefully it'll have captured whoever was in there the morning of Gil's murder.'

They give her a brief run-through of the rest. There are still the car park logs and visitors' lists from the university, and the woman who's all but a vegetable lying in a hospital in Coimbra. They have no idea how she fits into this investigation. Maybe she doesn't and it'll just be another dead end for them. And there's still Luisa and what the hell Gil was doing calling her.

A lot of roads and one of them has to lead to something.

The Chief stands. 'I want an update before you wrap up for the day.'

'Yes, Chief.'

40

Isabel hands over Voronov's coffee and takes a seat on the table behind him, cradling her own, eyes zooming in on the large monitor in front of them.

Once everyone is sitting down, Carla nods to herself and turns to the computer.

'Okay, first things first,' she says, and clicks on the little remote in her hand.

A webpage from the Registry comes up. It has a picture of an older woman with stern features, staring unsmiling out of the photo. She has short-cropped grey hair and red lipstick. Lines bracket the corners of her mouth and her forehead.

Isabel squints at the image. 'Is that the hospital patient that Gil was visiting? Mila Ferreira?'

'That's right. Daniel found her. She used to be a Guide. This is actually a cache page, basically a snapshot of the original webpage that has been stored in case the page becomes unavailable, so we can see what was actually on her profile.'

'Meaning her page was taken down by the Registry? Is there a connection with the case?' Isabel asks.

Daniel nods. 'I checked with the Registry. It's not much but Mila Ferreira was actually a specific type of Guide. She wasn't allocated to the government-mandated cohorts. She worked directly with NTI.'

'Doing what?' Isabel asks.

'She worked exclusively for the special cases that were overseen by them.'

'Like what? They have that kind of say?' Jacinta asks.

Daniel tucks his hands into his pockets and looks back at Ferreira's image on the monitor. 'Yeah. This is where it gets a little . . . grey. The only Gifted that the NTI would oversee directly after they've been tested are Gifted who are level eights and up. Maybe sevens depending on the situation. This would be in addition to their Monitor.'

Isabel takes in the face of the woman on the screen. She remembers Rosario's kind smile and patience. She wonders if Rosario's still working, still guiding young Gifted through their abilities with kindness.

This woman seems a million miles away from that type of Guide. 'So, not your regular Guide then,' Isabel says.

'No.'

'Do we know what happened to her?'

Daniel shakes his head. 'No one knows. She was found out cold on her living room floor. We're waiting for the higher-ups to give us clearance to dig deeper with the hospital. She doesn't have any known family that we can go to.'

Isabel sighs. Yeah. That seems to be their luck right now. 'All right. Let's get details of her previous address' – she rubs at the bridge of her nose, pinches it between her fingers to try to ease the tension there – 'we'll go have a look around there. Speak to the neighbours. See if they know anything of value. What's next?'

Carla heads over to the laptop. 'So, CCTV for the day of Julio's death. We've combed through most of it' – she blows out a long loud breath and looks at them – 'it isn't pretty.' She taps at the keyboard and the image on the screen begins to move.

The quality could be better, Isabel thinks. The image is grainy but it's clear enough that they can see into Professor Soares' lab. One of the double doors is still in place, the other is propped open. Through it, Soares is visible standing at his desk, the whiteboard large behind him. He's bent over something on the desk. He lifts his head. Even with the grainy image it's clear that his mouth is moving.

Anticipation curls in Isabel's stomach and she sits up, leaning closer to the monitor. In front of her Voronov is still, like her, probably not wanting to miss anything.

On the screen, Soares stands. The movement is abrupt and sends his chair rolling back. It bounces off the wall and wheels closer to the classroom door. Soares is yelling – or that's what it looks like, hand in front of him, finger pointing – and then he's airborne.

It's like an invisible hand picks him up and slams him back against the board. He slams against it, once, face cracking against the white. Red cuts across the board in a splatter. He's yanked back, toes dragging over the floor, whole body flopping like a rag doll, then slammed against it again. And again. And again.

He drops and is still.

Isabel stares. 'Jesus.'

The time on the top-right corner of the screen continues to tick away. The attack took less than a minute. For another full minute they sit in silence in the big room, the clock behind them ticking away, loud and mocking.

'There,' Voronov says.

Movement just behind the still-closed door of the lab.

A head, hooded, behind the square window of the door, then the person's foot as they make to come out. The killer stops, head turning but still low as if to look through the window. The image distorts, lines cutting across the screen, the whole thing flickering before the image goes black.

For a moment, no one in the room speaks.

Isabel grits her teeth. 'There's nothing. Not one thing that we can pick out for identification.' She glances at Carla. 'Carla, have you looked through the rest of the footage for that day?'

Carla nods and leans back in her seat. 'Yes. I don't know who that person is, can't pinpoint where they even get into the classroom.'

Isabel thinks back to the room, remembers the fire exit at the back, which would have been locked. 'He looked fine until he started yelling. He probably knew this person. It's possible that they could have come in through the fire exit at the back.'

Voronov shrugs and nods but doesn't say anything.

233

'I checked with the site manager and the tech team. No one gets in or out without a key fob, and they're religious about signing in visitors. Doesn't mean someone hasn't slipped through the net though. The car park is operated by key fobs too and the emergency exits lead down to that, but I don't know how they could open the gates undetected,' Isabel says.

'They could've waited and snuck out behind another car, or maybe parked outside and gone in on foot,' Voronov points out.

'True.' Isabel drinks her coffee. 'We still need to go through the log of who was in the building that day. If we get lucky we might get some more witnesses who haven't felt particularly comfortable about coming forward.' She shrugs off her jacket and pulls up the broken chair she'd ignored when she'd come into the room earlier. Straddling it, she scoots closer to the monitor and rolls right up to Voronov. 'All right, let's take it all the way back to the night before,' she says with a sigh.

'Don't think you brought enough coffee for this,' Voronov says.

Isabel resists the urge to flip him off and settles in for what's going to be an eye-watering night.

41

Isabel is in their investigations room, ass on the table and one foot on a chair. She stares at the board they have up. Her eyes are still gritty from all the footage they've spent the majority of the evening viewing.

All of their evidence and dates neatly written in, connections made and names jumping up at her. She stares at Ferreira's name on the board, trying to figure out how she connects to any of this – if at all. Gil had visited her regularly and yet the closest people to him had no knowledge of these visits. Célia, the only Gifted individual in this case capable of the kind of power necessary to commit the crime, nowhere near the scene.

And Luisa, a level 3 telekinetic trying to stay as out of their way as possible. That's bothering Isabel.

How the hell does this woman fit into all of this and why does she keep popping up?

The journal? Is that what it all comes down to?

Isabel's head feels too full and she knows she needs to get it together. She can't afford to let herself slip right now. The department is just about keeping Soares at bay, but that won't last long and when he lashes out, it's going to hurt.

Someone raps on the investigation room's door. Isabel snaps her head up.

Carla pops her head round. 'Isabel, sorry to interrupt. Gabriel Bernardo is here to see you.'

Isabel twists around to face her fully, eyebrows climbing high. At this time? 'Sure. Has he said what it's about?'

Carla grimaces. 'He asked for you specifically.'

Isabel pauses. 'Okay.' She shoves her sleeves back past her

elbows and pushes her hair back from her face. 'Get Voronov, he's in with Jacinta. I want someone observing, just in case. Take Bernardo to the interview room, I'll be there in a minute.' She glances out the door but the blinds are down and she can't see past them. They probably have him waiting downstairs anyway.

Carla nods and backs out of the room.

Isabel downs the rest of her coffee and takes a breath. Fuck, she's tired.

Gabriel is already in the room when she reaches it. Carla's sat him down and he's got something to drink. He looks up when Isabel walks in.

'Inspector,' Gabriel says, half rising out of his chair, hand out for her to shake. The corners of his mouth draw back in an attempt at a smile, but it falls short.

'Mr Bernardo—'

'Gabriel.'

'All right. Gabriel. It's quite late, what can I help you with?' She sits.

'I'm sorry I couldn't do more to help,' Gabriel says.

Huh. Not what she'd been expecting. 'Why? Do you think you could do more?'

For a moment, he's silent. He watches her quietly, eyes mapping her face, slowly.

Isabel settles more comfortably into her chair, staring right back, and waits. From him she feels curiosity, spreading edged in a pale pink. And apprehension. That same emotion that was present when she and Voronov visited him in his apartment.

'You heard me, didn't you?' he asks, eyes intense. 'Last time.'

Isabel has to keep herself from leaning away. His tone, the implied intimacy of it, makes her want to be as far away from him as possible. He doesn't look away from her. Doesn't so much as blink.

'Don't you have to ask my permission before you do that?' he asks. 'You're not allowed to look in my head without asking for my permission, right?'

She has to tread carefully here. What did he think? That she'd tried to steal thoughts right out of his head when she'd been there?

An accusation of that kind would be enough to get Isabel thrown off the case. Maybe suspended. Possibly fired.

'Gabriel,' she says, crossing her legs and shifting forward, resting her arm on the table and peering at him, 'it was a handshake. Not an open door into your mind.' Well, she thinks to herself, not quite. 'And you're right. We need to get your consent before doing anything like reading your thoughts.' She leans closer across the table. 'You said you wished you could've been of more help. Gabriel, is there something that you know that could help us?'

He breaks eye contact, shaking his head, and sighs. 'I'm sorry, I didn't mean to – it's just Luisa isn't coping well. This is all really getting to her. She told me that you know about her classification.'

'That's true. But I'm afraid I can't discuss that with you.'

'I'm sorry,' he says, 'she's just scared. I'm worried about her and I don't know how to help. The press – you know what they're like when it comes to anything related to Gifted. And now with the announcement of Julio's death and the connection being made to Dr dos Santos,' his mouth settles into a grim line, 'I'm not sure Luisa could take it if her name gets dragged through the press. She hasn't been coping well with high-stress situations and she knows she's still a person of interest in your investigation. If this gets out . . .'

'She hasn't been named a person of interest.' Even though, Isabel thinks, she very much is. 'Gifted people have never had it easy,' she goes on and folds her arms on the table. 'Sadly, it's something a lot of us have learned to live with.' She wants to know where this is actually going.

Isabel can't quite read the look Gabriel gives her then.

'You don't get tired of it?'

'Yes. But that doesn't change anything. A lot of people like the status quo. People that run in the same circles as Gil dos Santos, like Julio Soares and his father. Like yourself even.'

Gabriel stares down at his hands. 'Not all of them. Some of them are actually trying to help. Their research is important. Maybe one day—' He cuts himself off and shakes his head.

'Maybe one day what?'

Gabriel sighs. 'I'm sorry. It's not important.' When he looks back up at her the sense of softening is gone and he's just a mask of politeness. 'Professor Soares really was trying to help, in all that he did. He's a huge loss to the research community. If I can be of any assistance, I'll be happy to help.'

Isabel tilts her head. 'Even if that means it might not be helpful to Luisa?' She leans forward. Because the conflict of interest alone would mean that they would have to take any information from him with a pinch of salt. 'Gabriel, what aren't you telling me?'

The door opens and Voronov walks in. It's hard for her to read his face.

Gabriel looks up at Voronov.

'I think I've taken up enough of your time, Inspector,' Gabriel says to Isabel and stands. 'Thank you for seeing me.'

Isabel stands too, inwardly cursing, and nods in acknowledgement. 'Not at all.'

'Inspector Voronov,' Gabriel says and then walks around him and leaves.

Voronov stands at the door watching him go, then turns back to Isabel. 'What was that?'

Isabel pushes her fingers through her hair and expels a long breath.

'I'm not sure.'

42

Michael is sitting on the step by the gate to Isabel's building when she arrives. He's got one hand stuffed into the pocket of his coat and his phone in the other. He hasn't seen her yet.

Isabel stops in front of the gate, trying to keep the wind from unravelling her scarf. She contemplates turning on her heel, going to have a drink and not coming back until she's sure he'll be gone.

But she's tired. Bone-deep tired, and drained from having to work through the worsening headaches.

She continues the climb up.

The tram bell rings behind her, signalling its ascent.

Evening has settled and the streetlights cast wide pools of yellow light down the steep street. Because the universe is a bitch, it just makes Michael look even sleeker than usual and makes her aware of what a mess she looks right now, at the end of a long day and without decent sleep. It feels like the bags under her eyes could drag down her cheeks under their weight.

'What're you doing here?' Isabel says, stopping in front of him. She leaves enough distance so that they don't have to be in each other's space. Her keys jangle as she plays with them inside the warmth of her pocket.

Michael looks up from his phone, hazel eyes looking more like brown in the dark. 'I tried calling,' he says.

'Yes,' Isabel says, 'I saw. Did you notice I didn't pick up?'

Michael sighs and looks away, rubs a rough hand over the back of his head. Then he stands and looks at her once more. 'Yes. I did. I still want to talk to you.'

She does not have the time or the energy for bullshit right now. 'I've had a long day. I'm not up for whatever it is that you're doing here.'

Isabel unlocks the gate and steps through. His hand closes over her upper arm and she flinches back, slaps his hand away and backs up, glaring at him. 'Don't do that,' she says, tone flat. Because the pills have faded and she's too tired to maintain her walls. She's burned out, needs food and space so she can regroup. She doesn't need this arsehole touching her and making it easier for her to pick up his thoughts. She doesn't want him in her head like that. Never did.

Michael looks stunned. Then pissed off. 'God Isabel what the hell did you think I was going to do? I'm trying to talk to you.'

'And I'm telling you to fuck off.' She throws her hands up in the air. The pulsing in her head is worse, so much worse. 'I'm telling you I'm tired. I don't want to do this. I really, really don't. You can't respect that?'

Something must come through in her voice because instead of having another go at her over his poor wounded ego, he seems to look at her properly, eyes zeroing in on her face.

Then he makes a show of looking around them, but all that's making its way towards them is the tram, rising steadily up the street, still packed despite the hour, the last of the commuters having squeezed themselves in.

'Is it the headaches?'

'Yes.'

Michael watches her for a moment longer. Then he straightens up and his jaw sets, eyes narrowing on her. 'Come on, let's get you inside.'

Isabel groans and lets her head fall back. She stares up at the sky and wonders what she's done to deserve this. 'I don't believe this. Can't you just leave?'

'You're tired, you want to get inside. Let's go. The sooner I check on you, the sooner I go.'

'I don't want you coming in at all. It's pretty easy to understand, Michael. Don't think I can say it any clearer.'

'Why do you always have to do this?' he asks, the anger coming back into his voice. 'Why do you always have to make everything more difficult than it needs to be?'

Isabel laughs, incredulous. She turns on her heel. Fuck this. She's not standing out in the cold doing this.

She hears him shut the gate behind her and resists the urge to brain herself on the door. She has seen what that looks like only too recently and doesn't want to go there.

She flips the lights on as she goes in, yanking the scarf off her neck.

Michael follows behind her, not saying anything as she goes about turning on the heater and the TV. She tosses her scarf on the sofa and forces herself to take off her coat. The apartment is cold from being empty for so long and it's going to take a while for it to warm up.

When Isabel goes into the kitchen, Michael follows.

She doesn't ask him if he wants anything, since she doesn't want him there at all.

'Where's the kettle?' he asks when she starts pouring water into the small pan she uses for the tea.

'It broke,' she bites off. He'd bought the damn thing when they'd been together. It had broken. After she threw it at the wall. But he doesn't need to know that.

The pan clangs against the stove when she sets it down too hard. Isabel pushes past him to get the bag of lemongrass out of the fridge. She makes quick work of washing a section of it and then puts it in the pan.

Once the heat is up Isabel turns to face him, crossing her arms and legs as she leans back against the counter.

'Hurry up. I have things to do.'

For a moment he's quiet. 'What are you going to do about the pills?'

Isabel shifts in place. 'Look. Thank you for what you've done for me. But what happens from here on out isn't any of your business.'

'You came to me just last week and asked for my help.'

'Yeah, well. I think it's probably best if I deal with this myself.'

'And when they find you out?'

Isabel stills, then tilts her head and really looks at him. 'Is this you telling me you're planning on ratting me out, Michael?'

'No. I'm not going to do that.'

Isabel doesn't comment. She doesn't trust him. The only thing that she knows guarantees his silence on this is that if she goes down, he'll be going down with her. Failing to report her and supplying her with the S3 to begin with makes him complicit.

'I've been taking care of myself for this long.'

'With my help, yes.'

'Don't worry,' Isabel says, 'I'll manage.' Not that she has any idea how she's going to do that. One thing is certain though: even if it weren't for the revelation of what he's been doing with her sister, he can't help her any more.

The S3's effect on her is wearing off, which means soon it won't work at all and all of those voices will come rushing in. And that's where the real problem lies.

'Will you?'

'Is this what you came to talk about? Because if it is, then rest assured, I've got it handled. You can leave.'

Michael bites off a curse and steps back, turning his back on her. He rubs a hand down his face. Frustration pours off him and Isabel has to make a concentrated effort to keep her walls up and not hear whatever is going on in his head. She's relied on the S3 to help her keep her Gift tamped down for so long that when it wears off, she's struggling to adapt.

'No' – he blows out a breath and turns back round – 'it's not what I wanted to talk to you about. I wanted to apologise about how you found out. About me and Rita.'

Just hearing it makes Isabel wish she had the kettle back. Then she could break it again. On his face.

Michael comes further into the kitchen. Not a smart move. It's small enough as it is and if he comes any closer she might have to give in to the urge to knock him out.

She doesn't want him near her, doesn't want him in her space, period.

Michael leans a shoulder against the wall. 'We hadn't spoken in a long time. When you come over to the clinic we don't talk. There was never a right time. And Rita asked me to let her be the one to tell you but . . . it just never happened.'

'I know now, so it's all good.'

Michael sighs. 'Isa.' He looks at her. 'We were over, had been for a long time and we . . . I like your sister. I really like her and I respect her. It just . . . snowballed.' He stops, and she can hear him swallow. 'I'm sorry.'

'Right. Thanks.' She can hear the water start to bubble behind her.

He's staring at her. And the worst part? He looks sorry. He does.

He looks like standing there and saying these things to her is causing him pain. Because he's looking at her like he always did when they were together and something had gone wrong that couldn't be fixed.

I miss you.

His thought slips in and, God— Isabel sucks in a sharp breath as hot and cold rolls over her, the unexpectedness of the feelings wrapped around that thought leaving her winded.

And as Michael takes in her expression, he looks confused at first. But she sees the realisation start to dawn.

Isabel turns her back on him and opens the cupboard. She pulls out a mug. Just the one.

'You need to leave,' she says.

'Isa.' His voice is shaking. 'Isa.' His hands close on her shoulders and when she tries to shrug him off, he just tightens his grip and forces her to turn around. His eyes are wide when she meets them. 'Isa, you can – you heard me?'

Isabel shoves at his chest, hard. He stumbles back, still staring at her in that way. 'I said you need to go. And don't touch me. Don't put your fucking hands on me. Do it again and you're not going to like the way this goes.'

'You never—' He looks lost. 'You never told me you could – is it because of the pills? Because they're not working? Was this always—'

'Michael. I need you to listen to what I'm saying.' She enunci-
ates each word slowly. 'Get out. I don't want to talk to you about
my Gift. I don't want to talk to you about my sister. I don't want
to talk.'

His face closes off then and she can see him withdrawing. 'You
never did. Wasn't that part of the problem?'

'No. I talked. You just never listened. But it's fine. You've found
yourself another Reis who can give you what you want. You're
getting married, remember? And I don't think Rita or my mum
will be too impressed if they find out you've been by to visit.'

He flinches back. 'It's not like that.'

'You're right. It isn't. So it's best if you leave and don't come
back.'

Isabel waits for him to do as she's asked, can hear the water
boiling in the silence that follows.

Then quietly, he says, 'I'm not the only one still in this.'

And the fact that he can say that, and that she feels the hurt,
makes her want to snap something in two. So instead she looks
him dead in the eye. 'Yes, you are.'

She watches as his jaw tenses, skin going white around his
mouth. But then he's nodding and taking a step back.

'Listen,' he rubs his hand over his mouth, 'don't be stubborn. If
you need anything, you know. Just. Come by the clinic.' When he
looks at her again, his shoulders sag and sadness is etched into the
lines of his forehead and the downturn of his lips. 'I'll never turn
you away. You should know that.'

He leaves then, shutting the front door quietly behind him.

Isabel takes the water from the stove and turns it off. The smell
of lemongrass fills the small space. She hadn't even noticed.

She pours herself a mugful, brow puckered against the pain
radiating in her head.

She ignores the wetness of her eyes.

43

Despite the tiredness that had had Isabel itching to collapse the second she got home, she can't stay in the house after Michael leaves.

She gets out an old T-shirt and a pair of jogging bottoms instead. Her running trainers are like most of her other shoes, beat-up and soft. She tugs them on and pulls her hair up into a ponytail, though the majority of it escapes from the bottom. She zips up her jacket, leaves her phone behind and grabs her keys before making her way up the steep road, stretching her arms and legs as she goes.

When she gets to the top, her breath coming out in white puffs that fade in the air almost as soon as they materialise, she pops in her earbuds and puts on a playlist that is purely instrumental, a low-fi hip hop that never fails to relax her and keeps words out. She doesn't need more words.

She's sick of words and other people's emotions.

She wants her own slice of peace.

Isabel briefly stretches her calves, a lone figure at the top of the hill thrown into stark relief by the streetlight directly above her, and then starts jogging, her pace slow but steady. The warmth of the exercise slowly easing into her muscles until eventually it's throbbing in her cheeks, her chest, her forehead, her face flushed with it and her muscles protesting.

The cold night air keeps her alert though, crisp and unforgiving, as she settles into a rhythm. She sticks to the narrower roads, avoiding those filled with light and people, working her way along to the calm beat in her ears.

Every time her thoughts start to slip back to the conversation in her kitchen, to Michael's face and the way he'd looked at her, she pushes herself a little more, drags her mind away from it and into the aches in her calves and upper thighs instead, into the way her breath wheezes in and out of her lungs and leaves her throat feeling iced over from sucking in such cold air.

It's an hour later when she finally slows down, having come full circle to where the tram is parked at the bottom of the street.

She stands there for a moment, staring at the uphill climb back to her house, hands on her hips, head back and chest heaving as she tries to slow down her breaths. It takes her a few minutes before she's ready to start making the climb, pressing her hand into the wall along the way to steady herself.

Isabel glances at the empty tram as she passes. She can't help peering inside it every time now, just in case. But as usual, there's nothing but the darkened seats and the play of shadows from the streetlights.

She keeps climbing, her head down. The weight of the day is in her every step, but the soreness grounds her.

When she's close to the front of her building she looks up.

She stops.

Someone is standing in the exact same spot she had stopped to stretch just an hour ago. They're directly under the streetlight, the light washing away any discernible features.

They're standing very still, hands at their sides. Facing her.

Watching.

And all of a sudden, she's full of it – this full, desperate, volatile thing climbing up her stomach and into her lungs, turning her muscles rigid all over again. It's foreign, a billowing that latches onto her, forcing her to feel it.

'Hey!' she yells, and the adrenaline floods her.

They take off.

She's not thinking straight. She knows better than to throw herself into this situation. But she's going after them, pushing muscles that scream at her now to stop but she's not doing it. Because she recognises the weight of it. She'd felt it the other night

246

when she'd been staring into the dark of the tram, positive that something had been locked on her.

Frustration eats at her as she makes it to the top, panting at the climb and eyes seeking out the figure. Instead she hears it, hears running steps. The streets here are quiet enough that they echo. She takes off again, following the sound, and as she catches sight of them running, taking the zigzagging path that leads higher up the hill instead of her earlier route, she keeps going.

She shouldn't. The higher up she goes, the more deserted it'll become.

The sound of their breaths lingers in the night, like trailing crumbs for her to follow as the streetlights become scarcer.

Her lungs ache and frustration eats at her because she's done too much. She won't be able to keep up.

Isabel sets her jaw. Knows what she is about to do is useless even as she does it because the effects of the pill are still in place. She does it anyway. She pushes against the distance, throws her Gift against the barriers, feels the stretch of it, makes herself focus on the body growing smaller in her line of sight even as she pumps her legs faster. It's too much. Isabel pushes, focuses all her senses on that person, and it's like a part of herself thins even as it expands, going taut – trying to reach.

She has to know. She has to know who they are.

Panic. Not her own.

She sinks into the feeling, imagines herself dragging it towards her. She wraps it tight around herself even as she fights against the weight of the barriers imposed by the pill, tries to push them up and slip beneath them.

If she just pushes a bit more, she can do it.

Her breaths are hissing through her gritted teeth and her pace is slowing. She's going to lose them. When she's so close.

Come *on*, Isabel. Come *on*.

She gathers as much energy as she can and shoves through the barrier.

A scream rips through the dark.

White, searing pain cracks through her head and she stumbles, then hits the ground.

Another cry, weaker this time. Her knees and the palms of her hands are on fire, but she can't—

Her head is cracking open and she presses her hands to her temples like she can hold it together. It's hard to breathe. She can't see.

'I can't—' she gasps.

She can't.

Everything stops.

And then she feels nothing else.

44

Isabel feels a rhythmic pounding through her entire body.

There's a bright light being shone in her face. She flinches away from it and the drag of the blanket against her skin hurts.

The groan that leaves her feels like it comes all the way from her gut. She twists away from the light. The blanket wraps around her legs and the air is stolen right out of her lungs as the shift sets off throbbing all over her body.

It takes several seconds of lying on her back, hands shaking, taking quick and shallow breaths, for her to feel brave enough to open her eyes again. The pain is centred on her right side, but her knees, her hands, her face feel scraped raw.

There are people right outside her window speaking loudly and she grits her teeth. The throbbing of her head sharpens.

It takes longer than it should for it to dawn on her that the pounding is coming from her front door.

Cursing, she pushes herself up. Her throat feels dry. She tugs the blanket from around her and turns carefully to see where she is lying. On her duvet are little rust-red lines here and there, enough to let her know that she took some serious damage. Gingerly, she sets her feet on the floor, still in her trainers.

The person outside her house. The chase.

Her head breaking open and the blinding pain.

Another round of banging starts and someone is calling out her name. Not the people outside her window, though they still haven't shut up.

Hissing at the effort, Isabel stands. Her back curves under the weight of the aches. She presses her hand carefully to her ribs. Then presses harder.

When she opens the door, Voronov freezes, eyes all over her face.

It gives her a pretty good idea of how she must look.

'What happened to you?' He takes the rest of her in and before she can answer he's stepping inside and putting a hand on her shoulder. *Merda, did she get jumped? Does she need a hospital?*

Isabel flinches back but he doesn't let go.

'The Chief has been trying to call you since this morning.'

'Morning?' She winces. 'And why are you speaking like that?' she asks. 'And who the hell is that outside my house?' She presses her hands to her eyes and steps away from the door. 'Do me a favour and tell them to shut the fuck up or I'm going to murder someone, Voronov.'

Voronov stares at her. Then he turns and pulls the door closed behind him.

'Isabel, there's no one outside. What are you talking about?'

Confused, Isabel looks beyond him at the closed door. 'But . . .' She can still hear them.

She turns back in to her apartment to go and look at the window and she can hear Voronov talking to her, something off about his tone and just droning on until she can't take it any more.

She spins around. 'Jesus, stop talking and let me think!'

Except Voronov is standing in her hallway, still as anything, not talking. There's something wrong about his expression.

'What?' She steps away from him. Ironically, though her head is hurting, it's not the usual headache brought on by the S3. Instead it's radiating from what feels like a fair-sized bump on the side of her head, which she only dares brush her fingers over gently.

A glance at the clock in the living room shows that it's nearing noon. 'Wait, what did you say? The Chief?'

'I said,' he says, following her, 'the Chief's been trying to reach you since this morning. You didn't pick up. Jacinta tried to get hold of you too. I came over to check if you were okay.'

Isabel goes into the bathroom, flicking the light switch on and taking a good long look at herself in the cabinet mirror.

Shit. There's not enough foundation in the world to cover all of that up.

Scrapes mar the entire right side of her face from jawline to temple and the bruising is starting to show, a pale green-blue hue that will deepen as the day goes on. The skin under her eye is shiny and darker, the swell making it puffy.

Isabel swears under her breath and pulls the face towel from where it hangs by the sink, turning on the cold water tap and soaking it through.

Her hands are just as much of a mess and less than steady.

'Isabel,' Voronov says, and she notices how close he is then.

'What?' she bites out. She doesn't need him here. There's no way she wants to explain herself to him. Even if she did under-stand what had happened the night before.

'Isabel,' he says again, and this time reaches for her hand.

She yanks her arm back because she can't take touch right now – can't stand the idea of hearing his thoughts. Not when the pit of her stomach is mired in dread and she has the sinking feeling that she's crossed a line she can't uncross. Because Voronov is right.

There were no people outside her apartment. There was no one outside her window.

Those words hadn't been coming from anywhere but inside her head.

'Hey.' Again that edge to his voice. He grabs the towel from her. 'Don't be stupid. What do you think I'm going to do?' And it's the first time she's heard his tone slip like this, irritated and impa-tient. 'You're standing here looking like you got dragged by a car and your hands are shaking.' Except she can hear his thoughts spilling out like overflowing water.

Frustration builds up, her hands curling into fists as she turns her back on him.

Then after a moment she sits on the lip of the bath. Her fingers dig into the porcelain, eyes locked on the fluffy carpet.

She hears the tap switch on again but doesn't look up. The rush of water shuts off and she hears him wring out the towel.

His booted feet come into view and she presses her fingertips into the lip of the bath even harder.

'Come on, tilt your head up.'

Reluctantly, she does it. The normally fluffy towel feels like it's scraping over raw skin despite how gentle he's being.

'Are you going to tell me what happened?' he asks, moving it up to her temple.

'I was out for a jog last night. Slipped and fell.'

He gives her a look that tells her just how much he thinks that's bullshit, before turning back to the task at hand. 'All right.'

Isabel glances away.

'Your hands are in a bad way too. Stop clenching the bath like that before you make it worse,' he says.

She bites back the fuck you, barely. 'As you can see,' she says, 'I'm alive. You can go now.'

Voronov scoffs and shakes his head, expression grim. He uses the towel to tilt her head back a little further and presses it to her jawline. 'The Chief was trying to reach you to warn you. The whole team was contacted this morning.'

She pushes his hand away, careful to avoid touching skin. 'Why? Has something else happened?'

Voronov walks back to the sink and soaks the towel once more, then rinses it. He turns around and holds it out to her. 'For your hands.'

Isabel takes it. 'Well?'

'The press have our names, they were all over the precinct today.' He nods at her face. 'Good thing you didn't show up looking like that.'

'Fuck.' Isabel finishes wiping off her hands, ignoring the fresh sting it leaves behind, and throws the towel in the sink, the wet slap of it loud in the small space. 'How?' she asks.

'Don't know yet.'

Isabel stands, body stiff. 'I have to talk to the Chief.'

'I'd suggest you do that over the phone. And maybe take the day off.'

She shoots him a dirty look.

He lifts his hands in a gesture of peace and turns to leave the bathroom. 'I told you. The press is all over the precinct right now. And unless you're also planning to lie to Chief Bautista about what happened, then it might be a better idea for you to keep yourself inside for a day.' He glances pointedly at her scraped face. 'Or two. I'll see you later. Make sure you call in. Let me know when you're back.'

Isabel follows him as he heads to the door.

The voices are still there. Isabel keeps it from showing on her face and makes a concentrated effort to block them out. She needs to eat something and take a pill ASAP.

'Voronov.'

He pauses, already half out the door and glances back at her.

'Can you keep this to yourself? Please.'

He takes a good long look at her. 'I wasn't planning on saying anything to begin with.'

Maybe Isabel would feel a little bit shit about making an assumption, except she hurts all over. Except that she still doesn't know if she can trust him.

She just nods.

'Let me know if you need anything.' The door closes with a quiet snick behind him.

The voices still don't stop.

The heat of the bath is both soothing and a torture. Isabel sinks into it with a grimace, forearms trembling from the effort of lowering herself. Her knees, like the rest of her, are a mess and sting like crazy as they slip under the water.

Her conversation with the Chief had been brief and thankfully uncomplicated.

'You sound like shit and Voronov says you look it too. Stay inside, get better. I want you at a hundred per cent to deal with this circus. Take the day and check in with me tomorrow if you're still not good enough to come back. But Isabel?'

'Yes, Chief?'

'I mean it when I'm telling you to rest. But we can't afford to lose too much time with this.'

She'd thanked her and then spent a full five minutes with her head in her hands fighting down the panic trying to take her by the throat.

Isabel sinks into the water and breathes out, leaning her head back. She'd left the TV on, the murmur of an actual physical sound making her feel a little less crazy, and when she focuses on it, she finds it helps her ignore the other voices. The ones where no one is actually speaking to her.

It's all she can do to feel a little less freaked out until the pill kicks in. She'd knocked one back the second the door had shut behind Voronov but so far it's made no difference.

The steam has fogged up the mirrors and she can see the ceiling gleam with the damp. It'll be dripping in no time. It's why she usually keeps her showers short and sweet. The dehumidifier is old and switches itself on and off, so she's given up using it. It's tucked uselessly into a corner of the bathroom.

Isabel feels wrung out.

The person standing outside her place last night – they have been watching her now for some time. She'd been so close last night. So close.

She's going to have to report it.

She snorts at that and laughs quietly, sending ripples through the water.

And say what? That she took off running after them and smashed her face to pieces when her Gift snapped out of her control? She has no useful description, no proof, couldn't even tell if it was a man or a woman.

She'd pushed herself too hard. She'd had a long day and then having to deal with Michael on top of it all – Isabel's never pushed her Gift like that.

'Not a mistake I'm planning on making again any time soon,' she mutters.

She soaks for a while longer, until the water shifts from hot to warm and then to edging into something cooler. It sloshes off her when she stands, even though she does it carefully and wraps herself up in a towel.

The cold seeps in, leaving her skin a map of goose-pimpled flesh, and she finishes patting herself dry as quickly as she dares before slipping on the softest nightclothes she can find in her closet. The pyjama trousers are so old that the waistband has lost its elasticity and sags to her hips, and she tops it with a jumper just as worn and soft. She wraps herself up in a robe for good measure and pulls on woolly socks. She's always hated slippers. Even in winter, she hates the things.

As she's heating her tea, breaking news comes up on her TV – Bento Soares in front of his big house with its stunning backdrop, arm around his wife, both dressed in black.

'—do you feel about the progress the PJ is making into your son's case?' the reporter asks and points her mic in Bento's direction.

'The PJ has many hard-working individuals. At this time, we have no choice but to leave this in their hands. I have my doubts about the particular team that has been assigned to my son's case but have to trust that the PJ know their own people best.'

'Cabrão,' Isabel murmurs.

'I will be following the investigation very closely and I will ensure the PJ does its job diligently, so that my son and our family can get the justice we deserve.'

Isabel grits her teeth, staring at the unforgiving face of a man who hates her people and knows deep down that the Gifted community has no chance of making it out of this unscathed.

She knows *she* definitely won't.

45

With the press surrounding them the case comes under additional scrutiny.

Isabel is back to work the next day and ignores the stares that follow her as she heads straight for their case room. She doesn't even have the energy to deal with it.

There had been no sleep for her. It had been as if the voices of every individual in her building were being spoken directly into her ears throughout the night and she'd spent the night on the sofa, with the TV on, trying to block everything out. She'd eventually managed to doze off around 3 a.m.

The S3 had made no difference.

They start rechecking all evidence taken in since the beginning of the case, going through reports, phone logs, accounts, diaries, papers, anything that they can think of that might give them a break.

The scrapes on Isabel's face are still vivid; her knees are starting to scab over. Her wounds chafe against the denim of her jeans.

The team, already in the case room, all look up when she walks in.

Jacinta's mouth drops open and Carla's eyes widen. Daniel straightens and takes a step towards her before he catches himself.

Isabel waves their reactions away and eases herself out of her jacket. 'I'm fine. Hi.'

The tension lingers in the room.

'Fine,' Daniel mutters, 'looks like she kissed a wall with her face, and she says she's fine.' Before Isabel can open her mouth and tell him to shut it, he's heading towards the door. 'I'll get you a coffee.'

Isabel relaxes. 'Thanks. And can you close the door behind you? Still a little sensitive,' she lies, 'the less noise the better.'

Voronov catches her eye then but doesn't comment.

'I really am fine,' she says to the rest.

Another lie. She'd sat in her car for nearly forty minutes before coming inside, eyes closed and trying to centre herself. Bracing herself to enter the building and the bombardment of thoughts that would blanket her the second she stepped inside.

She can hear them all, like monologue upon monologue smudged in colours of emotion, and she has to cut through all of it and focus on one thing, one thing only. So that's what she'd done, hyper-focusing on the sound of her steps as she'd made her way through the precinct, giving people clipped nods as they'd greeted her but keeping her senses narrowed to that one thing.

And now, here, she does the same. The drag of the chair legs on the floor as she tugs it out, the hum of the electric heater, the thrum of an engine outside. Anything voiceless. She ignores the sweat gathering at the back of her neck and the small of her back.

She can do this.

'Update me,' she says, 'what have I missed?'

They don't immediately rush to fill her in and that's fine. But when the silence edges into too long, Isabel squares her shoulders and cuts a glare at them.

'Well?'

Carla shares a look with Jacinta, briefly catches her lip with her teeth, uncertain. Then she flips open one of the case folders and tugs out an A4 page with a picture printed on it in black and white. She slides it over to Isabel.

'The security footage from the internet café gave us this,' she says.

Isabel stares down at the image and it takes her longer than it should to actually absorb what she's looking at.

It's a decent image, clear enough. It's taken from the same side of the room as the counter, except from higher up. It catches a familiar face on their way out of the internet café.

That's Julio Soares.

'Julio is the one who accessed and wiped Gil's cloud?' Isabel glances up.

Carla's grim expression confirms it.

But Julio is dead now and they can't drag him in to find out what he was doing at an internet café, accessing Gil dos Santos' drive just a few hours after his colleague was killed.

Before they can say any more, Isabel's shaky control is blown to pieces as the room fills with an oppressive emotion that nails her to her seat. It comes down on her, heavy like tar, and she's not even aware of reaching out and grabbing the edge of the table to steady herself.

A few seconds later, one of the officers who mans the front of the precinct is rapping her knuckles on the case room door, her cheeks a blotchy red and mouth tense.

Voronov rises from his seat. 'What is it?'

'Bento Soares is outside and insisting on speaking to you. He's close to making a scene. I thought we might want to stop him before it gets to that point.'

Voronov takes in Isabel's face and she knows how she must look right now. She feels like what was left of the composure she managed to scrape together this morning has been stripped from her. 'I'll speak to him,' he says.

Isabel grits her teeth and pushes up to her feet as well. 'I'm coming,' she insists. She's already coated in his emotions, won't be able to peel them off her when they're this strong. Not until he's out of the fucking building.

You're barely fucking standing right now.

Isabel narrows her eyes on him. 'I'm *fine*.'

His jaw tightens and he gives a short nod, as if she needs his fucking permission.

'Put him in one of the interview rooms,' Voronov says, 'we'll be there soon.'

'Gotcha.' The officer leaves, walking quickly.

Voronov looks at Isabel. 'Want me to lead?' he asks, words sarcasm-heavy.

Isabel makes sure her back is ramrod straight as she walks to the door, ignoring Jacinta and Carla watching in silence. 'Yes.'

'All right,' he says, 'let's get this over with.' He waits until they're out of earshot of the case room, then steps closer to her, voice lowered. 'You're a stubborn arsehole. I don't know what's happening to you right now, but don't let him see it.'

'Goes without saying,' she grits out.

Bento Soares is pacing the room like a caged animal. Isabel feels it, that oppressive feeling doubling, a coiled rage that's tangled in grief and threatening to burst out of him.

His emotions are a dangerous combination right now and Isabel braces herself for the backlash.

Isabel has to force herself to slow her exhale, grounds herself with the shuffle of the noise of work outside. But not the voices.

Bento rounds on them as soon as they walk in. His handsome face is twisted in a snarl.

'At least you're here today. My son is dead and you're taking days off?' He's looking straight at Isabel as he says it.

So there's a snitch in the precinct. Great. Probably the person who had fed Bento Soares information was the same one who had leaked hers and Voronov's names to the press.

Voronov steps in, raising his hands in a calming motion. 'Mr Soares, I understand your frustration. We are following every lead we have at the moment trying to find the person responsible for this.'

'Oh? And when were you going to tell me that my son had been killed by one of them?' He cuts a look at Isabel, poison etched in every line of his face.

Isabel doesn't say a word, just stares back at him with as placid an expression as she can manage, nothing of what's happening inside her right then showing on her face.

'Mr Soares, I need you to calm down or we'll have to have you removed from the premises. The PJ is an inclusive organisation that respects all individuals and we won't tolerate that kind of rhetoric here.' Voronov's words are polite but there's no mistaking the underlying steel. He's standing taller and looking down on Soares.

'You're pathetic, that's what you are. Maybe instead of overdoing it as sympathisers, you might actually try doing your job. Because I can't see any of you rushing to find my son's murderer.' He glares at Isabel. 'Maybe I'm not the one letting prejudices get in the way.' He turns on his heel and walks to the door. 'If I don't receive any significant updates from you by the end of this week, I'm dragging both of you and the entire PJ through the mud.' He storms out, leaving a vacuum of silence in his wake. After a few seconds, the swell of rage dissipates too.

Isabel takes a couple of steps back until her back hits the wall. She rubs her face, aggravating the scratches there and not caring. The sharp sting helps her stay present in the room. 'Meu Deus.'

Voronov rolls his head on his neck and huffs out a breath.

Daniel pokes his head in through the open door, looks at both of them and then holds out a cup of coffee to Isabel.

'Thanks,' she murmurs.

'Think the whole precinct heard that,' Daniel says.

Voronov snorts but it's not an amused sound.

'It was going to happen eventually,' Isabel says, grimaces as she drinks. Everything else is rushing back in now that Bento Soares isn't engulfing everything in the building. How the hell is she going to handle this on a daily basis?

'Well,' Daniel says, 'while you were in here getting chewed out by that prick, university logs have come through.'

Isabel lowers her cup. 'The car park logs for the day Julio was killed?'

Daniel motions for them to follow.

The columns of data are being projected onto the board in the case room and Daniel quickly shuts the door behind them.

Isabel automatically eases back, eyes adjusting to the light. The logs are organised by date, times in and times out, names, length of stay and car registration numbers.

Isabel rubs her fingers over her eyes. She scans the names, skimming over all the unfamiliar ones and lighting on one that is very, very familiar.

'You see that, right?' she says to Voronov.

'I see it.'

Luisa Delgado.

46

Luisa had reluctantly agreed to come in the next morning.

Isabel wakes up the next day to another message from Rita on her phone, which she doesn't read, and to what feels like the thoughts of the entire neighbourhood drilling into her head.

She grabs the dog food she bought as an afterthought the previous afternoon and pours some out of the window, hoping she hasn't just doomed herself and the rest of the building to rodent visitors, then slowly starts to get ready.

The TV, which she kept on through the night again, keeps up a steady stream of noise as she forces herself to shower and dress. She skipped her run last night and wasn't going to make up for it this morning either. Her routine will have to undergo some changes as she tries to figure out what the hell to do.

The problem is that with Luisa's current level – a level 3 telekinetic – there is no way that she would be able to pack enough punch to control either Gil or Julio. Célia, on the other hand, was high enough on the Gifted ladder to be a possibility. Notwithstanding her solid alibis.

But then there's the journal. That journal hints at something bigger. It outlined a disagreement about a project that's clearly shady, and two of the people working on said project are dead, one of whom had clearly been trying to hide something – why else would Julio be sneaking around straight after Gil's death, going through his files?

At least they had eyes on Célia. After their briefing with the Chief the day of Julio's murder, Bautista had been quick to action that, agreeing that Célia might herself be in the firing line.

Whoever the mysterious Patient 2 is, they're flying under the radar. That person could be going around as a Regular, or a lower-level Gifted. Gil had been worried about their stability and according to Luisa's colleague, stable isn't really her middle name at the moment.

And the woman is everywhere. On the same train when Gil is killed, on his phone records, at the function and now on the car park logs the day Julio is murdered. In the journal, in entries dated a year ago, Julio alludes to the subject losing their Guide; which wouldn't mean much, except that it is around that time that Gil's visits to Mila Ferreira begin. And around that same time, Luisa's memory problems at work start.

Maybe Luisa isn't their murderer, but she's definitely a piece of the puzzle.

Their floor is quiet when Isabel arrives, murmuring a 'bom dia' to the officer on reception before heading to her desk.

Unsurprisingly, Voronov is already seated, jacket off and sleeves rolled up. He's got the journal open in front of him and a legal pad and a pencil in hand.

'Bom dia,' she says, dumping her stuff underneath her desk, 'are you ever not ridiculously early?'

'Just because my punctuality makes you feel threatened, Reis,' he says, and when he glances up at her there's an uptick of humour to his mouth. It's quickly gone. 'Feeling better?'

'A bit,' Isabel says.

She doesn't think about how a big chunk of her sleepless night was spent wondering if Voronov would go to Bautista about how he'd found Isabel that morning. About the pills.

He's not an idiot. He's seen enough to raise a concern with the Chief if he wanted to.

But he hasn't.

Yet.

She checks her watch. 'A few minutes before Luisa is due to arrive. What about the independent consultant?' They hadn't wanted to get Dr Alves involved at this point, not when it had become evident just how much this case would touch on Monitoring and pose a conflict of interest. The Chief had agreed to bring in an impartial Gifted specialist to witness the interview and provide some guidance after.

'Already here. She's grabbing a coffee and will be right back.'

'Oh. Good. You up for a trip after this?'

Voronov tilts his head in question.

'I want to go up to Mila Ferreira's house.'

'All right.'

They're notified then of Luisa Delgado's arrival. She is ready and waiting in the interview room.

Luisa tenses when they enter. She's in a soft, fluffy cardigan that swallows her up and her hair is pulled back from her face. The skin under her eyes has taken on that shiny green sheen that often comes with exhaustion and her shoulders are slumped.

'Luisa, thank you for coming.' Voronov reaches across the table to shake her hand.

'I don't really know what else I can help you with, Inspectors,' she says.

'We don't want to waste your time, Luisa, so let me tell you what we know,' Voronov says. 'At this point we know you're Gifted and a telekinetic. You were present on the train the morning of Gil dos Santos' death. Your car was also logged into the university car park the evening when Julio Soares was killed. You knew both of the victims and we know you were in contact with Gil before his death.' Voronov sighs. 'Talk to us.'

Luisa's eyes are wide and she's sitting so still that Isabel worries for a moment that she's stopped breathing.

'Luisa?' Voronov prompts. 'How do you explain all of this?'

Luisa swallows. She drops her gaze to her wringing hands. She clears her throat. 'I don't know.'

'That's not good enough,' Voronov says, still speaking gently.

Isabel inhales as subtly as possible. Luisa is a jumble of emotions, tangled so badly Isabel doesn't know which thread to tug on to unravel it all. It's not the pure punch that Isabel was subjected to in the same room as Bento Soares but it's no less intense.

'But I *don't know*! This is what I'm telling you.'

The confusion is real. Isabel can feel it lapping at her like a fog.

'I've been— for the past year—' Luisa stops herself, closes her eyes and takes a deep breath before continuing. Her voice is thicker, like she's holding in tears. 'I've been seeing a doctor. I have-have lapses in memory. Sometimes things are just a blur and I can't focus. They're doing,' she rubs at her temple, softly, her gaze going far away, 'they're doing tests.'

They wait for her to go on.

She swallows and then continues. 'I know I was at the train station. I remember driving there. I even remember parking the car, but then everything is a haze until my boyfriend picks me up. I told you before, I don't even remember calling him. I don't remember it.'

'What about the university?'

'Yes. I drove there. Professor Soares was giving a talk that evening, so I went with Gabriel and stayed for the talk, although to be honest I didn't understand all that much of it.'

'And then what?'

'We left.' She doesn't look either of them in the eye when she says it.

'Did you?'

She rubs at her temple. 'Yes. I remembered we chatted with Professor Soares after and then we left.'

'What time was this?'

'I don't know. I-I was tired. We went home.'

'Your home or his? Did he stay with you that night?'

'Mine. I had work the next day. And yes. He did. We haven't been spending much time together, so it was a chance for us to relax.' Luisa covers her face with her hand and Isabel watches as she tries to calm herself.

'Luisa, would you agree to a retesting?' Voronov asks. 'It would also be helpful if you agreed to release your phone records to us and, if you're okay with it, we'd like to speak to your doctor too. That would be a great help to us.'

Luisa drops her head into her hands and mumbles. 'Do what you like. I just want you to leave me alone.'

47

Isabel and Voronov make the two-hour drive to Coimbra, heading to the home Mila Ferreira had lived in until a year ago, when she was hospitalised.

The open road is like balm to Isabel's overcrowded head.

'At least she agreed to a retesting,' Voronov says.

'Hmm. A little too easily,' Isabel says. She's got her head pressed to the car window and it's blissfully cool against her throbbing temples. 'Doesn't bode well for us. Like the rest of this case.'

'We'll get there. I think Luisa is our key, here.'

'Yeah, I think so too. But what we need is for Célia to start talking to us.'

'You don't think she will?'

'Two of her colleagues are dead. Unless she's involved in their murder, she'd be stupid not to.'

'Maybe this road trip will be our lucky break.'

Isabel snorts. 'One can hope.'

Mila Ferreira's house is located in the Baixa and they have to park some way away from it.

The narrow street leading up to Mila's house is deserted. Some windows are open, but the blinds are down. Coimbra is well known for being a university city, and Isabel had expected more action.

'It's a bit quiet, isn't it?' she says as Voronov locks the car and checks his phone for the directions. When he starts walking, she falls into step with him.

'Time of day, maybe?'

It could be, seeing as it's nearing 3 p.m. And, despite it not really being a big thing any more, some people do still like to take their sesta. 'Maybe.'

The houses they pass are an odd mixture of those that are old and shabby, and others that shine with fresh coats of paint and gleaming doors. It takes them about ten minutes to find the correct place, passing only a handful of people on the way and ignoring the curious glances that follow them.

Mila Ferreira's house is one of the more polished-looking ones. Unsurprising, if she was on an NTI salary. Her door is a bright green that has yet to start flaking with age. The squat windows either side of it have gauzy white curtains that add a whimsical touch. Not what Isabel imagined after seeing the woman's severe face on the NTI webpage.

Isabel and Voronov look at each other. With a shrug, Isabel knocks on the door.

There's no noise from inside, not that they expected it. The report had said no next of kin, so this was always going to be a shot in the dark.

But just a few moments after they've knocked, the door of the house next to Mila's opens and a stocky man with a greying beard peers out at them from beneath his cap.

'Can I help you?' he says. His eyes are narrowed on them, not really bothering to hide his suspicion.

'Boa tarde,' Isabel points at Mila's door, 'are you Ms Ferreira's neighbour?'

He scowls at her, clearly unimpressed. 'Yes. I've been keeping an eye on the place while Ms Ferreira is . . . well. That's not important. What do you want?'

Huh. A little watchdog.

'We're with the police,' Isabel says and shows him her ID. 'We wanted to speak to someone who might know Ms Ferreira.'

'Oh.' The man falters. He looks at Voronov, who is waiting calmly at Isabel's side. 'Ms Ferreira doesn't have any family.'

'We're aware,' Isabel says and turns to face him properly, 'but you sound like you knew her well.'

'Well enough,' he says. 'I used to look after the place when she was away on business. Ever since the accident, I've been doing the same. My wife goes in once a week. She dusts the place a little, you know.' The initial defensiveness is gone and now concern filters through. 'Has something happened to Ms Ferreira? We hadn't heard anything in a while. The wife sometimes visits her in hospital, but she hasn't had the time lately.'

'No,' Isabel assures him, 'nothing like that. What's your name? Would you be able to let us in? So we can take a look?'

The man looks from Isabel to Voronov. 'I'm Joaquim. I can, but you're not allowed to go through her stuff. Can't let you do that without a warrant.' Smart man. Technically he doesn't have to let them in without the warrant either, but she's not about to point that out.

'We'd just like to take a look around,' she reassures him.

'Oh. All right. Well,' he blinks, looking lost for a moment, 'I'll just, uh, get the key.' Then he disappears back into his house.

Isabel looks at Voronov, amused despite herself. 'Looks like we've lucked out a little, hmm?'

Voronov just shakes his head at her and straightens again as Joaquim returns, brandishing the key.

'Wife was in cleaning two days ago,' he says. The door sticks a bit but then gives, leading the way into what is clearly an open-plan living and dining area.

Isabel stops just inside, feeling immediately uncomfortable.

The furniture has all been covered up under big white sheets, the TV screen is black and a small chandelier twinkles under the light spilling in through the front door.

'We covered everything up,' Joaquim says. He's got his cap in his hands and is twisting it to and fro as he talks. 'Didn't want it getting ruined. Covered everything upstairs as well. But we didn't touch anything else apart from that. We come in, sweep the floors and the kitchen area just to keep the dust off, air it out. Not much else to do.'

So maybe not much to find here after all.

'How well do you know Ms Ferreira?' Voronov says.

'Not much. She kept to herself most of the time but came around now and then when my wife invited her over to dinner. She spent most of her time in the city. She worked with those kinds of people. You know the ones.' He makes an expression like he's just bitten into something foul. 'Like the ones that caused that incident in Colombo.'

He clearly hadn't looked at Isabel's ID too closely then. 'You mean Gifted.'

That makes Joaquim look even more like he's sucked a lemon. 'I hate that term' – he waves it away – 'they should just call them what they are.'

'I see,' Isabel says calmly. 'Were you here when Ms Ferreira's incident happened?'

Joaquim seems happy to move on from his dislike for Gifted. 'No. I was away. I have a son in Serra da Estrela.'

'Right,' Isabel says.

'But it was my wife that found her. No one knows what happened. Wife said she was just lying down on the floor there,' he points at the empty spot just under the chandelier, 'says her eyes were wide open, staring up at nothing. Said it creeped her out because she was breathing and everything but it was like no one was there.'

'Is your wife around?' Voronov asks.

'She's helping out at the chapel today.'

'Did your wife say anything else about that day? Did she see anyone around?'

'Not that she said. She did say that she didn't feel comfortable being inside the house. She tried to wait with Ms Ferreira until the emergency services arrived but she said she couldn't do it. It took a month or so before she'd even come inside to help sort the place out, and even then I had to come in with her.'

'I see. Thank you, Joaquim, you've been very helpful,' Isabel says and both she and Voronov step back out of the house. She understands a bit of where Joaquim's wife was coming from. Being inside the house hadn't felt pleasant at all.

She sighs as they walk a little way away. 'Let's see who else might know something. And then I think we owe ourselves a treat.'

Voronov acquiesces easily enough, but Isabel doesn't miss the way he watches Joaquim locking up the house with distaste clear in his expression.

The Hospital de Santa Luz is about a half-hour drive from Célia's house. A building that has seen better days. It's a large facility though and, thankfully, they find their way to reception easily enough.

The person at the front desk is quick to inform them that visiting hours are now over, but picks up the phone to contact the department they need without fuss when Voronov shows her his badge. Isabel thinks to herself that the smile he gives the woman definitely goes a long way towards making her more agreeable. She's starting to think it's his superpower.

About twenty minutes later they're being led through the corridors by Mila Ferreira's doctor.

Isabel's nose tickles from the strong smell of antibacterial sanitiser. The floors are spotless and although the walls could use a lick of paint, it's a hub of clean and quiet efficiency.

For Isabel though it's a little more than that.

The hospital is a quieter place and walking through its corridors makes her feel as if she's wading into rapidly cooling water. The thoughts that butt up against her flimsy walls are feeble, nothing but faded, bruised yellows.

'This is Ms Ferreira's room,' the doctor says. They're at the end of a long and brightly lit hallway on the second floor and Mila's room is one of the last two.

Isabel looks around the open door and at the woman lying prone on the bed. She leaves Voronov speaking to the doctor and slips inside.

Hospital blankets always leave her wondering if the patients are warm enough. They look so flimsy. The room is bare of any cards or flowers. There isn't one personal thing in sight as she does a sweep of the room. It's sad.

She turns her attention to the woman on the bed instead.

The cropped grey hair that looked so sharp in Mila's professional headshot falls limply away from her face. Her face is gaunt and the lines even more pronounced. Although she's clearly unconscious, there's a tenseness to her face, like someone trapped in a bad dream.

Isabel stops at the edge of the bed.

For a second she's thrown back to her Jane Doe. Standing over her and wondering if she would be able to hear her.

Except Mila Ferreira isn't dead. In fact, she's doing everything except waking up.

Curious, Isabel lowers her walls. She doesn't plan on doing anything, just wants to see if there's anything, even the slightest whisper.

The noises around her fade away as she waits and listens, but not a word slips into the temporary silence in her head.

Then a stretch, like fingers stretching through rubber—

A hand lands on her shoulder. She jumps.

'Isabel?'

'Shit,' she hisses, pressing a hand to her chest and glaring up at Voronov.

He looks startled. 'Okay?'

'Yeah, yes,' she shrugs his hand away, 'fine. Sorry.' She glances back at Mila but she's lying as still as when Isabel walked into the room. The doctor has left but there's a nurse at the door who seems to be waiting for them. 'All done?' she asks.

Voronov looks at Mila and then back at Isabel and nods, turning to leave. 'Yes.'

Isabel falls into step with him. 'And?'

'The doctor says Gil dos Santos and a neighbour are the only ones who usually visit. No next of kin to speak of. Been looked at by multiple specialists and none of them have a clue. Brain function is fine, she's breathing on her own, no need for life support. They can't figure out why she's not coming out of it. There's no reason for her to still be under.'

272

Isabel runs her fingers through her hair. 'Great, just what we need. Something else that doesn't make sense.'

But as they leave she can't shake the feeling that there is something in that room, just beneath the surface.

48

They end up at Isabel's place. Isabel is carrying the boxes of pizza and Voronov has the bottles of wine.

Isabel flicks on the light as she walks in, toeing off her shoes and then nudging them out of the way of the door.

'Make yourself comfortable.'

'Thanks,' Voronov says behind her. She hears the door close but she's already ducking into the kitchen, turning those lights on too as she goes.

She opens up a window to let in some air. The light from inside spills out onto the dark slope her apartment looks over. The smell of oncoming rain fills the room and she breathes it in, letting it soothe her nerves. Having someone else inside her home helps her tune out all the other noise she doesn't want to hear. It's a pleasant surprise.

Setting the boxes of pizza on the counter, Isabel pulls out napkins and glasses, taking a bottle of water out of the fridge.

'No space in here,' she says to Voronov, who is unpacking the wine on the counter. 'You take the pizza into the living room; I'll bring the rest.'

When they are both settled on the floor of the living room, Isabel pours them each a glass and grabs herself a slice of pizza. The smell of onions, tomato and cheese makes her mouth water. She settles with her back to the wall and takes a bite, closing her eyes in pleasure at the first proper food she's had all day.

'You want the TV on?'

Voronov shakes his head. 'This is fine,' he says. He peels a slice off the cardboard box and Isabel focuses on the cheese stretching and stretching until it snaps loose.

They eat in silence for a while, the exhaustion of the last couple of days sweeping over them both. But it's not like it was the last time they shared a meal. There is no tension or defensiveness, just two tired colleagues grateful to be off their feet and out of the station for a small amount of time with pizza and alcohol at their fingertips.

Isabel takes a sip of her wine and once that first swallow has gone down, she tilts her head back against the wall, closing her eyes. The food settles warm in her stomach.

'I think Mila is the Guide Julio mentions in the journal,' she says. 'The timeline adds up.'

Voronov finishes his slice and reaches for his wine. He makes himself comfortable on the sofa. 'Could be.'

She drinks a little more. 'And Gil's visiting her, arguing with his colleagues over this project.' She thinks it over. 'That they've taken pains to keep under wraps.' She glances at Voronov. 'Do you think . . .' She rubs her thumb over the lip of her glass, chewing on the inside of her cheek.

'What?'

'Luisa. She doesn't fit into this any other way. What if Luisa is the subject?'

Voronov sets his glass down, considering. 'Yes, okay. That would explain some things – why Gil would've reached out to her. But the journal describes the subject as unstable and dangerous.'

'She could be dangerous. Isn't that what we're trying to prove?'

'Except she's been tested. She's a level three, her classification was actually assessed.'

'Right. Right.' Isabel's wine just about covers the bottom of the glass. She's surprised at how fast she's drunk it.

What Voronov is saying makes sense.

Except he's sitting next to someone who proves that the tests aren't foolproof.

'Should you be drinking?'

Isabel looks over at him. 'What?' She looks back at her glass of wine, which she was actually about to top up. 'I thought you wanted a drink?'

'I'm asking you if it'll clash with your pills.'

Isabel sets down her glass and hunches forward, rubbing a hand over her face with a groan. 'You're an arsehole,' she says, gives a bitter laugh. 'Is that why you came over here? Trying to catch me out?' Well, she thinks, guess what, they're useless to me now so good luck trying to catch me popping one.

He shrugs a shoulder, leans forward and tops up her glass. 'Not entirely. Though I was hoping you'd feel more comfortable talking here.' He sits back. 'I just need to know it's not something that you'd have to do time for. But if you want to tell me what they're for, I'm not going to say no.'

She stares at him with narrowed eyes, then smooths her features into something a bit more agreeable and nods, toasting him in thanks for topping her up. 'Sure, Voronov. If you tell me what really happened with your partner and why you've been branded an anti-Gifted arsehole.'

He smirks, though it doesn't hold any kind of mirth, not any more than her laugh did.

'Call me Aleks.'

49

The pizza and the wine help.

Isabel sits beneath the window, her back to the wall, radiator close by and a blanket over her legs. She's got one of the boxes of pizza open on her lap and her glass beside her. She's settled in for this.

Voronov is on the sofa, sitting cross-legged. It's the most casual she's seen him, with his shoes off and socked feet, top buttons of his charcoal-grey top undone. The colour does insane things for his eyes. Not that she'll ever tell him. He has his own box of pizza on his lap. She'd taken one look at the pineapple and judged him on the spot.

'So?' Isabel asks.

He gives her a look. 'I'm supposed to be going first?'

She shrugs. 'House rules. Come on. Don't leave me hanging here, *Aleks*.'

Voronov takes a bite of pizza, reeling in the stringy cheese and taking another gulp of beer before continuing. 'I'm surprised,' he says.

'About what?'

'I didn't expect you to be so calm about this.'

'What did you expect?' she asks.

He finishes off the slice and plucks a paper napkin from the stash that was included with the pizzas. He speaks like he's considering his words. 'You're guarded. All the time.' He meets her eyes. 'It makes sense. I thought having someone with my history as your backup wouldn't sit well with you.'

Isabel savours another slice. 'At first, it did. When I realised who you were. But the Chief wouldn't have put you with me if she'd thought you'd framed your partner.' The taste of cheese and tomato so perfectly put together blisses her out. 'I have to give you the benefit of the doubt. But I'm not going to pretend I didn't look you up. Because I did.'

He acknowledges that with a nod of his head. 'Fair enough.' He's silent for a moment and finishes the rest of his wine. Starts on another slice. The sound of the TV next door filters in, muffled by the wall. He gets up and she hears him filling a glass with water.

'The newspapers covered everything,' he says, sitting back down. 'I did rat him out.'

Isabel sets her slice down and pulls her knees to her chest, sets her chin on top of them.

Voronov downs the water and then plucks his wine glass back up. 'The rumours weren't wrong. Seles was good at what he did. Better than most. Which is probably why it rankled even more. We worked narcotics.'

He sighs and brushes his hair back from his face, eyes going unfocused. 'In recent years there's been a rise in a drug slipping into the black market, marketed as creating a "Gifted effect",' he says, giving her a telling look. 'I'm sure you can guess what it does. We'd been on it for about a year. Got close, but never found the source. They're smart about it. Operate mostly online, use the dark web; shut down storefronts and they pop up again the next day. It's hard to trace as is, even harder when they're constantly moving it around.' He scratches at his chin. 'We managed to find someone. Took us three months to find this guy. He was the one receiving and distributing. Gifted.'

'What happened?'

Voronov grins, sharp and mean. 'We nailed him. Had him eating out of the palm of our hands.'

Isabel blinks. 'You got him?'

'Yeah.' His smile fades away with that, taking on a bitter edge. 'But somewhere along the line Seles turned. We knew that just taking the distributor down wouldn't stop anything. It would slow things down for a while but eventually someone new would crop up somewhere. We knew it'd be more difficult to pin down the second time around.' He reaches for the bottle of wine and starts picking at the label with his thumbnail. 'Our leads started falling through, but it wasn't because we were given the wrong information. They were being warned ahead of time and clearing out before we got there.'

'Oh shit,' she says.

'It was Seles. I am – was – friends with his wife. We grew up together actually. She came to me for advice. Said the case was taking too much out of him. That not being able to spend all that much time at home was depressing him, that he was refusing to see a therapist about all the shit we were seeing.'

He shakes his head as if still disbelieving.

'It wasn't true.'

'Partially. He wasn't lying about the toll it was taking on him. But I was working the case with him. Sure, it was tough, but there was no reason for him not to be going home. As for the therapist' – he shrugs – 'we'd seen a lot worse. Not that we couldn't have done with a trip to the head doctor. But I couldn't fault him for that. It's not something any of us willingly do unless we're being pushed to do it by the boss.'

Isabel can't argue with that.

'I thought he was cheating on her.' He laughs. 'Which pissed me off. She's a sweet woman. It would've pissed me off even if she wasn't. It wouldn't be the first time someone cheated on their spouse.'

Yeah. Isabel's heard it all. The thing is, people don't realise how much gossip actually goes on in a police station. All the dirty secrets that aren't really secrets because someone always talks to someone, who talks to someone else. And the truth is they all spend more time at work than they do at home. People get carried away. Things happen. And then continue to happen.

'Did you talk to him about it?' she asks.

'No. I didn't think it was my place. But I kept an eye. And one night, curiosity got the better of me. He left early. Didn't go home though. Headed across the river, over to Alcochete. I still thought he was sleeping around at this point. Maybe paying someone for it, considering the area.'

'He wasn't.'

'He wasn't,' he confirms. 'He was being paid for information.'

'Fuck.'

'When you work in narcotics, you get to know a lot of names. How he got them to trust him, I don't know. But he did.'

'What did you do?'

'I let him keep doing it. Collected evidence.'

'And turned him in when you had enough.'

He shrugs.

'Did you ever try to talk him out of it?'

His expression hardens. 'No. He lied to me. He put our investigation in jeopardy. And the effect these drugs were having on the people taking them—' His mouth thins and he takes another drink. 'No. I wasn't going to reason with him.'

Isabel watches him as he goes back to peeling the label off the beer. 'How did the rumour start?'

'Others thought I should've tried a bit harder to bring him to his senses. That I shouldn't have gone straight to Internal Investigations.'

'Fuckers. That's bullshit.'

'Someone made a half-arsed comment about things going down differently if he had been a Regular.'

'I doubt it,' she says and she means it. She hasn't known Voronov for long but from what she's seen of him, she knows he's as fair as you can be in this kind of environment. If you've fucked up, it doesn't matter what someone is and what they're not. Voronov will go for them.

'No one likes a snitch,' he says.

'Fuck that. Hang on. I'm getting the other bottle.'

He lets out a loud laugh at that, one of those ones that come straight from the chest. It makes her a little pleased. Voronov's not humourless then, by any means.

When she comes back she sets the wine on the coffee table, picks up her blanket and her box of pizza, and sits down next to him on the sofa.

Then he looks at her, looks back at the bottle, then back at her again.

'Liquid courage?' he asks.

Under different circumstances, she might've done. But considering that he's seen her take pills and he's not an idiot, she lets it slide.

'Focus on eating your messed-up pineapple pizza, heathen.'

He smirks around his bite but doesn't say anything. 'So. What does it do?'

Isabel sighs and drops her head back onto the sofa. She swallows. Then turns to look at him.

She'd agreed to be honest. But though she appreciates and respects his sense of justice, she wonders if this will tip his moral compass. The last thing she needs is to be reported and suspended.

When she looks at him, she finds him staring down at her, face serious.

'I won't report you.'

She smiles a little. 'Hiding some telepathic powers, are we?'

'I doubt you're distributing whatever it is you're taking. And whatever it is you take, it doesn't look like it's because it gives you a high.'

Isabel stares at him. This is something she's never talked about. She keeps her cards close to her chest. Always. The only reason why Michael had found out at all is because he'd been able to supply her with what she needed, something safe that she didn't have to risk her career and health for by buying from a dealer on the street.

Sebastião knows, but that hadn't been by choice either.

'All right.' Isabel steels herself and prays that she's not about to make a mistake. But he's her partner and for once she wants to know that someone has her back, that they know what's going on with her. Wants not to have to pretend to be fine. Because although she loves her brother, she can't be honest with him about what the pill does to her. Oh, sure, he knows what it's for, what effect it has on her power. But he doesn't know what it costs her.

As for Michael, she hates that he even knows about it at all. That she's had to keep going to him for something she needs even after they parted ways. Especially knowing what she knows now about him and Rita.

'Around the time I was taking the exams for Inspector, there were these trials going on, for suppressors. They pre-emptively rolled out the S3 pills. They were meant to be over-the-counter, small things to help people control their Gift. I was going through some things at the time. Started having some issues with control.'

'You started taking them?'

She nods. 'Yeah. I was, what, about twenty-five at the time? Gift levels can fluctuate for a time but then settle. Sometimes they settle late. At the latest they settle by age nineteen, twenty at a push. There's no documented case of anything higher than that.' She looks at the pizza but her appetite is gone. 'I used it for about a month. Maybe a little more, until I was a bit more settled. Then it was recalled.'

'If it was recalled . . . doesn't that mean there's something wrong with it?'

She snorts. 'They weren't too concerned with that. They'd been heavily trialled. It was the government's wonder drug. It would lower Gift levels and the Regular public would feel safer. The drugs were being regulated, people were taking suppressors or being recommended they go on it, which meant a lot less power wielded by Gifted.'

'So . . .'

'The government took it back, but it wasn't made illegal or anything. That would've caused an uproar in the Gifted community. Made it seem like the government and the pharmaceutical company hadn't cared enough about Gifted lives and had put them at risk unnecessarily by rolling out a drug that shouldn't have been out. They were careful about how they framed their reasons for recall.'

'Why do you think they recalled them?'

Isabel looks at him. It feels like she has a tight hand squeezing around her throat. But she manages to work past it. Clears her throat.

'Because of Gifted like me. Remember the Colombo incident?'

'The girl?'

'Yes. She slipped through the cracks. Really badly. But not because of S3. Her situation was different; she was misclassified.' Isabel shakes her head, thinking about it. 'Still don't know how that happened but,' she shrugs, 'no system is fail-safe. In her case, it failed. Badly.'

'How does it relate to you?'

'Well, Aleks,' she turns to look at him, 'I wasn't misdiagnosed. But my Gift was going a little crazy because I was emotionally distraught for a while.'

Voronov's eyes narrow on her. 'Your classification is a level five.'

She smiles, the edges of it bittersweet. 'It was. When I tested. And I stayed that way for a long time. Then when that changed S3 helped me keep it that way. It dumbs down our Gift, so to speak. And what sucks for the government is that after taking it, it's untraceable on the system.'

Understanding dawns. 'So it could be used to cheat the system.'

'Bingo.'

'But they have the Monitoring system.'

Isabel laughs, grim. 'Yeah. They do. But the last time I checked there's no level nine or ten under Monitoring. The highest Monitoring covers is an eight.' She gives him a pointed look. 'Where do you think those level nines and tens go?'

Voronov glances away from her. 'How do you still have the pills?'

Isabel keeps watching him, trying to make out what he's thinking and not bothering to hide it either. What she's telling him

– she needs to know that he really meant what he said. And Voronov is a man of his word. Isabel believes this. But it's not every day she stakes so much on someone's word alone. She's not even sure why she's doing it now and with him.

'When I went off them . . .' She searches for the words.

How do you explain to someone who has never experienced it how much the strength of her own Gift scared her?

'It's like my awareness, what I was able to reach and hear, had expanded. At times, I couldn't even block it. I thought people would look at me and know. That I'd be hauled away to one of their therapy farms out in the countryside and no one would come looking for me.'

It had been Sebastião's face in her mind when she'd started panicking. The thought that she'd be taken away in the middle of the night and he would never even know what had really happened. He would just think she'd disappeared one day.

'You're so sure they would do that?'

She wets her lips. Just talking about it has her stomach turning. 'Yes. I know they would.' She forges on. 'I was seeing someone. A doctor. He helped me.' She shrugs a shoulder. 'Since then I've been getting them through him.'

'And the headaches?'

'It's the suppression. It's unnatural. The blockage causes the headaches. Except recently it escalated beyond what I can take,' she admits. 'I went to see Michael – my doctor – but I think . . . I've reached a point where S3 isn't an option for me any longer.

And it scares the shit out of her that she doesn't know how the hell she's going to cope without the safety barrier it provided.

'Isabel.'

'What?'

'What level are you now?'

Her heart leaps in her throat and when she looks at him, she knows she looks wobbly. 'I'm not sure I want to know.'

After a moment Voronov nods. He holds out his hand to her.

She looks from his hand up to his face.

'You said physical contact helps the connection.'

'Yes.' She doesn't have it in her to tell him that it doesn't seem to matter any more.

He doesn't say anything else but instead leaves his hand there.

After a small hesitation, Isabel takes his hand, nervous when it practically swallows hers.

But within seconds she knows what he's doing.

She would've heard it even without the touch, as long as she'd tried. But she wouldn't have felt the truth behind it.

This stays between us.

The voice is undeniably Voronov's. And the truth behind them is there plain as day, set in stone; she feels it without a doubt.

For a moment, Isabel thinks she might tear up. But then she sucks it up and just lets her head fall back in relief.

He's not going to tell anyone. He has her back.

She doesn't even notice that she doesn't let go of his hand, and he doesn't let go of hers.

50

Isabel's eyes hurt and her entire right side and shoulder throb with discomfort. It'd be nice to not wake up to pain at some point. The clock reads 4.31 a.m.

When she forces her eyes open past a squint, she finds that she's on her living room floor. By the feel of it, she hasn't even changed out of her clothes. Her teeth feel grainy when she runs her tongue over them and her mouth feels like it's been stuffed with cotton balls. She needs water. And a shower.

Groaning, she pushes herself up. The pizza boxes are scattered around the living room along with the empty wine bottles. On her sofa, feet sticking out over the edge because the man is just ridiculously tall, is Voronov. His head is tilted back against the armrest and he's sleeping.

Isabel groans again, hanging her head. A look out of the window shows her that it's still dark out, but the sky is lightening. Outside, she can hear the birds already awake.

They'd fallen asleep with all the windows open.

Isabel stands, meaning to shake Voronov awake and tell him to go and sleep on the bed, but then she hears the rustle outside. It's followed by a low whine.

She can feel the alcohol still swimming around in her system as she drags herself over to peer out of the window.

It's the two strays, cuddled together on the ground. Something isn't right though.

'Hey,' she says softly. A pair of eyes open in the dark and stare right up at her, ears twitching. He or she is curled around the other one, which doesn't so much as blink. Isabel frowns. 'What's wrong? Is something wrong with your little friend?'

Isabel squints to see if she can see what's wrong with them but she can't.

Maybe it's the alcohol. That's what she will blame it on later on that day. Right now, she's focused on what she needs to do right at this moment. She goes back into her bedroom and grabs the first two T-shirts she finds. Both come out of the laundry basket she hasn't looked at in a long time.

When she goes back into the living room Voronov is sitting up, frowning. His hair is sticking up at the back and there's a crease on his cheek from the imprint of the sofa cushions. There's a deeper shadow on his jaw from stubble that's grown in during the night.

'What are you doing?' he asks. He sounds stumped and watches, confused, as Isabel swings one leg over the windowsill.

'Get up,' she says. 'I'm probably going to need your help. And don't make too much noise. You'll scare them.'

He frowns. 'What?' He pushes himself up off the sofa and walks over to the window. He looks a lot steadier than she feels.

She's going to break her neck.

'Shut up. I'll be fine.'

Did I say that ou—

'Obviously, you're being loud as fuck,' she mutters, and swings her other leg over, T-shirts around her neck. The slope means that even though she's on the ground floor, there's still a decent gap between her feet and touch-down. Her arms tremble from the effort of lowering herself slowly. Dried grass crunches under her feet and the brindle dog tenses. The other one, the white one, just opens its eyes. In the dark they glow eerily, looking as if they're swallowing the light flooding out of Isabel's window. The one on top starts growling, a low rumble that makes her cautious.

'Come on,' she says, tone soothing. She crouches down and removes the T-shirts from around her neck. The dog curled in on itself isn't budging, so isn't much of a threat right now. The brindle with the floppy ear growls at her, clearly protecting the other one, and Isabel knows to take care. Dogs can be vicious when they're backed into a corner and she's not her steadiest right now.

287

This woman is crazy. 'Isabel, what the hell are you doing?'

'What does it look like I'm doing? One of them is hurt, okay?'

'I'll come down and—'

'No!' she hisses, daring to look up over her shoulder at him. The light from the kitchen is bright and throws him into darkness. She can't make out his expression. 'Just stay there, I'm going to have to hand them up to you and then I'll need help getting back in. So just shush and stay calm.' She takes a deep breath and turns back to the task at hand.

She approaches slowly. The growling intensifies and she holds the T-shirt low so the dog doesn't panic. The brindle doesn't move though.

'Shh, shh.' Isabel tries to stay relaxed as she reaches out her hand, T-shirt wrapped around her palm and wrist to protect it from any serious damage if this takes a nasty turn. She holds her hand out slowly and waits, patient. It takes a while. Her breath rattles in her lungs and she can hear the dry trees around her, naked twigs shifting in the sweeps of the wind raking the slope. The growling stops. A wet nose glances off the backs of her fingers as it sniffs her hand. 'Yes, you know me, don't you?' The other stays still, just watching blearily through slitted eyes, its white paw tucked under it.

Isabel pulls her hand back and, still whispering soothingly, wraps the T-shirt around it, making sure to cover the dog's muzzle in case it turns on her. It whines then, sharp and wounded, and she winces, feeling like an arsehole.

When she finally picks the dog up she grunts under its weight. It's an effort to hold it high enough that Voronov can pull it up but they manage. The second one is easier – it isn't as responsive, which is even more worrying. She gets that one up safely to Voronov too.

Isabel waits for Voronov to return to the window to help her up. She wipes a hand over her face and is surprised when it comes away damp with sweat. She sighs, blinking into the darkness. Her eyes sweep down the line of the slope to the road.

What the hell is she going to do with two dogs, she wonders.

There's a car parked close to the gate. It's not one of the neighbours'. Locals don't drive down or park on the main road because of the trams. Whoever's parked there will have to move it before the trams start up in a couple of hours.

The streetlight glances off the door when it moves and Isabel realises it's been open all this time. She stares, trying to see whether there's a person sitting on the seat, can just about make out their legs hanging outside the car. It looks like the person is twisting round to look at her apartment building.

Isabel takes a few steps down, Voronov and dogs forgotten.

There's a sense of dread wrapping around her. Something is familiar here.

The car. Isabel's seen this car before.

She freezes, hand pressed to the wall of the building, stands under its shadow. He shouldn't be able to see her.

'Isabel!'

She startles at the hiss of her name and turns back to see Voronov hanging out of the window, scanning the darkness for her.

'I'm here,' she calls out, voice soft, 'I'm coming.'

Voronov is waiting and helps her climb back in.

He's muttering under his breath. 'You're fucking crazy, the dogs could've attacked you,' he grunts as he drags her back up.

'Aleks.' She slumps down onto her ass, starting to shiver, her body chilled from being outside.

She looks up at Voronov.

'Gabriel Bernardo was watching my house.'

51

It's just a little after 9 a.m. and the vet's is mostly empty. Luckily, Isabel's problem isn't anything they can't handle. Floppy-ear is fine but the white dog has an ear infection they will have to treat with antibiotics. The thing that probably won't recover as easily is Isabel's wallet.

After she'd climbed back in the night before and they'd tucked the dogs into blankets, she and Voronov had gone out to check the road, but all that had greeted them had been the sounds of the city waking up, the tram bells ringing as people had started arriving, sleepy and huddled in their warm clothes, not quite ready for the day to start. There had been no sign of Gabriel Bernardo.

Voronov had left soon after, to freshen up before heading in.

Isabel's grateful for the soothing calm that fills the vet's. Despite the clinical smell, it still feels like a comforting space, so far removed from a place primarily inhabited by human minds.

Sebastião is still shaking his head in disbelief. 'Dogs. Not even one, but two.'

He'd already been up when she'd called him, too used to rising early even though this was his morning off. He'd met her at her house and driven her over here. Something Isabel had been grateful for, considering the wine from the night before had definitely made a dent in her already barely-there control. She had no faith in her ability to keep anything at bay this morning.

The bell above the vet's door jingles as the door opens to admit an elderly man with a cat carrier in one hand and a cane in the other. The young man at reception rushes around the counter with a warm greeting to help him. Apart from them, Isabel and Sebastião are the only ones in the waiting area.

'You look tired,' Sebastião says.

Isabel snorts. 'I feel tired.'

'Is it the investigation?'

Isabel shrugs. 'Among other things. But yes, the case.' She watches the receptionist coo at the cat in the carrier. The old man is chuckling and patting the young man's shoulder. He follows the receptionist into the back and Isabel and Sebastião are alone in the quiet again.

Sunlight streams through the shopfront, flooding the pale-green room and making the animal stickers ringing the reception counter gleam. There's a whole wall filled with shelves of expensive, vet-endorsed food brands, grooming products, health products. Isabel's going to stop at the pet shop and then at the supermarket instead.

'Is it bad?'

'It's complicated. And I have the feeling this one's going to leave a mark, Sebastião. It's just . . . taken a turn that I don't like, that's all.' She thinks of Bento Soares at the precinct, bursting with grief mingled with rage.

Sebastião is quiet for a moment. 'You're being careful, aren't you?'

'I am.'

'Dad was careful too.'

Isabel looks at Sebastião. 'Yeah.' She smiles. 'I've been missing him. I mean' – she shrugs – 'I always miss him but right now, I'm feeling it more.' What she wouldn't give for one of Dad's hugs right now.

Sebastião reaches out and pats her hand. Isabel breathes in sharply as she feels the brush of his thoughts. She inhales through her nose and breathes out through her mouth. Focuses on keeping her measly walls up. She needs to work on them. Too used to the S3 doing most of the work for her. She doesn't have that luxury now.

The speed with which her Gift had changed – she's terrified.

She hasn't felt like this since the day she'd sat in that chair, in the waiting room with those other kids, waiting for her dad to come out and tell her that her whole life was about to change.

'Have you still not spoken to Rita?'

'No.' Despite the whole thing, Isabel's starting to feel guilty about the number of unanswered calls and messages on her phone. Michael's visit hadn't made her feel any more like having that conversation, though. 'Have you?'

'She came around yesterday,' he sighs, 'she was down, really upset.'

It's hard to resist Rita when she's like that. It's like kicking a puppy and it always leaves Isabel feeling like utter shit. Even now, she can feel the pressure building to go and speak to her, to soothe, even though that really isn't Isabel's job in this scenario.

Sebastião squeezes her hand. 'It's a situation of her own making, Isa. And she needs to learn that actions have consequences.'

'Mum doesn't see it that way.'

'Tia Maria has her own issues that I hope she'll overcome some day. It still confuses me how she can be two so completely different people over something that shouldn't matter at all. I guess Dad just weathered it all so well that I could never understand why she couldn't do the same,' he says.

Isabel chooses not to think about that even though it never really goes away. 'She wasn't always like that,' she murmurs and it's easy to pluck from memory her mother's laughing face, so beautiful in its smile. The way that if they couldn't sit together on the bus when Isabel was young, she'd always look over at her, checking in. Her mum used to smile so much. 'But I suppose that's in the past. I don't have any expectations any more.'

'Liar,' Sebastião says, voice soft and sad. 'What about the headaches?'

Isabel sinks down on the seat, plants her booted feet flat on the floor. 'The pills aren't working any more so I've stopped taking them. No headaches but . . .' she chuckles, at a loss, 'sometimes one problem walks out and another one walks right in.'

'What do you mean? Are you okay? Do you need help?'

All of her wants to reject it, but the truth is she has no one else who can help her. It rubs her raw on the inside to know she's going to have to eat her own words.

'I'm going to ask Michael for help.'

Sebastião seals his lips together, but he doesn't tell her not to. Like her, he knows her options are limited. Isabel is walking a thin line as it is. It's either swallow her pride or suffer the consequences.

'I have no choice,' she says.

'I know.'

'I'm going to ask him to carry out a retesting' – she keeps her voice down, just in case – 'a real one. I need to know what I'm dealing with here, Sebastião, or I'm going to lose my mind. I have no idea how to even begin taking this on.'

'You did it before.'

'I had a Guide before. This time I'm on my own.'

'You're not on your own.' He bumps his shoulder against hers.

'Yeah. I know.' Isabel closes her eyes. 'I know.'

Sebastião comes back with her and helps her settle the dogs back in before leaving her, with a tight hug and a promise to check in on them for her later.

She should be rushing out of the house. They still need to figure out how Luisa fits into this whole thing and what role Célia Armindas has in this. Is she the perpetrator or the next victim?

But Isabel needs this. Just a moment where everything slows down, so she can gather herself. She makes sure to notify the Chief she's running a little late and takes her time. She gives the dogs a quick scratch behind the ears. She still has to name them.

Then she heads into the bathroom and takes a long shower so hot that when she finally steps back out, her skin is red. Steam billows out of the bathroom door when she opens it.

She squeezes at her hair with a towel one-handed and starts on the tea. All the while her phone sits on the counter, unavoidable. Isabel knows she's going to have to pick it up and make the call.

She's already told Sebastião. That was the part she'd been dreading the most.

No. That's a lie.

She doesn't want to ask for help. Especially not from him. But just like the headaches, the fear has settled in is eating at her. The escalation of her powers is too much. The S3 is now totally ineffective.

Isabel takes her tea and heads over to the sofa, still drying her hair. She sets the mug down on the floor and picks up the phone, feeling like her jaw has been screwed into place. She unlocks the screen and scrolls through her contacts and her thumb hovers over the name, just the idea of dialling sticking in her throat so badly that it feels as if there's a chunk of food there obstructing it.

Isabel takes a deep breath and presses it.

He picks up on the fourth ring and sounds out of breath. 'Isabel?'

'Michael,' she forces the words out, 'I need to ask for your help.'

52

Come afternoon, Isabel is outside HS Pharmaceuticals – Gabriel Bernardo's place of work – having given her name at reception and told them that she'd wait outside.

She'd stopped by the precinct to check in before coming here. Voronov hadn't looked happy at her coming on her own, but Isabel had a feeling this meeting would go better without him here.

HS Pharmaceuticals is housed in one of those super-modern buildings that are always a shock to the system in a city like Lisbon that is made up of so many old things. The windows have a blue sheen to them, and the building is huge enough that its shadow falls across those on the opposite side of the avenue.

The road outside splits around an island of gardens in the middle, lined with benches and punctuated by kiosks and huge flower beds. Isabel tucks her sunglasses over her eyes, the crystalline brightness a bit too much for her when her head is so sensitive.

She takes a seat on one of the benches, setting one paper cup of coffee down next to her, keeping the other in her hand as she draws her coat tighter around herself. The cup warms her palm through her glove. Gloves aren't usually her thing, not even when it's freezing, but she's been taking extra care, making sure there's something between her skin and others whenever possible.

She watches people going about their daily lives with a degree of trepidation, just waiting for their thoughts and emotions to touch her.

Isabel has had to return to the basics of when she'd first learned to control her powers. Half an hour to meditate, another half an hour to build her walls. She's been keeping as much distance as possible between herself and other people. It's not much of a barrier but it helps her feel better, helps her compose herself whenever it's not enough and she slips up and lets the thoughts flood in.

Would've been nice if this wasn't happening in the middle of a murder investigation.

She plucks the lid off her coffee and blows on it lightly.

Gabriel comes out through the rotating doors, tugging a jacket on. He has his hair up like before but this time he is wearing prescription glasses, which surprises her. He hasn't worn them in their previous meetings.

There's a hitch in his step when he spots her.

Isabel smiles, holding up the second coffee cup and waiting for him to cross the street.

He stops in front of her, sliding his hands into his pockets, still looking unsure.

'Inspector,' he says.

'Isabel,' she corrects, and holds the coffee out to him. 'Sorry, it's just plain black. Not sure what you take extra. I have some sugar in my pocket if you like?'

Gabriel looks at it like he's never seen coffee before. Then his eyes flick back to her face, apprehensive.

Isabel's smile turns wry. 'You don't drink coffee?'

Gabriel takes the cup. 'Thank you,' and then he takes a seat next to her.

'Sorry to come to your work like this.'

Steam peels into the air as he lifts the lid to take a sip. 'I can't stay out here long.' He won't meet her eyes.

'Gabriel,' she says, kindly, 'what were you doing outside my house?'

Gabriel stares down into his drink, a muscle working at his jaw. The dark circles under his eyes have got worse.

Isabel looks around them. 'There's no one here except for you and me. I haven't reported it. I haven't done anything like that.'

She twists in the seat, bringing a leg up onto it. 'I want you to talk to me.'

Gabriel says nothing, keeps his gaze locked on the cup of coffee.

'Gabriel.' She waits until he lifts his head and meets her gaze. 'Talk to me.'

'I'm sorry.'

'You don't have to be. Just be honest. Why were you there? Why did you run?'

'You need to be careful,' he says, voice low and soft, as if he is scared to speak the words into existence.

Isabel draws back, surprised. 'What?'

'I wanted to speak to you but then I panicked. I didn't want to be seen.' Gabriel turns to look at her. Despite the brightness of the day, his skin looks sallow, drained. 'What's it like?'

'What?'

'I've worked on the development of a lot of Gifted-level medicine. I know someone on suppressors when I see it.'

Isabel freezes.

'Debilitating headaches are part of it, you know. They can get so bad that people can't function. The higher the level the worse they are. Both times we met you kept wincing, when you thought someone wouldn't notice, and you always keep your distance, even from your partner, even at the function where it was packed with people. Like you were trying to erect a physical barrier. We saw it all through the trials. But suppressors have been discontinued.'

Isabel doesn't know how to react, shocked that this has come out of nowhere and after a handful of previous encounters.

'Luisa says you asked to look into her mind.' He glances down at her gloved hands. 'Do you do it through touch? Your level must be so high. Do you understand when someone's level is high, the danger they could be in? You know about that, right?'

Isabel recovers herself enough to reply. 'Not from personal experience, as you seem to think,' she says.

'It's why higher-level Gifted require monitoring. It starts to corrode parts of the brain, impacts the amygdala. Empathy and memory become affected. It can lead to a lack of emotion, which could be dangerous – less willingness to control oneself. It's why S3 was created to begin with, to keep things from reaching that stage.' Gabriel stops and drinks.

'Why are you telling me this?' She reaches for him but then realises what she's doing and stops herself. 'Do you know about what they were working on? Is that what this is about? We have two people who have had their lives taken. If you know something, you need to tell me.'

'The people you're looking into are very smart, Isabel. They know a lot about these things. You need to make sure you're watching your back because they have a lot of power.'

He gets up and walks to a nearby bin and throws the cup in there, still almost full. Stuffing his hands back in his pockets, he walks back over and stops in front of her.

'I really am sorry about yesterday. Please take care of yourself. I have to go back now.'

Isabel watches him cross the road and follow the slow spin of the revolving door back inside the building.

She can feel the frantic pulse of her heart at her throat. Her throat feels dry and there's a detached feeling of panic trying to claw its way through her chest, but she can't quite connect to it, as if she's not sure that she just sat through that conversation.

She stays on the bench, the cool sunlight on her face and the susurrus of the city in her ears, until her coffee is finished.

53

'You called for me?' Isabel asks, coming into the Chief's office.

The Chief looks up from the documents she has in hand. She doesn't have to say anything. Because the look on her face says it all.

'What's happened?'

The Chief pushes back from her desk and stands up, her movements stiff and aggressive, underlining the stamp of anger in her expression. Her hands are clasped behind her back as if she's keeping herself from doing some serious damage.

'Isabel, take a seat.'

Isabel blinks at her. She'd expected the Chief to throw a serious roadblock at her about the case, some kind of mistake or another piece of intel that has somehow slipped through the cracks.

'Just – for once in your life shut your mouth and take a seat. Voronov is on his way over, too. This concerns you both.'

At that, Isabel is thrown back into that moment, that one moment as a child when her life changed and she wasn't able to do a thing about it. Her body goes cold instantly and then flashes hot. She has to breathe in deeply through her nose to keep herself calm.

Chief knows. She knows about the pills.

Voronov.

'All right,' Isabel manages to force past clenched teeth. When she takes a seat, it's like all her bones hurt and she can't bend her joints. Neither of them say anything else.

Voronov's knock sounds in the room – yeah, she recognises his fucking knocks now, but even if she hadn't, his signature bleeds through the door. It's not just him. She's been slowly adjusting to the way things just come to her without her having to pull them to her.

'Get in here, Voronov.'

The door opens and closes. Isabel can't bring herself to look at him. She doesn't know what she'll do if she does.

'What's going on Chief?'

'Sit.'

Isabel hears the groan of the chair as he sits.

The Chief can't seem to shake the unwanted energy clinging to her because she doesn't sit herself; instead she starts pacing back and forth behind her desk.

'We've had a complaint made.'

Isabel looks up, unprepared for this.

Complaint. Not an allegation.

Isabel looks at Voronov and finds his eyes on her face. All of a sudden she feels guilty. His eyes narrow on her and she feels like he's seeing right through her. Isabel wonders if this is how people feel when *she* looks at them, this sensation of knowing that someone can read everything going on in your head.

'Irina dos Santos.'

Both Voronov and Isabel speak at the same time. 'What?'

Isabel scoots forward on her chair.

'Wait, wait, Irina dos Santos made a complaint? Against who?' Isabel asks.

The Chief finally sits down and when she looks at Isabel, Isabel feels her stomach drop.

'She's filed an official complaint against Inspector Isabel Reis.'

Isabel sits back in her chair and looks away, too angry to speak. Because if she's been called into the Chief's office for this then it means whatever dos Santos' wife complained about has stuck and Isabel is about to hear something from the Chief that she really, really isn't going to like.

'What could she have to complain about?' Voronov asks. 'I was with Isabel the whole time. She hasn't broken any protocol or done anything that can even—'

300

'Upon first contact, Inspector Reis failed to identify herself as a Gifted officer.'

Isabel freezes. She drops her face into her hands. Her mouth goes dry as dread spreads down her chest, heavy and sickly.

Voronov is silent for a moment and then swears under his breath.

'I don't even know what to say to you both.'

Isabel focuses, focuses hard on building her walls high because she can't be bombarded with anything right now. She really can't. She seals those walls tightly around herself and keeps breathing.

'This doesn't make sense,' Voronov says, 'that woman had no issues with us. We've been keeping her posted every step of the way.' He's slamming the side of his hand into his other palm as he's talking, anger so obvious that if Isabel wasn't dealing with her own temper, she would've been surprised at hearing him so blatantly emotional.

The Chief sighs and leans back in her chair, eyes turning up to the ceiling. 'No. She didn't. But Bento Soares does.'

Isabel closes her eyes. *Foda-se*.

'How?' Voronov bites out.

'His lawyer is the one who called and made the complaint on Mrs dos Santos' behalf. He's wanted Isabel off the case since this all started.'

And, Isabel thinks, he's found a way to do it in the most damaging way possible.

'But you can't—'

'Voronov. Believe you me; I understand. Especially when we have two dead bodies and nothing to show for it. I want to tell that bastard to fuck off as much as you do. But this crosses over into issues of consent. And we have to be hopeful that he doesn't convince her to take this further. Isabel.'

Isabel drops her hand and looks at her boss.

'I'm working on it. I want you on this case. I don't intend to let this arsehole dictate how we work here. But you're going to have to give me a little time. For now, I have to suspend you.'

Isabel shakes her head. Can't even open her mouth to speak right now. She's been stripped of her words.

She yanks her badge off and slaps it down on the desk before standing.

'Thanks, Chief.' There's nothing else she can say. The Chief's hands are tied.

'Isabel,' the Chief calls, stopping her before she can get through the door, 'take it easy for now. Go home and stay calm. I'll handle this.'

'Yes, Chief.'

She doesn't look at anyone as she picks up her shit and leaves.

54

THEN

Isabel is twelve the year her father dies.

Her dad's funeral happens on a sunny day. The sky is a stretch of clean blue and the sun is a weight of brightness. The winter cold is fierce and sinks into Isabel's bones like needles.

Sebastião stands beside her, his arm around her shoulders, steadying her, protecting her. Her mother and sister stand on his other side.

Isabel's eyes are fixed on the casket, on her dad's perfectly still form lying there. Every time she looks at his face, she feels like she's losing air. It's too peaceful.

He looks empty.

They'd told her he would look like he was sleeping, but her dad has never slept like this. His mouth was always a little open, little snores escaping his chest rising and falling. He wouldn't have lain there like this, in the cold, dressed in a suit.

Isabel has never seen him in a suit before. She doesn't like it. She doesn't think he'd like it either.

Her mum had gone with Tia Simone to pick it out.

Tia Simone had picked his tie, white and green diagonal stripes that matched the football team he'd been crazy about all of his life. Isabel likes that part of it.

Isabel thinks of the way her mother hasn't looked at her once yet. Sebastião had been the one to knock on Isabel's door that morning to wake her.

Sebastião had been crying the night before. She knew he'd cried again. His eyes are still red from it now. It's worse for Sebastião. Now he has no mum and no dad. Isabel holds him tighter.

But she thinks about how her mum leaves the room every time Isabel walks in. Maybe Sebastião isn't the only one without a mum and dad now.

Isabel's eyelashes feel heavy, sticking together, wet from her tears as she looks over at her sister and mum.

Rita stands there in her pea coat, hand tightly held by their mum, her large doe eyes made bigger as she stares at the coffin like she doesn't understand what it is. She's only nine. Maybe she doesn't understand what's happening like Isabel does. She tries not to, but Isabel feels envious in that moment, because she can see how tightly her mum is holding on to her sister.

'Isabel,' Sebastião says quietly. The priest's voice is strong and steady as he gives a final sermon. Sebastião turns Isabel so she's no longer looking at her mum and sister. 'Don't look, okay? Just stay here with me, okay?'

He blocks her vision and his face blurs in front of her.

'Okay,' Isabel chokes out and tears spill over her cheeks. She wipes her face on Sebastião's coat, the wool soft.

The worst of it all is that she can feel them.

All of these people and their emotions the colour of deep, dark wounds, forcing their way into her mind when she just wants to be alone.

In the middle of them all she can feel her mother the most. Her mother's presence used to be a glow of affection. It had made Isabel feel happy, safe, comforted. Now it doesn't give Isabel any of those things.

It's like an absence of self; so hollow and empty, as empty as her mum's expressions whenever she looks at her.

The same way she's been looking at Isabel since she went for testing at NTI and came back classified as a Gifted.

But her father had been there.

He'd been there, cupping Isabel's cheeks in his hands and pressing a kiss to her forehead, smiling at her, telling her it would be fine. She's just special. She's a Gift. That's why they call people like her Gifted, because they're a Gift.

But now he's left her.

Isabel's mouth feels sore from trying to bite back her sobs, her bottom lip trembling under the press of her teeth. She doesn't want her mum to hear. She doesn't want to make everything worse. She has to keep it in, trap it all in her chest where it sits heavy and choking, making it feel like she can't breathe.

Sebastião brushes his hand down her hair and murmurs that it'll be okay and he's there, and Isabel prays that he won't be taken away from her too.

Isabel can't hear what the priest is saying any more, stopped listening a long time ago. She pulls away from her brother. The cold is even worse now on her damp cheeks and she wipes at them with the sleeve of her coat.

Only when she's stopped sniffling and her eyes are smarting does she look at her mum and sister again, even though Sebastião has told her not to.

Isabel freezes, her breath trapping in her throat.

Her mum is looking right at her. The hate in those eyes is so visceral that Isabel would've stumbled back if it weren't for Sebastião's arm around her.

It's instinctive, is what Isabel will realise when she's older, the way her mind throws up a block. Self-protection. Because in that one moment, Isabel knows she doesn't want to feel a single thing that her mother is feeling right now.

Isabel doesn't want to know for certain what she's known since the moment her father brought her back from the NTI with her results in his hand.

55

Isabel has only been home an hour when her door buzzer goes off. She comes out of the bathroom still squeezing her hair with the towel. The dogs peer out from their new-found spot. She's surprised that neither of them bark.

Rain batters the windows and the sky outside is heavy with clouds, the grey muting any daylight trying to break through.

The buzzer goes again and she just sighs. The anger that had spurred her when she'd walked out of the station has left her and she feels like her strings have been cut, the strength sucked out of her marrow.

She leaves damp footprints on the floor as she walks over to the intercom. She's regretting not pulling her slippers out from wherever the dogs have hidden them. The borrowed heat from the shower is already disappearing.

'Yes?'

'It's me,' Voronov says, over the sound of rain pouring down outside.

She presses the buttons to unlock the gate and main door without replying and goes into her bedroom to put something on. She's finished dragging on an old jumper and trousers and is slipping a thick pair of socks onto her feet when she hears his knock.

The dogs do bark this time and it makes her smile a little. Even the little white one is showing a bit of spirit, which is good. Isabel's been keeping an eye on her like the vet had told her to and she'd been worried that she wasn't showing enough interest in her surroundings. Looks like that is changing.

Isabel opens the door, staring at the mess of water that Voronov leaves on the landing as he comes inside uninvited. She pulls the towel from her head to mop up the rain.

'What are you doing here? You should be down at the station,' she calls after him. 'Or do you think the case can afford to lose two of its main investigators?' She finishes mopping up and walks back inside.

Voronov is standing in her living room looking down at the two dogs sniffing at his feet as if he'd forgotten that they lived with her now. Clearly they remember him, because they're wagging their tails, entire bodies wriggling with it. He squats down and starts rubbing his hands over them, sending them into a frenzy of excitement. Isabel leaves him to it and goes to put the towel in the washing basket.

He's taken off his coat and shoes and is sitting on her sofa when she returns. His dark hair is wet and sticks to his face, dripping onto the floor as he continues to stroke the two dogs that don't want to leave him alone.

'You thought I'd told the Chief about you,' he says.

Isabel shifts awkwardly. 'Yeah.'

He jerks his chin down and she can't see his face. 'I told you I wouldn't do that.'

'I know.'

'So, you don't trust me.'

'I do. It's just in that moment . . . sorry. I didn't know what else it could be. All I knew was that it was something bad, and that was the only thing I could think of. And you're the only one I've told.'

'Right.'

'I'm— look. Sorry.' She pushes her hair back from her face. 'For the record, I'm not worrying about you going over my head every time I turn my back. I panicked and thought stupid things.' She throws her hands up in the air. 'Does it even matter right now?'

'Yes.' He looks up at her and she gets that feeling again, like they're cutting through flesh and bone to see into her core. 'It does matter. I told you I wouldn't do that, and I won't.' He heaves a sigh and turns his face away from her, then stands. 'I understand

307

where you're coming from though. So.' He walks over to where she's standing, and she tilts her head back to look up at him. He leans on the wall next to her, body facing hers. 'Are you okay?'

Isabel tightens her arms around herself, ducks her head. She can't quite meet his eyes like this.

'No,' she says, eyes fixed on the top button of his sweater. 'I'm pissed off, I'm tired, I'm frustrated. I'm sick of what I am being used against me. I'm tired of having to watch my back every time I open my mouth and someone decides to misinterpret what I say or accuse me of violating people's privacy.' She laughs. 'The irony is, a level five can't even do what Irina and Soares' lawyer are basically implying I did. I mean I could.' She glances up at him. 'I spoke to Michael.'

Isabel has her walls up, but the change is so strong that it bleeds through. Voronov had walked in here angry. A little angry with her, mostly angry at the situation. But now it's like everything frosts over.

Isabel licks her lips. 'I've asked him for a retesting. An actual one.'

He frowns. 'Is that a good idea?'

'I need to know what's going on up here.' She taps her head. 'I can't protect myself against what I don't understand and the S3 are useless to me now. Things that would've been held back by the pill and my training are bleeding through.' It scares the crap out of her.

He breathes out and that frost disappears. 'Jacinta's going to be filling in as case lead until you come back,' he murmurs.

'I know. She messaged me already,' she says. 'She's good at what she does.' She'll keep the case on track. 'You guys need to keep an eye on Célia. So far she's managed to keep to herself but we need her to start talking.'

The look he gives her is a curious one. 'I thought you'd be angrier.'

'You mean like you are?'

He turns his face away at that.

'I am angry. So angry I could choke on it. But,' she laughs then, 'I'm also tired as fuck. You know? I'm really tired right now, Aleks.'

'Okay.'

'You have to go back.'

'I know,' he murmurs. 'But a little longer won't hurt.'

56

Just looking at the house makes Isabel feel queasy.

She leans her head back on the headrest and forces herself to keep looking at it, reminds herself that she's not sixteen any more. She doesn't have to look over her shoulder as she closes the door behind her, the morning dew making her shiver as she squeezes her eyes shut and prays and prays for her mum not to wake up.

Even with that, it takes Isabel a while to convince herself to get out of the car and walk up the pathway to the house.

It's a beautiful home. It always was. It's a home that Isabel's dad worked hard for. It's all on one floor, sprawling out with its sloped roof and neat windows, neatly trimmed grass all along the front and plants in terracotta pots, still looking green and vibrant despite winter.

Isabel closes the gate behind her and walks to the door.

She'd spent the rest of yesterday licking her wounds and staring at her living room ceiling, trying to bury the helplessness threatening to paralyse her. So this morning she'd found some balls and decided to tackle a problem that she could still take care of.

Maybe it makes her a coward, but she'd called ahead to make sure her mum wouldn't be there. She doesn't want to see her. Doesn't want to see her mum ever again if she can help it. It doesn't matter that Sebastião thinks her mother will come around some day. It's no longer a question of her mother coming around. It's a case of Isabel knowing she'll never be able to forgive her mother for everything she's put Isabel through. For going as far as putting a dent in Isabel's relationship with Rita too.

The door opens and Rita stands there. She looks like she's just rolled out of bed, face soft with sleep and hair in a hasty bun that is slowly sagging to the side and threatening to fall out of the hairband.

'Hey,' Rita says and her voice is a bit croaky. She steps forward, giving Isabel a brief hug and kissing her on the cheeks. 'Sorry, I kind of lay back down and fell asleep again before I knew it.'

'You look tired,' Isabel says, steps in and closes the door. Her nerves spike as she does so. The sound of that door closing at her back makes her hands itch to yank it back open.

Meu Deus.

It even smells the same inside. Like lemongrass tea and wood polish.

'Isabel?'

Isabel jumps and looks at Rita, who is watching her with puckered eyebrows.

'Sorry, just got a bit distracted.'

'Okay. Want something to drink?'

'Sure,' Isabel says and follows her in through the house and into the kitchen.

It's warmer here and Isabel pulls off her scarf, forcing herself to sit down at the table and relax her muscles.

'Are you off today?' Rita asks. 'You want tea?'

'Yeah, thank you.' Isabel shrugs out of her coat. 'And no. I'm not off right now.' She braces herself. 'I've been suspended.'

Rita jerks round to look at her, mouth dropping open. 'You? For what?'

Isabel waves it away. 'It doesn't matter. Well. It matters, my Chief is dealing with it. I have to leave it in her hands for a while and hope that it gets resolved quickly.'

Rita hovers there, worry lining her features. She looks ridiculous standing there like that, a tuft of lemongrass in one hand and a pot filled with water in the other.

'You want to maybe put the lemongrass in the water and put it on the stove?' Isabel asks, amused.

'Oh. Right.' Rita quickly gets everything ready and then goes to grab a huge Tupperware box that's filled to the brim with familiar rounded biscuits that Isabel knows crumble on the tongue and taste like cinnamon. Her mum used to make them every Sunday, enough to last the week. They always had some for tea.

Isabel shakes her head when Rita offers her some. 'No thank you. I'm having to be more careful with the sugar intake,' she says, and at Rita's incredulous look she taps the side of her own head. 'I've been a bit more sensitive lately. Or should I say my Gift has been a little more sensitive lately. I'm trying to get it to calm down. It means I have to watch what I eat a bit.'

'Oh.' Rita seals the box back up and sets it on the table before tucking her hands between her knees. 'Um, Sebastião mentioned you get a lot of headaches.'

'I do,' Isabel says as Rita shifts in her seat, her discomfort obvious. It must be sinking in, how little Rita knows about her. And knowing her sister, Isabel can imagine the guilt. The problem with Rita is that she always feels the guilt; she knows when something she's doing is wrong. She'll feel bad about it. But there's a timer on it and it never runs for very long.

Rita's got a talent for burying things that upset her and not thinking about them again. That's partly their mother's education and partly growing up in a house where siding with Isabel meant their mother's bad temper would extend to her too.

'But it's getting a lot better. Anyway, sorry to just come by out of the blue. I know you probably have things to do, but, well, I had a couple of things I wanted to say.'

Rita's eyes flick up to Isabel's face, wary.

'I'm not going to lie to you and tell you that what you've done is okay. No matter what Mum says.'

Rita drops her gaze to the table and reaches out to run her thumb along the Tupperware's seal, rubbing it back and forth. She doesn't say anything.

'Look,' Isabel blows out a breath and shrugs, 'shit happens. I get that sometimes . . . things are messy and that's just the way it is.'

Isabel thinks about Michael in her apartment, eyes on her like he might never see her again and the words he'd thought burning into her mind like a brand. But it isn't her place to say any of that, especially when Isabel still isn't sure what her own feelings are on the subject.

'You're marrying him. You love him, right?'

At that Rita glares at her. 'I'm not an idiot, Isabel, of course I do.'

'Hey, that's not what I meant. But I just thought, if you're going to go out with my ex-boyfriend for a year behind my back, then it should be for something more, something special, I guess. That's all.'

Rita's flinches at the ex-boyfriend label. 'I didn't mean for it to happen.'

'I believe you. I don't think you deliberately set out to fall for Michael. Like I said. Shit happens.'

Rita sighs. 'I'm sorry, Isabel.'

'Yeah. Well, it is what it is, right?' Isabel forces a smile. 'I think . . . you should do what you want. If you really want to marry him then I wish you all the best. I really do. I hope you make each other happy.'

Rita opens her mouth, at a loss for words. But then she shuts it again. 'Will you come to our wedding?'

Isabel chokes out a laugh in disbelief. 'Rita. Are you seriously still asking me that?'

'You're my sister.'

'I know. And I'm sorry but I can't do that. You have to understand where I'm coming from here.'

'But you're telling me to be with him!'

'I'm not telling you to do anything. I'm saying you should do what you want. And I'm saying you don't have to feel any guilt towards me for doing it. But I still won't be coming to your wedding. And, if I'm honest,' she leans forward and peers into her sister's face, 'I don't think it's fair of you to ask that of me. If you think about it, really think about it, you know I'm right.'

313

Rita stays silent.

'You'll have Mum there. Sebastião has already agreed to give you away. It'll still be a ceremony filled with people who care about you. But this is as much as I can give here. I can't do more than this. Just. Be happy.'

Rita turns away and Isabel hears the sniffle she tries to muffle with her hand. She doesn't turn to look at Isabel as she gets up to go to the boiling water and composes herself. She keeps her back to Isabel as she wipes at her face.

'You still want tea?' Rita asks. Her voice wobbles but doesn't break.

Isabel watches her sister, feeling drained and sad.

'Yeah. I can still have some tea.'

57

It doesn't take long for Isabel to decide she's not going to stay at home doing nothing. She has faith that the Chief will resolve everything. It doesn't matter who has the audacity to come after the woman, the Chief doesn't take things lying down and she never lets people meddle with her team.

As she leaves the building with the two dogs trailing after her, she feels displaced.

Not in a bad way. It's a test for herself.

Nerves beat through her as she prepares. Slowly lowering her walls.

If there's ever a time to do it, it's right now, when the streets aren't packed with people and just the thought of their every worry and problem finding their way into her head is almost enough to convince her that this is one of the stupidest things she's ever done.

Isabel can't remember the last time she left her house in no hurry and with nothing more demanding to do than this. The dogs trail obediently at her side, which surprises her; she thought they would have been tugging her left, right and centre and she'd been braced for a disaster happening as soon as they stepped outside the gate. Images of them taking off after a cat and her rolling down the steep street might have crossed her mind a time or two.

Sebastião had laughed at her when she'd told him what she'd named them, apparently shocked by her lack of imagination. She'd named the brindle Tigre and the little white dog Branca. It worked and they didn't care.

It's stupidly early. Just after seven in the morning and the people awake right now, walking under the pink morning sky, are wrapped up tight and yawning their way through their commute to work. But the kiosks are open and so are the local cafés tucked away from the main streets that will fill with tourists in a couple of hours' time.

People's thoughts as they walk by her manifest in her mind with a crisp clarity that leaves Isabel stunned. The only thing that keeps her moving is the dogs surging forward to sniff the next street corner. Isabel follows them, keeping enough attention on her surroundings that she doesn't barge into someone, but mostly she just focuses on leaving herself open and listening.

Maybe it's because it's the first few hours of the working day, but people's minds are mellow; as their words form in her mind, they bring with them colours that reflect their sentiment. Soft yellows as they think about what they have to get done today, or as they remember that they've agreed to meet someone after work – that one is tinged with pink towards the end – or as they think about what they'll have to pick up for dinner on their way home.

Had she ever noticed that people's thoughts had colours too? That their voices were dipped in them just like emotions?

Isabel's throat tightens and she keeps making her way, letting herself swim in and out of the voices around her, even while the world remains silent to her ears.

It's so unobtrusive. The thoughts aren't forcing their way in; they're just there, in the space between her and others. She's not pushing her way into anyone's mind, doesn't have to forge any paths. All she's doing is listening.

Isabel makes her way to the river, taking the long route through snaking streets and hidden courtyards. Lisbon is a maze of them.

The river is quiet at this time too. They'd remodelled it a few years back so that there are now wide, yawning steps that span the length of the riverbank all the way to the Terreiro do Paço terminal, where the boats that ferry people across come and go at all hours.

She grabs a coffee from a nearby café. It's a small space with just enough room for stock and for someone to move around a few steps. There's a see-through glass box on the counter displaying a few cakes, but Isabel can smell the sweet scent of roasted chestnuts a little further down the river bank.

'Bom dia,' she says, 'small coffee please.'

Five minutes later Isabel is sitting on one of the higher steps of the river, dog leads and coffee resting next to her and chestnuts on her lap. The dogs are two steps down from her, playing in the water as it laps over the steps, chasing the waves and barking excitedly when a wave comes too close.

Isabel pats her pockets absently to make sure she has the treats in there. It's one way to make sure they come back. Dogs that have had to scrounge for scraps for most of their lives will have a hard time running away when there's an open bag of treats waiting for them right there.

The river is soothing.

Her breath billows in the cool air.

It starts to sink in, then. How much she's closed herself off from her Gift. She doesn't even know the extent of what she can do. She has this thing that she's been born with and she's spent years suppressing it, scared to let it show because so much of her life depends on it.

But what had that got her? Years of physical pain. Years of failed relationships with family, friends and lovers. She's been burying a part of herself, thinking that if she can control it then she won't end up like other Gifted. She won't be taken away somewhere in the middle of the night and never be seen by her family again.

Tigre runs up to her, setting his wet paws on Isabel's lap and panting in her face, trying to lick her.

Isabel laughs and pushes him away. 'Stop!' she says. 'Look what you're doing.' Branca chases after her friend and then she has two dogs on her lap. 'All right, all right. Let's keep walking.'

By the time they get home it's lunchtime. Isabel lets them back in the house and goes to see what she has in the fridge that she can throw together. The dogs sniff around before settling down in their preferred spot, Tigre curling around Branca and licking her a couple of times.

After making herself a quick something, Isabel sits down and props open her laptop.

Fuck Bento Soares if he thinks he's going to be keeping her down at all.

After two hours of scouring through everything they've got, Isabel has the scans of Gil's diary up on the screen and is flicking through them, looking for anything that could've led up to Gil's visit to the hospital. Why visit someone comatose, repeatedly? He wasn't a friend, nor was he family. Was the fact that he'd been going up there a significant factor in his murder?

Isabel is still looking at the scans when her phone starts ringing.

'Hey,' she says.

'Hi,' Voronov says. 'Thought I should check in.'

'Yeah? You realise that you have no obligation to keep me posted while I'm suspended? In fact,' Isabel leans back in her chair, checking on her two new housemates and finding them snoring on top of one another, 'I think updating me might get you in trouble.'

'If they find out.'

'Wow, rule-breaker.' She smirks. 'Any progress?'

'No. We've been keeping tabs on Célia but there's been no unusual activity around her. The Chief's been pulled in by the higher-ups wanting to know the status of the case.'

'Soares?'

'Yeah. He's not letting up.'

The fact that he's a bigoted arsehole aside, the man has just lost his son. Isabel isn't surprised that he's using every tool at his disposal to see some results.

'I'm looking back through Gil's diary,' she admits, 'trying to see if there's anything we've missed.' The pointed silence on the other end of the line makes her smirk. 'What? You thought I was

318

going to sit here and do nothing? Have you got to know me at all during the time you've been here?'

'Enough.'

'Yeah, yeah,' she says, knows her smile is coming through even over the phone.

'Listen, if you're going to keep working the case,' he lowers his voice, 'be careful. The Chief is working on getting you back in, so best thing to do is to stay under the radar.'

'I know. You don't have to tell me that.'

He sighs. 'I'll call later.'

'Okay. Bye.'

She puts the phone back down, pushing the conversation to the back of her mind because that's something to think about later on. Voronov is right. She's going to have to tread carefully.

But she's not letting this go.

58

Isabel has taken breaks and paced her apartment and sat back down so many times that she's lost count. In the end she relocates to the sofa.

At some point her neighbour arrives home and decides that playing music as loud as possible is how she wants to spend the rest of her day. It triggers a small headache but not anything compared to what Isabel is used to dealing with.

She's on the verge of getting up to give her eyes a rest for the umpteenth time when she spots something.

The documents that had been found on Gil, commenting on a study pertaining to trials.

She'd read through them a couple of times already and, without context, they had seemed irrelevant as she hadn't known what study Gil had been commenting on.

But as she's scrolling down now, she sees it nestled in a bit of text. It says:

the proposed goal has its origins based on E5 trials.

Isabel pulls the laptop closer and frowns down at it. She rereads the entire paragraph but E5 isn't mentioned again. Not in that paragraph and not in the rest of the notes. What's E5?

She logs on to the system – risky if someone decides to check that she's being a good little Inspector and staying away from the case. My case, she thinks, and continues on anyway, going straight for the evidence folder.

Looking through what had come up on Gil's laptop, she finds no mentions of E5 anywhere, but she knows she's seen the term somewhere. She closes the investigation logs and switches over to a search engine instead.

She gets a bunch of links to mobile phone makes and systems, a city church in England and a university. Apparently, it's also a postcode. She kisses her teeth and goes back to the search box. She types in 'E5+Gifted'.

Some more phone deal links; Gifted care plans; recruitment—

It comes up as part of a forum discussion. When Isabel clicks on it, it takes her to the thread but tells her, in white letters on a purple background, that she won't be able to view the thread unless she's signed in.

'Seriously?' she mutters. 'This better not be fucking porn.'

It takes a few minutes and she has to make them send a confirmation link email to her twice, but eventually she's in.

Mostly it's conspiracy theory bullshit about the government creating drugs to enslave Gifted, or about islands that Gifted are shipped off to never to be heard from again – Isabel thinks that one may have merit – but then E5 is brought up as an example on a thread about the government attempting to weaponise Gifted. Something about it acting as an enhancer that they'd trialled for.

Isabel stares at the screen for a moment.

Something like this would've been all over the news. So, either it's utter bullshit, which is highly likely given everything else that's on this forum, or the trials didn't succeed, and it never got rolled out.

How to—

She jumps up and runs to her bag, upending it onto her bed and sifting through the contents until she comes up with the card for Dr Nazaré Alves.

Dr Alves gets up and waves from her seat when she spots Isabel at the door to the bar.

Isabel takes off her coat, folding it over her arm as she makes her way to the last booth where Dr Alves is tucked into the corner, a bottle of what looks like cider in front of her.

'Hi again,' Isabel says, 'thank you for coming today.'

'Not at all. It's my day off so a drink is nice.'

'Day off?' Isabel scoots into the booth and when she manages to catch the bartender's eye, she points to Dr Alves' drink and holds up a finger, getting a nod in return.

Dr Alves smiles. 'You did say it wasn't about work.'

'I believe what I said was that it's unofficially about work.'

Dr Alves laughs. 'Same thing. So, what is that you need to know so badly that you're risking getting in trouble by coming to see me?'

The bartender sets a sweating bottle of cider in front of Isabel. She thanks him before taking a swig. 'I know what happened with the S3 roll-out,' she starts and sees Dr Alves wince. 'What?'

'Nothing. It's just that was a disaster.'

'Tell me about it. Those were heavily pushed by Monitoring, weren't they? The study and trials?'

Dr Alves nods. 'Yeah. It still is in cases where a Gifted's powers are difficult to control or spiralling. But usually this is for individuals who are already being monitored.'

Just hearing that sends a lick of unease down Isabel's spine. 'Was there ever an ongoing study or trials into the development of a drug called E5?'

Dr Alves frowns. 'E5?' She takes another drink, leaning forward. 'Yes. I mean, that was a long time ago and I don't know much about it, but I think one of the big three pharmaceutical companies was pushing it, trying to get the government to back it.'

'But they didn't?'

'No, there were concerns about the implications of the government being involved with that type of trial. I don't know all that much about it, but they were worried about the nature of it and possible damage.'

'Concerns that it might be a play to weaponise Gifted?'

Dr Alves inclines her head in assent. 'Something like that. But I think there were other factors.'

'And E5 was actually an enhancer?'

'Yes. As far as I know that was its purpose. It was like a counter-part to S3. At one point the government was looking at the possi-bility of funding further research into the differences in stability within Gifted levels. There's a rising belief that perhaps the middle-level Gifted have stronger mental and emotional stability. S3 and trials for other drugs such as E5 could play into that.'

Isabel sinks back into her seat. Mulling all of this over.

'Does this affect your investigation?'

Isabel smiles. 'Can't comment at this point. Besides, unofficial, remember?'

'Right.'

'Dr Alves, you said it was one of the big three pushing this. Which ones?'

'Sorry, I meant the big three that deal in medicine specifically aimed at Gifted individuals.'

'Right. And which one of those was trialling E5?'

'HS Pharmaceuticals. They had some big-name buyers that were very invested in the outcome of that trial; I heard it caused them problems after the trials weren't backed by the government. Had it been a regular pharmaceutical company, I think they would've been fine. Private investors would have stepped in. But because medicine surrounding Gifted is such a charged issue, the government was able to put a stop to it. To my knowledge they haven't attempted anything like it again. Which isn't to say that other companies won't. Someone will get to it eventually. It just won't be in this country any time soon.'

Isabel tilts her head and thinks it over. 'This might be pushing it a bit, but you wouldn't happen to know who was involved in those trials, would you?'

'No. I know that NTI was involved at some point; they were part of the team being asked to supervise the trials. As for HS Pharma, they had their newest talent involved.'

Anticipation skitters over her skin.

'And who was that?'

'Gabriel Bernardo.'

59

'Gabriel Bernardo was in charge of trials being conducted by HS Pharmaceuticals to produce enhancers,' Isabel says.

She thinks back to their conversation outside his workplace. Had he been trying to tell her then?

Jacinta stops in the process of taking off her coat. She looks between Isabel and Voronov. Voronov is by the door, stooping down to play with the dogs.

'What?' Jacinta says.

'I was going through Gil's notes.' Voronov sets the bag of takeaway on the counter and Isabel starts taking down plates. 'I know we combed through the whole thing and it didn't seem relevant. But I found something. He referred to E5.'

As they plate up, she fills them in on the rest.

When she's done, they're both quiet. She sets her plate aside. 'Look, I know this is still a vague connection, but it could lead to something. We need to follow this up.'

Voronov shares a look with Jacinta.

'Daniel kept digging after the Chief called you in,' Jacinta says, 'and we were able to get a warrant for the Registry to show us Luisa's actual test results. Given that Patient 2 was an identity that Gil, Armindas and Julio were keeping under wraps, we were looking for the actual paperwork; the assessments, the scores, everything that would've been completed before it was added to the system.'

'What did they find? Did they make a mistake with Luisa's classification?' Isabel asks. Because if a mistake had been made then they had a near-solved case on their hands.

'No. They don't have any of those records.'

Isabel stares. 'What do you mean they don't have the records?'

Voronov finishes the food on his plate, shaking his head as he chews his last bite. 'There's nothing. None of the files are in the Registry, they can't find them. They're not there.'

Isabel shoves up to her feet. 'Wait. Wait. So where are the files? Who the hell was responsible for the files?'

'That's the other thing,' Jacinta says, and she looks grim. 'The year logged for Luisa's testing is the same year that both Célia Armindas and Gil dos Santos began working at NTI. At the time they were overseeing individual tests.'

Isabel remembers the smiling Dr Carvalho who had taken her through each test, always there, always watching and recording. 'Do we at least know who administered the tests? At least one person would have had to have been in charge, would've actually gone through the results with the parents.'

'Nothing. All we have as proof that they were even there to do the test are the log dates. The Registry doesn't have anything else.'

'This is insane,' Isabel says, 'what does Armindas have to say?'

'Nothing,' Jacinta says, 'she's been putting her PA to good use and dodging us.'

'Don't we have a watch on her? We need to corner her. She's kept her mouth shut from day one. Threaten her with obstruction.'

Jacinta says, 'I've got Carla hounding her. We're thinking of going down there next. What we really need in that room with her, though, is you.'

Isabel looks up. She has to tread carefully here. 'There are two problems with that. First problem, I'm suspended. Second problem, we'd still have to get her consent. She'd have to let me actually look in her mind.'

Not true. Being in the same room would be enough. Just as in this room she can sense Voronov and Jacinta's thoughts. She can't hear them clearly, but only because she's actively working not to.

But she can't tell Jacinta that.

'Even if she does consent, none of it will be admissible if it's taken from someone who is suspended. And then the Chief will have all our asses. I can't afford to be reckless here, none of us can.'

Jacinta sighs.

Isabel paces over to the window, beyond frustrated. 'There has to be something to make Armindas talk.' Something that doesn't require her to be there personally, or at least that won't mean she has to use her Gift.

Something occurs to her. 'Soares is making a lot of noise about this. He's gone as far as getting me suspended.' She turns to look at them. 'How does his son's death fit into all of this?' She understands that Gil and Armindas were working on something shady, something that looks as if it dates back to their start at NTI. But what about Julio?

Voronov folds his arms. 'Actually, we have found a connection there too.'

'You have?'

Voronov nods. 'When we tried to check who oversaw Luisa's tests we also looked at everyone who was working at NTI at the time.'

She frowns. 'Julio would've been too young—'

Voronov shakes his head. 'He was an intern.' He smiles a little then.

Isabel remembers about the higher levels. 'If Luisa is the unknown subject at the centre of all this, those memory lapses she's been having could be related. All three of them – Gil, Julio and Célia – were involved with testing the unknown subject. And two of them are dead. Célia Armindas is in the thick of this.'

Luisa's memory lapses also coincided with Mila Ferreira's admission to the hospital. Mila Ferreira worked directly for NTI. They could have assigned her to whomever they wanted and she may be the only outsider who knows what really happened with Patient 2. Except that she's currently unconscious.

So, Patient 2 loses their Guide. Gil gets cold feet. Célia and Julio turn on him? And then Julio follows shortly after.

She shakes her head, disbelieving. They have every piece. Now they just need to connect up the puzzle. 'We need to figure out what happened during Luisa's test.'

If Julio's notes were to be trusted, someone with dual abilities. God, the press would have a field day with this. They had a new monster on their hands.

She looks at Jacinta and Voronov. 'Célia Armindas needs to talk.'

'So our next move is?'

'I don't know.'

Except that's not entirely true.

There's someone else who may be able to shed some light on this situation.

Isabel finishes her coffee. She doesn't share that thought with Voronov and Jacinta though.

They'll need plausible deniability.

60

After Jacinta leaves for the night, Voronov lingers.

It's chucking it down hard enough that as they stand just inside the door to Isabel's building, visibility isn't great.

She rubs at her arms, trying to warm the skin.

'We'll pick it back up first thing, speak to the Chief too,' Voronov says. He's got his hands tucked into the pockets of his jeans and is staring out at the rain bouncing off the ground.

'Okay. Let me know if anything comes up,' Isabel says, 'I doubt there'll be much I can do until the Chief sorts this out but I want to stay in the loop.'

'Of course.' He's watching her carefully and she hopes all he sees on her face is weariness. 'You're okay, though?'

'Yeah. I'm good.' She pats him on the shoulder and nods her chin at the downpour. 'You better run.'

Voronov gives the rain a dubious look and nods. He hikes his jacket up over his head and jogs to the gate. Isabel stands at the door and watches him, his shape made hazy by the rain as he heads up the hill to where he's parked at the fork of the road.

It's not until she sees him drive off that she ducks back inside and then starts to get ready.

She wants to make a move before she loses her nerve.

At this time, the hospital ward's sounds consist only of beeps, quiet scratches of pen on paper and the sound of the nurses' steps. If Isabel listens hard enough, she can hear a TV from behind a door too.

She isn't experiencing the same quiet now as on her first visit here, though. Instead, they match the restlessness of the rain outside, like a living beat under the physical noises that fill the building. Agonised pleas and prayers, soft words that are looped on repeat. Isabel wipes a hand hard across her face, like she can brush them away the same way as she does the raindrops.

Isabel's wet boots squeak on the floor as she approaches the nurse at the front desk. After a token protest about visiting hours and her flashing her ID, she signs in.

She pushes her hair back. The strands that escaped from beneath her hood in her dash from the car are wet and stick to her cheeks. The nurse at the front desk hadn't looked too impressed.

Isabel pauses by the door.

The room is squeaky clean, and the bed looks recently changed. The machine at Mila's side continues to beep, the rhythm steady and healthy. Everything functioning just the same. Apart from whatever is happening in her head.

She looks smaller than last time, or perhaps it's the darkness outside and the blankets drawn higher up to her shoulders that make her seem so.

Isabel stops behind the visitor's chair that's positioned near Mila's bed.

She takes off her coat, winces when she realises how badly she's dripped all over the floor. She pushes her sleeves up above her elbows and scoops her hair back, wiping a hand down her face to get rid of the little drops of rainwater.

The door to the room remains open – she doesn't want to draw any suspicion. It's bad enough that she's here. But the clock is ticking, she doesn't know how long until the next patients' round is made and she doesn't want to be questioned about her presence here. This is the missing piece. This is it.

Isabel perches on the edge of the chair, scrubs her hands repeatedly over her jeans. Her fingertips feel like ice points.

'You're really going to do this, Isabel?' she mutters under her breath. 'You're really going to do this?'

She stands as abruptly as she sat down and steps close to the bed.

Glancing back at the door, she strains to listen out for footsteps. But even if someone does walk by, they shouldn't notice anything out of the ordinary.

Isabel's fingers are trembling when she reaches for Mila's hand. She curses under her breath, rubs her hand against her jeans again and closes her eyes, head tipping back as she breathes in through her nose and out through her mouth. She calms the pulse she can feel echoing through her, as if her blood is making the veins swell and push against her skin all over.

When she tries again, her hand is steady.

Mila's skin is warm when Isabel touches it. Isabel's every muscle is stiff, ready to beat back any unwanted thoughts and emotions even though that's exactly why she's here.

'Come on, don't be stupid Isabel. You've done this before. Just do it. Just do it.'

She closes her eyes again and drops the feeble wards barely keeping things out of her mind.

And it's—

Goosebumps roll out over her skin and it's like sinking into an abyss.

Everything around her mutes and there is no sound, like she's wrapped herself in a black curtain of silence and can't see beyond it. She's never felt anything like it and for a moment, she doesn't know where to go from here.

'Mila,' she says, 'can you hear me?'

Nothing. There's nothing here but Isabel standing alone, sightless and desperately sending her presence out to seek Mila's.

This quietness is so unnatural.

This is a waste of time. Maybe this is why she hasn't woken up. Maybe there's nothing left of Mila Ferreira. Just a shell.

Except Isabel is sure she'd felt something the last time she was in this room.

'Mila.' She tries to sink deeper into the darkness, to see if something appears, anything that'll indicate what—

Isabel blinks and brings up a hand to block against the sudden brightness. When she finally drops it there is someone in the darkness with her.

Her back is to Isabel, her feet bare, thin hospital gown hanging off thin shoulders and lank grey hair curling at the tips where it stops just under the nape. The woman stands utterly still.

Isabel is unnerved and almost withdraws from Mila's mind completely, catches the reflex just in time to keep herself tethered.

'So, you are here,' Isabel breathes.

No response.

'I'm sorry,' Isabel says, 'to come here without your permission.' She takes a few steps, wary of the dark that remains around them. 'There are some bad things happening. On the surface. Mila – I think the person you were a Guide to, Luisa, is the reason behind these things. And I need to know if you're here because of her. Can you help me?'

Nothing.

'I think we can help each other.' Isabel moves closer, feels the black around them pressing in and wonders what exactly this is, how deep she's gone into Mila's consciousness.

In between one blink and the next Isabel finds herself an inch away from Mila and she has to control the urge to recreate the distance that had been there before. They're so close that each one of Isabel's exhalations disturbs the lank strands of Mila's hair.

She forges on, ignores the unsteadiness of her own voice. 'NTI are hiding whatever your involvement was in their tests. Célia Armindas isn't talking. Gil dos Santos and Julio Soares are dead. We know you're involved somehow but not how. Help me. Help me so we can figure this out. What happened to you, Mila?'

And then Isabel is on her back. The room she's in is familiar and unfamiliar all at once. The chandelier blinds her, sunlight reflecting off the crystals and making it hard to focus on the face peering down into hers. Isabel can't move. Her arms are pinned to her sides and it's as if a giant paperweight is on her, keeping her from rising back up.

That weight keeping her down is sinking her deep, dragging her away from the room around her. Isabel struggles to see around the blur of Mila's eyes, knows that this is Mila's memory that is being shared with her.

A face resolves itself in front of her eyes but only for a moment.

Green eyes under thick black eyebrows, and a snarling mouth that Isabel is all too used to seeing curved in a polite smile.

The black swallows up that face and Isabel is alone.

Fingers dig into the curves of her shoulders and the world whirls around her. She throws a hand out, clutching at anything that she can as she can't make sense of up or down. She flinches with her whole body, expecting the ground to rush up to meet her.

'Isabel, come on.'

She recognises the voice that accompanies the words spoken into her ear with a warm whisper of air, and reaches up to clutch at the steadying hands.

'Isabel, you're bleeding. Merda.' That's followed by more swearing that Isabel doesn't understand. Voronov has switched from Portuguese to Russian.

She flinches again when something soft presses to her nose. It takes her a moment to realise it's a tissue and she raises a shaky hand to hold it in place. She can feel blood now, dripping from her nose, warm and thick, onto her upper lip and chin.

'What did you do?' he's muttering. 'She's a vegetable—'

'Aleks? How did you— no, she's not,' Isabel says and her voice sounds choked and nasal from the blood clogging up her nose. There's a fine tremble taking over her whole body and she lets Voronov lead her from the room. Around her the sounds change and she thinks that maybe they're back out in the hallway.

Voronov gently nudges her until her back is resting against a wall. The warmth radiating from him tells her that he is staying close. Isabel sags against it. Her head feels so slow, like it's been pressured from all sides and then suddenly released. Her sight changes, going from a dark tunnel to spots that echo within spots. She feels herself slip and locks her knees at the same time as she reaches out to steady herself, her grip weak as she latches onto some part of Voronov.

'What did you do?' He sounds strained.

The spots fade and with it, Voronov's clavicle comes into focus. He's standing in front of her but he's looking over his shoulder, back at Mila's room.

There's a streak of red on Voronov's T-shirt. The palm of her hand is covered in red too; it glistens on her skin. Her stomach turns and she turns away from him as her throat tightens, the underside of her tongue shrivelling. She struggles only for a few seconds before she breaks, bending at the waist, the acidic bitter taste of sick coating her whole mouth.

A gentle hand pulls her hair back from her face and another rubs circles into her lower back.

'Isabel. Come on. I'm going to call—'

'Stop.' She's still got her hand fisted in his T-shirt and now she squeezes tight to keep him from going anywhere. She swallows and wishes she hadn't. 'I'm fine. I just-I've never . . .' She looks down at the sick on the floor and quickly looks away again. 'Have to get this cleaned up.'

Despite her stomach still feeling unsteady, she's going to need food as soon as possible. Whatever she did has drained her dry.

'I need something—'

Voronov hauls her up. 'Food. I know. Let's go.'

'I know who it is. I saw him.'

'How.' The word is bitten out and Isabel side-eyes him. But she doesn't have the energy to do more than that, not right now. She's depleted and reeling from her own actions. Her hands are trembling but she's doing her best to ignore it.

'I managed to look into her mind.'

'She couldn't consent.'

Isabel closes her eyes. 'I know. It's why I didn't tell either you or Jacinta. Didn't want to involve either of you. You followed me?'

'Isabel—' He cuts himself off and Isabel keeps her eyes closed. Doesn't want to see the expression on his face. Doesn't want to see if she's just lost a friend. She has precious few of those. But now's not the time for that. She has to focus.

'We can talk about this later. We have to figure out where to go from here.'

'It's not Luisa. It's Gabriel. Gabriel Bernardo. It was all him.'

61

The next day, Isabel is back at the station. She'd walked the dogs quickly first thing that morning before rushing over. The fewer people saw her walking into the precinct, the better, especially with the press poking around.

The night before, they'd called Jacinta. She'd had to skirt the particulars and Jacinta isn't stupid, knew that Isabel was holding something back but didn't push. She'd agreed to have the team comb over all the information anew, searching for any connection to Gabriel Bernardo.

She follows Voronov and Carla over to where a laptop is connected to the smartboard, a calendar displayed on it.

'Soares' laptop turned up something interesting.'

To anyone else, Voronov probably looks the same, but Isabel can see the line of tension that had been there all throughout their trip back from the hospital the previous night.

Isabel takes a seat and sniffs. She'd woken up with a telltale scratch in the back of her throat. Not what she needs now at all. Voronov pulls out the chair next to her and sits too.

'Okay, after I confirmed the day of Gabriel's testing, I was able to find out who was in charge of it. Like with Luisa's results, there are no records of his tests either, only his testing date. Julio had appointment schedules filed under Monitoring, but for an unnamed subject. There are no records for this, nothing has been logged and everything is classified. The appointments start two months after Gabriel's retesting. The retesting itself was a regular routine one.' Carla stands in front of the smartboard and taps something on the laptop and the screen in front of them changes.

'Okay,' Isabel says.

'But we took the appointment dates listed and cross-referenced with Gil's and Célia's calendars. The same days were booked out for them. It's been going on for eleven years with one meeting every month. This is the only project that does *not* have accessible documentation. Everything is under lock and key. The subject's name is redacted from any records that do exist and the results are buried under so many encryptions that it would take someone with serious skill to be able to break them open. The only living person who I believe can now access the results is Célia Armindas. Here's the thing. Two weeks before dos Santos' death, there was an entire week of closed sessions with the unnamed subject.'

Isabel turns to Voronov. 'What do you think?' she asks.

Voronov sighs and shrugs. 'Our problem is still Célia not talking, although with this, I think she might now. And we'll need to confirm Gabriel's whereabouts during those appointments.'

The appointments might go too far back to alibi, but if they can at least prove that he could've been present for a good number of them, that might be enough.

Isabel could easily get them the information they need but they've agreed that giving Gabriel any hint of the extent of her powers could be disastrous.

He's been playing with them. Coming into the station, being outside her house. The touching concern for her safety. Luisa's role in this whole thing had been nothing but a smokescreen, orchestrated by Gabriel.

No. They need to be able to manage him as much as possible.

If he's really the person that Armindas, Julio and Gil had been working on, there's no telling what his level may be. And if he's really the one responsible for Julio and Gil's deaths, then he's already proven that he's capable of violence.

There are no friendly offers of beverages from Célia Armindas this time. She strides to her desk, sits down and shuffles a couple of papers before tossing them back on the desk. She rocks back on her expensive chair, fingers tapping at the armrest with nervous energy. She watches them through narrowed eyes.

'Inspectors, I've told you already that I don't have anything else to say that could be of help to you. With the recent tragedies that have taken place and how both Dr dos Santos and Professor Soares worked very closely on this centre's projects, I'm sure you can appreciate that everything is very chaotic here at the moment. I don't have time to be asked the same questions twice over.'

Isabel speared her with a look. 'Maybe if you'd answered the questions truthfully the first time around, we wouldn't have to be here repeating them.'

Célia snaps her mouth shut.

'I think it's in your best interest to tell us everything you know about Gabriel Bernardo and his dealings with NTI,' Isabel says.

It's like the noise gets sucked out of the room. Célia's eyes flare wide and dart from Isabel to Voronov.

'Célia,' Voronov says, 'we know that you, Gil and Julio were working on an unnamed test subject. We know this began shortly after Gabriel Bernardo was retested. We know all of the dates on which this happened and that these tests with the unnamed subject became more and more frequent, peaking in the week before dos Santos was killed. We have strong reasons to suspect the subject is Gabriel Bernardo.'

'What would happen if it gets out that the heads of national testing were keeping their very own lab rat to experiment on?' Isabel asks.

Célia slaps her hand down on her desk. 'That's not what that was! How dare you?'

'We don't know what it was,' Isabel says. 'You refuse to tell us. Do you understand that when this blows open, you'll have done yourself no favours by refusing to assist us? Two men are dead. Both were involved in an unnamed subject testing and you're the only one left to tell the tale. I think you should be more concerned for your own safety, rather than worrying about what kind of trouble you'll get into with the board of ethics. I think you need to start talking.'

Armindas shoves up from her chair, sending it spinning across the floor. It bumps into the glass wall and stops. She starts pacing. Eventually, she sighs.

'Gabriel's registered as a Regular. When he was tested that's what he presented as. But there were some anomalies, so we agreed to retest at a later date. We spoke to Gabriel's father and we agreed on six months. We'd thought that the anomalies were just that, a fluke, something that would be smoothed over with time. At this point, only Gil was working with Gabriel. He was on good terms with the family.'

'Go on,' Isabel says.

'Six months later, the retest proved otherwise. He tested as Gifted. It was a very low level. This was unusual. We hadn't seen this kind of development before, but it wasn't anything to be alarmed over. It could've all been brushed under the carpet. Easily corrected. Gabriel's father didn't feel the same way. They come from a very traditional family. Gabriel being Gifted is unacceptable to them. He knew we were having trouble raising funding for a particular project we had pertaining to the stages that Gifted could access. He offered Gabriel as a test subject. We kept his name redacted; all files sealed. He wanted his son fixed. Or as close to a Regular as could be achieved, as if there is such a thing.' She bites her lip and pauses by the corner of the desk, absently plays with a pencil on its top. Then she stops and sits on the corner of the desk.

'So, what happened?'

Armindas blows out a slow breath.

'His level continued to escalate. It was slow at first, but obvious. And then it started to get dangerous. In no time at all he was presenting as mid-level Gifted. And not just that but as a dual-category. Can you imagine? It was all happening so fast. The data we were getting from his case alone was incredible and with the family funding the research—'

'They bribed you,' Isabel says.

Armindas gives them a tight-lipped nod. 'It was supposed to be safe. We were monitoring him.' Her shoulders slump. 'But Gabriel's fast development wasn't without its side effects. Higher-level Gifted can develop some very serious issues. It begins to affect their empathy and decision-making skills. It's something that can be managed and barely even noticed in a low-level Gifted. But this isn't the case for a higher level. It can turn them into very unstable individuals.'

'Is that what happened to Gabriel?'

'The last visit – we realised just how bad it had got. Gil wanted to pull the plug on everything. He was scared,' she says. 'Gabriel had become bigger than any of us had expected. Gil thought we should come clean with the Registry, face the music, put things right. He didn't want a tragedy like Colombo on his hands. A few days after that, he died.' She shakes her head. 'I knew right away it wasn't a fit.' She laughs. 'A fit! Gabriel is capable of a great deal. Things people would find impossible to believe. Soares wanted to keep this under wraps. It's what we were arguing about the night of the fundraiser. I wouldn't denounce anyone, but I wanted out. Julio was so angry with me' – she laughs – 'he said I was being delusional. That Gabriel would never resort to that kind of violence. I don't know how he didn't see it. Gabriel was becoming more and more unstable.' She presses a hand to her mouth. 'Gil was right. We should've reported it. But if we'd been caught—' she looks up at them, jaw set, eyes angry, 'do you have any idea the lengths Monitoring would have gone to to hide something like this?'

'What about Soares?' Isabel asks.

'Julio thought we could get it under control. That we could still fix this and be able to get away with it. He fought with Gil over coming clean to Monitoring, wanted to keep Gil quiet.' She swallows. 'Gil wanted to turn Gabriel over to them.' She drops her gaze then, staring at the fingers she's trailing back and forth over the edge of the desk. 'He thought we could get in contact with

Monitoring and sort it out quietly. Julio thought we could handle it ourselves.'

Isabel draws in a sharp breath at the implications.

Armindas isn't talking about the day-to-day monitoring that the majority of higher-level Gifted were enrolled into.

She's talking about the other kind. The one where they show up to take you away in the middle of the night and no one ever hears from you again. The one where if you do come back, it's years later and your mind is never quite the same again.

Isabel stares at her. 'Because of the decisions the three of you have made, two people are now dead. We have no real concept of just how much damage Gabriel can do on a larger scale. And you refused to come forward.'

Armindas looks away, pressing the back of her hand to her mouth.

'Call the Chief,' Isabel says, 'we need to get a grip on this.' She flicks a look at Célia, who is still staring off into space, lost in her own head. 'The Chief's going to have to put a proper detail on her.'

Because right now, Armindas is the only one capable of making sure they have anything on Gabriel at all.

'We need to find Gabriel.'

62

THEN

It never starts the way Isabel thinks it will.

She keeps to herself, always. She tidies up her room, she washes the dishes and cleans the kitchen and the bathroom and irons when it's her turn. She rarely makes a peep.

She wishes she could predict it. But she never can.

The first time her mother locks her in, Isabel is thirteen. It's the anniversary of her father's death.

When Isabel wakes up that morning, the house is quiet.

She looks over at the bed next to hers. Rita lies, curled onto her side, facing Isabel. She's got her knees tucked in high against her chest and one arm hanging off the side of the bed.

Isabel watches the rise and fall of her sister's shoulders underneath the sheets and blankets. Rita is still so small, really petite. She eats like a little bird. That's what their Tia Simone says when they go there for lunch with her and Sebastião. She always tries to make Rita eat a bit more but gives up because Rita gets upset and starts crying.

The first time that happened, Isabel's mother got so angry she called Tia on the phone and yelled at her. Told her if that ever happened again then she'd never let them go over for lunch again. Isabel had been standing in the kitchen, back pressed to the kitchen wall and her heart beating really fast, gnawing at her lip because the thought of not being allowed to go there, to see her tia and her brother, made her want to open the front door and run all the way there so her mother would never have the chance to make good on the threat.

341

Isabel gets up, stops to make her bed first before she gets dressed, goes to the bathroom to brush her teeth. She closes the door quietly behind her so as not to wake up her sister.

The ticking of the clock is loud in the hallway.

When she reaches the living room the smell of alcohol is strong.

Isabel peers around the door. Her mother is on the sofa. She's sitting hunched over, a blanket over her shoulders and her head in her hands. Isabel can't see her face because her hair hangs down and covers it. She's barefoot, her feet flat on the marble floor.

There are two bottles of wine on the table. One is empty and the other one is halfway gone. The glass on the table is full.

'Mãe?' Isabel asks, tentative. She steps into the room.

Slowly, her mum's head comes up and the eyes she trains on Isabel are like something out of a nightmare. They're shot through with so much red that Isabel takes a step back.

Isabel freezes in place. Just like she does in her nightmares. And when her mother stands, she can't move. She wants to, she can feel every bone in her body screaming at her to run away because it's not normal. The way her mother is looking at her isn't normal.

'Can you hear what I'm thinking?' her mum asks. Her voice is so hoarse; it sounds like it does when her mum catches a cold.

Isabel shakes her head. 'No. I can't do that,' she says. Because she can't. That's not something she can do. 'Mãe?'

Isabel can't move. Fear has her frozen in place and she wants to cry but she can't. She can't do any of that.

'I don't want to see you,' her mum says. And then she starts sobbing. Her face just falls, like it's too heavy for her to keep her expression. Her voice becomes deeper and choked up. 'I don't want to see you, can't you understand that? You're like a demon in my house. Why can't I get rid of you?'

Isabel drops her gaze to the floor, digs her nails into the sides of her thighs and tries to breathe through it. It's okay. Her mother won't do anything. She won't do anything. She'll say mean words and then she'll walk away, like she always does. Isabel just has to keep quiet, keep her head down.

It'll go away. It'll go away. It'll go away.

When her mother grabs her arm, nails cutting into Isabel's skin, grip too tight, Isabel yelps and jumps back. She looks up at her mother and the fear is just how it is in her nightmares. It renders her helpless.

Her mother isn't even looking at her any more. She pulls on Isabel's arm so hard Isabel sobs and clutches at her shoulder because it hurts. When her mother begins to drag Isabel after her, her slippers slide on the smooth floor.

Isabel trips and falls but that doesn't make her mother stop. She just keeps pulling her by her arm, yanks so hard when Isabel tries to cling to the corner of the corridor that Isabel's hand slips and her face hits the floor. Her teeth cut into her bottom lip. She starts crying for real then, her shirt riding up and the floor burning the skin over her ribs.

'I don't want to look at you,' her mother repeats, 'I don't want to look at you.'

Isabel doesn't look up when her mother lets go of her. She curls in on herself and prays that her mother will leave her alone now.

Then she hears the door open. Her mother grips her under her shoulders and drags her into the dark, drops her there, still muttering under her breath. The stench of alcohol washes over Isabel's face but she still doesn't take her hand away from her mouth.

She realises then what her mother's going to do.

'No, no, mãe, *please*!' She reaches out, trying to grab onto her mother's leg, but she doesn't reach her in time.

The door slams closed and leaves her locked in darkness.

63

Tigre is peering at Isabel from the bottom of the bed, eyes eerily reflecting the light streaming in from the window as he watches Isabel. Next to Isabel, Branca just goes on snoring like she's heard nothing. Isabel is disorientated and it takes her a second to figure out what dragged her from sleep.

The phone. The phone is ringing. Isabel curses and reaches for it without looking.

'Yes.'

'Reis. Get your ass out of bed.'

The Chief's voice snaps her out of her drowsy, disturbed state. 'Chief?'

'Armindas is missing. We need all hands on deck.'

That strikes her dumb. *Foda-se*.

'The suspension—'

'You don't need to worry about that, understand me? You need to do as you're told. I want you here in twenty minutes.'

'Yes, Chief.'

Isabel gets there in less and will probably get more than one ticket, but she doesn't care. She walks into the station and goes straight up to the case room. She's bleary still and the lights make her swear under her breath. It's one thirty in the morning and her body is not happy with her. Without the constraints of headaches and work times, she'd got used to sleeping through the night.

She's there though, her hair plastered to her head from the rain. She doesn't even know exactly what she's got on, because she hadn't bothered to turn on the lights while getting dressed. Her trainers hadn't held up too well on the short walk from her car in the pouring rain and they squish with her every step.

The Chief sticks her head out of the case room just as Isabel strides in.

'Get in here.' She disappears back inside the room.

Isabel hurries to catch up, cold and out of breath. God. Sometimes she wonders about the Chief. Her sixth sense borders on creepy. Given how NTI was being shown up as incompetent as hell during their investigation, it wouldn't surprise her if the Chief herself has slipped through the cracks and is walking around as a happy-go-lucky Gifted, free of government intervention.

Everyone is gathered in the room. Only Jacinta looks as if she's also just been dragged from her bed. Carla and Daniel look wide awake. But then they're used to working the graveyard shift. Voronov looks as composed as ever. It's only when he looks over at her that she sees the bags under his eyes and the paleness of his face.

'How did we lose Célia?' Isabel asks as she sheds her coat and goes to stand by the others. 'I thought we were keeping it hushed up about where she'd gone.'

The Chief is pacing the length of the room. Isabel has to ward against her emotions because they're leaking all over the place. Isabel doesn't want to burn out by tuning in to people accidentally.

'She didn't want to go to the safe hotel we suggested. So we agreed to a different space.'

'Where?'

'She has a house in Sintra. We agreed to let her retreat there as long as she stayed confined to the house for the time being, and posted some of our people there.'

Isabel frowns. 'So where are our people?' The woman couldn't have just walked out from under their noses.

The Chief grits her teeth. 'Incapacitated.'

'Jesus,' Isabel stands and starts to pace herself, 'incapacitated?'

Jacinta sighs long and hard. 'Their injuries seem to be self-inflicted.'

Isabel freezes. She turns to look at them. 'You're telling me he found her?'

'We don't know that for certain. We can't make accusations without cause,' the Chief snaps. 'We need to focus on what we have.'

Isabel grits her teeth. 'Chief, with all due respect. We have plenty of cause. And focus on what we have? We had Célia. And now we don't. If we lose her, we have nothing.'

'We've dispatched officers to Bernardo's house, but there's no one there. NTI has also been checked and so has Célia's apartment,' Carla says.

'We have to work under the assumption that it might not be Gabriel,' Daniel says with a shrug. Because he's not wrong. Tunnel vision never does anyone any good. But in this case, Isabel is willing to bet her house and newly acquired canine friends that the only person behind this is Gabriel Bernardo. Because she knows. She *saw* what he did to Mila.

'I just don't want to get there too late and find another person who has brained themselves to death, with no witnesses or anything else to tie Gabriel to these crimes,' Isabel says.

'None of us want that, Isabel,' Carla says.

'I know, I know.' She covers her eyes. She stops. 'Luisa.'

Voronov looks at her.

Isabel stops pacing. 'Luisa Delgado. She's the one constant. Did anyone talk to her?'

'We tried contacting her when searching for Gabriel but couldn't get through. We've tried tonight too but still no answer.'

Shit. 'Okay, keep trying. Whoever contacts her first, let the rest of us know. Voronov, let's go.'

64

They make the drive to Luisa's place in silence.

The lights of the Vasco da Gama bridge light up the night and the river rushes on beneath them as the car eats up the stretch of road. They follow the serpentine strip, leaving the lights of the city behind them, heading towards the darker depths of Setúbal.

'If you need me to switch with you, just let me know,' she says.

'I'm okay for now,' he says. 'What's our plan when we get there?'

'If we get there and she's there you mean? Because if she's not then we're fucked. Tracking her will take time we don't have.' A car passes them, heading in the opposite direction, and leaves them alone on the road again. The traffic at this hour is non-existent, so they should make good time. 'I'm going to get pushy when I'm in there.'

Voronov glances at her out of the corner of his eye.

'It'll be fine.'

He's quiet for a moment and when she looks at him, his jaw is tense, his hands gripping the wheel tighter than necessary.

'What?'

'Have you gone through the retesting yet?'

'No. It's not a facility that's equipped to deal with it and Michael's going to have to be careful about it. If I'd taken it at NTI then I would've had results right away but doing it by a back-door place is a little different.'

'You're sure we can trust him?'

We.

Isabel bites back a smile. 'On this matter? Yes. I trust him.'

'Just be careful tonight. We can't afford to do anything we can't explain away or whatever happens will be worse than a suspension.'

Isabel knows he's right. 'I'll be careful. I promise.' She faces forward and hopes that she's able to keep that promise.

Luisa's building is a contrast to Gabriel's. There are none of the luxury touches that they'd seen in his.

The apartment building is a part of an estate, all of the buildings lined up next to each other, neat square gardens fitted in between each one, with picnic tables and benches and flowers that see maintenance regularly. It might not be the most affluent of estates, but it is well taken care of.

They find Block O – there aren't any gates preventing people from getting in – and go up the open stairs. They follow them to the top and out to an open corridor. Some people have taken it upon themselves to add a little sloping roof over their doors but the majority of them don't have anything.

Plant pots line the floor, spilling over onto the floor in curls of leaves.

The door they find themselves in front of has nothing around it, though it's painted neatly. The night is silent.

Isabel knocks and as the sound echoes in the air, she gathers her power and casts it out. She pictures it in her mind, a silvery web slipping, phasing through the walls to capture any presences within.

When she doesn't immediately pick anything up, Isabel worries that she's wasting her time, but she keeps stretching it, a new comfort in her growing control of her Gift giving her confidence. That mellowness that she always senses on her early morning walks reveals itself. One by one, by one, it's so faint and yet she still gets a sense of peacefulness from it. No thoughts go with it, nothing with a direction to it, only vague images or blankness.

Everyone is sleeping.

She turns to the door in front of her and in her mind's eye reels the net back in until it's hovering over the house in front of them.

'Isabel?'

'Give me a second,' she murmurs, closing her eyes and concentrating.

She picks it up. The signature vibrant and present. In the middle of the colour that makes up Luisa, a dense purple, she sees something tiny, like a speck. Dark and oily, something there that shouldn't be there. She knows that instinctively and recoils from it.

She opens her eyes and Voronov is staring at her like she's lost her mind.

Isabel straightens up and knocks on the door again. Louder this time.

'We know you're in there and I know you're awake. If you don't want this to get a lot louder, and for your nice neighbours to wake up and come to see what's happening outside your door, I suggest you open up. We don't have time for your games.'

If the night wasn't so quiet, her voice wouldn't have carried as much as it does. But as it is, she can hear it travel all the way down to the end of the corridor.

Voronov is looking from her to the door like he doesn't know what the hell is going on.

A few seconds later, they hear the sound of the chain being undone and the door opens. Luisa looks as if she hasn't seen sleep in days. She is a far cry from the put-together woman they'd spoken to that first time. Her hair is escaping her hairband and her thin robe is tied tightly around her waist. She clutches it together at her throat too, as if trying to protect any visible inch of skin.

'We need to come in,' Isabel says, itching to push the door open herself. But she reminds herself that they have to be as by the book as possible.

Luisa steps back and opens her door wider. 'Come in.'

Isabel goes ahead, Voronov following behind her. Luisa takes a little longer before closing the door and Isabel knows she's checking whether any of her neighbours woke up at the noise.

The apartment is in darkness. The only light is coming from the TV. There's a blanket on the sofa, a mug on the floor beside it and remote controls there too. Cushions are tucked between the armrest and the seat of the sofa, indented like someone has been sleeping there.

'Mind if we turn the light on?' Isabel asks.

Luisa wraps her arms around herself. 'Go ahead.'

The light flicks on, illuminating the place. It's a big living room, everything tasteful.

'Is Gabriel Bernardo in your house right now?' Isabel asks her.

Luisa shrinks in on herself. 'No.'

'Mind if we check?' she asks.

'No.'

Voronov doesn't waste time following through on that.

Isabel watches Luisa the whole time. She's wrapped tight in the robe and she's barefoot on the tiled floor that Isabel is sure must be freezing. She won't look at Isabel.

'Have you seen him today?' she asks.

'No.'

'What about Célia Armindas. Have you seen her?'

'I don't know who that is. Just like I didn't know Gil dos Santos or Julio Soares. I don't know any of these people.' She's talking in a monotone.

'Right.'

Voronov comes back into the room. 'Not here.'

'I think you should leave now,' Luisa says.

'Let's say we believe you,' Isabel says, softening her voice. 'And you have nothing to do with this. The details you've given us are vague and your boyfriend isn't giving you any answers, is he? I bet you've asked him, and he hasn't told you. He's told me, though,' Isabel finishes.

Luisa looks up and meets Isabel's eyes then.

'I don't know what you're talking about. There's nothing to tell.'

'Isn't there?' Isabel asks. 'What, just because that's what he's said? You're fooling yourself. You're fooling yourself while he uses you to cover for himself.'

'You're wrong.' Luisa grits the words out. Her arms stay wrapped around herself, her fingers digging into her sides.

'I'm not. I could even show you. I could show you how he waited outside my apartment, watching me. I can show you what he did to Gil. And his Guide. I can show you all of that.'

'You're a telepath,' Luisa spits out, moving into Isabel's space. Anger blooms red over her skin and muddies the air around them. Isabel feels it lap against the tentative wards she has in place. 'You create lies. I know what your kind can do.'

'My kind? You mean *our* kind. You have a Gift. And I don't lie. You'd know. You'd be able to see the truth of it. You can't plant lies in people's heads, the mind senses and rejects them. You know that.'

'That's a lie too.'

Isabel stares at her because the conviction in Luisa's tone speaks of knowledge. It speaks of someone who knows what they're talking about.

'You'd only know that if you'd experienced it yourself,' Isabel says, treading carefully here. 'Because how else would you be able to tell?'

Isabel doesn't look at her.

At their side Voronov looks lost.

'Luisa. Who's put lies in your head?'

Luisa stays silent but Isabel can see the tremor in her chin now and the sheen of tears in her eyes.

'Can I see?' Isabel asks, gently.

A sob that sounds as if it's been wrenched from her core pours out of Luisa's mouth. She starts to cry, but the sobs that rack her frame are silent and kept inside as Luisa refuses to let them escape.

'I can help you,' Isabel says, 'I'm not like him.'

And that seems to do it. Because as she continues to cry, Luisa peels an arm away from where she'd been wrapping herself so tightly and holds it out to Isabel.

'Luisa,' Isabel says, 'I can't do anything unless you give permission.'

Luisa breathes in in hitches, as if she can't gulp in large amounts of air because of how hard she's crying. But she calms herself for a moment, chin tilting up and throat working as she tries to quiet herself. 'Y-yes,' she chokes out, 'you have my p-permission to look at my memories.'

Isabel looks at Voronov, who is looking apprehensive. 'Sit down for me,' she tells Luisa and the other woman collapses onto the sofa, like she doesn't have the energy to do anything any more. She leans back, eyes squeezed shut and her lips tightly sealed.

'It's okay.'

Isabel looks at Voronov one last time and then goes under.

At first it's the same, finding a pathway and peering into what's happening. Luisa's thoughts and emotions are all around her, variations of the purple colour Isabel had seen when she'd been on the other side of the door.

But then she starts to see the anomalies. What Isabel finds makes her think of cuts that have healed over, but still leave a white scar long after the scabs have gone.

They're paved pathways. Old ones. And not normal ones either because normal pathways wouldn't leave this kind of trail; they wouldn't so much as leave their presence. It's like someone's cut through Luisa's psyche and then tried to sew it shut.

Isabel tightens her grip on Luisa's hand. Then she carries on.

Step by step she follows those trails and notices that as she does, Luisa's thoughts become quieter and quieter until Isabel can't hear them any more, until there's just silence and the purple associated with Luisa starts to pale.

Right there, where those trails end, is an inky blackness that feels foreign, misplaced, and Isabel knows instinctively that it doesn't belong.

She hears Voronov say her name but it comes from far away, like he's at one end of a tunnel and she's at the other.

'Wait,' Isabel says, but she doesn't know if she's spoken it aloud or not. And then she does something stupid.

Isabel reaches right for it and lets it swallow her.

65

People talk a lot about out-of-body experiences.

Isabel thinks that the way she feels when she touches someone's mind, when she's seeing things from their eyes, must be a lot like one.

But this time, it's something very different.

It reminds her of the lagoa she always drives to in the summer in Alcochete, where she wades in lukewarm waters, hypnotic in its warmth, and then she swims a little further out into its deepest parts where ice cold wraps around her and steals the breath from her lungs.

That's how she feels. Like she's waded out too far into the Atlantic and now the current won't let her go, except instead of blue waters, she's surrounded by black ink that weighs her down.

The worst thing about it is that it's familiar. It reminds her of those fleeting ghost touches against the back of her neck.

And it dawns on her what it is.

Shock ripples through her and for a moment Isabel feels the live essence around her take on an awareness that makes her freeze. She feels like a dozen eyes have opened and locked on her. As though, if she makes the slightest movement, they'll find her in the darkness and swallow her up.

Disorientation threatens to sink her. But Isabel regroups, gathers herself and tries to make sense of what she's seeing, willing herself to see—

She feels herself snap into place. It jolts her whole body and she gasps, stumbles and when she looks up again her body has a weight to it and she's walking. Isabel walks and the dirt trail crunches under her feet as she climbs up. She's holding onto

354

something tightly, something soft but firm. She looks, and finds herself staring at Célia Armindas' dirty, crying face.

Isabel's eyes widen, her mind already jumping to what this is but unable to comprehend it.

'What—' The voice that forms the word isn't her own, but she knows it. Célia's scared eyes look up at her, horrified and confused. *Isabel.*

The sound of Gabriel's voice in her mind is enough to make her want to throw herself out of there but she can't. Not yet. She needs to see. Where are they?

Rocks. There's no one around but she can see rocks, can see the uphill stretch of a dirt road that curves to the right. And the sea. She can see the sea. Desperately, Isabel tries to look, pushes back as she feels Gabriel trying to take back control. Can he even see what's happening with her in here?

Then she spots it, way below. A marina.

Isabel isn't in control. Can't force that hand to release Célia. And even if she can she knows it won't matter. Because his power isn't just telekinesis.

She'd forgotten.

He has dual affinities.

I'll play with you another time, he says.

Isabel is ripped out of there, and she feels her gut swoop, her ears popping. She opens her eyes and winces from the brightness of the room. She's breathing heavily and she's cold all over, can still taste the salt of the sea air on her tongue.

Voronov's head blots out the light and she can hear him saying her name but can't move.

Luisa comes into view too and she's pressing something white into Voronov's hand. He leans over Isabel and as she slowly starts to feel settled again, sensation coming back, she feels the cloth he's pressing to the thick, hot wetness that's coating her nose and upper lip again.

'Aleks,' she says. It comes out as a groan. 'I think I know where they are.' She shoves him aside, trying to get to her feet, but Voronov just clamps a hand around her arm and holds her.

'For fuck's sake, Isabel, hold still!' He sounds angry, but when she looks at his face there's fear there. She can feel it, cloying and desperate. His touch on her face is gentle.

'Aleks, you have to listen to me; you have to call the team. Gabriel is in Sesimbra. They're near the marina. Call them now.'

He looks at her in disbelief, like he's wondering if she's really lost it this time. He drops his gaze, grabs her hand and presses it stubbornly over the cloth that he's holding to her nose and holds it there, the look he gives her telling her that she better not let it go.

He pulls his phone out of his pocket and stands. 'How do you even know this?' He puts the phone to his ear.

Isabel becomes aware that Luisa is staring down at her. When she looks up, Luisa is trembling, eyelashes wet and her skin sickly pale. She looks ill.

'Because he's in my head,' Luisa says, 'isn't he?'

Isabel can't bring herself to answer. She doesn't have to.

That they don't crash is a miracle. They speed all the way there, the siren lighting the dark streets around them in flashes of red and blue.

The others are on their way, with Carla electing to stay behind just in case, just in case they're wrong.

Isabel stares unseeing out the car window, the surroundings blurring, because she can't fathom what she's just done. What she's just seen.

She feels sick to her stomach.

That kind of power—

What someone could do with that kind of power. What Gabriel had done with it.

And now Isabel has done it too. Bile climbs up her throat, but she forces it down, clears her throat and forces herself to focus, to drag herself from staring sightlessly out of the window.

'Are you okay?' Voronov asks. He doesn't take his eyes off the road; his hands are steady on the wheel. At the speed they're going and with the narrowness of the road in front of him, even with the sirens he'd be an idiot if he did.

'No,' she says. 'But we don't have time for that right now.'

'Okay.'

66

It takes them another fifteen minutes to reach Sesimbra. Isabel can already see Jacinta's car parked there. Voronov pulls in behind it and gets out, calling to them to find out where they are.

'They're at the end of the beach, starting from the first hotel,' he says.

Isabel nods. 'All right, you take the trail. I'll go with you and go down to the rocks.'

Voronov gives her a sharp look.

'Now is not the time to give me bullshit about it being dangerous. Let's go. You can do it later. Let's just find them.'

His face is grim but he doesn't argue with her. They start up the dirt trail; it goes past the marina and heads up towards the houses. It occurs to Isabel that the dos Santos household is only a half-hour walk away from them. She wonders if there's meaning in that.

Isabel shakes that thought away and then pushes on ahead. She does exactly what she did outside of Luisa's house and lets her wards sink away, ignores the tiredness in her bones and gives herself over to her Gift.

'Go,' she says to Voronov. She can feel his worry and anger so acutely and sees all the colours that go with it. But if he's next to her, it might keep her from finding Célia's signature. Isabel isn't used to working at this capacity. She can't afford any distractions. 'I'll catch up to you. Check in in fifteen minutes.'

It takes him longer than it should, but he finally nods and sets off without her.

Isabel makes her way to the rocks.

67

Isabel feels like she's built of static energy. The buzzing under her skin is driving her wild.

The flashlight lights up the dirt trail winding itself away from the beach. It leads up and up towards the housing developments that were meant to provide the buyers with beautiful views of Sesimbra.

Isabel is on high alert, her senses cast out like a web to pick up anything, anything she possibly can. It's been a while since her Gift has been working at such high frequency and the only reason she is still coherent is because it's two-something a.m. on a week-night and the beach is empty.

Her feet scrape over the path, the crunch of dirt and stone loud in the night. The waves crash against the side of the cliff and she can taste the sea salt in the air. There's no railing at the side of the road, just overgrown grass that has dried and died in the winter.

Isabel's flashlight sweeps its wide spot of light over and over as she carries on up.

Carla and Voronov are searching lower down, Carla by car and Voronov on foot. Isabel feels for the phone in her pocket and prays that it has enough battery.

Isabel almost misses it.

It's a mantra, barely legible, like a whisper. Like someone who is battling unconsciousness.

I'm sorry . . . I'm sorry . . . I'm sorry.

Isabel stops. The back of her neck is damp, as is the skin at her temples. She's lost track of how long she's been on this uphill climb.

'Where are you coming from?' she murmurs.

Because that voice isn't someone speaking out loud. That's someone speaking in their own mind.

Isabel takes a few breaths to settle herself and closes her eyes. Tries to see it.

She gasps. She hadn't really expected to see anything, but there it is, in vibrant green that is fading with the words, the colour an echo in the dark.

From her left.

It's coming from her left.

She finds herself staring down at the slope leading down to the rocks. The sound of the waves crashing into them becomes abruptly menacing.

Locking her jaw, Isabel steps up to the edge and swings her flashlight over the side.

The rocks gleam wet and black.

'Célia,' Isabel calls out, 'can you hear me?'

Quiet. And then—

A cry, weak and buried under the sound of the sea.

'Merda. Merda, merda, merda.' How is she supposed to get down the—

Isabel sucks in a sharp breath as her light catches on an arm curled around a rock. And it's not holding on, it's caught in between rocks while the person trapped, floats up with the viciousness of the waves and—

Her stomach turns as the body slams against the rock with the rise of the next wave.

Fumbling in her pocket, Isabel takes out her phone.

'Isa—'

'Aleks, I've found her. Head towards the fort, go past it and up the dirt trail. She's trapped in the rocks. Still alive. I don't know where Gabriel is. Get here. And call an ambulance.'

'Wait for me. Don't go down there, Isabel.'

'I have to, she won't make it otherwise. Just hurry.'

'Isabel—'

Isabel hangs up and shoves the phone back into her pocket. She shoves the flashlight in her mouth and, looking around her, shrugs out of her jacket. She tries to find Gabriel in the shadows but she sees nothing. He could kill her too. He could send her flying off the cliff edge and break her on those rocks. Fear pumps through her veins and she forces herself to remain steady.

As her jacket drops to the ground, Isabel realises she won't be able to use the flashlight either. She lets rip another string of swearwords as she heads back down the road to where land gives way to rock. She's going to have to pick her way through the rocks and hope that the lighthouse far away will provide enough of something for her not to slip and drown.

It's funny that something that she used to do as a child with her dad could terrify her now.

You can do this, Isabel, you can do this.

She hears the echoes of Célia's thoughts again, wondering if she's alone again, if whoever had called to her had left.

'Célia,' Isabel calls out, hands gripping the rocks tightly, 'hold on, I'm coming to you. Voronov is bringing help.' She makes her way cautiously, knowing that if she rushes and slips up it's not going to be pretty. She stays crouched low and close to the cliff side.

The expanse of rocks starts to narrow down, getting closer and closer to the wall of the cliff side as she approaches the spot where she'd seen Célia barely clinging on.

She doesn't know how long it takes her to get there. It feels like hours before she is finally pressed flat against the cliff side, staring at the damaged arm still trapped in the rocks.

How the hell is she going to get Célia up?

Gritting her teeth, Isabel moves over the last few rocks separating them.

A large wave hits. Her instinct to jerk back is what does it. Her foot sinks in between two rocks and she falls back. She feels the crack of the rock against the back of her head and cries out as pain splinters through her. She's winded, air driven out of her from the fall and the pain, but she rights herself, breathes through it as she steadies and presses a hand to the place where she was hit.

She stays lower this time and manages to reach Célia even as another wave slaps up against her and leaves her soaked to the bone.

Bracing herself and trying to stay out of the path of the waves, Isabel peers over the peak of the rock and sees her. Célia's eyes are barely open and she's bobbing with the sea. Her face looks drained of life. The angle of her trapped arm has bile rushing up Isabel's throat.

'Célia, look at me,' Isabel says, voice urgent, 'look at me.'

She gets a moan. Célia moves her head, pressing the side of her face against the rock.

'Célia, can you move your other arm? Can you reach for me?' Isabel grits her teeth, reaches down and grips Célia's chin, tipping her face up. Célia's skin is like ice. It feels like she's not even touching something human.

Célia doesn't respond, her head just lolls back and she moans.

Isabel tries it another way.

It's hard. Isabel's head hurts but she goes back into her own mind space and follows the track of those echoes back to their source until she's in the middle of a green so vivid, it feels like she's actually seeing it.

Célia. Can you hear me?

It hurts . . .

Isabel closes her eyes briefly in relief.

You need to open your eyes and look at me. Do it now.

Célia's eyes open.

'*Now give me your arm. Give me your arm!*' Isabel says it both aloud and in Célia's head, needing to reach her in any way she can.

Nothing happens.

Isabel's about to yell at her when there's a twitch of movement. A shaking, weak hand emerges from the water, and Isabel doesn't wait. She reaches down further, grabs Célia's hand and pulls, grunting at the effort. She hooks her feet into the divots of the rocks to brace herself and drags Célia up.

A weak scream splits the night. Célia's bad arm comes loose as she's pulled forward. She shudders, eyes rolling back into her head.

The wave comes up with a roar. Salt water fills Isabel's mouth and she chokes as it goes up her nose and leaves her lips stinging, but using the momentum she yanks at Célia's arm.

She cushions Célia's fall, does her best to take the brunt of it. Rocks jab into Isabel's back, making her sob out a cry of pain. Célia is a limp weight, lying far too still against her. The only sign that she's even alive is the short bursts of air puffing out against the wet skin of Isabel's neck.

Shock.

'Okay, okay,' Isabel whispers. She wraps herself around the other woman and closes her eyes and breathes. 'Stay with me. Stay with me.'

'Why would you do this?'

The new voice behind her makes her freeze.

He's here.

68

'Why did you come, Isabel? It would've been fine after this.'

Isabel twists around to find him standing by the wall of the cliff. He looks . . . he looks betrayed.

Isabel doesn't say anything, remains nestled in the rocks, heart pounding in her throat. She doesn't let go of Célia.

'You understand me,' he's saying, 'so why are you doing this? You're like me.' He sounds hoarse, it's hard to hear him over the waves. 'Do you know what people like them can do to people like us? What they were planning on doing to me?'

And Isabel has never felt so helpless in her life. 'What were they planning on doing to you?'

'Gil was going to come clean. After all these years. He was going to go to the Registry and Monitoring. Tell them everything.' He smiles but his eyes are flat. 'You know what happens to Gifted people like you and me don't you? If you're a seven then maybe, maybe they'll let you live your life, slap a Monitor on you. But if you go above that . . . what do you think happens to the nines and the tens? What do you think happened to that girl in Colombo?'

Isabel keeps her hold on Célia, can taste the sea on her lips, drying them out, and licks them compulsively, her own body starting to shiver from the wet and the cold.

'It's why you took suppressors, wasn't it? That fear.'

Fuck. She glances down at Célia and prays that she's too out of it to hear what he's saying. 'I don't know what you're talking about.'

'You're lying,' he says, calm, 'you don't have to lie to me. I've been on your side from the start, you know that. If they get their hands on us, we'll disappear, just like the girl from Colombo. We'll disappear and we won't come back. You've heard the stories, don't pretend you haven't. The government and the people like to turn a blind eye to all the cases. Have you looked? For yourself? Have you ever thought to look at the number of missing cases for Gifted people? Have you ever checked to see what their levels are? Because I have.' His jaw firms and he straightens up. 'And that's not going to happen to me. No one's putting me in a cage.'

And how is it that she's staring at a killer, at someone capable of taking away someone's consent, taking away their ability to live, their very life – and how can she feel her chest ache from the things he's saying?

He's voicing everything that weighed on her every time she popped a pill, every time her mum looked at her, every time a retesting came around and she worried that this would be the time they would realise what she hid.

But not this way. Deus, none of this was the way to do it. 'Gabriel—'

He lifts a hand towards her and she feels it.

It's terrifying.

Something unseen tugs at Célia, trying to rip her out of Isabel's arms. Isabel tightens her grip and makes herself as much of a dead weight as she can, trying to keep Célia down with her. The power is violent.

'Stop,' she grits out. 'Don't do this.'

It pulls again. Isabel's grip weakens and Célia nearly slips through.

'Gabriel!' she snaps out.

This time when he pulls, Isabel rolls with it, taking Célia with her. They both hit the rock opposite. Isabel tastes blood in her mouth and the right side of her face is agony.

She defends herself.

Gabriel's thoughts are made up of yellow. A poisonous yellow that's green around the edges. Isabel dives right for them.

His surprise is such a puff of innocence in the face of the dark oily malice oozing from his core. Isabel grits her teeth and follows her instinct and goes right for it.

It's an out-of-body experience.

It reminds her of seeing someone else's memories, that feeling of dislocation.

This time, when she opens her eyes, she's staring at two women wedged between the rocks at the edge of the water. One of them familiar, Célia, unconscious. Probably dead now. And the other . . .

She's staring at her own face.

I knew it, the thought echoes in her own head, so close, so touched with wonder. *You're just like me. Your Gift is so amazing.*

'You should've listened to me, Gabriel,' she says softly, and it's disconcerting, so disconcerting to hear her own words coming out in Gabriel's voice, spoken with a cadence that she has never heard in his voice. Isabel steps forward.

Fear spikes. It's not her own.

Isabel keeps moving, moving the foreign weight of Gabriel's body around her, one step at a time over the uneven surface of the rocks.

Don't!

But Isabel does exactly what he did. She moves him, bit by bit, her control tenuous over the body she's wearing. And as she gets closer to the water, she feels his body begin to shake, her control over him not absolute. But it's strong enough.

Isabel's at the edge, Gabriel's protests screaming loud in her mind as she stops right there.

To her left, Isabel's own body is still, staring vacantly ahead, Célia collapsed on top of her.

Just one more step and he'll hit the water.

Cold metal touches the back of her head.

'Isabel.' Voronov. 'I need you to come out of there. I've got this.'

'He's not safe,' she says, and pauses, still thrown when her words emerge in Gabriel's voice. She forces herself to continue. 'He could rip that gun out of your hand in a second.'

'Hold on to him long enough for me to get the cuffs on him. The blindfold should help. He can't touch what he can't see. Not even with his powers.'

'We don't know that.'

'Trust me. There'll be no going back if you make him step off that edge. Don't put me in that position. Leave him while we still have time.' He lowers his voice. 'People can't even suspect that you've been able to do this.'

She feels Voronov's fingers closing around her wrist – Gabriel's wrist – and she lets him.

'I'm going to reach for the other one. Hold him for a bit longer for me but then leave when I tell you to. Isabel?'

She breathes through it, flexes the fingers of Gabriel's hand. Voronov's hand is warm.

'Isabel?'

Inside, Gabriel is battering against her hold, throwing his entire power into it. But that's the small difference between them. His Gift is so great and vast; she doesn't stand a chance against his telekinesis. But her telepathy is even stronger than his.

He can't win this one.

'Okay.'

Only then does Voronov reach for the other hand. The cuffs pinch the skin and she winces.

When the cloth wraps around her eyes, Isabel lets herself sink out of the mist of yellow with a sigh.

She blinks. She's cold. She hurts.

Isabel looks to the side in time to watch as violent rasping breaths lift Gabriel's threat. He's sucking in air like he hasn't breathed in years as he's pulled back by Voronov, who forces him to sit back against a rock.

Voronov tucks the gun away and looks over at her. He wipes the water from his face and moves carefully to crouch in front of her and Célia.

'The ambulance is here,' he says calmly, eyes mapping out her face. He brushes her hair back from her face. 'They'll be here in a moment.'

Isabel swallows. Her throat feels dry and her head is pounding. Her eyes sting. 'Okay,' she croaks.

He shrugs out of his hoodie and carefully wraps it around Célia without jostling her too much. 'It's best if we wait here, we shouldn't move either of you.'

Behind him, Gabriel continues to suck in air in that odd way, a makeshift blindfold around his eyes. It occurs to Isabel that maybe they should check on him but she's not sure she can move right now. And she doesn't want to be anywhere near him.

Isabel hears Carla call out from somewhere, a warning that they're almost there and to get ready.

'That was a close call,' Voronov murmurs.

Isabel closes her eyes and leans her head back.

She's not sure that's true.

The damage feels like it's been done.

69

Dr Alves refers to it as a Gifted's form of hypnotic suggestion. Except it's more sinister than that. Isabel stands and watches through the one-way mirror as Luisa sobs into her hands. Turns out she did remember Gil's call. Gil had realised what Gabriel had been doing to her. He'd got Luisa to agree to meet him that day. Luisa said he'd wanted her to help him, to prove how dangerous Gabriel was.

Except having her on that train was ultimately what had got him killed.

Gabriel had known everything.

Dr Alves is gentle as she explains to Luisa what has been done to her. She tells her that they will arrange for her to talk to a professional, do everything they can to support her going forward. If she testifies.

Gabriel had gone into Luisa's mind without her consent and he'd managed to forge a link. One that doesn't just disappear when a person withdraws from someone else's mind. He'd used those links to control Luisa, to put her in the right places at the right times without once having to dirty his own hands.

It was the E5 that had helped Gabriel get what he wanted. After searching his house, they'd found large quantities of the failed drug stored away.

There's no way Luisa's telekinesis would have been enough to control someone else's person the way Gil and Julio had been controlled. Gabriel had been doping her up with E5, temporarily enhancing her abilities. Then he'd got into her mind.

Luisa's memory lapses and increasing state of confusion were attributed to Gabriel's takeovers. The doctor who had sat with

Luisa had explained that it had been Luisa's way of coping. It had just shut down when the foreign entity – in this case Gabriel – took control and played her like a puppet.

Isabel had asked Dr Alves if it would be possible to remove the link Gabriel had left behind in Luisa's mind. The look on Dr Alves' face hadn't been promising but she'd said they would have to wait until Luisa was seen by other professionals with a deeper understanding. Apparently, they were bringing in a specialist from Switzerland. What had taken place here would be sending shock-waves throughout the Gifted community and those who dedicated their lives to studying them.

The whole of NTI is under investigation, meaning that the country ends up having to scramble to find an outside alternative to come in because Testing season is approaching. Isabel hopes that maybe, just maybe, they can't find a suitable company and the Gifted get a break for once. She thinks growing up without the stigma might be a nice thing.

Tigre licks one of Isabel's toes, drawing her attention down to himself. 'No,' she says, 'this toast isn't for you. Live with it. Where's the treat I gave you?' Isabel goes back out into the living room and finds Branca curled up in a corner of the sofa. She opens one eye, the perfect picture of laziness as Isabel makes her way to sit at the other end of the sofa with toast and coffee in hand.

Unfortunately for Isabel, she'd been benched again, but this time only while they investigated her story of what exactly had happened on those rocks the night Gabriel had taken Célia.

Gabriel is keeping his mouth shut, refusing to say a word, not even to his lawyer apparently. Dr Alves told Isabel that ever since they'd started force-feeding him suppressors, he'd just shut down on them. Apparently, whatever they were giving him put S3 to shame.

Isabel tries not to think about that.

She tries not to think about the mandatory sessions she needs to have with the department's therapist either. Or the envelope on the table in front of her. The edges are scrunched because she keeps shoving it out of sight. It's addressed to Isabel in Michael's looping handwriting, with a familiar logo at the left-hand corner.

She's been staring at it for the past hour.

Isabel sets her toast down and dusts her hands off on her jogging bottoms before reaching for the envelope.

She ignores the tremor in her fingers as she picks at the corner and slides her thumb in, slicing open the rest of the envelope.

Her heart beats a rapid tattoo against her chest and her head feels light as she pulls the folded paper out. Just the one sheet. She sucks in a steadying breath as she opens it, closing her eyes and praying—

She looks at the result on the letter, printed in neat black typed letters.

The buzzer rings.

Isabel jumps and slams the paper face down on the table. Rubs at her eyes and then glances over at the intercom. She puts the letter back in the envelope.

She nudges Tigre off her lap where the dog has decided to try to make himself comfortable in the hopes of getting some toast, and then shoves the letter into one of the kitchen drawers as she trudges over to the intercom, one sock well on its way to coming off her foot.

'Yes?'

'Can I come up?' Voronov's voice carries loudly in the hallway.

Isabel presses the buzzer and checks her reflection in the mirror.

They hadn't really had a chance to talk about that night on the rocks. What she'd done.

When she opens the door to him he's dressed as casually as he had been that day. He looks her over. His gaze lands on her feet and he smirks a little at the half-off sock.

'Hey' he steps in.

'Hey,' she says.

'Have you had breakfast yet?'

She glances over at her burnt toast. 'Kind of.'

'Come on then. We can grab a proper breakfast on the way to the station. Chief wants to see you.'

'Are you paying?'

'Isn't it your turn?'

'I thought I was still benched anyway,' she says, grabbing the first jumper her hand lands on. 'What does she want to see me about? And why didn't she call?'

'I was on my way over here when she called me. I told her I'd stop by.'

'Okay. So?'

'It's about the Jane Doe in the morgue. The one you were working on.'

An image of the woman lying on the slab. It feels like years ago now. Isabel turns to look at him.

'What about her?'

Voronov grins. 'Some new information has come to light. And the case was never officially closed.'

Isabel finishes stuffing herself into her clothes and only stops long enough to grab her bag and keys. She quickly fills Tigre and Branca's water bowls and leaves their toys out for them. 'I'll be back later,' she says, patting them both on the head.

'All right, let's go.'

THE END

Order the next book in the gripping
Inspector Reis series . . .

HOUSE OF SILENCE

Out May 2022.

HODDER &
STOUGHTON

THRILLINGLY GOOD BOOKS
FROM CRIMINALLY
GOOD WRITERS

CRIME FILES BRINGS YOU THE LATEST RELEASES FROM
TOP CRIME AND THRILLER AUTHORS.

SIGN UP ONLINE FOR OUR MONTHLY NEWSLETTER AND BE THE FIRST
TO KNOW ABOUT OUR COMPETITIONS, NEW BOOKS AND MORE.

VISIT OUR WEBSITE: WWW.CRIMEFILES.CO.UK
LIKE US ON FACEBOOK: FACEBOOK.COM/CRIMEFILES
FOLLOW US ON TWITTER: @CRIMEFILESBOOKS